P9-DWM-945

Intimate Strangers

Intimate Strangers

Juliette Mead

POCKET BOOKS

New York   London   Toronto   Sydney   Tokyo   Singapore

This book is a work of fiction. Names, characters, places and incidents are products of the author's imagination or are used fictitiously. Any resemblance to actual events or locales or persons, living or dead, is entirely coincidental.

POCKET BOOKS, a division of Simon & Schuster Inc.
1230 Avenue of the Americas, New York, NY 10020

Copyright © 1995, 1996 by Juliette Mead

The 1995 edition was published in Great Britain by Simon & Schuster Ltd.

All rights reserved, including the right to reproduce
this book or portions thereof in any form whatsoever.
For information address Pocket Books, 1230 Avenue
of the Americas, New York, NY 10020

Library of Congress Cataloging-in-Publication Data

Mead, Juliette.
   Intimate strangers / Juliette Mead.
     p.   cm.
   ISBN: 0-671-53794-6
   I. Title.
PS3563.E165415   1996
813'.54—dc20   96-7659
                                               CIP

First Pocket Books hardcover printing November 1996

10 9 8 7 6 5 4 3 2 1

POCKET and colophon are registered trademarks of
Simon & Schuster Inc.

Printed in the U.S.A.

To my much loved, mid-Atlantic parents,
Tom and Eleanor Mead

I am enormously and sincerely grateful to my editor, Dona Chernoff, for her enthusiasm, hard work, and relentless refusal to pull her punches. My equally sincere thanks to my agents, Emma Sweeney and Jane Bradish-Ellames, for all their efforts on behalf of this book.

My husband, Guy, and my sons and daughters, for continuing to believe that I tell good stories, and for continuing to listen to them. My dog, Boot, who provides enough material to deserve a book to himself, and who will no doubt eat a copy or two of this one. He is the only living creature who appears as a character in this book, and in his case, all similarities are wholly intentional.

My friends Helen Pate McLean and Jonathan McLean, who exchanged their lovely home for ours, and Carol and W. L. Biggs, who taught us the essence of Southern hospitality, and all those we met in a certain small town in North Carolina, who were, without exception, warm and generous in their welcome to strangers.

I have various friends who read the first draft of the book, and whose advice and encouragement were invaluable: Annette Falkner, Beate von der Seipen, Elise Ballantyne, Tina Jenkins, Amanda Lay, Emilie and Rich Powers, and Tim Woolley of Woolley & Wallis, Salisbury. I can only ask them to continue to read, advise, and encourage.

Finally, but not for the last time, to my parents, who always made sure there was a rocking horse in the garden.

"Love in the form in which it exists in society, is nothing but the exchange of two fantasies and the superficial contact of two bodies."

—*Nicholas-Sébastien Chamfort, Maximes et Pensées, 1796*

The Husband (musing)
"She has not meant to wound me, nor to vex—
Zounds! But 'tis difficult to please the sex.
I've housed and gowned her like a very queen
Yet there she goes with discontented mien.
I gave her diamonds only yesterday:
Some women are like that, do what you may."

—*Ella Wheeler Wilcox, from "A Holiday" (1850–1919)*

"There is no infidelity where there has been no love."

—*Honoré de Balzac, letter to Mme. Hanska, August 1833*

Intimate Strangers

"In general, Worldwide Home Exchange members tend to be the best of house guests. Perhaps this is because they understand that their own homes are just as vulnerable as yours and the golden rule of 'doing unto others' . . . takes on a new pertinence . . ."

—*The Worldwide Home Exchange Club Directory 1993*

Prologue

April 1993

BY THE TIME MAGGIE HAD SHOVELLED THE BABY INTO A DRY sleepsuit and was snapping the last button, she heard the front door slam, and Oliver's feet bounding up the staircase. She was unbuttoning her jeans as Oliver strode into their bedroom. Her husband was as fair as she was, a tall man with rangy good looks and a lazy grin, which he now directed towards his son and heir.

"Where have you been?" Maggie hated sounding accusatory, but did so more often than she would have cared to admit.

"Pub." He picked up Arthur and swung him into the air. "How are you, old chap? Not exactly dormant, I see." Arthur beat the air with his arms, delighted by the prospect of a late-night romp with his father. "I went with the Brig. He twisted my arm, Mags. Honest injun. We were only gone half an hour."

"Only half an hour? What was wrong, Ol? Did they run out of beer? No pretty barmaid around tonight? Nothing to tempt you?"

"Stop bitching, Mags. It was business. Charles and Lucy were there, and Edward. They all sent their love. Didn't they, Wart? Oh yes they did. Oodles of love to Mummy." He laid the baby back on the bed, and began tickling the velvet soles of his feet.

"Oh, he's never going to go back to sleep if you start doing that. He was barely awake when I brought him in. He'd be asleep now if the bloody answering machine had been on. The phone woke him up." Maggie sat on the edge of the bed in her bra and pants and pulled off her socks, glowering at her husband.

"Your machine," he said jauntily.

1

"Yes, but you turned it off."

Oliver shrugged. "Let's not fight about it, Mags. Let's save our strength for more important fights. You're not going to bed now, are you?" He glanced at his watch.

"I'm hardly dressed to go to the Ritz."

"Come back downstairs. I want to talk about this holiday. I'll put his nibs back to sleep, and you pour the whisky. Mine's a large one." He winked at her, and Maggie relented, and smiled back.

"In your dreams it is. Good night, sweet little bunny. Sleep tight." Maggie and Oliver had grown accustomed to three-way conversations. Maggie talked to Oliver whilst she talked to Arthur, and Oliver talked to Arthur whilst he talked to Maggie. Arthur didn't exactly talk—he was only nine months old—but he made himself understood. An eavesdropper might not have known which comment was addressed to whom, but there were subtle shifts in voice tone that identified the addressee, if the context didn't. Oliver Callahan was many things, but a sweet little bunny wasn't one of them.

Maggie slipped on a dressing gown, and after checking that Lily was sleeping quietly, she retreated back to the small sitting room where she had been sitting before summoned upstairs by Arthur's bellow. She poked the fire halfheartedly. It was mid-April, but still cold enough in the evenings to warrant a fire. Her notes were strewn all over the floor of the room that she insisted on calling her office, although everybody else referred to it as the den. She shuffled them into a pile, and stuffed it into a folder. Oliver hated the way she worked. He claimed there were only three things required of a successful journalist: efficiency, efficiency, and efficiency. Maggie countered that the only reason he could afford to say that was that *his* work was done in the comparative order of the study he had claimed on the ground floor of the house, or in the offices of the *Daily Telegraph,* whereas almost all of hers, as a freelance journalist, was done at the kitchen table, or leaning against Arthur's cot in the middle of the night, or in the den. She had no computer of her own, no filing cabinet, no in-tray, and if she didn't sort herself out relatively soon, as Oliver so frequently reminded her, it looked like her sporadic freelance career would disappear as well. By the time Oliver came downstairs, miraculously baby-free, she had poured two tumblers of whisky, pulled out a shabby file labelled "House Swaps

1993" and was curled up in the armchair nearest the fire. Oliver looked smug.

"That was quick," Maggie acknowledged grudgingly. She was genuinely appreciative that Ol had settled Arthur back in his cot, but still felt that he deserved some punishment for nipping off to the boozer without a word to her.

"It's all a matter of discipline, Mags. As you know, I won't brook insubordinate behaviour, and Arthur knows it, too. As soon as you left the room, he took one look at me, tugged his forelock in a suitably servile way, said 'Right you are, boss,' and went straight to sleep. Knows the hierarchy, that boy. Discipline. Authority." He waved a fist in the air.

"He just knows you are not as much fun as I am. You either bored him to sleep, or the alcoholic fumes on your breath must have knocked him unconscious."

"Now, now, Mags, none of your lift just because I had a quick pint—half, I mean—with the Brig. I had to. He absolutely insisted. He's in a terrible lather. Trying to block some sort of new road the Department of Transport have recommended. The Brig wants us to chain ourselves to the trees. You'd think it was the battle of El Alamein, or something. I had to lend support, do my bit for the community, didn't I? I told them we probably wouldn't be here for the showdown in the summer, but we could instruct our Yanks to lie in the path of the bulldozers. The very least I could do was make sympathetic noises."

"You mean slurping, swallowing, bear-belching noises?"

"Exactly. Community spirit down at The Fox in Garters. He wants some press coverage."

"Ol, since when have you written an environmental article?"

"First time for everything. Anyway, Mags, you could turn your hand to it. You could ghostwrite it under my name, to lend it a bit of credibility."

Maggie ignored his suggestion. "I think we're going to be stuck here all summer if we don't get some more favourable responses." She looked idly through the file on her lap. "The only replies we've had from the directory are the ranch outside Midland, Texas, the two-bedroom apartment in Manhattan, and the luxury duplex in Rancho Santa Fe, California."

Oliver shuddered. "I am not, repeat *not*, going to spend eight weeks—which, for all I know, could be a significant portion of my remaining life span, in the Jacuzzi of "one of America's most prestigious residential communities." He snatched the book off Maggie's lap. It was a slim, vanilla directory called The Worldwide Home Exchange Club, and listed perhaps a thousand homes around the world that people wanted to exchange for holidays. Across the top of the cover was the slogan "Holiday in Rent-Free Splendor . . ." He flipped first to their own entry, and read it aloud:

"Lovely spacious nineteenth-century family house with large gardens situated in idyllic rural location near Salisbury, Wiltshire. Four reception rooms, eight bedrooms. Stonehenge—five miles; Historic Bath, Winchester, and Longleat all within easy driving distance. Cleaning included. Central heating, fridge, washer/dryer, dishwasher, TV, stereo. Two cars. Three dogs.

"Small London flat possibly available.

"Oliver and Margaret Callahan, Bockhampton House, Bockhampton, Salisbury, Wiltshire. (H) journalist. (W) journalist. Three adults, two children (ages four and nine months). Prefer USA for long swap—six to eight weeks."

He put the book down and looked balefully at Maggie.

"Sounds bloody awful, doesn't it? No microwave. No tennis court. No bloody Jacuzzi."

"You wrote it, chum. You always claim you are the one with the gift for a finely turned phrase. You always say that if one of us is going to make a living out of writing, it's going to be you. Anyway, you exaggerated quite enough already about the central heating."

"We *do* have central heating." Maggie arched her eyebrows. "Some of it. It's just not very efficient. Anyway, it will be the middle of bloody summer! No one will even know if there's central heating or not." He glared at the entry again. "We should have put in a photo. That would have clinched it. Why didn't we put in a photo?"

Maggie gave him a dazzling smile. "Correct me if I'm wrong, my darling, but as I remember, you resented paying the extra seven pounds fifty."

"Bloody hell. Rancho Santa Fe, here we come."

Maggie and Oliver sat downstairs for another hour, looking through the register of houses. Three months previously, on a friend's recommendation, they had impulsively filled out a membership form to join the Worldwide Home Exchange Club. Oliver had persuaded the *Telegraph* to commission him for a series of articles, a sort of lighthearted version of "Letter from America," and Maggie had decided to take two months off from writing her freelance pieces. She could always dabble in some of Oliver's if she felt withdrawal pains. After six years of marriage and proofing his copy, she could have written an Oliver Callahan article with one hand, if not both, tied behind her back. In due course, they had been sent the booklet, with their entry printed in it, and instructions that they should write to the owners of those houses that appealed to them, and propose a swap. They had written seven letters, mainly to people on the East Coast (Oliver had a knee-jerk aversion to the West Coast) and to a couple of entries in Mexico, just for the hell of it. Oliver wasn't at all sure how the *Telegraph* would feel about "Letter from the Yucatan." So far, they had not received a reply from any of the people they had approached, but had received three unsolicited letters from people who had liked *their* entry. They referred to them by location: Midland, Manhattan, and Rancho Santa Fe, although Oliver occasionally referred to them by their owners' assumed attributes: The Cowboy, The Legal Eagle, and The Dickhead. At a pinch, they would accept the Texan cattle ranch. Neither of them knew Texas, or the Southwest at all, so at the very least it would count as "an experience." Manhattan was, through no fault of the city, deemed unsuitable: a two-bedroom apartment simply wasn't big enough to accommodate the two of them, Lily and Arthur, and their nanny Leah, and Maggie didn't relish the idea of entertaining two small children in the middle of New York City for eight weeks. Rancho Santa Fe had been ruled out altogether. Oliver said that the owners' claim that they lived "in one of America's most prestigious, if not *the* most prestigious, residential communities" made him want to vomit.

Maggie looked up from the additional supplement to the directory they had received a few days earlier that listed the late entries.

"Ol? You know where I'd *really* like to be? I'd like to go to the South."

Oliver didn't look up. Having rejected all the Tennessee entries, he was now looking at Vermont.

"The South? You mean Florida? Disney World?"

"No, I mean the proper South. The Old South. You know. Civil War stuff. Sherman's March. The Confederacy."

Oliver put a finger in the book to keep his place and looked at her with a smile.

"You never really got over *Gone with the Wind,* did you, Mags?

You're just dying to slip into a hoop skirt, sit on the porch, and say, "Well, I declair! Mistah Rhett!" as Clark Gable sweeps you into his arms . . ."

"Yeah, that's the problem. I'd only have you, and you're nothing like Rhett Butler. Ashley Wilkes, perhaps." She smiled back into his long, narrow face. "You know, Ol, it's never occurred to me before, but you actually *do* look a bit like Leslie Howard. Your nose is a little on the big side—beaky rather than aquiline, and your jawline isn't as firm as his—and you look a touch debauched rather than noble—but on a dark night, if you just glanced quickly—"

"And happened to be accompanied by a guide dog and a white stick, yes, yes, I've heard it all before, thank you very much, Mags. A bit less of the cheek, please. You just get your nose back in that supplement and find us somewhere to go or *you're* going to stay put in one of England's *least* prestigious residential communities and I'm going to Manhattan alone."

Christy Moore McCarthy was sitting on the back porch of her house reading *Business Week*. She wasn't particularly gripped by the article on small cap stocks, and hadn't been interested in small cap stocks for about three years—maybe longer, if she were honest with herself—but she read it anyway. Christy read everything. She read *Business Week* and she read the *Washington Post,* and she read *Vanity Fair, National Geographic,* and *Cosmopolitan.* She would have read *Popular Mechanics* if they had had a subscription to it. She read novels, and children's stories and plays. She read romantic fiction, detective fiction, and horror fiction. She read books on zoology, sociology, theology, criminology, and ecology. She read biographies, and history and poetry. She read anything she could get her hands on. Most of all, she read "literature." Once she had even read a science fiction novel. She had a curious mind, a hungry appetite, and an active imagination. And since she had stopped working as a Merrill Lynch broker six years ago, she had an awful lot of time on her hands.

She read *Business Week* cover to cover, and then put it down. It was only April, and still midmorning, but the porch was getting hot. By midsummer, its new coat of white paint would be blistered by the sun. Christy went into the kitchen to make a pitcher of iced tea. She made it the traditional way, with real tea leaves, real lemon juice, and real sugar. She had no need to watch her weight, and anyway, she liked tradition. Her mother, Blanche Hewlett Moore, had always claimed that you could tell whether someone was a lady or not just by watching them make tea. She poured the hot tea over a tall glass of ice, and listened to the cubes crack and shatter. Her mother wouldn't approve of that. Her mother would have insisted on letting the tea cool before it was served, but Christy had less patience than her mother. As Christy returned to the porch, the mailman pulled up the back drive.

"How're y'all doing today, Mrs. McCarthy?"

"Just grand, thank you, Sam. It's getting real hot, isn't it?"

"Ain't it just. Gonna get right much hotter too."

"I expect you're not wrong there! You take care now, Sam."

He waved goodbye, and Christy looked through the pile of mail, and opened a thick brown envelope. It was from her friend Myra in New York. Inside the envelope she found a book, a cream-coloured directory called The Worldwide Home Exchange Club. She read the short pink note that accompanied it.

Dear Christy,

This arrived in the mail a few weeks back and Marty and I can't get away this year because of Mitch's summer school. (God how I wish my kids were still as little as Jake! Soon we'll have to deal with his *girlfriends!*) I was about to trash it when I thought how you and Gabe were always talking about making a long trip to Europe, and I got to thinking how this might just *inspire* you to go do it! We've done three exchanges through this outfit and had a great time, so why not give it a whirl? You just pick the houses you like the sound of, and write them, or better phone them, because the nice places get booked up fast, and I've had this hanging around the apartment forever.

Hugs to Gabe and Jake and ring me when you've looked through the book. And it's about time you came to the city—you must be dying to get out of the sticks!

Myra

Myra was wrong in her conviction that Christy longed to return to New York. Christy had left the city six years ago, when she conceived Jake, and "retired" to full-time motherhood and Oak Ridge, a house outside the small town of Lawrenceville in Marlon County,

North Carolina. She had never once regretted the move, and if there *was* something missing from her life, it surely wasn't New York. She had loved it when she lived there, but now she didn't want to go back. When Christy made a considered decision, she acted on it, and she didn't regret it. Her friends who hadn't taken the same decision reassured themselves by thinking that Christy had made a mistake. But she hadn't. Christy Moore McCarthy had been raised in the strictest of genteel Southern traditions, and the two dietary supplements given with mother's milk to all upstanding Southerners, male or female, were determination and tenacity. Christy had them both in spades. Christy didn't make mistakes, she made decisions. It was that simple.

It took Christy the rest of the morning to read through the directory, and when she had finished, she didn't call Myra. She called her husband at his office in Charlotte, two hundred miles northwest of Lawrenceville.

"Hey, darlin'! Is everything okay?"

"Everything's fine, Gabe, just fine."

"What are you doing?"

"Nothing much."

"C'mon, Christy! Tell me everything you've done since you woke up. You know how I like to be able to imagine what you're doing at any time of day."

"Like I said, Gabe"—Christy struggled to keep the irritation out of her voice—"nothing much. Just reading. Johnny's coming by in a while to give me another lesson."

"Work on your backhand, okay, honey? Like we were doing this weekend."

"Okay. Gabe? How much vacation are you going to take this summer?" She had to phrase the question that way. Her husband was entitled to as much vacation as he wanted, as one of the partners of a small but noted North Carolina law firm. Some of his peers took the whole summer off, but not Gabe, who felt that simply wasn't fair to the junior partners and associates. She heard him draw his breath in over his teeth.

"Hard to say at this stage, honey. Maybe two weeks. It depends what kind of a backlog we've got . . . Did you decide where you want to go?"

"Yeah. I want to go to Europe."

"Honey, we went to Paris for New Year's. I thought we could

maybe go to Vermont or something, get away from the goddamn heat . . ."

"I want to go to Wiltshire."

"Wiltshire! Where on God's green earth is Wiltshire?"

"In England. Stonehenge is in Wiltshire." She expected him to follow her train of thought.

"Stonehenge?"

"Oh, Gabe! I *told* you about Stonehenge! It was in *Tess of the D'Urbervilles* . . ."

"Oh, yeah. I remember now; you were all worked up about being Tess, weren't you? Was that the book where there was a guy like me in it? Didn't you think I was like the hero?"

Christy laughed. "No, Gabe. I did *not* think you were like the hero. You aren't anything like Angel Clare, and anyway, he isn't a real hero . . . not in the end."

"Well, that's a real relief, darlin', because the idea that anyone called *Angel* reminded you of me would have been kinda disturbing . . ."

"The guy I thought you were like was Gabriel Oak. In a different book. Same writer, though," she added to reassure him. Gabe needed no reassurance. He had read both *Tess of the D'Urbervilles* and *Far From The Madding Crowd,* and had only confused the male protagonists in order to amuse Christy, and give her the chance to patronise him. He would have stood on his head if it made her smile. His wife continued, "You should read both books. You could take them on vacation. To Wiltshire."

"Honey, I don't even have the time to read *one* book on vacation . . ."

"Gabe, could you get a sabbatical or something?"

"A sabbatical? 'Fess up, Christy; what's going on in that pretty head of yours?"

"I only meant, could you take a longer vacation, a month maybe . . . Could we go away for longer? Jake would love it, and he'd really benefit educationally . . ."

There isn't a parent on earth who hasn't *at least once* justified an indulgence of their own by claiming it was for the sake of their children. Parental love is one of the few incontestible defences of selfishness.

"I'd have to see . . ." Gabe said doubtfully, but didn't want to dash Christy's hopes. "Maybe."

"Okay. We'll talk about it when you get home. Can you come home early?" It was a Thursday. Gabe normally flew from Charlotte to Fayetteville, their nearest domestic airport, on Thursday evening, and worked from home on Fridays. It was one of the advantages of having exchanged his New York practice for a partnership in North Carolina.

"Do you want me home early, Christy, darling?"

"Sure I do! Early like *now.*" She made her voice husky and suggestive, and Gabe laughed.

"I'll do my best. Give Jake a hug for me if I don't make it back by bedtime."

"I surely will. See you. I'll be waiting," she purred.

She put the phone back gently in its cradle, and went upstairs to change into her tennis clothes. On the rocker on the porch, the Worldwide Home Exchange Club directory lay open, with only one entry circled in red:

"Lovely, spacious nineteenth-century family house with large gardens situated in idyllic rural location near Salisbury, Wiltshire. Four reception rooms, eight bedrooms. Historic Bath, Stonehenge . . ."

Christy couldn't wait for her husband to come home. As soon as Johnny, their tennis coach, had finished with her, leaving her a set of exercises for strengthening her wrist and thereby her backhand, Christy went back into the white antebellum house where she and Gabe and their son Jake had lived since leaving New York, and dialled a number in England. She had a long conversation with a charming woman called Maggie Callahan. They both talked at great length about their houses, and agreed to exchange detailed information and photographs. They discussed provisional dates, and the best airports to fly into. They talked about their respective husbands, children, and animals. They marvelled at the coincidence that both their husbands worked in part from home, and how useful it would be for them to have computers, printers, and fax machines when on holiday. They concurred that they should leave their existing cleaning and gardening arrangements in place. They agreed that six weeks was the absolute minimum amount of time required to make the project worthwhile, and settled on eight. They agreed about everything. Most importantly of all, they agreed to swap houses.

One

IT TOOK CHRISTY PRECISELY FIVE WEEKS TO ACHIEVE HER OBJECTIVES. By the 20th of May, not only had Gabe agreed to take eight weeks' vacation and go to Wiltshire instead of Vermont, but she had also exchanged several letters with the Callahans, and secured their formal undertaking to vacate their house for hers on the 3rd of July, and vacate her house for theirs on the 28th of August. Keen as she was to spend the summer in England, she didn't relish the idea of not being able to get into her beloved Oak Ridge again, and having to spend the rest of her days in deepest Wiltshire. She had also offered Maggie the use of their beach house, which had delighted the English lady. Christy had barely opened the letter containing the photographs of Bockhampton before she had fallen in love with the house; it was everything and more than she had imagined. Christy had dismissed Maggie Callahan's warnings that the house was a touch on the shabby side, and that the central heating was dodgy. She refused Maggie's offer to buy a microwave, saying that she wanted to live *exactly* the way the Callahans themselves lived. She told Maggie to make no changes to the house or garden whatsoever. For her own part, she had already booked their flight to London, arriving early on the 3rd, arranged for the tennis court to be resurfaced and the air-conditioning to be overhauled, and she had laid in a supply of "English Breakfast" tea. Christy put it in the freezer. She hoped it was suitable, and that it would stay fresh for the next six weeks. Only six weeks to go, and she had so much to *do* . . .

Most of their friends thought they were crazy to open their home to complete strangers. Mary-Jo, their closest neighbour in Lawrenceville, had been horrified. "But, Christy!" she had exclaimed. "What about your privacy? They'll go through your bank statements—and all your *personal* things . . ." Gabe had dismissed the notion with a laugh. "You've just blown your cover, Mary-Jo. *You* may be the type of person who would go through people's private papers, but that doesn't mean that the Callahans are, any more than we are. We are ordinary people; you are—something else." Mary-Jo had giggled coquettishly, but wagged her finger at him. "Well, Gabe, honey, if you have any problems with these people, don't you come running to me. I'll be sure to say I told you so." She had smoothed the silk of her figure-hugging dress, and prepared to leave the porch. "Now don't get me wrong; I'll look after these folk real good, just like they were genuine neighbours, but I still say you should put everything away that you wouldn't want your nearest and dearest to know about . . ."

Christy inspected her house and grounds as if she were seeing them for the first time. Oak Ridge had been built in the 1860's, and was not strictly a "plantation" house, more of a large and relatively luxurious farmhouse on the edge of Lawrenceville, surrounded by fields of cotton, tobacco, and soybean. The McCarthys had made some improvements since moving in. They had constructed the tennis court, and supervised the redesign of the garden and lawns, and last year Christy had finished the summer house down by the lake. Critical as her eye was, Christy knew it to be a lovely home. The house was a little formal, but retained the character of a family home. The kitchen and breakfast room were well equipped, but far from modern. Christy had left the original wood flooring throughout the house—its perpetual creaking and wheezing were part of the character of Oak Ridge and vastly preferable to the tap-tapping of a tiled floor, or the unnatural silence of fitted carpet. She walked slowly up the sweep of the large staircase, her hand automatically running above and below the carved banister to check for dust. On the second floor, the classical layout was repeated: four large bedrooms, their high ceilings dominated by huge wooden ceiling fans, windows and beds draped in billowing white cottons and lace to emphasize a cool, breezy effect. All the rooms—even Jake's—were quite bare and uncluttered, tributes to Christy's simple and elegant taste, and to her maid Ellen's hard work. Last of all, Christy opened the door of her husband's tiny office. Her mouth tightened as she saw the mess of papers scattered over the desk and floor, the ashtray heaped with old cigar butts, and the regimental line of dirty cups and glasses. She knew how much Gabe objected to Ellen's or his wife's intruding into his private sanctuary, but time was pressing, and they would have to sort it out in the next couple of weeks. As she glared at his desk, hands on hips, she heard the back door slam, and shrieks of laughter rang through the house. Mariella, her au pair, had returned from collecting Jake from school. Christy's heels clicked down the stairs as she went to greet them.

Jake hurled himself into her arms as if he hadn't seen her for weeks, rubbing his black curly head against her stomach, talking and giggling at the same time so that he was almost incomprehensible.

"Mommy, Mommy, Mommy—guess what Billy did—just guess what he did—it was *so* funny, he looked like an elephant—"

Christy calmed Jake down enough to allow him to describe how Billy Fairfield, his best friend at school, had a mouthful of water that he had spewed over their kindergarten teacher. Jake thought this act had scaled a new peak in the art of comedy. Mariella waited to one side, watching Christy cautiously to see whether her boss would be amused, or whether she would be held responsible for this disgraceful act. Christy was in a good mood. She frowned, and shook her finger, but her lovely smile broke through in seconds, even though her tone was reprimanding.

"That was very, *very* naughty of Billy."

"Yes it was. *Very* naughty," Jake agreed delightedly.

"Poor Mrs. West."

"Yes, poor Mrs. West. *Naughty* Billy." This again from Jake, his face a picture of joy. Christy laughed, hugged him, and looked up at Mariella. "Would you take Jake down to the lake for a swim before dinner, Mariella? I went in at lunchtime and it was as hot as a bath. I need to get some things ready for England."

"When are we going to England, Mommy?" Jake asked. "Are we going tomorrow? Are we going on an airplane?" He imitated one. "Are we going now?"

"Soon, darling. We're going real soon. You'll be there before you know it."

"What about Jackson? We going to take Jackson?"

"Honey, we're not allowed to take dogs to England, but the Callahans will look after him real well for you, and they've got three dogs over there—I'll show you the pictures of them."

"*Three* dogs? Great!" Jake, as fickle as most five-year-olds, at once forgot about Jackson and galloped off after Mariella. As Christy watched him go she again thought what a tragedy it was that her son was so innocently dependent on animals for companionship. She would have given anything to have been able to give him a little brother or sister, but it wasn't possible. It was one of those things that just hadn't worked out quite as she had planned.

Christy returned upstairs with a couple of cartons for Gabe's papers. As she sorted them into piles and laid them neatly in the boxes, a sentence or phrase occasionally caught her eye. Again and again, people asked for her husband's advice. A hand-written scrawl from a colleague: "Gabe, I think this looks okay, but I'd appreciate you having a final check." "GTM—FYI: a letter of thanks from NationsBank. Well done, sport!" "Gabe. Here's my estimate for the Morgan Lewis deal. Could you run over the numbers when you've got a minute?" Some of the clients from his old New York firm were still referred to him, former colleagues missing Gabe's judgement after nearly six years. Christy felt a tiny frisson of—what? Pride? No. Resentment? She respected Gabe, of course she did, and she was proud of him, proud that he was so highly esteemed by his peers in the legal profession. Nonetheless, there had been a time when Christy herself had brought home armfuls of work, memos marked for *her* attention, requests for *her* advice, notes of congratulation on *her* handling of a major stock placing. What did she get now? Nothing. The only people who asked her opinion were Mariella, Ellen, and the occasional builder or decorator working on one of their properties. Christy knew perfectly well that no one had pushed her out of her job—least of all, Gabe. It had been her own decision to leave Merrill, and one that she had never regretted. Never. But once in a while it would be nice if someone other than a member of her household asked her opinion about something. Just because she had stopped work to be a good mother didn't mean that her brains had addled overnight. Of course, *Gabe* still asked her advice. He frequently consulted her about whether or not he should take on a case, how he should handle a tricky client, when to promote a talented but overconfident junior. It just wasn't the same. In her heart of hearts she knew that her husband genuinely wanted to know what she thought, and generally acted on her instincts. But it still wasn't the same, it wasn't the way things used to be. She wanted someone else to depend on her, someone who wasn't married to her, wasn't paid by her, and ideally, was taller than three foot six. She finished packing up the papers, and if the last ones on the pile were a little less neatly arranged than the first, a little more crumpled, Gabe would be the last to notice.

At seven o'clock, Christy went to Jake's bedroom and found her son in his pyjamas and Mariella tidying away his clothes. She said good night to Mariella, and sat down on Jake's bed. He was waiting for her. His newly washed hair had been smoothed down by Mariella's patient brushing, but dark, unruly curls, inherited from his father, were springing up around his forehead as they began to dry.

"Have you chosen which stories you'd like?" asked Christy, as she settled herself on the edge of his bed.

"Yup. These five." He shoved the books into her lap.

"Jake. You know the rule. Three."

"No, five. Five's not a lot."

"Three."

"Oh, *Mom!* Three's for babies. Three's hardly any—"

"Jake." She cut him off mid-whine. "Let me explain something to you, something you should remember all your life. There are things you can negotiate in life and things you just can't. This is one of the things you can't. You heard me. Three stories, bud."

Jake fell asleep before the end of the third story, and Christy returned downstairs to fix drinks ready for Gabe's arrival. She prepared mint juleps, pounding mint leaves and sugar into a green slime, and splashing in Maker's Mark bourbon over lots of ice. She was carrying the two tumblers and the crystal pitcher out to the porch when she heard Gabe's car scrunching on the gravel of the back drive. He removed his jacket and tie as he walked up the porch steps, presented her with a bunch of flowers, kissed her head, and poured out the drinks. It was a domestic ritual they adopted as soon as the weather turned towards summer and tipped over 70 degrees, generally in mid-April or early May. For a few moments they sipped their drinks in companionable silence, Christy leaning against the railing and gazing at the crape myrtle bushes in the courtyard. Gabe sighed contentedly.

"It's good to be home, darling."

Christy tensed automatically. This was also part of the ritual. "You always say that."

"I always feel it."

"You're so . . ."

"Predictable? Boring?"

Christy regained her composure and gave him the warmest smile she could muster. "No. You're so . . . supportive. You're always in a good mood, you always bring me flowers. You know what I mean. You're just very appreciative."

"I have a hell of a lot to appreciate, Christy; you most of all. Does it bother you?"

"Bother me?" She shrugged. "No; how could it? I'd have to be pretty weird if I let that bother me." She stood stiffly at the edge of the porch, plucking dead leaves off the plants that lined the balustrade, and wishing that Gabe showed a little less appreciation and a little more passion. "I'm glad you notice things, Gabe."

"Sometimes I think I bore you, though. I think you think I'm a pain in the ass."

One of the things that Christy found most irritating about her husband was his fear that he bored her. If he had ever really felt that way, he could damn well do more about it than just acknowledge it from time to time. Tonight, she interpreted this questioning, and his pause as he waited for her rebuttal, as his way of patting himself on the back for making her happy. His complacency insulted her. She screwed her eyes up tight, and counted to ten before turning to face him. She tapped him on a cheek that was turning stubbly, and Gabe took the opportunity to grab her hand.

"I surely think you're silly. How could you bore me? You're a fine husband, and a fine father, and I'm proud of you." She slid down onto his lap. "How was your week?"

"Too long. Dull. Martin's screwed up the Buckland purchase, and we're going to be liable. I told him a hundred times not to rush them, and now they've pulled out and we're heading right up shit creek." He closed his eyes as Christy's long fingers wound themselves in his thick hair, coaxing the curls onto his forehead. "But we've been there before. I dare say we'll be there again. It'll take months to sort out the mess."

"Not months, Gabe. You've only got till July first."

"Don't worry, Christy. We'll be on that plane if I have to fly it myself. I know how much this vacation means to you. I'd move heaven and earth to make you happy."

"You shouldn't be always thinking about me, Gabe. What about you? Don't *you* want to go? I wish you'd think of yourself for a change. Aren't you excited about it?"

"Sure I am, honey, but you know me, I'm pretty much happy

wherever I am, provided you and Jake are there too. I'd be happy just spending the rest of my life sitting right here." Not for the first time, it struck Christy how little her husband demanded from life. "Did you talk to the Callahans again?"

"Just to Maggie. Everything's set. I've even cleared out your office."

"Christy! We're not leaving for months! I need all those papers—"

"We're leaving in six weeks, and all your precious papers are fine. I kept them all in place, I just tidied them up. I figured if I left it to you I'd end up doing it the night before we fly. It's fine, Gabe. Trust me."

"I do trust you, darling. I trust you to find a way to do exactly what you want to do regardless of what I say"—she again tapped him playfully across the cheek—"and that's why I love you. One of the reasons why. One of the many." He kissed her and stood up, lifting her at the same time. "Have I time for a shower before dinner?"

Christy listened to his steady footsteps going up the stairs. She could hear him going first to the master bedroom, and then to Jake's before tracing his steps. She basted the pot roast. He *was* a fine father. He should have had a houseful of kids, although he never blamed her for not providing them, and always said that Jake was the whole world to him. He loved her, too. He even took the time to say so, and Christy believed him. As far as her husband was concerned, there was nothing missing from their lives.

Oliver stomped around Lily's bedroom dragging one leg behind him. "Aaargh! Grrr-aaa-wlll!" he roared.

Lily sat up in bed, watching him calmly. "That's not very good, Daddy. You're not scary. Mummy's scarier. Lots."

"Well, fine, thank you very much, young lady. I'll accept your opinion when you are the casting director of the Royal Shakespeare Company, and not until then. I'll have you know some of the finest actors in the land—Alan Howard, Kenneth Branagh, or Ken, as I call him, Anthony Hopkins, Gielgud himself—have consulted me on the portrayal of monsters, ogres, and all forms of unpleasantness. As for Mummy, although she is undoubtedly scary at certain times— like first thing in the morning—she is a *neophyte* in the monster business"—he heard Maggie come into the room behind him—"and even though she's shaping up nicely, she has a great deal to learn. A very great deal. You just watch your pa, and learn from the master."

Oliver repeated his performance, watched by two pairs of implacable green eyes. Maggie and Lily remained unimpressed.

"Okay, so I'm a little rusty. Arthur thinks it's a damn good interpretation."

"That's 'cos Arthur is just a baby," Lily explained matter-of-factly.

"Lily, it's time to go to sleep. It's very late, well past your bedtime. Ol, Edward called and said he wants to drop by and use the fax. He said he could use a whisky, too. You better go down—he'll be here any minute."

"Oh, Mummy! Daddy's going to read me a story!"

"It's too late for stories. If you wanted stories you should have gone to bed earlier." Maggie spoke firmly.

"That's not fair!" Lily cried. "Pul-lease, Daddy! You promised!"

Oliver looked proudly at Maggie. "My audience calls, and I cannot deny them."

"Okay. I'll go down and see Edward. But no monkey business, you two, d'you hear?"

"Monkey business? Now that's something I *can* do!"

Maggie left the room as Oliver began scratching his armpits for Lily's amusement.

She heard a noise in Oliver's office and went to join Edward, who had already arrived and let himself in. She found him trying to send a fax to a London antique dealer. Edward Arabin was a partner at Bishop & Moodey, the Salisbury auctioneers. More importantly, he was one of the Callahans' nearest neighbours and closest friends. Ten years older than Oliver, he carried his age easily, and apart from the salt and pepper sprinkled through his dark hair, could have passed for being in his late thirties.

"Sorry we weren't here, Eddie. We were putting the children to bed."

"Little bastards still up, are they? You should have them put down, Maggie, really. That's what I'd do."

"That's because you haven't got any children, Eddie."

"Too right. One of life's small mercies. How are you, lovely?"

"Oh, I'm okay. A bit tired."

"You look gorgeous. Perfectly edible." He brushed her cheek with his lips, and stood back, holding her away from him and with his head cocked on one side, appraising her as if she were a painting.

"Perhaps I can detect slight shadows under the eyes—rather alluring, in fact. It suits you. Maybe you shouldn't go on holiday."

"Well, we *are* going, Eddie. I told you. We're swapping houses with an American family called the McCarthys."

"Ah, yes! Our American cousins! How could I have forgotten? So when's D-day? When are the Yanks landing?"

"We'll leave on the second of July; they'll arrive here on the third. Come into the den and have a drink with me. Oliver will be down soon."

"I'd much rather come into the den and have a drink with you if Oliver *wasn't* going to be down soon . . ."

Maggie looped her arm through his. "Do you know, Edward, you have the most jaded, hackneyed pick-up lines I've ever heard, but I love you for it. It's good for us mums to have a local roué around. You do cheer us up."

Edward kept up his banter as Maggie poured their drinks, but he was watching her closely. There was something a little hangdog about her tonight, and he suspected it was something to do with Oliver.

"So. How is he?"

"Who?"

"Your lover, of course. Who do you think I mean, Maggie? 'Im upstairs."

"Oliver's fine. You'll see for yourself, in a minute."

"And you? How are you, really?" Edward sat in an armchair and stretched out his long legs.

"How am I, *really?*" Maggie echoed. "Oh, Edward. I don't know. I'm looking forward to this holiday, but I just can't seem to work up much enthusiasm. I think I'm just tired, honestly. Arthur's not sleeping very well, teething or whatever. *Teething* seems to be the catch-all phrase that parents use when what they mean is being a right bastard." She smiled wanly at him, inviting him to laugh at her. He didn't. "Did you see my piece in the *Mail?*"

"No, Mags, I didn't. I don't read the papers unless you warn me you've got a piece coming out."

"I've never seen you read anything in any paper except for the cricket articles . . ."

"Only stuff that's worth reading. In the good old days, when I was a lad"—Edward was in his midforties, and thought that the best way to deal with jokes about his age was to exaggerate it—"the

19

quality papers wrote quality stuff. Now it's all lies. Lies, lies, and marketing."

"My piece was about child care and parenting. About whether mothers should stay at home and look after their children rather than going back to work."

"Good God, Mags, you are turning serious in your old age!"

"Oh, it wasn't serious. My serious days died about five or six years ago. Just around the time Ol and I got married, curiously enough. The article was an attempt to justify to myself having a nanny when I barely work any longer."

"You shouldn't be bothered about justifying anything. You're quite alright as you are."

"Ah, but I do bother, Eddie. That's my Achilles heel."

"You don't have an Achilles heel, darling. You have two perfectly beautiful heels, and don't let anyone tell you otherwise."

Maggie warmed under the glow of his approval. Edward always made her feel happier about herself.

"Anyway, let me have a copy of this article; it sounds right up my street."

"Since when were you interested in child care?"

"I'm not—but I'm interested in you." Maggie had often had the sensation of a door opening in her relationship with Edward, and although she had no inclination to slam it shut, she was too wary to nudge it further open.

"Thanks," she said lightly. "Always the gent, aren't you, Eddie? Do you want a top-up?"

She was refilling Edward's glass as Oliver came into the room.

"Edward, old man. Keeping the wife company?"

"Not having one of my own, I find keeping other men's wives company one of my favourite pastimes, Oliver. Maggie was just filling me in on your American visitors. D'you want me to show them around, give them a bit of a tour?"

"Not your kind of tour, Eddie. Not that many tourists would want to see eighteen pubs in one evening." Oliver lobbed a cushion at Edward's head.

"Seriously, Edward, could you take them out to something? Take them to a point-to-point, or round the Cathedral, or something?"

"Of course I could, Maggie. I'd be delighted. Perhaps not the Cathedral, though . . . let me think." He frowned, pulling his dark bushy eyebrows together in the effort of concentration. "I could

always take them to the cricket! A village match, or even Lords."
He nodded towards Oliver. "You'd have to stump up for the three
tickets, old man. I'm not laying out twenty-six quid a seat for people
I haven't even met and am unlikely to get off with."

"Two tickets, Eddie. I'm not bloody paying for your bloody day
out. You can buy your own bloody ticket, and if you *do* get off with
Mrs. McCarthy, I'll expect a refund on her ticket, too."

"Fair enough, Oliver, but don't bank on it. I've never had much
success with married women, more's the pity." He kissed Maggie's
cheek. "Look, I'll have a think about the test match. If I can work
it, I'll pull it off; if not, I'll entertain them some other way. Fear
not. Well, my lovely, I must be off. Do you two want to come over
for a spot of dinner next week? Thursday? Charles and Loopy Lucy
are coming."

"Not if you're cooking, Eddie. Our dogs eat better than the muck
you dish up." Oliver was still smarting at having been bulldozed
into paying fifty-two pounds for a cricket match he wouldn't even
see. "I'm up in London on Thursday anyway."

"Are you? Thanks for letting me know," Maggie said sharply before smiling at Edward. "I'd love to come, provided I can get the
nanny to babysit."

"Excellent. Then you can play hostess for me, lovely. I'll see
you then."

Edward patted Oliver's shoulder, and wandered out of the house
and down the lane to his own home. He was thinking about the
Callahans—more particularly, what was wrong with them. He had
known both Oliver and Maggie ever since the day they had moved
into Bockhampton, and he had taken an especial interest in Maggie.
There was something about her—something tremendously appealing
that he couldn't quite put his finger on. Oliver was far easier to
define; he was an out and out bounder, but an immensely charming
one. But Maggie . . . Maggie was different. Special. Recently, she
had seemed increasingly depressed, and Edward was worried about
her. By the time he completed the walk to his front door, he had
come to the simple conclusion that either Maggie wasn't getting
enough sex, or Oliver was getting too much.

Two

A message on the Callahans' answering machine:

Hey, Maggie; this is Christy McCarthy. I just wanted to let you know that we're all set—and we've set up Jake's old crib for your little boy, and some toys for the little girl. It's a crying shame we won't meet you on the way over, but we'll be waving from the airplane! Y'all take care now, and don't hesitate to call me if you need anything else. . . .

ON THE EVENING OF THURSDAY, THE 27TH OF MAY, MAGGIE POURED a glass of wine in the kitchen, listening to the radio with one ear and to her nanny arguing with Lily with the other one.

"Mummy, Leah's being horrid. She won't let me watch the *Jungle Book* and I want to and she's horrid and not my friend and will you tell her to go away and you can stay with us and why are you wearing that dress?"

"Don't you like it, Lily?"

"No. It's boring and black. Why don't you wear something pretty and bright yellow with lots and lots of frills?" Lily's arms stretched out in imitation of a huge hooped skirt as she pirouetted for her mother.

"Yellow suits you, darling, but it doesn't suit me. It makes me look like a banana. And anyway, it would get covered in dog hairs. Black dresses don't show Boomer's hair." At the mention of his name, the obese black labrador at her feet thumped his tail half-heartedly. Lily watched with narrowed eyes as her mother snapped earrings on.

"You're not going out, are you, Mummy? You're not leaving us?"

"I'm going to have dinner with Edward, Lily. I won't be gone long. And Leah will be here with you."

"Why can't Leah go to dinner with Edward?" Lily wailed. "You could stay here and read us stories *all night*. I hate Edward."

"No, you don't, you like him very much, and you should never say you hate anyone, Lily. It's very rude."

"But I *do* hate him. And sometimes I hate Arthur." Lily's whining stopped as she mentally ran through the list of people she sometimes hated. A contemplative look came over her face. *"And* William. *And* Horrid Miranda." She was warming to the task, naming all her supposed "best friends" at nursery school.

"That's enough, Lily. I won't be long, Leah. I don't even want to go, to be honest."

"Bullshit, you'll have a fab time. What's the story with the plans for America?"

"We're all set. Oliver's got his commission from the *Telegraph* and thinks he's going to be the new Alistair Cooke. The McCarthys have been incredibly efficient, done all the insurance and whatever. I asked them to put your name on the car insurance so you can have a bit of freedom, and go off on your own for a while."

"That's brill. I have a mate in Atlanta who wants me to visit."

"Fine. You don't know when you'll get the chance to go back to the States, so you should make the most of it. I certainly intend to." Maggie gave the two children a squeeze, which Lily tried hard to wriggle out of as it blocked her view of the TV screen.

When Maggie let herself into the barn that Edward Arabin had converted several years ago, she could hear the voices of the Wickham-Edwardes raised in argument. There was nothing unusual in this. Charles and Lucy argued nonstop, considering it almost their duty to amuse their hosts or guests by exaggerated marital bickering. If Maggie had heard once how Lucy had had her pick of the county, and had made the mistake of accepting Charles's proposal, she'd heard it a thousand times, and if Maggie had heard once how Charles had married a beautiful blond nymph who had metamorphosed into a ten-stone harridan within twelve months, she'd heard it a thousand and one times. The truth was that Charles had been and probably still was the pick of the county, and Lucy remained barely over eight stone and the belle of, at the very least, South Wiltshire. For this particular row they had appointed Edward to

judge the grudge, and he sat in long-suffering silence as they presented their opposed cases about the redesign of their garden. Edward slumped opposite them, his elegant fingers pressed to his
forehead in pain as he listened to them bicker. He rolled his grey
eyes at Maggie as she came in. Lucy and Charles barely drew breath
to greet her before continuing, but Maggie's entrance allowed Edward to excuse himself to get the new arrival a drink. When he
returned, the question was put to the vote:

"Can you imagine anything worse, anything more tasteless than
a row of cypressa and a rockery? It's disgusting. It makes me think
of some nasty little suburb like Borehamwood."

"Don't be such a stupid snob, Lucy; your whole concept of gardens depends on 'The Englishwoman and Her Garden'; you can't
have one-hundred-year-old mulberries, damn it, unless they were
planted a hundred years ago. What we need here is imagination,
vision . . . new frontiers—that's what gardening is all about, isn't
it, Edward?"

The conversation was interrupted by the arrival of two of Edward's friends who had driven down from London. When they sat
down to dinner—Edward's speciality of smoked salmon with brown
bread, a steak and kidney pie, and a selection of English cheeses—
Lucy turned to Maggie and demanded to know all about the American who were coming to stay.

"We can't help but be curious, Maggie. It's not often we have
strangers in the Valley after all, and I don't think any Americans
have been here—not to stay, that is. Probably not since the war. Is
he desperately good looking?"

"I hadn't really thought about it, but yes, he is, in a way. Judging
from the photo they sent. Sort of big and tall and dark. I suppose
Americans would call him a jock."

"How *lovely*," Lucy purred. "And what about her? What's she
like?"

"Very pretty," Maggie said firmly. "Really lovely. She says she's
thirty-six, but she looks ten years younger, very slim . . . She was
wearing tennis clothes in the photo, and had mile-long tanned legs—
slim but sort of athletic—and masses of wavy dark hair, huge eyes"—
Lucy's narrowed perceptibly—"and cover girl smile, perfectly white
teeth; you can come and have a look at the snaps they sent if you
like, Luce."

"No thanks. I'll wait until she arrives in person. She sounds simply too frightful for words. How exactly do you mean 'slim but athletic'? Muscular calves?"

"Oh, God, no; I mean slim but in really good shape—like an eighteen-year-old's."

"Bitch. I can see it's going to be a question of lock up your husbands, isn't it? Not to mention the local bachelors. What's the betting we don't see Edward for the whole of the summer—he'll be fawning over her at your house all the time. At least Oliver will be out of harm's reach. You are wicked, Maggie, to place a femme fatale in the neighbourhood and then bugger off a million miles with your own man. It's not fair on the rest of us."

"You'll be fine, Luce. I'm sure you're a match for Christy McCarthy. Anyway, she's not a femme fatale, she's a happily married woman—"

"I hope you're not suggesting the two are mutually exclusive, Maggie." Lucy bridled. "I mean, I'm a happily married woman, too, in a manner of speaking, and I like to think of myself as desperately 'fatale'; marriage doesn't mean *anything* when it comes to holiday romance. In *fact*—quite the opposite."

"She has a five-year-old son, and she's chosen to come here because she's passionately interested in English literature, particularly Hardy—"

"Oh, *God!* Don't say she's clever, too! It's just too, too much!" Lucy closed her eyes in pain.

"I haven't the foggiest if she's clever or not. Reading Hardy doesn't exactly make one clever, Luce. The McCarthys are simply a nice, young, uncomplicated American family, hoping to spend a nice, uncomplicated English country holiday."

"Are they *rich?*" Lucy lowered her voice infinitesimally, which was as close as she ever came to discretion.

"I've no idea! It's not the sort of question you ask when you're swapping houses. Not the sort of question *I'd* ask, that is. They seem—comfortable, at least. They have a very nice-looking house, plus a beach house. We haven't exchanged bank statements. Anyway, Luce, I'm not asking you to spend all your time with them. Just have them over for a drink, or something. Be nice."

"Come off it, Mags. When have you ever seen Lucy being 'nice' to an attractive younger woman?" Charles had been listening patiently to the conversation, waiting for an opportunity to have another dig at his wife.

"What do you mean, 'younger', Charles? I'm only thirty-nine, for heaven's sake, so she's barely younger than I am, however pretty she might be. And I'm perfectly nice to Maggie. I always have been."

"Precisely. I rest my case." There was a very short, but very uncomfortable silence, during which both Charles and Maggie reddened.

"Maggie, I didn't mean you're not attract—"

"It's alright, Charles, don't say—"

"You're a perfectly lovely young woman—"

"Charles, you *are* an ass." His wife groaned.

"No, you don't understand, what I *meant* was—"

"Just drop it, Charles. Maggie knows perfectly well that she's entrancing, and so do the rest of us. You'd have to be blind not to. Now leave it, or I'll be forced to agree with your wife for once that you are an ass. A complete ass." Edward reached to squeeze Maggie's hand, but found that she had tugged the sleeves of her dress down over her fingers in a familiar nervous gesture, making it impossible for him to touch them. He refilled her glass instead.

"Did anyone see that extraordinary programme on the box the other night—the one about animals' sex drives?" Charles was now trying to change the subject.

Maggie nodded. "It was *The Sexual Imperative*. Yes, I saw it. Baboons and mice. Australian desert mice, to be exact. It was amazing, wasn't it?"

"Are you particularly interested in baboons, then?" asked Richard, an advertising executive from London who had whizzed up for a breath of country air, as he put it.

"No, it was just a very interesting idea about which animals mate for life, and how they conduct courtship. You know, the selfish gene meets the sexual imperative, that sort of thing."

"How *exciting*! You mean, like what these baboons get up to? All sorts of weird sex stuff? No wonder Charles watched it!" Lucy was interested, but not enough to have forgotten her husband's recent faux pas.

"Not really weird, Luce. It was about the difference in courtship rituals of the desert mouse and the baboon; the baboon is effectively monogamous, and the desert rat isn't; their females react to them very differently."

"Which one is better?"

"In what way, better?"

"Well, a better lover, I suppose. Better at *it*. One would assume that the desert mouse is the better—how can I put it without being vilely vulgar?—*bonk*—as he does it more often—has more practice, so to say."

"I don't believe that anyone has ever proven that monogamy bears any relation to infrequency. Scientifically speaking, that is. Anyway, that wasn't the point, Lucy. I suppose they're equally good at *it*. The point was, which one ensures the reproduction of its own genetic line more effectively, and why is there such a difference between them. The desert mouse reaches sexual maturity, and just belts off to find a female, then he fights her, then they bonk, for about twelve hours, and then he goes off and finds another one, and it all starts over again. The baboon just picks his mate and sticks with her all his life, and does everything to please her so she has no reason to stray. It was just an interesting comparison."

"I know which one I'd rather be, haw haw!" laughed Michael, Edward's other London friend.

"You may think that, but there's a bit of a sting in the tail for the mouse." Maggie waited until she commanded their attention. "After about four days—or four partners—the mouse keels over and dies. All those hormones, you see—it's such a strain on the heart and the immune system."

Michael looked crestfallen and Lucy beamed. "I'd say he got his just deserts for not sticking around to help with the children. Did they relate it to men? Male human beings, if you could call them that?"

"No, they didn't, but it makes you think, doesn't it?" Maggie swung her hair forward, so that it half shielded her face. "I mean, you have to wonder if the mouse, on his deathbed, suddenly has a great crisis of conscience, and thinks it's just not worth it. Maybe he tries to leave a note for his sons—do as I say, not as I do, or something."

They all laughed. "But what about the lady baboon?" Lucy interjected. "Don't you think she gets frightfully bored with all that slavish devotion—I mean, Lord! The idea of some great ape plodding round after you all day saying, 'Dear, can I get you another cup of tea?' How tedious!"

"They didn't really speculate on the females."

"They should have. I mean, this desert mouse girl has a real problem. Why does she put up with it? Surely if she put her foot down and refused to do the dirty deed, the boys would have to change? The mice, I mean."

"You'd think so. Maybe they like it. Maybe there are females around who just like really aggressive, sexy macho men and they don't mind if they hang around or not."

"There's something in that." Lucy giggled. "I mean, if one had a baboon at home, and a mouse or two on the side, one might be relatively content. . . ."

Dinner passed easily, in the relaxed and rather lazy way that mid-week dinner parties in the country normally pass. No one was in a great hurry to leave, no one really cared about the impression they were making, and there were no urgent topics to discuss; apart from the two interlopers from London, Edward's guests were likely to see one another, if not the next day, then certainly the day after that. There was therefore a languorous quality to the evening. A little after midnight, the small party was still assembled around the large oak table.

"Eddie, I must leave. I told Leah that I'd be back early."

"No, you must *not*. You know perfectly well that it's still early, and I won't allow *you* to break up the party when you have the least distance to go, and an entirely competent Aussie looking after your house." Edward Arabin stared, rather pointedly in Maggie's opinion, at his London friends.

"C'mon, Mike, we ought to be leaving." Richard spoke firmly, but his rear remained glued firmly to his seat. "Perhaps a small whisky, old man, and then we'll be on our way."

"Afraid not, Dick. I don't serve after-dinner drinks to people who are driving. One of my few points of principle."

"We could always crash here, Edward. . . . I've got nothing much on tomorrow, have you, Mike?" Richard looked hopefully across the table.

"Not possible, I'm afraid. I have an auction to conduct first thing in the morning, and you'll be much better off leaving now when there's no traffic . . ." Edward rose to his feet without allowing Mike to reply.

It took Edward a matter of minutes to bustle the two men through their farewells and out the front door. When he returned from waving them off, Charles and Lucy had revived their garden row, and Maggie was searching halfheartedly for her handbag.

"Mags. A quick whisky. I haven't had a chance to talk to you properly all night. Now come and sit down by the fire"—he took her arm firmly—"and relax. It's early."

"Well . . ." Maggie slumped down onto the sofa, too tired to go home to bed, and grateful to Edward for stopping her attempts.

"Charles, we must leave."

"I rather fancied a whisky myself—" Charles began.

"No you didn't. You've had quite enough as it is. And Eddie said he had a lot on tomorrow."

Maggie again half rose from her seat, restrained by Edward's hand.

"I've got nothing whatsoever on tomorrow. Just wanted to get rid of those buggers. You can stay if you like." It wasn't the most enthusiastic of invitations.

"Thanks awfully, old man. A malt, perhaps?" Charles sat back in his chair.

"Charles!" Lucy made the word sound like a hissing cobra. "It's time we left, don't you think?"

It was a pretty standard end to a dinner party. Maggie and Charles bobbed up and down, unsure whether they were outstaying their welcome, with Lucy standing, coat on, hand wrapped around the doorknob. Charles finally shuffled off, and Edward and Maggie smiled at each other as they heard Lucy's voice ringing out through the night sky: "I simply will not, will *not*, tolerate a rockery in the garden. It's incontestable grounds for divorce, d'you hear me, Charles?"

"In that case, it sounds like a bloody good idea to me. . . ."

Edward touched his glass against Maggie's. His grey eyes smiled at her, as one hand swept his thick hair back.

"Alone at last. Now, lovely, what's worrying you?"

Maggie closed her eyes, and rubbed one of them wearily, not caring whether she smudged her mascara. There was no need for a preamble with Eddie.

"Is it that obvious? I never was much of an actress. I feel such a fool, Edward. I turned thirty-five last month."

"Mags! You didn't tell me! I would have baked a cake."

"I didn't think there was much to tell. Don't get me wrong, Edward. I'm not saying I'm depressed about hitting my midthirties, for God's sake. It's just that by now I should be a perfectly independent, mature woman, and have everything sorted out, and in fact, I haven't begun. I've achieved nothing. Sometimes I feel like I'm about sixteen."

"That's alright, lovely. Sometimes you look sixteen. And anyway, being thirty-five and feeling sixteen is infinitely preferable to being thirty-five and feeling forty-four."

Maggie shrugged. "It's not really about age. What I'm trying to say is that I feel odd when Oliver isn't here. He's spent a lot of time in town recently. I don't feel complete, and it makes me angry that I can't function normally without my husband." Maggie wasn't really telling the truth. She wanted Edward to know that she was unhappy, but she didn't want to voice the cause of it.

"Maybe it says you have a very good marriage. Maybe it says you are both only complete when you're together."

"Maybe." Maggie shrugged again. "Maybe not. I don't think Ol has any problems when he's not with me. He enjoys it. Maybe it means I'm a pathetically dependent creature, and that I just feed off Oliver . . ."

"Oh, Maggie, Maggie, Maggie . . ." Edward shook his head. "I love you very much, but sometimes you do make me angry. You're no more dependent on Oliver than he is on you. I thought that was the marital ideal. The goal."

Maggie smiled at him cynically. "So you *do* admit there is some sort of goal in marriage, Eddie? You, the die-hard bachelor?"

"Not for me, Mags. There are people I know who I think should be married—people who suit being married—and I think they should aspire to a goal, and for them there *is* a goal. Not for me."

"Oh, Edward! That sounds so sad! I wish you could find someone. There's so much about marriage that would suit you—and you are certainly attractive—you're young enough—"

"Maggie, I'm nearly forty-six—"

"That's not old, Eddie."

"I'm not saying it is. I'm saying that if I haven't wanted to be married in forty-five years, I'm unlikely to want to do so now. It's not for me, Mags. I'm not unhappy about that. It's just not for me. I love to see people who are happily married, and I admire them—I celebrate them—but it's not for me. It never has been. It never will be."

"Why not?" Maggie stared at him so hard, she was almost glaring.

"Some people thrive under shackles . . . I don't mean that rudely. I mean some people really *do* flourish under the sense of permanent attachment, a sort of discipline, if you know what I mean. I've never met anyone who I thought I wanted to be with—could bear to be with—for the rest of my life. It's that lifetime companion business, you see. It is one hell of a risk saying you're going to love someone for the rest of their life; what if they stop being lovable?"

"Maybe you've just never met the right woman . . ."

"I've met plenty of right women, Maggie. Ten—maybe fifteen. Some of them have even loved me. I've been fortunate enough to meet plenty of utterly wonderful, utterly lovable, utterly entrancing women. Do you know that Shaw line? 'The fickleness of the women I have loved is only equalled by the infernal constancy of the women who have loved me.' Ah well. It's just not for me. The thing is, I'm a true, full-blooded romantic; I'd be bound to be disappointed. Love is for romantics, and marriage is for pragmatists—realists, if you like. They don't set their sights so high, so there's no disappointment. I wasn't designed for marriage. It's all a question of expectations, I dare say. It's all very well if you expect to be married to a bitch—or a bastard, in your case. Your expectations will almost certainly be fulfilled—at least they won't be disappointed. But if you expect to be married to a god . . . well. Heaven preserve you, because nothing else will."

"Didn't you ever love anyone enough to propose?"

"What a question," Edward said mildly, smiling at her.

"Did you?" Maggie persisted.

"True confession time, is it, lovely?" Edward sighed. "Well, yes. I did. I did love someone, a long time ago, and I did propose."

"And?"

Edward spread his hands wide. "You can see for yourself. Here I am. No wife. She turned me down. Fickle, you see. Like Shaw said. All the best women are."

"Oh, Eddie. I'm so sorry. How sad. You never said anything about her. Did you love her very much?"

"Oh yes, very, very much. I loved her . . . badly. But I survived. I think."

"Was it unrequited? Did she marry someone else?"

"Not exactly. You see, she was already married at the time I proposed. I'm not sure if she loved me or not. I thought she did, but one can't be sure, can one? The more time passes, the more I think she never really took it seriously. You see? I'm faithless, too. When we parted, I swore I would never forget how much we loved each other, and here I am doubting that she loved me at all. I suppose the truth is that she simply didn't love me enough to be able to leave her husband, and so she made the right decision, and sent me packing. Clever woman." He smiled crookedly. "Perhaps she wasn't that fickle after all. That's the ghastly thing about infidelity. One's interpretation of who was unfaithful depends on which side of the fence you happen to be standing. To me, she seemed fickle; to her husband, and probably the rest of the world, she was a very model of constancy. Lord. It was a long time ago, but oddly, I still don't find it very easy to talk about."

"I'm so sorry," Maggie whispered. "I had no right to ask."

Edward moved onto the sofa beside her, and put his arm around her.

"Mags, I hereby give you permission to ask anything you like. Don't worry about me. I'm happy. Let me give you the benefit of my worldly wisdom. This is the way I see it. Where I went wrong was that I thought love and marriage was all about a dream coming true. Well, it just can't be. You see, dreams are all mixed up. One minute, there you are, dreaming that you're eight years old and back at school with your favourite teacher, and the next minute, your boss walks into the classroom—in his adult incarnation—and starts dipping your hair in the inkwell. Dreams *are* dreams because they exist outside the realm of possibility. Fantasy is no respecter of reality. So if you're a romantic, and I suspect you are a bit, then my advice is to keep them well apart."

"But what about you? What about the future?"

"The future? Ah, I see the way you're heading." He grinned. "You mean when I'm ninety? Ninety, and I don't have anyone to look after me? It can't be that sort of contract, Maggie. You can't, at my age, marry someone in fear of loneliness and old age. I'm sure there'll be someone who'll look after me . . . if I pay them enough." He kissed the top of her head.

Maggie, her head swimming a little with whisky drunk far too fast, answered impulsively.

"I'll look after you, Edward! I promise you!"

Edward laughed. "Maggie, you are so very dear. The warmest of all hearts. What would I do without you? But let's make a deal. If you are going to look after me in forty years, let me do my side of the bargain, and look after you now. . . ."

Maggie stiffened a little, pulling away from his sheltering arm.

"Why doesn't anyone think I'm capable of looking after myself?

32

I have two children, I look after the house, I have a job—sometimes;
I have responsibilities . . .”

“Maggie. You also need looking after. Everybody does. Your children, Oliver, me, you . . . And as Oliver’s not here, why shouldn’t
I look after you? You’re tired, you’re fed up, let me help you . . .”
He pulled her back to lie against his shoulder once again.

Maggie thought about the first time that she had met Edward
Arabin. It had been that first week they had moved into Bockhampton, and she had been trudging up a track, pushing Lily in a buggy
through deep mud, when Edward’s Jag had nearly run them down.
Indignant, splattered with dirt, Maggie had stood hands on hips
ranting about his maniacal driving. Edward had slowly uncurled
himself from the Jag and offered her a large linen handkerchief.
Twenty minutes later, he had been sitting on a packing crate in their
drawing room drinking whisky out of a tooth mug, and filling her
in on the local gossip. Since then, she and Oliver had hardly gone
a week without seeing him.

“Eddie, I don’t know if Oliver loves me any longer.”

Edward swirled whisky around in his mouth and took his time to
reply. He had been waiting for Maggie to give him some guidance
as to which direction the conversation should take, but his heart
sank at her words. He had hoped to avoid this particular topic.
Although Oliver Callahan was a good friend, Edward had long
doubted that he loved his wife in the way in which she deserved to
be loved. He considered telling Maggie what he honestly thought,
but decided on consolation rather than education.

“As we’ve already ascertained, I’m not an expert in marital relations. I’m sure Oliver loves you very much. I suspect that you are
at a point where you are exhausted by your charming but demanding
children, and need a break. Perhaps Oliver does, too. I suspect you
have some romantic notion of marriage being perfect, and never
going through a rough spot. I don’t know, Maggie. I simply know
that you are a lovely woman, and a good friend, and that Oliver is
a lucky man, and that I am jealous of him.”

Edward had expressed various opinions in this last sentence, but
the one that really pricked up Maggie’s ears was the last one, that
he was jealous of her husband. This was therefore the one point she
tried studiously to avoid.

“Charles made it perfectly clear that he doesn’t think I’m
attractive.”

"Correction. Charles made it perfectly clear that *Lucy* doesn't consider you a *threat*. Charles himself has wet dreams about you. He's told me himself. Several times, the old bugger." He shook her a little in the cradle of his arm. "Lucy doesn't consider you a threat because, like you, she is an intelligent woman, however hard she tries to prove otherwise, and she knows perfectly well that you wouldn't have anything to do with Charles. Ergo, you are not a threat to her, and she would never be bitchy to you. Ergo, Charles thinks *Lucy* doesn't consider you attractive, and so he is safe to fancy you rotten without Lucy ever being upset and giving him a hard time. Come *on*, Mags. Use your head. You're too bright to need me to explain all this to you."

"Sometimes I don't think anyone fancies me." Maggie knew exactly what she was doing, and how she sounded as the words came out of her mouth. She was a little the worse for drink—that was true. She was just drunk enough for her behaviour to be excusable, but she wasn't so drunk that she didn't realise that she was fishing for compliments, and she wasn't so drunk that she was unaware that she was treading on ice that might just not support her weight. It was a bizarre world where treading on thin ice might land her in hot water. For a year or two Maggie had toyed with the notion that Edward was attracted to her, and she to him, but she had always kept the concept at bay until now. She liked the idea that there was an unspoken but acknowledged secret between them.

Edward frowned. He turned her so that she was facing him, gripping her upper arms firmly.

"What are you doing, Maggie? What are you saying?"

"I don't know. Talking rubbish, I suppose. Could I have another whisky?"

"Help yourself. I'd like to make sure that you can still walk."

Maggie rose smoothly, and walked steadily across the room to where Edward had left the bottle of Glenfiddich. Her black dress was very simply cut, but the skirt had a deep slash that exposed her well-shaped leg up to the upper thigh. As she turned and walked back towards Edward, she consciously swung her hips so that her leg was exposed to the maximum.

"Okay. I admit you can walk. I'm not sure what else you're playing at." Edward's finger stroked her cheek.

"I should go home."

"No. You can go home later if you want. It's just past one. From

34

what you've told me, Leah will have gone to bed, and won't be waiting up for you. Nor will Oliver. So we have plenty of time to talk. You can finish what you started." Edward was no longer touching her. He was looking at her rather strangely, his face only inches away, but not touching any part of her. Maggie suddenly felt extremely hot, and hoped that she wasn't blushing; she took a couple of deep breaths, and leaned back against the sofa, her eyes closed. "D'you think he has affairs, Eddie?" she asked in a lazy drawl.

"I honestly don't know, Mags. He's never said anything directly, and I haven't asked. I wouldn't want him to say, frankly."

"Why? Because of poor little me?"

"I've never thought of you as poor little Maggie. I simply don't care to know that sort of thing about Oliver. It doesn't interest me."

"And you only want to know about things that interest you?"

"Yes."

"So you wouldn't want to know if *I* had affairs? It wouldn't interest you?" Maggie had kept her eyes shut, her head tipped back against the top of the sofa, her chin jutting out.

"Yes. I admit that *would* interest me. But I wouldn't ask you."

"Why ever not? We're good friends. You said I could ask you anything. It would be churlish of me not to return the favour." Maggie opened her eyes, and looked at him sideways, without moving her head, her eyes narrowed and green.

"Maggie. I'm a little confused by your behaviour right now—"

"Oh. I'm sorry. I suppose I'm embarrassing you." Edward laid a finger gently on her lips, silencing her.

"Let me finish. I don't know if you are playing a game. I don't know what you want me to do, or how you want me to respond. I do care about you a great deal, Maggie. I don't want to upset you, but you're not being exactly straight with me. I'm nervous of saying the wrong thing."

"You're nervous of saying that Oliver is having five affairs, and that you don't fancy me." She gabbled the last words, rushing them as if she didn't intend Eddie to hear them.

"My God, Maggie." Edward groaned, his head in his hands. "I don't know if Oliver is having *one* affair, let alone five. If you really want to push me to make a guess—"

"Yes, I do."

"Then alright. I suspect he might be having, or have had, an affair. Maybe. He's never said anything to me directly. I simply suspect that he's the sort of man who might." Maggie didn't say a word. "What concerns me more, more than Oliver, is what you think about me, and what you think I think about you. I don't think you really want to deal with that. And what is this nonsense about my not fancying you?"

"Oh, Edward! I should have gone home!" Maggie moaned.

"But you didn't."

"No. Look. I *know* Oliver's had an affair. After we'd been married for about a year, he told me about a fling he'd had with a woman at the *Telegraph*. Louise. After *one year of marriage,* do you hear me? And he didn't exactly volunteer the information. I was still working at the *Guardian*. We were living in Clanricarde Gardens; d'you remember that grotty little flat I told you about? I thought we were blissful newlyweds. He started coming home late; he had odd engagements that came up at the last minute. For a while I didn't think anything of it. God, I was so *stupid!* Then one night, a colleague of his mentioned something about this woman, Louise she was called—I still can't bear the name—and he said it in such a funny way—as if I *knew* something. As if *he* knew something. I asked Oliver about her, and Oliver was very odd—he lied, of course, you know how he lies—he said he didn't know her. Couldn't place her. Finally, a month or two later, I was chucking a pair of his cords in the washing machine, and I shook out the pockets, because they're always full of change, and a condom fell out. I asked him why he had it, and he went bright red. First of all, he said he was carrying it around to *give* to a *friend* at the *office*. As you might imagine, I didn't believe him. Then he said it was an office prank; some berk had put it in his pocket hoping I'd find it. Then he flipped completely and said that the truth was, the truth, you hear, was that he had thought it might be *fun* for us to use a rubber— he said it would add a certain *piquancy* to our relationship, make us remember the good old, bad old dangerous days before we got married." Maggie looked at Edward with an unreadable expression in her green eyes. "Can you believe it? He must have thought I was a complete idiot. I've been on the pill since I was eighteen. Finally he broke down and admitted it all. It burst out of him like pus from a pimple. We talked for weeks. I decided to be mature. He was really sorry. I forgave him, I guess. Then, when I became pregnant with Lily, I think he felt really guilty, and he was very attentive for a while. I don't know what he did between Lily and Arthur. But

I'm sure now that something's going on, somewhere, with someone. He hasn't said anything, but I can just feel it."

"Did you ever really forgive him for Louise?"

"Yes." Maggie nodded vigorously, then paused. "Well. Forgive him? No. Not really, I suppose. I've tried to forget about it, but I haven't been very successful."

"And have you ever asked him since if he's having an affair? Since Louise?" Maggie shook her head slowly. "There's no point. First, I'd never know if he was lying or not, and secondly, I don't think I'd want to know the truth even if he could tell it."

"And what about you, Maggie? *Have* you had affairs?"

"No." She dipped her head nervously, and then grinned at him. "Well, only in my imagination. You know, like good old Jimmy Carter. I guess I've sinned in my heart, if not in the flesh."

"Why not?"

"I don't honestly know. Sometimes I think it's because I love Ol too much. Sometimes I think it's because I honestly take my marriage vows very seriously. Most of the time I think I can't even be bothered. Sometimes I think it's because no one's ever asked."

"Maggie Callahan, will you go to bed with me?"

The simple question rang through Edward's sitting room.

"Maggie Callahan . . . will you come to bed with me?"

For once, Maggie didn't shake her hair over her face, she didn't cover her hands, and she didn't close her eyes. She had been longing for this question, even if she didn't know the answer to it. She looked straight into Edward's eyes, boldly and naturally, and said: "If I say yes, Edward, what would that mean to you?"

He took up her hand, and raised it fleetingly to his lips before holding it firmly in both his own. "It would mean that I could make love to a woman I have wanted to make love to for a long time. It would mean that we could talk honestly to each other, and enjoy each other. I suppose it would be a fulfilment of a fantasy for me, and perhaps a little bit of an escape for you. I don't know, lovely. It's not wise to talk about what would happen before it happens. There are some things you just have to do, and hang the consequences."

"And infidelity is one of those things?"

"Maggie. Dear Maggie. That's not for me to say. I'm a single man. I have no infidelities, and I don't ever want to worry about what you—and Oliver—worry about. That's your choice. All I can tell you is that I very much want to make love to you. When I told you earlier that I had met lovable, entrancing women, you are one of them. Now, if you walk out of my front door right now, I can assure you that you won't become any the less lovable and entrancing. I might have to cross you off my list as a potential lover, but then, until tonight, I never really thought I had a chance anyway. So it won't be a crushing disappointment. I have never, from the moment I saw you in the lane, covered in mud, thought of you as anything other than—what? Not "attractive." That doesn't express what I felt—feel. I have never thought of you without thinking of you as a perfect—dream, something, I don't know—a deliciously tempting, lovely thing that is out of my grasp unless you choose otherwise. All I can offer you is my very honest friendship, my very honest desire for you to be happy, and my very, *very* honest libido, which wants you more than any woman within at least a hundred-mile radius. I can't say any more than that, lovely. I would never have said it at all if you hadn't suddenly started playing Salome."

"Oh, Eddie—that's dreadful. That means that if we go to bed, it's because I flirted with you, and led you on, and how could you help yourself when I threw myself at you?" She said it with a slight smile, but there was an edge to her voice. "How can I respond to that?" Maggie continued. "You're basically saying that you don't care if you sleep with me, and you don't care if you don't. How do you expect me to feel?" Her cheeks were flushed, her eyes were flashing, and her breathing short and shallow. She had taken the first step, by blurting out what had always been unspoken between them. Now she longed for Edward to make a move, longed for him to take things past the conversational boundary, to the point where she could simply give in. Most of all, she longed for him to take full responsibility for whatever happened.

Most seductions hinge on timing and setting. Whereas marriage can be seen as an endless, death-us-do-part series of long corridors lined with open doors, there is only the tiniest window of opportunity in illicit sexual relationships. A second out of time, a word or an expression out of place, an unfortunately positioned photograph, and that window can either be flung open or slammed shut.

Edward did his best to help. He leant forward and kissed her hard on the lips. Her mouth didn't open, but that didn't matter; the relaxation of her upper body against his expressed her welcome of the kiss. And then—Edward stopped helping. He sat back again, deep into the sofa they shared, and looked at her.

"Maggie." There was an almost humorous lilt in his voice. "This is very simple. You are trying to make it complicated, and it simply isn't. If you have any desire—any curiosity—to sleep with me, then for Christ's sake let's go upstairs and get on with it. I'm not an eighteen-year-old—I can't sustain an erection for two hours. If you don't want to sleep with me, then, God bless you, go home, or sleep on my sofa. Or I'll have the sofa, and you can have my bed. If you *do*—and God only knows how much I hope you do—then come upstairs with me now, and let's have no talk of afterwards, or Oliver, or marriage. Let's talk about you, or me, or not talk at all. That's what I want right now, Maggie. I won't ask you for more."

Maggie knew that Edward was speaking the truth, and saying exactly what he wanted. She also knew what she wanted, which was to be able to fling herself into Edward's arms and hang the consequences. There had been a moment when she would have followed him upstairs willingly—when she would have floated up the stairs—but that moment had passed, and with it, all excuse of an instant of impetuosity. There had been too much talk already, too much analysis. If she went with him now, she would have to justify it rationally. Passion and rational discussion are not compatible bedfellows.

"Edward, I think I must go home. I am very flattered—really—and very tempted. But I'm also more than a little drunk, and I don't think I should do this when I honestly don't know how I'll feel about it tomorrow. You're my best friend around here—maybe anywhere. I don't know if I can go to bed with you and then carry on as if nothing ever happened, and I don't know what I might feel about you, and me, and Oliver, afterwards. I'm sorry."

"Don't be. Now, let's see about getting you back to Bockhampton."

"I can drive, Eddie—it's only a mile—"

"No, I'll take you back in your car. I may not be enough of a gentleman to worry about trying to seduce the wife of a friend of mine, but I'm too much of one to let his wife drive home half cupped. I've always been a bit of a one for double standards. I'll drop you off and walk home. It'll do me good. It'll help me cool down. I haven't got a shower."

Edward drove Maggie home without another word passing be-

tween them. At her door, Maggie took his face between her hands
and kissed him tenderly.

"Edward, we'll be alright, won't we? I haven't ruined everything,
have I?"

"Of course you haven't, darling. You could never ruin anything
as far as I'm concerned.

He set off down the lane, turning his collar up against the chill,
and whistling jauntily until he had heard Maggie's door close behind
him, and seen her bedroom light go on. Then he fell silent, and his
pace slowed. The idea of a hasty one-night stand with Maggie held
little appeal for him. The possibility of it had shaken him badly,
although he had tried to conceal that from her. He had assured her
that what had happened—or not happened—between them would
not affect their friendship, but he was less confident of this than he
had pretended. He had long admitted his deepening attraction to
Maggie to himself, but it was quite a different matter now that it
was openly acknowledged between them. He either wanted considerably more than a one-night stand with Maggie, or he would prefer
considerably less.

As Maggie prepared for bed, she also experienced a confusion of
disappointment and relief. She was disappointed that Edward hadn't
desired her enough to push her into bed with him, and relieved that
she didn't have to face the consequences. The contradictory nature
of her emotions annoyed her, but they didn't surprise her. Maggie
had always accused herself of indecision. As she turned off the light
and curled up in bed, she recognised a sensation that she hadn't
experienced for a long time. One of excitement.

It is all too easy to draw a heavy black line between the immoral
and the virtuous. Most of the time that line is faint, and pencil thin.
All of us want to condemn infidelity, and those of us who condemn
it most violently are probably those who are most aware how close
they themselves come to it. This is why infidelity is such a compel-
ling idea. Most of us can't say for sure which side of the line we
would end up on.

The next morning, trying not to think about Edward, Maggie
began the dreaded task of preparing the house for the McCarthys.
There was no way she and Oliver could hope to make Bockhampton
"pristine"; they had neither the time nor the money to do any
serious work on the house, and anyway, Maggie loved its idiosyncra-
sies and imperfections. They had not been able to afford to redeco-

rate since they had inherited the house from Uncle Leo, and many of the rooms cried out for a coat of paint. They could cry all they liked, Maggie thought grimly, because they weren't going to get one. But there were other things that she and Oliver had lived with for so long that they no longer noticed them—missing lightbulbs, no handle on one of the bathroom doors, the fact that the key to the back door was long lost, probably thrown into the rubbish by Lily. Maggie's first task was to complete a "to do" list; she drew three neat columns, and wrote at the top of each: "Maggie," "Oliver," and "Other." As she started to fill in the chores under the appropriate heading, the lists became radically unbalanced. Oliver had only one duty: to sort out his office and put his papers and files in some sort of order. Maggie assigned herself about fifteen jobs, mainly to do with packing and cleaning and the niceties of leaving fresh flowers and a bottle of champagne for the McCarthys, but these paled into insignificance when compared to the list assigned to "Other." This unspecified person had to weed the garden, mow the lawn, and feed all the roses; "other" also had to take down, clean, and rehang all the curtains; have the cars serviced; have the stove checked and cleaned; polish the parquet; have the boiler looked at; glue the loose leg back on the kitchen table; polish the silver; arrange for carpet cleaners to come in and do the house. . . . As Maggie looked at the list she began to regret suggesting a swap in the first place. It would take all the remaining five weeks to get themselves and the house organised. Maggie resigned herself to the truth. This miraculous "Other"—a team of staff to rival the shoemaker's elves—was not going to materialise. There was nothing for it but to go over the list and reassign it between the people who could be counted on to help: Leah; Joan Mason, who helped her with cooking and cleaning; Mr. Gordon, their very occasional and part-time gardener; and Maggie herself. She knew that Ol would fly into a panic if asked to do anything vaguely practical, but she reallocated him the job of sorting out the dogs.

Once the list had been completed, and every possible chore put on paper, Maggie decided to go down to the local stables to see if she could get a ride.

"Hi, Mog." Maggie leant over the stable door where her friend Imogen was shovelling shit. "Any chance of a ride this afternoon?"

"Hi, Maggie. Course you can. Bonny's off—bad leg—but you can take Samson down to the school, and I'll be with you in two ticks."

"Samson?"

"Yeah. He's Bonny's brother. He's a poppet. You go get him ready—his tack's all there—he's in the upper yard, third on the left. I'll join you up there."

Maggie sauntered down the stables and peeped over the door into Samson's loosebox. She whistled.

"Mog?" she shouted. "What *is* this?"

Imogen joined her at Samson's loosebox. The big black horse ignored them both.

"Well, Maggie, I can't be sure, but I'd say it's a horse . . ." she drawled.

"That ain't no horse," Maggie said with conviction. "It's a tower block. He's bloody enormous."

"He's a touch over eighteen hands. He's a lamb, aren't you, my baby?"

"Imogen, I can't ride *him* . . . I won't even be able to get *on* him, for Chrissakes . . ."

"Don't be pathetic, Maggie—we've got a mounting block—"

"I'll need a bloody stepladder, more like," Maggie muttered.

"He's lovely. Absolutely *genuine.*"

Imogen always described all her horses as "genuine," and Maggie still hadn't understood what it meant. Imogen didn't actually have a single horse that Maggie would have described as a lamb, and yet they were all . . . *genuine.* Maggie had come to the conclusion that all it meant was that the horse didn't behave as something other than its true nature; in other words, if the horse was a bastard, it behaved like a bastard, and if it was a temperamental shit, it behaved like a temperamental shit. So much for genuineness. Shortly later, Maggie was—somehow—up on Samson, and trotting round the school, observed by Imogen's hypercritical eye.

"For God's sake, Maggie—legs, legs, *legs!* What the *hell* do you think you are doing, having a massage? Having a cup of coffee? Concentrate! Let me see a longer leg—don't let him treat you like that—don't let him walk all over you—tell him what you want, for fuck's sake—"

"I *am* telling him what I want. He's just not listening—"

"Then tell him more. He's intelligent, Mags—he knows what he's doing, he just hasn't got a clue what you're doing—more leg, for God's sake—that's it, that's *it—keep him there* . . . Better. Much better. . . ."

Samson threw his head back so that Maggie could see the white of his eye, and gave a short series of little, twisting bucks.

"Isn't he darling? Such a lamb—so playful . . . For God's sake, Maggie—shorten your reins—talk to him, for pity's sake, you're not a sack of flour!" Imogen shouted, and then, after a pause, added, "Are you?"

Imogen did not fit the stereotype image of a horsy woman; she was pretty, neat, rather elegant, and had worked in PR in the City for a number of years before retiring to Wiltshire to pursue her dream. Nonetheless, she shared a peculiar trait with others involved in the world of horses. She was inclined to treat horses as if they were people, difficult but fascinating teenagers who needed to have a structure of authority in which to function, who needed a firm hand and a gentle voice. She was inclined to treat the people who rode them as if they were dumb beasts.

Maggie bit her tongue. She wasn't exactly enjoying this experience, but it beat cleaning the carpets. . . .

While Maggie was struggling to control Samson, Christy McCarthy was preparing shrimp remoulade. She had invited Mary-Jo and her husband Frank to dinner, along with Lindy and B. J. Richards. Christy had cooked carefully, thinking that it might be the last dinner party she had before they went to England. Everything was prepared by the time Gabe got home, and laid out on the buffet in the dining room: the shrimp as a first course, an amazing Moroccan dish with chicken and preserved lemons that she had found in a back copy of *Gourmet* magazine, and raspberries with soft meringue— also from *Gourmet*—to follow. It was quite an upmarket dinner for Lawrenceville, which normally favoured Southern-fried chicken and Bar-B-Q steaks, but Christy *was* upmarket, and liked to set standards. Many of the women in Lawrenceville would ask for her recipes, and imitate her menus, claiming "Christy gave me the recipe; I think it's a New York dish . . ." Some of the time, Christy cooked very simply, or rather, let Gabe cook very simply; Gabe was a local legend as a barbecue chef. But tonight she had shooed him out of the kitchen, and given him responsibility purely for the drinks.

"I just can't for the life of me understand why they would want to come to Lawrenceville, of all places . . ." Mary-Jo tossed her blond curls. "I mean, do they realise that this is Nowheresville?

Why would any European want to come to some little Southern backwater town?"

"Hey, Mary-Jo—Lawrenceville isn't that bad . . . we all choose to live here. It's a good place . . . would you want to spend eight weeks in New York City? Or Chicago? Or Los Angeles?"

"Heaven forbid! But, Gabe, they could have gone to Charleston, or Savannah even—" Mary-Jo originally came from Charleston, as indeed did Christy, and tended to see Savannah as the poor cousin of the premier Southern city.

"Mary-Jo, I think they're just a nice, ordinary family and want to spend a family vacation. We figure they'll spend more time at the beach house rather than at Oak Ridge. Their kids are little, same kind of age as Jake, and they seem a pretty laid back kind of family."

"Well, we should still organise some trips for them . . . I could take them to the Triangle, or maybe Carowinds—their kids would like that—and we could have a party for them, couldn't we, hon?" Mary-Jo turned to face her rather laconic husband Frank.

"Whatever you say, Mary-Jo."

"And Frank could take them to the tobacco auctions—that might be kinda interesting for him—and I could take her shopping of course—"

"Mrs. Callahan might not have the stamina to go shopping with you, Mary-Jo." Christy smiled at her friend.

"I suppose the stores about here don't really compare to England . . ." Mary-Jo looked worried.

"I don't see why these folks should be disappointed by Lawrenceville," Lindy Richards interjected firmly. "After all, they chose to come here. They'll have a good time at the beach, and we can all get them round for a meal or something. We'll take care of them, Christy; you just go have a real good time."

Christy patted Lindy on the arm gratefully. Although Mary-Jo was theoretically her "best friend," Christy had a lot of respect for the Richards. They were a little older than the McCarthys, and had lived in Lawrenceville all their lives. On the surface, Lindy was tougher and blunter than many of the women Christy knew locally, more like a New Yorker, although she was a Southern girl born and bred. She called a spade a spade, and she always spoke the exact truth, without any attempts to soften the blow. She commanded the respect of most of the neighbourhood, and particularly the respect of the McCarthys. Her husband B.J. was a real gentleman of the old

school—charming, funny, big-hearted, with an utterly relaxed attitude to the business of life, and a firm grip on his own particular
version of Christianity. He was known only by his initials; Christy
had never heard anyone call him by a proper name, and when she
had asked local people what the "B" stood for, they had either never
heard his name, or hadn't used it for so long, it had been forgotten.
So he was B.J., or occasionally, in very intimate moments, such as
when he and Gabe and the other good ol' boys went fishing, Beej.

"Hey, Gabe, I could take them to a ball game, wha'd'ya think?
That would be different—show them how real men play ball. . . ."

"Good idea, B.J. I hope to hell we don't have to go see any of
those weirdo English games where the guys just walk up and down
between two sticks—you know what I mean—that game, what's it
called? Christy'll know."

"Cricket."

"Yeah. Cricket. That's it. My last business trip to London some
Brit lawyer took me to a cricket game, and boy, I was never so
bored in all my life . . . the players have this real funny uniform,
doctor's trousers, and they're all padded up, and just when you think
they've finally scored a home run, nobody moves. . . . It's weird, I'm
telling you. And the crowd! The crowd just go crazy when nothing's
even happened—one of the outfield catches a ball that my boy Jake
could catch with one hand tied behind his back, and they all jump
up and shout—it's a kind of crazy atmosphere. . . . They can keep
it, far as I'm concerned."

"I'm real glad to hear you say that, Gabe, because I wasn't planning on going to any ball games during our vacation. . . ." Christy
smiled, and then squeezed into the small space in between Frank
and B.J. "Now, Frank, tell me everything you've been up to, and I
mean *everything* . . . I hear you've taken on some new acreage up
towards Martinsville?"

Gabe watched his wife at work, while keeping one ear bent politely towards Mary-Jo's endless chatter. Not for the first time, he
admired Christy's social skills. Frank wasn't an easy man to bring
into the conversational circle; he was shy, and a little aloof, and
unhappy when the topic turned away from things with which he
was familiar—and those things were strictly limited to farming—and
even then, only to crop farming in the Carolinas—Civil War history,
and fishing. His preferred subject was most definitely crop farming.
Yet Christy, alone of all the women of Lawrenceville, managed to

draw him out. She could coax him out like a splinter. Gabe knew that Frank had been in love with Christy—quite deeply in love, despite the obvious attractions of his own wife—ever since Gabe and Christy had moved to Lawrenceville. That knowledge made Gabe love his own wife even more, if that were possible.

Gabe had decided that Christy was the woman he wanted to marry within a week of meeting her on the Wall Street cocktail party circuit. She was beautiful, and much in demand, and Gabe had been prepared to work long and hard to win her favour. After a whirlwind courtship, he had hesitantly proposed, and he had been almost taken aback by her immediate acceptance. She had told him that her mother would never forgive her for not doing things the proper way and making him wait for an answer. When Gabe had met Blanche Hewlett Moore, he'd understood what Christy had been talking about. The Moores were a prestigious family in Charleston, but not nearly as prestigious as the Hewletts. The Hewletts even had a street named after them, and not just any street, but a street south of Broad, or SOB, as Charlestonians called it. Blanche Hewlett Moore was a beautiful woman, nearly as lovely as her daughter, and also a very formidable one. She had made it perfectly clear to Gabe that she was mightily relieved that Christy, at the ripe old age of twenty-six, was finally doing her duty and settling down. She'd also made it clear that she expected her daughter and son-in-law to do everything properly from now on in. They had certainly done the wedding the proper way—an enormous social affair in Charleston, hosted by Christy's parents and attended by everyone who counted in the state. Right after the reception, they had flown to Paris to honeymoon at the Ritz; Blanche had told him that the Ritz was the only hotel he could possibly patronise. Gabe could still see Christy in the pale pink suit she had chosen as her going-away outfit, topped with the pale pink hat that Blanche had insisted on, and that Christy had trampled underfoot in a rush of independence as soon as their car was out of sight. In those early days of marriage, Gabe had glimpsed an occasional rebellious streak in his wife, a desire to kick over the traces, but these eruptions were only evident immediately after visits to or from her mother.

When they had been married just twelve months, Blanche had come to stay with them in New York. Her visit had coincided with Christy's telling him that she felt it was time for them to start a family. Nothing could have pleased him more. His mother-in-law

had called her daughter every month, regular as clockwork, to ask
if she had conceived. After six months, Christy had installed an answering machine, and refused to pick up the telephone. Blanche had
had to wait a long time. It had taken Christy over three years, and
as many consultants, to become pregnant. When her condition was
confirmed, her mother was the first person Christy had called. Her
boss was the second. She had resigned from Merrill that same day,
and within a week had put their apartment up for sale and persuaded
Gabe to start looking for a job in North Carolina; she didn't want
to live on her mother's doorstep. She had begun the search for the
perfect family home. There had been no disagreement between
them—Gabe could barely remember a time when he and Christy
had disagreed. Now he came to think about it, there had barely
been any discussion at all. They had just naturally arrived at the
same conclusion. They had both felt strongly against raising children
in New York, and had been eager to return to the South. Neither
of them believed that children could be given the security they
needed if both parents pursued careers. No, unlike many of the
couples they knew, he and Christy didn't fight. They were on the
same wavelength. Sometimes, he saw a brittleness come over her
face, but it always passed within a few minutes, and he never chose
to interfere in her private thoughts. Watching her now, Gabe was
reminded of one black period, an awful time, right after Jake was
born, when they should have been their happiest. The consultant
had told them that Christy would never be able to conceive again.
Christy had fallen into a depression. She had been unable to drag
herself out of bed for four weeks—his Christy, who could barely sit
still for twenty minutes. He had been as gentle with her as he knew
how, and had finally convinced her that as far as he was concerned,
Jake was enough. The next morning, the storm had passed. Christy
had woken before him, prepared his breakfast, and commissioned a
team of designers to redecorate Oak Ridge from top to bottom.
That had been the first of several massive refurbishment schemes,
and ever since then she had been a model wife.

He watched her closely these days, fearful of over-enthusiasm
when she talked about how *happy* she was in Lawrenceville, and how
delighted she was to be able to spend so much of her time with
Jake, how *glad* she was to be improving her tennis, how *thrilled* she
was about her work as a fund-raiser for the local charity for Native
Americans, how *satisfied* she was that she could devote all her atten-

tion to one child. Sometimes when he watched Christy's too bright eyes and too broad smile he had the impression that she was performing—that she was trying to persuade someone—maybe her mother, maybe himself, that she was happy. She could give almost too perfect a performance, and he listened for signs of discontent. He heard far more than she ever said. But there were times, like tonight, when he believed that Christy meant what she said, that there was nowhere she would rather be than Lawrenceville, and that there was nothing that she would rather be than his wife and the mother of his child, and that there was no man in the world for her but him.

When you love somebody very much, there is nothing in life more gratifying than the certain knowledge that you make them entirely happy. Love can be very self-protective, and sometimes cowardly. A person in love can almost always convince themselves that they are loved in return, if they concentrate their minds on it.

When their guests had left, full of excitement about the Callahans' arrival, the McCarthys retired upstairs. Christy looked at the piles on her bed. She had selected about five suitcases' full of clothes and was now beginning the process of elimination.

"What do you think, darlin'? If I take the two silk shifts—the cream and the green—will that be enough for formal wear? I'm sure people in England dress up more than we do—I *could* take the taffeta as well, but it takes up so much room, and it's *so* dressy . . . I'd surely hate to look overdressed. . . ."

Gabe smiled to himself. He was touched that Christy asked his opinion, but he knew her well enough to realise that she would make her own decision regardless of what he said. Christy had style, and she combined this with the good judgement always to ask him what he thought in such a way that he would confirm her own choice. He listened to her now, waiting for a clue.

"The silk shifts are kind of casual formal—you know what I mean?—they're formal cruise wear—the taffeta is like opening night at the Met, and I don't guess we're going to do much of that in Wiltshire . . . I *could* take the Saks black . . . maybe that would fit in . . ."

"Christy, if I were you, I'd take the two shifts, because you could wear them during the day or the evening, and because you look so gorgeous in them, and I'd take the black dress, because it's sexy and sophisticated . . . and then in *my* bag, I'll pack that lilac lace number, because I can't resist you in it."

He'd hit the spot. Bull's-eye.

Christy pushed him back on the bed, so that he fell on top of the neat piles of her clothes.

"You are one hell of a man, Gabe McCarthy . . . golden tongued, smooth as silk, and great taste. Not as great as mine, 'cos I picked you, but real good . . ." She kissed him hard on the mouth, a little perfunctorily for Gabe's taste, and rolled off him. Gabe began to undress, placing his clothes carefully in either the laundry hamper or back in the closet. Christy watched him as she put her clothes neatly into the suitcases. It mattered to her that her husband stood up to inspection. These were the times that she liked Gabe best, when she could just look at him and know that he stacked up pretty well. These were the times that Christy thought she'd made a pretty good investment. "Gabe, you're lookin' real good. You look even better than when we got married."

"You take good care of me, darling. And I'm a happy man."

"You sure are a good-looking one."

Christy was proud of her husband. There were days when she saw it as her greatest—perhaps her only—achievement, Gabe's good looks, his taut stomach, his easy, winning ways, his charm, his success. . . . She took credit for him, and how he appeared, as she gave him credit for her triumphs. Not that she had many of them these days. Not that Gabe was perfect. One thing he lacked was a little more edge and bite—a touch of smooth and polished aggression; the killer instinct. So far, his natural charm had paid off, and she was working at sharpening up his edges. In Christy's experience, there was a great deal more artistry involved in redefining a man's soft edges than in sandblasting his rough ones. It was a question of setting high standards and not backsliding, she reasoned with herself. She could apply the same energy to working on Gabe that she had applied to shifting lines of stock for Merrill Lynch. She refused ever to give her mother grounds for criticising her performance as a wife. If Gabe fell short of a professional ideal, her mother wasn't going to know about it. And if Christy had the odd moment when she doubted whether Gabe was her perfect dream lover, her mother wasn't going to know about that either. And if their lifestyle sometimes bored Christy to the very back of her very fine teeth, was it any of Blanche Hewlett Moore's business? Christy had married Gabe because he was the type of man that she had been told from the cradle onwards would make her happy. If she wasn't all that happy, then neither Gabe nor her mother were ever going to hear about it. Maybe it just wasn't meant to be. She could live with that. Fate was something she could come to terms with. Sometimes Christy had the sensation that her marriage had been all laid out for her like a role in a play; the lines, her stage directions, her entrances and exits were all there, and all she had to do was get herself onto the stage on cue. If that was what it was all about, then Christy was determined to be word perfect. So far, she had failed only once. Her role had specified a large family; it was what she and Gabe had always assumed, and she hadn't been able to provide it. That was the only time that the script had gone wrong. When she thought about it, and she tried very hard not to, that was when she had first felt dissatisfied with her life, and it wasn't going to happen again.

She undressed rapidly, down to a silk camisole. Gabe lay on the bed, on top of the sheets, reading her copy of *Business Week*. She clicked on the overhead fan, and stretched out languorously beside him. Gabe laid his hand gently on her stomach, but continued reading. Christy picked up a book off her bedside table and read as well. After a few pages, she felt Gabe's hand on her inner thigh. She felt the weight and warmth of it lying there. She read one more page. As his caress became firmer, Christy put down the book, stifling a sigh.

Gabe always made love to her the same way. He began by resting a hand on her thigh, and then let it slip, as if by accident, between her legs. At that point, he would place his other hand gently on one breast, and begin to kiss her. Christy could time his movements almost to the second. Gabe was a quite a good kisser; he was slow and gentle, which Christy enjoyed most of the time. Sometimes she felt it dragged the whole process out too much, and she was dying to hurry him along. He was slow and gentle in every aspect of his lovemaking, which Christy enjoyed considerably less than his kissing. You could have too much of a good thing, and Gabe went in for just too much stroking, but she would never have told him to stop it—she would never be able to criticise him directly like that. Her mama had always told her that men do things best if you let them get on with it the way they want to. This didn't mean that Christy was entirely passive; she went to great lengths to please Gabe, and also to show him that he pleased her. It was the least she could do to repay him for being such a good husband, or so she told herself. In some ways, her effort was far greater than his. Tonight, it certainly was. She was relieved when Gabe, who had been struggling manfully to hold back his orgasm, began to pant, and then groaned. He finished as he always finished, with a whisper:

"Sweet thing, was it alright? Was it good for you?"

"It was great, Gabe. It was real good."

He kissed her on the forehead, and rolled away from her.

"Sleep well, darling."

Christy fell asleep fantasising about meeting a stranger on a dark and wet night. She dreamt of being lashed by rain and and a pair of vicious, passionate eyes. Some nights Christy had terrible thoughts, terrible dreams. Some nights, she pretended she was on a train, an old-fashioned carriage with wood panelling, looking at a man opposite her. It didn't matter who the man was or what he looked like—it could be any man. She would imagine her eyes locking with his as she signalled her acquiescence. She'd see herself walking down the corridor ahead of him, her body swaying with the irregular rhythm of the train. She'd watch herself enter a private compartment, followed by the man; she'd have a bird's eye view of herself lying on the hard, uncarpeted floor of the train and see herself making love to him, quickly and violently, and then she would imagine dressing again in a prim dark suit, taking one last look at the man, sated but shocked, and closing the door behind her without a word. They were terrible, terrible thoughts, but they weren't for real, and only Christy knew about them.

Three

An interoffice memorandum at Winkler Barrows,
Charlotte, North Carolina:

DATE: *June 29th, 1993*
TO: *Lilah Biggs*
FROM: *Gabe McCarthy*
RE: *Vacation Plans*

Lilah,
   *As of July 2nd and until August 28th, you will be able to
reach me at the following address:*

   Bockhampton House
   Bockhampton
   Compton Purlew
   Near Salisbury
   Wiltshire SP7 8LH
   England

   Tel: 011-44-873-655381
   Fax: 011-44-873-655385

   *I will be available for any business needs, and I believe I
can page into conference calls from Wiltshire when needed.
Please sort my mail and fax me whatever needs attention. Make
sure that everyone in the office knows how to contact me.*
   Thanks, Lilah! Don't know what I'd do without you!
                                    Gabe

MAGGIE LEANT AGAINST THE DOOR, WAITING FOR OLIVER TO FINISH his conversation on the phone, and signalling him to wind it up fast. He was lying on the parquet floor of his office, rhythmically curling his knees to his chest in an attempt to flatten the small of his back. Oliver considered himself a martyr to backache, and spent a lot of time on the floor, or on his masseur's table. He had recently developed a new pain, in his neck. When he complained about it Maggie told him he simply *was* a pain in the neck.

"Gotta go, Peter. The wife's making faces at me. I'm clearly required to deal with some sort of domestic crisis. What it is to be needed." He stretched one leg over his head—someone had suggested that the root of his lower back pain might lie in taut hamstrings. "Maggie? She's fine, absolutely fine." Maggie blew a kiss. "She sends her love . . . I certainly will." He blew a kiss back at Maggie, passed on from Peter, who was Ol's editor at the *Telegraph*. "Yup. We're off the day after tomorrow . . ." "Of course we're organised! You know me, Pete. Mr. Efficiency." "Yup. Talk to you then. Cheers."

Oliver rolled across the floor and put the phone back in its cradle.

"Pete says 'bon voyage.' He also says he wants the first piece for a week on Saturday. I'll have to start writing as soon as we get there."

"Ol, we are not going to be able to leave unless you help me a little—there are at least a hundred things still on the list, and you've been holed up in here doing God knows what—"

"Mags, I have been working." Oliver looked wounded. "I am the breadwinner, after all. I have to put food in the mouths of our babes, and look after our long-term interests. . . ."

"Well, that's just fine, but you haven't even sorted out the office"—Maggie's arm swept out, embracing the disarray—"and we've only got a day and a half left to clear everything out. I've asked Leah to pack all the children's things, and make the beds, and Mrs. Mason's coming in after we've left to go over the house again, but you have to do this room, and you have to pack, and—"

"Maggie, I'm afraid you'll have to do that for me. I've just heard from Pete that I've *got* to be at the editorial meeting tomorrow afternoon. They need to go over the layout, they need to check the outlines, and Pete says I've got to be there in case someone tries to sabotage the whole thing. . . ." He was now folding a bent knee across his body, trying to touch the floor with it. Maggie stared at him blankly.

"You're not telling me you're going to London tomorrow? For fuck's sake, Ol, we've got to be at Heathrow at eight A.M. on Friday! You can't leave tomorrow. That means you'll get home really late, and we'll have to pack the car, and I can't—"

"I thought about that. So long as I leave right after the meeting, I should get back here by eight tomorrow night. I'll go by train so there won't be any traffic problem. I'll have to leave quite early, because I'm meeting the new girl for lunch before the meeting so that we can go over some of the ideas together—she's going to do all the editing. All you'll have to do is pick me up at the station tomorrow, and then we can finish everything off together. . . ."

Maggie slid down the door until she was squatting on her haunches. "Ol, don't do this to me. I can't face it. You're kidding, aren't you?"

"Maggie, how do you think we can afford this jamboree at all? If it wasn't for the *Telegraph*, we wouldn't be going. I can't exactly turn round to Pete and say, 'Sorry, guv'nor, can't make the meeting because Mags needs me to sit on the suitcases while she closes them,' can I, darling?" Maggie shook her head in disbelief. "It's not as if an occasional eight-hundred-word piece in *Country Living* is going to pay for the trip, is it? I mean, with all the goodwill in the world, sweetheart, you were the one who said you didn't want to be obliged to work for the next couple of months . . . somebody has to do it. . . . This is a *job*, Maggie. I know it's very difficult for you to understand, in your position as a lady of leisure, but I have certain obligations. . . . Come on, Maggie; we're a team, remember?"

"Like fuck we're a team. You go off and have a good time while I do all the work. Some bloody team. And if there's one thing I won't put up with, Oliver, it's your patronising me as if I'm some sort of idiot who's never done a day's work in their life. You are insufferable. I can't believe you're doing this. I can't believe I married you. I don't want to go away at all. It's not bloody worth it."

Oliver, still reclining on the floor, grinned at her. "You're really sexy when you pant like that. D'you want to have a quick snog here or do you want to go the whole hog and go upstairs?"

"Just fuck off, Oliver."

"Ahhh . . . poor baby. Poor Mags."

"You never take anything seriously, do you? You never think of anyone but yourself. You don't even bloody listen to me."

"I hear you, I hear you, Maggie," Oliver said long-sufferingly, still doing his knee exercises.

"It's not the same thing, Ol. You may hear me but you don't bloody *listen*. I'm going. I can't bear even to look at your self-satisfied face, you creep."

He stretched out a hand. "Give me a pull up, darling . . ."

"Pull yourself up," Maggie snapped. "I've really had enough of you, Oliver. You're a lazy, selfish bastard."

"So you *do* want to have sex?"

"What I want to do is kill you, but as it happens, I've got to clean the Aga." She slammed the door of his office and stomped into the kitchen to tackle the ancient stove.

"You're so beautiful when you're angry!" Oliver shouted through the door.

Oliver did eventually come to help her. He dumped a pile of books on the kitchen table at about eleven o'clock that night. Maggie was cleaning the silver, her temper set on a slow simmer.

"Mags, when you pack, make sure you put these in, would you? You can choose what clothes I need, but God knows if Lawrenceville has anything resembling a book shop, so I want to make sure to take the reference books I'll need. You won't forget, will you?"

"No, Ol, I won't forget." She didn't look at him, and her voice was icy.

"Okay. Now then. Let's cheer up, have a whisky, and I'll write that list you wanted me to do."

They sat in the den until the early hours of Thursday morning writing a guide to Bockhampton and Salisbury for the McCarthys. This involved trying to explain on paper how to relight the Aga if it suddenly went out, how to use the fax and reset the answering machine, where the fusebox was—neither Oliver nor Maggie could remember, so they had to search the house before they could complete this item—and a long list of essential phone numbers of friends, doctors, plumbers, kennels, insurance companies, garages, and other individuals vital to the smooth functioning of life at Bockhampton House. Maggie added a list of recommended shops and services, and the names of the local restaurants that she and Oliver patronised. When they finally went to bed, Oliver turned out the light, and said smugly, "See, Mags? Everything's just about done. You can put your feet up tomorrow and have your hair set."

"Oh, sure! You know what I have to do tomorrow? I have to do the whole of the garden, finish polishing the silver, re-hang the curtains, wash the dogs, pack my things—pack *your* things— Since when do I have my hair done anyway?"

"Maybe you should get it done. Might improve your looks a bit— show you cared."

"What the fuck do you mean by that? It's not as if you're God's gift to women."

"C'mon, Mags. It was a joke. Stop bitching. Life's not that bad, you're just feeling sorry for yourself. . . ."

"Sorry for myself? Hell, no, Oliver. I consider being your unpaid housekeeper a positive *treat*. Nothing gives me greater pleasure. I see it as my vocation, honestly I do. I've rarely looked forward to anything more! Sometimes, I lie awake just thinking how lucky I am to be married to you. I mean, it's not as if you've ever been *unfaithful* to me, or anything so sordid. No, not you. You are a model of fidelity, you're wise and warm and supportive, you shoulder all the responsibility for our domestic life, and you are so amazingly appreciative of my few, slight efforts, that I regularly fling myself onto my knees and thank God for giving you to me. Truly. You are a gift from God. A miracle. A bloody great God-given miracle."

They lay silently next to each other in the big four-poster. Oliver couldn't resist having the last word.

"I do believe it's your sarcasm that keeps the fire burning in our relationship, Maggie," Oliver said quietly.

"My sarcasm? For God's sake, Oliver, that's it. You've really blown it now. I'm not going to lift a bloody finger for you. You never show *any* appreciation of *anything* I do, or how hard I work—"

"How hard *you* work? How about how hard *I* work? What recognition do I get?"

"Why should you get any? You're doing exactly what you want to do when you write, and it's just a convenient excuse for not doing anything you don't want to do." She mimicked him, " 'Sorry, Mags, I'd love to help—I'm up to my ears in work, though.' 'Sorry, Mags, I'd love to mow the grass, but I've got a deadline.' 'Sorry, Mags, I'd truly love to cook dinner, but I've got a date with the new bimbo at the office.' 'Sorry, Mags, I'd really *love* to change Arthur's nappy, but

I'VE GOT A BLOODY BACKACHE AGAIN!'" Maggie was sitting up in bed shouting her head off.

"Just shut up for one minute, could you? Do you want to wake the kids?"

"Hell, no, I wouldn't want to do that! Wouldn't it be awful if you had to put them back to bed for once?"

"There are plenty of women who'd give their eye teeth to have your life, Maggie."

"Would they? They can have it—I'd rather have their bloody teeth any day! What, let me ask you, is so great about my life?"

"This." Oliver's hand snaked suddenly under his pyjama top—which Maggie was wearing.

"You think so, do you? You think having sex with you is compensation for all the rest of the shit I have to put up with?" Maggie was trying to move away from him and maintain her fury. "You have such a high opinion of yourself, you really think that, don't you? Well, let me tell you something, Oliver Callahan, you're *not* the only man I've ever slept with, and I don't know what makes you think you're the best. Did Louise tell you that?" As Oliver's hands went to work, her voice became throaty, her words spat out in a rush, punctuated with long, strange pauses. "You flatter . . . yourself. . . . You—really do. . . . Sometimes I wonder . . . why . . . you need to . . . sleep . . . with me . . . at all. You'd have just . . . as good a . . . time all by . . . yourself . . . Better . . . maybe."

"Why don't you just shut up and let me get on with it?" Oliver growled, and began to nip at her neck, his hands back up to her breasts, his knee flung across her thighs.

"So now I'm not even supposed . . . to talk?" Maggie groaned.

"That's right. Stop it. We could conduct a controlled experiment to see if you're even capable of keeping your mouth shut for five minutes."

"Is that how long it's going to take you to finish? Five minutes? My—that would be a record! And I don't think in this situation you are quite the person to be talking about control!" she mocked.

"Shut up, damn you!" Oliver grabbed her hair, and jerked her head back to expose her throat. His hands went back under the duvet and grabbed her buttocks roughly. Maggie wrapped her legs around his waist and forgot all about their row, and all about Louise, and, for a little while, all about Edward.

Later, a good forty minutes later, she remembered how much she had to do. Oliver was snoring. She jabbed her elbow in his ribs.

"What?"

"Ol. Did I ever tell you what an amazing husband you are? What an amazing lover you are?"

"As a matter of fact, you did. It was a long time ago, but I distinctly remember it."

"Well—I lied." Maggie smiled to herself in the dark. She'd had the last word. She normally did, post-coitally.

Despite Maggie's bitching, most of the jobs were completed, through the combined efforts of Maggie, Leah, Joan Mason, and Bill Gordon, and despite Arthur's attempts to undo whatever Leah had last done, by late afternoon on Thursday. There was still the packing to do, but Maggie decided to do that after the children had gone to bed, and she had picked Oliver up from Salisbury station. Joan Mason, a woman whose capacity for hard work was legendary in the Valley, made Maggie a cup of tea before she left.

"Now, Mrs. C., you sit yourself down and rest your feet. I'll be back tomorrow morning after you've left to have a go at the carpets and finish off the bits and bobs, and I'll sort out a spot of lunch and supper for the McCarthys so they don't have to shop or cook as soon as they arrive."

"I don't know what I'd do without you, Joan," Maggie replied sincerely. "Is there anything we can bring you back from America?"

"I don't think so, Mrs. C. I've managed to find everything I've ever needed right here or in the town for the past fifty years. I can't see what they have in America that you can't get in Salisbury. . . ."

"You're probably right," Maggie said with a smile. "Anyway, if you think of anything, *anything* at all, you have only to ask. . . . You have our number over there?"

"Pinned to the fridge. Now why don't you go and have a lie-down, Mrs. C?"

Maggie nodded. Try as she might, she had never persuaded Joan Mason to call her Maggie, although one Christmas, when Oliver had pushed her to stay for a glass of sherry, she had addressed Oliver as "Mister Oliver" and then, blushing girlishly, explained that she always thought of Mr. Leonard Callahan, Oliver's deceased uncle, as Mister Callahan, and still couldn't bring herself to give the title to anyone else. Joan Mason had been very fond of Uncle Leo.

Maggie watched Joan peddle down the lane, precariously balanced on her bicycle, and then called to Leah.

"Can you hang around and watch the children when I pick Ol up, Leah? He should be arriving around eight o'clock, but he'll call when he sets off."

"No worries, Maggie. I'm all packed next door. I might tuck up early and kip here, if that's okay; then Mrs. Mason won't have to worry about the flat tomorrow." Leah had come into the kitchen to get the children's tea.

"That's fine—it would be a real help. Look, I'm going to spray the roses one more time, so shout out to the garden when Ol calls, okay?" Maggie dropped a kiss on Lily's and Arthur's heads and went out into the garden.

It was a lovely early summer afternoon, quite warm, and Maggie sat outside to enjoy her last evening at Bockhampton for a while. The garden looked better than it had all year. Bill Gordon, a prickly and eccentric old man, whose conversational skills peaked at muttering about why 'them up at Westminster' should bring back hanging, had ten green fingers, and the garden blossomed whenever Maggie and Oliver called him in for damage limitation. Maggie felt a little sad about leaving Bockhampton at this time of year. Ever since they had moved here from London, she and Oliver had switched their annual holiday from the summer to the spring, as they both loved the summers in Wiltshire. Now that Lily was growing up, and starting proper school next September, they would have less flexibility about when they chose to go abroad. It was a sign of times changing, and Maggie felt that she was on the point of entering a new stage of life, one of settled, regular routines, school runs, family life, middle-age spread and mediocrity. . . . It wasn't that she didn't want to go to the States—she did, in a way. She sat on Lily's rope swing under an apple tree and imagined how the garden would look in a month's time, with her beloved roses in her favourite overblown stage and the sweet peas that she and Lily had planted scrambling up the wigwam. Despite the peace of the evening, she was overwhelmed by a sense of foreboding. She was uncomfortable about Oliver, more than she had ever been. His attitude to her was changing subtly. Before, when she lost her temper with him, he would either attempt to tease her out of it or detach himself. The past few weeks they had barely spoken without rowing, and their fights had been put on ice, rather than resolved, in bed. It didn't bode well for spending eight weeks in each other's company. The more she fought with Oliver, the more she thought about Edward. She hadn't seen Edward since the night she had gone to dinner with him. They had bumped into each other at the baker's the previous week, but Maggie had rushed out, shouting some lame excuse over her shoulder. Edward had looked puzzled; not exactly hurt, but a little shocked. She had spent ten minutes trembling in her car after that encounter, and Edward hadn't phoned her since. Maggie knew he hadn't even tried to call, because she had left the answering machine on all the time just in case he did. She checked her watch. A quarter to six: she'd have to get a move on to have everything finished before Oliver arrived.

An hour later, she heard Leah calling her name, and dropped the rose spray as she raced in to pick up the phone.

As she ran into the house, Leah pulled a face. "Not great news, Maggie."

"What? He's alright, isn't he?"

"Oh, yeah. He's alright. He's hanging on."

"Ol? Hi. Where are you?"

"I'm still in town, Mags. Still at the office."

"Oh, *Oliver!* Why?"

"There's been a cock-up, Mags. I'm sorry, darling—we've got to meet again. Later tonight. Pete's scheduled a secondary meeting." He winced. "And after that, I've got to have dinner with Pete and some TV producer bloke—there's a chance of a TV series here, Mags." He lowered his voice conspiritorially. "I can't say too much about it right now, if you get my drift. Early days, you know? It was Pete's idea—it's too good a chance to miss. They're thinking of a sort of bird's eye view of the Southern states—making a six-part series—I've got to meet the producer before we go, so it's a once in a lifetime's opportunity. I'm so sorry, Mags. There's nothing for it but for me to stay over tonight and meet you at the airport." Maggie could hear a lot of background noise over the phone, some sort of 70's pop music, and someone laughing. She felt suddenly cold.

"Oliver? Where are you, exactly?"

"I said, didn't I? In the office. In Peter's office." Oliver was gripping the telephone, with his eyes shut tight to block out the crowded pub lounge, and his jaw clenched. "Everyone's here—they want to change the supplement into a tabloid, you know, like *The*

Times, and there's all hell breaking loose. I've got to stay, Mags. Peter's insisted. Shut up, you lot! I can hardly hear myself!"

Maggie heard the noise diminish a little.

"Oliver, I don't see why you have to stay. You could drive back late. After dinner." Oliver sighed audibly. "Maggie, I can't. God only knows when we'll finish—you know what telly people are like. Anyway, I didn't bring the car—remember? Look. I'll make it up to you. Tomorrow night, when we get into town, you and I will go out to the finest place that Lawrenceville has to offer. Okay? I'm really sorry, darling. I know I'm leaving you in the lurch, but this is important. Imagine what a break into television could mean for me—for us. I'm sure Leah will help you, okay?"

"Yes. That's fine." She spoke briskly. Maggie knew perfectly well that Oliver was lying; some or all of his story was untrue.

"Look, if you really feel that desperate about it, I'll cancel the dinner."

"Don't bother. I don't want you to come back." All she wanted was for him to get off the phone.

"Mags, I'll call you when I get to the flat, okay? It won't be late—I hope."

"Don't call. I'll only have the machine on. I wouldn't mind getting at least three hours' sleep tonight."

"And I'll see you at Terminal Three check-in, United Airlines, at eight o'clock tomorrow, okay?"

Maggie heard another shriek of laughter.

"Are you sure you're in the office, Oliver?" She gave him one last chance, her hand itching to slam down the receiver.

"Of course I am—I'm not going senile, Mags. There are just a lot of people around."

"Fine. Oliver—what about your passport? Where is it?"

"My passport? Oh, I've got it on me . . . I must have shoved it in my briefcase. Fortuitously. All you need to bring is the tickets."

"You put it in your briefcase? How uncanny. That was a stroke of luck, wasn't it? Or foresight."

"Yup. Now, Mags. Try to get a good night's sleep, alright? I *will* phone if it's not too late. I'm really, really sorry I'm not there to help. Have you got tons to do?"

"No, not really. It's just about finished."

"Mags, you're a star. I love you. Big kisses. Can't wait for tomorrow."

Maggie didn't comment. Her stomach was knotted so tightly she didn't feel able to utter more than one syllable.

"Bye."

"Bye, darling."

Oliver hung up the pay phone, feeling sick. The saloon bar of The Eagle and Child was as noisy as ever, and he knew, even as the words had come out of his mouth, that Maggie would know he wasn't in Peter's office. The truth was, he *was* going back to the office to pick up Pete in about an hour's time. Oliver cursed himself. He had had a perfectly good and legitimate excuse for not going back to Bockhampton. Why had he lied to Maggie? Why had he said they had a secondary meeting scheduled? No one at the *Telegraph* ever scheduled a secondary meeting—primary meetings were barely on the agenda—and Maggie knew more about the *Telegraph* than most of the idiots who worked there. . . . Why he hadn't just explained about the BBC producer, and told her he was in the pub with a few mates waiting for Pete to get free, he'd never know. Whenever he felt guilty, he had an instinct to embroider the truth, however valid his excuse. It had just slipped out, and once a white lie had slipped out, it would cause too much hassle to correct it. Shit. He really didn't want to piss Maggie off. He had attempted a pre-emptive strike, playing his best hand to stop her getting angry, and he'd overdone it, and he'd lied to her, and she'd clammed up on him. Bugger. Sarah, the new researcher on the desk, sidled up to him when he put the phone down.

He was muttering "Shit, shit, shit . . ."

"Grief from the wife? Trouble on the home front? Can I get you another drink?" she purred.

"Hmm? No thanks, Sarah."

"Come on, Oliver—don't let the bastards get you down." She smiled at him, and put her hand gently on his arm in a gesture of sympathy. She was a tall girl, in her early twenties, with chestnut brown hair and a broad, gap-toothed grin. She struck Oliver as gloriously straightforward and uncomplicated. Oliver looked down at her legs. Not bad, he mused, a bit too straight—he preferred a little more definition between calf and ankle—but they did give her a schoolgirl air. He could just imagine her with grey socks fallen round her ankles. She reminded him of a rather overgrown schoolgirl hockey captain. Possibly more of a right wing, now he came to think about it.

"Sorry, Sarah. My mind was on something else."

"We all know what your mind's on, Ollie—" Guts Bishop, a fat lobby correspondent, said with a lewd wink.

"Oh, alright then—twist my arm . . . Gin and tonic, seeing as it's Guts' round—and easy on the tonic, Sarah, love. . . ."

Sarah had managed to create a job for herself on the *Telegraph* out of thin air, and had so secured herself in Peter Forbes' good books that he had appointed her to "help" Oliver and a couple of other regular columnists. Sarah made no effort to conceal the fact that her admiration was reserved exclusively for Oliver. She had told him very earnestly when they first met that she hoped he would be her mentor. He watched her as she stood at the bar twirling that glossy brown hair round her finger like a twelve-year-old. If dinner ended early, he might just pop back into The Eagle and Child for a bit of consolation, if Sarah was still hanging around. Maggie was already furious with him despite his relative innocence. If he was going to have to grovel, he might just as well have something to feel genuinely remorseful about.

Maggie hung up. Leah materialised at her shoulder, proffering what looked like a large gin and tonic, which Maggie accepted.

"Bummer, eh? What's the toad done this time?" Leah asked.

"It's okay, really. All I have to do now is pack. I'm not going to bother any more with the garden. It looks fine. Or with the house. Stuff 'em."

"Maggie, maybe I shouldn't say this . . . but don't you think he's a bit of a piker?"

"A piker?" Even after a year Maggie had trouble understanding Leah's Australian dialect.

"You know, skiving off . . . leaving you with all this shit at the last minute . . ."

"No, Leah, I don't think so. He's just doing what he has to do. It's his job, that's all. Anyway, we're pretty much finished. I just need to tie up a few loose ends."

"Whatever you say; you're the boss," Leah said with a shrug. Maggie normally leapt at the chance to criticise Oliver. "I'll bung the kids in bed, what d'you reckon?"

"That would be a real help."

Maggie's hand still rested on the telephone, and as Leah left the room, she tapped out a number.

"Edward? It's Maggie."

"Hello, darling! I thought you'd gone off to the land of liberty. How does the old song go? 'My country 'tis of thee, sweet land of liberty', rum, tum, tum, tum—" His voice sounded perfectly normal, as if they had chatted that morning.

"Tomorrow morning. Edward, I wondered if you fancied a fare-well drink? Ol's stuck in London, and I'm pretty much sorted out over here, and I'd like to take a break . . ."

"Delighted. Shall I come to you?"

"No, I'll come to you, if that's okay. I'll be about half an hour."

"No longer. The anticipation might kill me."

Maggie went upstairs and turned on the shower before stripping off her clothes. She stepped under steaming hot water, and stood still while it drenched her. She wondered if Oliver had been at The Eagle and Child. It was his home away from home after all. It was where she had met him, on her first day at the *Telegraph*, a little more than seven years ago. Once she and Ol had become a serious item, he had stopped suggesting that they meet there. Although it was a long time since she'd been in the pub, she could see perfectly the long bar, lined with hacks, and the grubby telephone kiosk in the corner. The more she thought about it, the more she knew Oliver had been at The Eagle. Maggie thought she had come to terms with Oliver's compulsive lying, and now regarded it as a peculiar reflex action. He was just as likely to lie if asked if he'd just farted as he was if asked if he was having an affair. He might well have been lying about the TV producer. She rarely challenged him these days, relying instead on her own instincts, but the refrain "Are you lying to me now? Are you lying to me about this? Are you cheating on me?" ran through her head with increasing frequency.

It occurred to Maggie that it would be useful if she had a friend who could walk in and say, "My God, Oliver's changed! I simply wouldn't recognise him any longer! Amazing what difference six months makes!" but it didn't work like that. People might make those comments about one's children, but not about one's spouse. But she wasn't going to waste time thinking about Oliver. Oliver was a permanent problem, and one she could think about tomorrow. Her more pressing concern was Edward. She was nervous about seeing him, the type of nervousness that combines apprehension and excitement, but she felt completely resolved, and the act of having made a decision gave her a sense of do and dare. She pulled on a pair of jeans, a worn shirt of Oliver's, and a pair of boots, and towel-dried her hair roughly. On her way downstairs, she went into the nursery to tell Leah she was popping out for an hour or two.

"Mummy, you mustn't go out with wet hair. You'll catch a cold," Lily said severely. She had always been a practical and serious child, with an overdeveloped sense of responsibility. Arthur, engrossed in trying to undo the buttons of Leah's shirt, mumbled something incomprehensible.

"That's an old wives' tale, silly."

"I'm not silly, I'm Lily!"

"I know you are, pudding." Maggie kissed them both, and gave Lily an extra squeeze. "I'll be back soon. I just need to do some last-minute errands."

"When are we going to America?"

"Tomorrow, darling. Tomorrow morning—the second you wake up."

"Goody. Is Daddy coming?"

"Oh yes. He's going to meet us at the airport."

"Is he going to buy me a present?"

"Maybe. Sleep well, sweethearts."

On her way to the front door, Maggie threw the clothes she had just removed and the children's clothes into the washing machine, and switched it on. No point leaving Joan laundry on top of every-thing else. She grabbed a bottle of champagne out of the fridge. She had bought two that morning, one to leave as a welcome for the McCarthys, and one to share with Oliver on their last night at Bockhampton. Too bad. Ol's loss would be Edward's gain. As she drove to the barn, she slowed down to a crawl to overtake Imogen on Samson, and rolled down the window.

"We're off to the States tomorrow, Mog. See you in a couple of months, okay?"

"Sure. Where are you heading now? D'you want to drop in at the yard for a farewell drink?"

"Maybe. If I've got time. I've got some stuff to do, and I don't know how long I'll be."

"I'm in all night. If you want to come by . . . come by! You could say goodbye to Samson."

"Samson will be glad to see the back of me." Maggie waved as she drove on.

Edward was in the garden when she walked through the gate.

"Hello, darling! Isn't it a gorgeous evening . . . What have you got there? Champagne! Lordy. I would have put on a jacket and tie if I knew you were planning something formal. Now let me get some glasses, and we can stay out here for a bit and watch the ducks."

Given that Edward Arabin wasn't a gardener, wasn't married, and didn't seem to give a damn about his surroundings, he had one of the loveliest gardens in the area. Sitting on a deck chair looking at the river, Maggie envied him the extraordinarily peaceful atmosphere that pervaded the barn.

"Oliver's got the chance of a series on the telly off the back of these American articles."

"Really? What kind of series?"

"He didn't have time to say—something about an Englishman's view of the South, I imagine."

"Could be interesting. . . . It could also do a great deal for his career. How d'you fancy being married to a TV star, Mags?"

"It could have its advantages."

"Like what? A double-page spread in *Hello* magazine?"

"Well . . . money, I guess."

"Not if it's the BBC."

"It's a first step at least."

"Oh, undoubtedly. You don't look that happy about it, Maggie."

"Don't I? I *am*, though. I couldn't be happier," Maggie said firmly. "Could I have another splash, please, Edward? I am very happy for him. Not that I wouldn't like to get the same sort of opportunity myself, but I've never had the chance. And Oliver's a much better performer than I am. I'm sure the camera will love him. Not to mention the audience."

"Do I detect a spot of professional jealousy?"

"Perhaps just a tiny smidgen. Oh God, Edward, you can't be jealous of your own husband! I can't, at least."

"I don't see why not. I'm perfectly capable of being jealous of anyone and everyone."

"Well, it's different when you're married."

"Is it? I wouldn't know." There was a wistful note in his voice.

Maggie couldn't think of anything to reply, so she stared across the river that ran at the bottom of Edward's garden, and pretended to be absorbed in watching a couple of swans. As she sat there, feeling rather than seeing the sun set behind her, she felt surprisingly calm and sure of herself.

"It's lovely here," Maggie said blandly. 'Wonderful to have the river right at the bottom of the garden. You know, thinking about this swap, I realised that I don't think I could ever leave the Valley for good." Maggie was annoyed with herself. She hadn't come over to talk about Edward's garden, or for yet another banal conversation about the swap. She kicked off her boots, crossed her ankles, and rested her bare feet on Edward's lap. He looked down at them, touching one of her toes.

"You have remarkably beautiful feet, Maggie. I don't think I've ever seen such beautiful feet."

"You do say the oddest things, Eddie. I'll look at them in a new light from now on." She raised her feet a few inches in the air and pretended to study them critically before letting them drop back.

"I feel a little bit odd sitting here with you and discussing Oliver."

"Why, Eddie?" Maggie didn't want to look him in the eye. "It isn't as if we haven't done it a million times."

"True, but I rather had the feeling that you were avoiding me."

"You did? How odd."

"Not all that odd. I haven't seen you for four weeks. You haven't called. We met at the baker's last week if you remember, and as soon as you saw me you jumped a foot in the air like a cat and ran out of the shop."

"I had Arthur in the car."

"No you didn't, Mags. I followed you out of the shop and watched. You sat in your car for ten minutes, and there wasn't anybody else in it. Not even a small one."

"Oh, I'd forgotten."

"So why *have* you been avoiding me? Because of our last conversation?"

"No, not really. I mean, yes. I *have* been avoiding you in a way, I suppose. I just didn't know how to behave, I guess."

"We agreed that it wouldn't affect us. I thought we were going to pretend that nothing had happened."

"Nothing did happen."

"Exactly."

"That's what I've come to see you about, Eddie." Maggie bent down to pluck a stray daisy from the lawn, and began to pull its petals off, her eyes glued to her lap. Her mouth had gone dry, and when she summoned the courage to speak, she didn't recognise her own voice. "I wondered if you could do me a favour?"

"So long as it doesn't involve money. Or not a lot of money, at least."

"It doesn't."

"Fire away."

"I wondered if you would kiss me again." Maggie smiled shyly at him, flicking her hair back. "I mean, could we kiss each other again?"

Edward looked away across the riverbank.

"Maggie. I don't know what to say."

"You don't have to say anything."

Edward pulled her onto his lap, and buried his face in her still-damp hair. "You smell wonderful."

Maggie laughed in her throat. "Don't, for heaven's sake, say that I smell of newly mown grass."

"I wouldn't dream of saying anything so crass. I don't know that I'm capable of saying anything at all." He kissed her hard on the mouth, and then softly at the corners of her lips, her temples, her eyes, and back to her mouth. Maggie coiled her arms around his neck, and clung to him, her legs twisting between his.

"D'you know something, Eddie? All the times I've been here, all the years I've known you, I've never seen your bedroom?"

"My God, Maggie. You have a very strange was of putting things. Maybe I'm just too old, too out of touch. Maybe I'm getting the wrong end of the stick."

Maggie shook her head slowly. "I don't think you are too old at all. Not for me." She leant forward and pressed herself against his chest. "If I'm not expressing myself very well, it's just that I know how I feel inside, but I'm not sure what to say. I don't know whether to say everything, or keep it simple." She gazed into his gentle eyes. She felt as if she and Edward were having a quite separate conversation that had nothing to do with the words coming out of their mouths. "I love you, Edward. I want to go to bed with you. I don't want to talk anymore, particularly about Oliver. Right now, I just want to be with you and forget about everything."

"You don't know what this means to me."

"I do. I really think I do. I know what it means to me at least." Maggie stroked his face, and was struck by how beautiful he looked, his wise, honest eyes fixed on hers while he cradled her face in his hands.

Edward rose from his chair, lifting Maggie in his arms, and carried her into the house like a baby.

Edward's bedroom was a long, gallery-like room built under the eaves of the barn. Like the rest of his house, it was an Aladdin's cave of treasures and knickknacks collected over the years. At the end of the room there was a large bed covered in a blood-red cloth. Maggie flung herself on the bed, her hands behind her head.

"This is amazing, Eddie," she said, stroking the fabric. "What is it?"

"Goat's hair. Dyed, of course. From Uzbekistan. Or so the dealer promised me. He also promised me it was two hundred years old, but my guess is you could knock a nought off that." Edward was uncharacteristically nervous. He sat down beside her, and rested one hand on her hipbone. Maggie lifted her hips off the bed, and wriggled out of her jeans. Edward undressed. He was broader shouldered and had far more chest hair than Maggie had expected. His hair was as soft and silky as the camel hair rug. He held her tightly against him.

"Maggie . . . you are even more beautiful than I had imagined . . ."

"*Have* you ever imagined me naked, Edward?"

"Countless times, for my sins. That's why I am such a devoted admirer of your feet. They are the only part of you I regularly get to see completely naked. A sort of promise of things to come. . . ."

"So you're not disappointed?"

"God, no. Bodies are one of the very few things that can be better in reality than in dreams." He began to caress her, with gentle but experienced hands. "Not in my case, of course. In my case, I expect the anticipation would be finer than the reality."

"Oh, you're wrong, Edward. You couldn't be more wrong. You feel . . . perfect."

"Maggie, can I ask you just one thing? I know you don't want to talk, but one question, please. Is this the only time? Is this the first and last?"

"Oh, Eddie, darling Eddie, I just don't know. Please, let's not talk about what happens next—I'm not very good at predicting things . . ."

"Alright. Okay. It's enough. If it's just this once, it will have to be enough. I love you, Maggie; I know that at least."

A couple of hours later, Maggie pulled into the yard, and parked at the back of the stables, near Imogen's cottage. Curtis was away; at least his extremely flashy car was missing. Curtis was a retired West Indian cricketer, and had lived with Imogen as long as Maggie had known her, although they had never married. Imogen referred to him as her "functional equivalent" of a spouse. Maggie, conscious of political correctness, called him Imogen's "partner" and most of the people in the Valley called him either "Imogen's boyfriend" or "that black bastard," depending on their leaning. Maggie shouted her arrival as she let herself in. No one really knocked in the Valley.

Imogen was sitting in front of the television polishing her boots.

"Hi, Mog. Is Curtis out?"

"He's at the pub." Imogen nodded at the armchair. "Have a seat, and help yourself to a drink. There's some whisky behind you."

Maggie did as she was told. She really liked Imogen. She was a very frank and independent woman who did exactly as she pleased, and Maggie knew that she could be trusted implicitly. *She* was "genuine"—far more than her horses.

"So, Mags, what's going down? All ready for your Big Adventure?"

"I have to go home and pack in a little while, and then we're all set. I just didn't feel like going straight home."

"No? Where have you been?" Imogen kept her eyes on her boots.

"I've been with Edward Arabin."

"Oh yeah? How is he? I haven't seen him for a week or two. Not since Samson threw him."

"What is it with you, Mog? Do you just save Samson up for when you're really pissed off with your friends, and then let him loose?"

"Nope." Imogen spat, and rubbed harder. "I save Samson for people I really like and care about."

"You've never let Oliver ride Samson."

"That's not because I don't like him. That's because Oliver thinks riding has something to do with sex—he can't separate them. Oliver really only rides in order to show off his thighs in jodhpurs. Samson would sense that, and he'd resent it. He objects to rival testosterone. Frankly, Oliver and Samson have a lot in common. They're both show-offs, and they wouldn't work well together. You and Samson do work together. So do you and Oliver, I guess." She chucked one glistening boot on the floor, and began on the other one. "So. How's Edward?"

"I've just spent the evening in bed with him." Maggie blurted out the words. She had sworn to herself on leaving the barn that she wouldn't tell a soul, and her resolve had lasted a bare fifteen minutes.

Imogen didn't miss a beat. "And how is he?"

"You mean, his general state of health, or d'you mean how *is* he?" Maggie laughed, and met Imogen's twinkling eyes.

"I mean both. I mean, I hope you haven't killed him, and I mean I've always been a little curious myself about what he'd be like."

"He's great. I'm not saying he's the last of the red-hot lovers. It's much better than that. He makes you *feel* great, if you know what I mean." Maggie leant forward in her seat, closer to her friend. "The funny thing is, I don't feel bad about it. I went over there deliberately to make love with him, and between you and me, a little bit to pay Oliver back—I can't even remember what for—and I did it, and I don't regret it. I was really nervous, and he was simply—wonderful. I suppose I thought of it as revenge—to have a fun bonk with a good friend, but it was much, much better than that. It was somehow—special. I feel as if I've been released, as if I'd been in a straight jacket, and somebody came up and snipped the ties. It was just—really nice. *Nice."* Maggie laughed again. "You can tell I'm a journalist, can't you, Mog? At least an ex-journalist. I have such an extraordinary fluency with words. . . ."

"Who needs words, Maggie, when it comes to sex? It *was* just sex, wasn't it? It wasn't the dreaded Love?"

"No. Love? Who needs it?" Maggie was trying to sound more flippant than she felt. She coloured a little, and shook her head vehemently. "Love? Don't be ridiculous, Mog; I'm not a complete fool." She met Imogen's cool gaze. "No; it was sex alright. I do love Edward, but I really just wanted to have sex with someone who was interested in me, and who I fancied, and most of all, who I respected. Eddie fit the bill."

"Not just because he happens to be the nearest thing to Bockhampton in trousers?"

"God no, Maggie—I was fired up enough to have driven a long way for the right person. It was just good luck that person happened to be a mile away."

"Aren't you having sex with Oliver?"

"Yes—we are—quite a lot actually. We're also fighting quite a lot—d'you think there's a connection there? Like animals?" Maggie's thoughts turned immediately to the fighting and fucking regimen of the desert mouse. She shrugged, feigning a casual attitude that she didn't feel. "Maybe I just felt like a change; like it would be rejuvenating to do it with someone else."

"Curtis will be gutted."

"Imogen, you mustn't tell . . ."

"Of course I wouldn't . . . I couldn't hurt Curtis so badly. Christ, it would crush him if he knew you went out looking for a bonk and chose Edward Arabin rather than him! He thinks that as the Valley's token black, he ought to have first call on all the naughty business going on. Poor innocent lamb. I'd never tell him. More to the point, are you going to tell Oliver?"

"What do you think?"

Imogen looked at her carefully. "I think you're not—not immediately anyway. But I don't know; you and Oliver have a funny relationship."

"Funny ha ha?"

"It doesn't amuse me much—maybe it does amuse you and Ol. I meant funny peculiar."

"I don't know what I'll say to Ol. Right now I don't feel like speaking to him ever again. I may wake up tomorrow and feel sick with shame and guilt. . . . Who can say?"

"You're going to spend a mighty long flight tomorrow sitting next to him all the way. You better think about it."

"If there's one thing I absolutely know I am *not* going to do, it's think about it. All I do know is that so far, I don't feel ashamed at all. I feel quite euphoric. I feel released."

"It's the hormones, dear. They'll get you every time."

A little later, Maggie realised it was eleven o'clock, gave Imogen a squeeze, and headed home to pack. Despite her confident assertion to Imogen, as she drove she did think about Edward, but little about Oliver. Thinking of Edward made her feel completely happy. She trusted him. She was convinced that he would never do anything to hurt her, and the knowledge that he now stood guard over a special part of her gave her a sense of confidence that she hadn't felt for years. She felt aroused, and safe, and relaxed all at once. As she flung open the front door, she saw Leah's suitcase, and the children's case, and the nappy bag, filled with toys and essentials for the journey neatly arranged in the hall, waiting to be loaded into the car. On top of the pile was a note from Leah:

Hi, Maggie! I've finished the stuff for me and the kids. The Toad phoned. I said you were running around doing his chores.

He said to say again how real sorry he was and give you all his love (vom) and he'll see you tomorrow.

Leah had drawn a happy face—a little circle with a huge grin— and an exclamation mark. Maggie looked at it and burst into choking sobs.

Oliver dined with Peter Forbes and an independent producer, Danny Bujevski, at Chéz Gerard in Charlotte Street. The meeting had gone as well as Oliver could have hoped, and the producer seemed genuinely enthusiastic. Both Bujevski and Peter had left early, shortly after ten, to avoid getting flak from their wives. Oliver had no such worries, but he *had* phoned Maggie from the restaurant to try to make amends. When she wasn't there, he pictured her sitting over a glass of wine with Mog and bitching about him. He hopped in a cab and returned to The Eagle. The bar had emptied somewhat since the early evening rush, but Sarah, Gus, and the editor of the Health and Medicine page were still slumped at a small table littered with empty glasses. Sarah's face lit up as Oliver came through the swing doors.

"Oliver! Just in time for last orders. Your round, I believe." Gus leant back in his chair contentedly.

Oliver rubbed his hands together. "For once, Gus, I don't object to standing you a drink. Don't take this as a precedent. I've just got something to celebrate. What'll it be? Brandy? A bottle of champagne?"

They took him up on the offer of champagne, Gus ordering a brandy chaser to be on the safe side.

"So what's the good news, Ollie? Won the pools?"

"Oh, nothing so specific . . . Just holidays, blue skies ahead . . . I'm filled with love for mankind. . . ."

"And womankind, Oliver?" Sarah prompted. "What about women?" He liked her healthy, open face and big teeth. He liked the way she looked at him with puppyish devotion, and laughed at every quip he made. He liked the fact that she was young, and not all that bright, and so tremendously easy to please. She reminded him a little of Louise.

"Ah, Sarah; if you knew me better, you'd know I've always loved womankind." He winked at her. "It's the love of mankind that I find difficult."

When the pub closed, Oliver offered to drop Sarah at her flat, leaving Gus to handle their entirely plastered medical expert alone. They got as far as the Callahans' studio in Notting Hill.

Christy locked the door of the tiny bathroom, and conducted her cleansing ritual. She had miniature plastic bottles of all her beauty products in a little case in her handbag, packed with cotton balls and facial tissues, so that she could cleanse, tone, and reapply her makeup during the flight. She even had a little spray of facial mist to "counteract cabin dryness," or so the label claimed. They should be landing in London within the hour. She drew the faintest smudge of eyeliner under her violet-blue eyes, eyes that she hadn't closed for a moment on the flight. As she walked back down the gangway, she could see her husband, fast asleep, and Jake and Mariella in the row behind. Bless Gabe for booking business-class seats for all of them. Breakfast was being served. Christy motioned the flight attendant to leave trays for her sleeping family, but not to wake them. She'd try it herself before deciding whether they should eat or sleep.

"Ladies and gentleman; we will be landing at London's Heathrow Airport in approximately thirty-five minutes, and we at American Airlines would like to present a short acclimatisation video for your entertainment and assistance. . . ." Christy checked her lipstick in her hand mirror, and then turned her attention to the screen above her, which ran a series of flickering images of Britain—the Horse Guards, Westminster Bridge, Bath's Royal Crescent, Edinburgh Castle . . .
"Welcome to England," said the voice-over in honeyed tones. "We hope you'll take the time to appreciate the rustic charm and stylish sophistication that make it one of the world's finest locations . . . London"—there was Big Ben—"is England's cosmopolitan capital, where commerce, government, and pageantry reign supreme . . ." The scene changed, showing various churches and buildings that Christy didn't recognise. "But just as there are answers, there are questions . . . The windswept monoliths of Stonehenge"—Christy stabbed Gabe in the ribs, her finger directing his confused stare—"are all that remains of a lost civilisation. . . . Where were they lost? And why?" The scene switched again, and the voice prattled on, but Christy was no longer listening.

"Gabe! Did you see it? Isn't it great—that they actually showed Stonehenge? It's an omen—I just know it is!" Her huge eyes were sparkling with excitement.

Everything went like clockwork. The lines at Immigration were short, their luggage arrived intact, and Jake behaved like an angel. At the Information desk they were handed an envelope addressed to Mr. Gabriel McCarthy, with a set of car keys, a map to Bockhampton, and a hastily scrawled note from Maggie Callahan: "The car is parked in bay number 23 on the first level of car park 1A at Terminal 3. Welcome!" Christy waited patiently with her son and Mariella while Gabe went to get the car. Ten minutes later, he was outside the terminal, driving a rather shabby Volvo. For about half an hour, they devoted their attention to finding their way out of the airport and onto the M25, which had clearly been designed by a sadist, if not a whole team of them. Once they were on course, they had plenty of time to take in their surroundings; the traffic inched along, not assisted by torrential rain and the fact that Gabe couldn't immediately find the controls for the windscreen wipers.

"Okay, honey, you're doing good. Now all we have to look out for is something called the M3 and a sign to Portsmouth." Christy was careful to say "Ports-muth" and not "Ports-mouth"; she had been doing her research.

"All *I'm* looking out for is the asshole on my right, Christy—you watch the signs, okay? It feels real strange driving on the wrong side of the road." The driver behind them honked repeatedly, for no reason that the McCarthys could understand, and then overtook them, flashing a V-sign, to gain perhaps fifteen feet of road. Gabe raised his eyebrows. "This may just be the last time we get in the car till it's time to go home."

Once they were on the M3 Gabe put his foot down, tickled to be able to drive over fifty-five miles an hour, but they were still in the slow lane, and everything else on the road—including some of the smallest and oldest cars that Christy had ever seen—roared past them. The rest of the directions were easy to follow, and at eight-thirty they passed the sign announcing the hamlet of Bockhampton, set the counter to measure one and a half miles, and watched for a pair of stone pillars to appear on the left. Christy held her breath as they pulled into the drive, which arced into a parking bay in front of the house. Ahead of them were open fields, with a herd of grazing cows. To their left was a large, stone house, exactly as it had looked in the photographs, and behind it a gate leading to a walled garden.

"Are we here already, Mom? Is this it?"

"Yes, Jake, this is *it.*"

"Where did they say they'd leave the keys?"

"They didn't. You sure they're not in the envelope?"

As they unloaded their bags, they heard furious barking, and saw the front door open to release a flurry of tails and fur and noise. Three dogs bounded down the steps to greet them, and behind them on the porch stood a tall, well-built woman with iron-grey hair screwed up into a bun.

"You'll be the McCarthys," she said matter-of-factly. "I'm Joan Mason. I do for the Callahans." She shook hands briskly with Gabe and Christy, nodded at Mariella, and turned a steely gaze on Jake.

"So. This is the youngster, then?"

"Yes, this is my baby, Jake." Christy pushed him forwards.

"Jake. Queer name for a child. Well, I suppose you do things differently over there in America. How do you do, young man?"

"Very well, thank you, ma'am."

Mrs. Mason bent to pick up the two largest suitcases, brushing away Gabe's remonstrations, and led the way into the house. "Now. If you'll follow me into the kitchen, I dare say you'll be in need of some breakfast after your journey."

Christy's eyes took in everything around her. Just inside the door was an enclosed tiled hallway, full of boots and coats, fishing equipment, a couple of cricket bats, and a large oak coffer. On the walls hung several yellowing black-and-white photographs of strange elderly men posing with fish. On either side of the hall double doors beckoned, but Christy didn't dare to peek until Mrs. Mason had given her the go-ahead. She followed the housekeeper meekly into a spacious farmhouse kitchen, where the table was set for four.

"Now you just sit yourselves down while I finish your breakfast."

"Mrs. Mason, we sure are happy to be here. I hope you haven't gone to any trouble?"

Joan heaped plates with bacon and eggs, sausages, fried bread and fried tomatoes, and piled toast dripping with butter and marmalade in the middle of the table.

"It's no trouble, sir. Only what Mrs. C. would have wanted, I'm sure. You must be longing for a bit of a sit-down after that terrible aeroplane business. I don't hold with them myself."

"Airplanes?"

"That's right. Nasty great things. I've never seen the need to go anywhere I can't reach with my own two feet. If God had wanted us to fly, he'd have given us wings, as my William used to say. . . ."

"Well, you've certainly got a point there!" Gabe winked at his wife. "This sure is a lovely house."

"It serves its purpose, I suppose, as houses go. Keeps one out of the rain. Now don't let your food get cold. You tuck in."

Christy watched in amazement as her generally picky son ate everything on his plate without a murmur. Jake, who tended to greet any food that wasn't obviously a peanut butter and jelly sandwich with the horrified cry "What's *this?*", tucked in happily. Christy was on the point of telling Gabe to avoid the bacon—she religiously watched his cholesterol level—when a look from Mrs. Mason made her think again, and she bent her head obediently and tucked in. There was something surreal about all this. Only fourteen hours ago they had set off from Oak Ridge, in the sweltering Carolina heat, and now here they were, chatting to a strange woman in a strange house, watching the rain pour down on an English garden, and eating a cooked breakfast. Christy was longing to explore the house. She jumped as she felt a wet nose up her skirt.

"This must be—"

"Boomer," Jake finished for her, patting the fat black labrador. He had spent several weeks studying the dogs' photographs and memorising their names. "And that's Snuff," he pointed at the Jack Russell, who growled amicably, "and that's Luck-i-us."

"Lucius," Mrs. Mason corrected. "Queer name for a dog, I must say, not that it's any concern of mine. Particularly queer for a common mongrel. Now. Shall I be showing you the geography of the house?"

Gabe hid a smile.

"Oh yes, please, Mrs. Mason, that would be grand."

They formed an orderly line behind Mrs. Mason, who led them back down the corridor and flung open the first set of double doors, revealing an enormous room with two bay windows and dominated by a mahogany dining-room table that must have been able to seat eighteen comfortably.

"This is the dining room," she explained unnecessarily. "It's a dreadfully cold room, summer or winter, but Mrs. C. puts a heater under the table when it's used in the evenings. That door goes back through to the kitchen, and then there's a back door into the kitchen garden for your vegetables. Now if you'll follow me . . ."

She crossed the hall and opened the doors of the drawing room. It was the same size as the previous room, but had a large fireplace on one wall and doors into the garden at the far end. Near the door stood a baby grand piano.

"Oh!" Christy exclaimed in delight, "does Maggie play?"

"I'm sure I don't know," Joan Mason replied severely. "My job is simply to polish it." Behind her back, Gabe and Christy smiled. The Callahans had mentioned Mrs. Mason in one of their letters, but hadn't said very much about her. They had clearly wanted her to be a surprise.

They were ushered into another large, panelled room. "This is Mr. C's private room. I don't suppose you'll be coming in here much. I certainly don't. Mister Oliver likes everything to be just the way he left it." Oliver's room was lined with books, and along one wall were the computer, printer, and fax. There were also a couple of comfortable armchairs, and a long, flat mahogany table, heaped with piles of papers. "Mrs. C. mentioned that you might be wanting to use the . . . machine." She pointed accusingly at the fax. "I've never understood why the Royal Mail wasn't good enough for them, but then it takes all sorts." She led them into another, smaller room at the foot of the stairs. "And this is the sitting room." There was a television, a small fireplace, a pair of sofas and chairs, and a heap of toys in one corner. Again, French doors opened into the garden.

"Why, it's simply lovely!" Christy exclaimed. "It's a genuine family room, isn't it, Gabe? And look at the fireplace! Isn't it darling?"

Mrs. Mason sniffed noisily in response.

"Now if you'll come upstairs, I'll show you the—sleeping accommodation. Mrs. C. and I decided which rooms you were likely to use, and I've made up the beds, but if you'd prefer a different arrangement, you need only tell me."

The master bedroom was huge but sparsely furnished, with a large four-poster bed draped in faded tapestry, a small sofa at the foot of the bed, a dressing table, and a large chest-on-chest. The window overlooked the garden. Next door was a small nursery—"Master Arthur's room," Mrs. Mason announced formally as she opened the door—and another guest bedroom. Across the hall were two bathrooms, another double bedroom, and a twin-bedded room with a Beatrix Potter frieze all around the walls. "And this is Miss Lily's room."

"Jake! Isn't it lovely? You'll be happy, here, won't you, honey?"

"It's a girl's room." Jake scowled.

Mrs. Mason put her hands on her hips and scowled right back at him. "Now I'm more than happy to change the arrangements for your parents, but not for you, young man. This room is perfectly adequate for Miss Lily, so it's good enough for the likes of you. If you'll follow me upstairs" —she puffed up a narrow flight of stairs— "you'll see that there are another three bedrooms on this level, and a third bathroom."

"It's charming, Mrs. Mason. Really charming. And you've arranged everything so nicely—the flowers and all."

"Mrs. C. did the flowers, madam. I don't hold with flowers in a room where people sleep, but Mrs. C. likes things that way."

"Well, I think we'll be real happy with things just as the Callahans have them. Mariella, will you be alright here?"

Mariella nodded, her black eyes shining at the thought of having a whole floor to herself.

"Now, I'll be off home. I'll be back in on Monday, and my number's next to the fridge if there's anything you need or can't find. I imagine you'll be wanting to get some sleep." She started back down the stairs. "My regular days are Mondays and Wednesdays, but I can always pop in special if you need something; my cottage is only down the road. Mrs. C. has left some papers for you on the dining-room table, which should explain everything, and if you have any questions, you just give me a call. Don't you go asking me anything"—she wagged her finger threateningly at Gabe— "about those machines in Master Oliver's study. I haven't the foggiest idea how they work, if they work at all. And I'd be grateful"— she turned to Christy—"if you'd give me fair warning when you're expecting company; I'll need to air the linen." They had arrived back at the kitchen. "Now I've left a spot of lunch and your supper in the fridge, so you can stay put until tomorrow. I shouldn't think you feel up to shopping. I've fed the dogs"—she bent down to look at Jake eye to eye—"so don't you be giving them any scraps off the table, young man. They're fat enough already." She struggled into her coat. "If there's nothing else, madam—"

"Oh, do call me Christy!"

"If there's nothing else, Mrs. McCarthy, I'll be off."

Christy followed her into the hall.

"Thank you so much for looking after us. Everything's just grand. We'll be very happy here, I just know it."

"Everyone else has been. It's that sort of house, I suppose."

Christy watched Joan cycle down the drive, and hugged herself. Everything *was* perfect—just perfect. And if one could improve perfection, Mrs. Mason just had, by leaving them alone. She felt Gabe's arms wrap round her from behind. He imitated the theme tune of *The Twilight Zone.*

"Who was that strange woman? Or rather, *what* was she?" They laughed.

"I think she's just part of the landscape."

"D'you want to grab a nap, honey? You must be exhausted."

"I couldn't now—I want to look at everything again, and read Maggie's letter, and get to know the house, and settle Jake, and look at the garden, and then we could go see the village—"

"Okay, okay! Back up some, Christy! We've got eight weeks here, darling—you don't have to do it all at once!"

As Joan Mason peddled down the narrow road through Bockhampton, she smiled to herself. She'd done Mrs. C. proud. Maggie had told her not to stand on ceremony with the McCarthys, and just to treat them as she did the Callahans, but Joan had watched enough television to know what Americans expected of English life, and had enjoyed calling the American woman "Madam." She had been particularly proud of "sleeping accommodation" and referring to Lily as "Miss Lily," when in fact she never referred to her as anything other than "that young scamp" or "you scrap of mischief." Well, if the McCarthys were expecting to see a bit of ye olde Englande, *she* certainly wasn't going to disappoint them. She was whistling as she reached her own cottage.

In his garden, feet up on the rickety table, Edward Arabin sipped his coffee and thought about Maggie. He hadn't stopped thinking about her since she had left the barn the night before her departure. He went over and over his conversations with her over the past few months, trying to discover a pattern in order to understand her motivation. The more he thought about it the less he understood why she had come round to his garden that night and taken up his earlier offer. He loved Maggie, had done so for years, but he had no right to make demands of her, and he had trained himself to expect nothing from love. There was a certain irony in the fact that he had ever really loved only two women; one of them had loved her married state too much to leave it for him, and the other one had slept with him only because of her married state. It was obvious what Maggie had been getting at the night of the dinner party. She meant that women, however much their rational minds told them to select the baboon, would always be more drawn to the desert mouse. She believed that women were the willing victims of male sexuality. The only problem was, he knew in his heart that her theory was wrong. He went inside to find a postcard—and scrawled a note to Maggie and Oliver.

Four

**A postcard of Stonehenge to Maggie and Oliver Callahan,
Oak Ridge, Lawrenceville:**

Greetings, Happy Campers!
Just to say that we're already missing you—bereft would be
a better word; but we'll struggle through. Haven't yet met the
Yanks, but promise I'll pop over and wag the flag. Mags—I've
been thinking about your theory on the baboons and desert mice,
but I've decided the focus was wrong; you only think about the
male of the species, and you should have zoomed in on the
female. After all, isn't it the female—of all species—that selects
the partner, and initiates sex? We males are such malleable
creatures! Keep me abreast of any follow-up research.
Love to you both, and the children,

Edward

OLIVER HAD RISEN EARLY, AND JOGGED DOWN THE DRIVEWAY TO THE
mailbox of Oak Ridge. Ever since dinner with Danny Bujevski Oliver
was determined to get in shape for the cameras. He hadn't been
jogging for five years, so a half-mile seemed a good place to start.
And an even better place to stop. The only things in the box were
a pile of mail-order catalogues addressed to the McCarthys and a
postcard from Edward Arabin. He read the card and flipped through
the catalogues as he strolled back to the house, marvelling at the
Americans' appetite for "leisure wear." Tomorrow, he promised
himself, he'd jog there and back.

He found Maggie and the children sitting in front of a glorious
array of cereals—Lucky Stars, Marshmallow Loops, Choco-Lites,

Fortune Cookies—a choice so weird and wonderful it could take Lily days to pick one. He flipped Edward's postcard across the table to Maggie.

"Don't know what Ed's on about—sounds uncharacteristically cryptic to me."

Maggie was pouring milk onto Arthur's cereal. As she read Eddie's message, the carton slipped through her fingers, spilling milk all over the table. She blushed and mopped it up, but Oliver was peering into the fridge and didn't notice her clumsiness.

"It's not cryptic. It's just about a conversation we had at that dinner you couldn't come to—remember that telly programme on the sexual imperative?"

"Well he obviously doesn't know *you* very well, does he, darling? Or he wouldn't have put the bit about females initiating sex, would he?"

"What does ini-shating sex mean, Daddy?"

Oliver smiled at Lily. "It's something few women understand, darling. Try asking your mother. Ask her if she knows." He grinned wolfishly at Maggie.

"What does ini-shating sex mean, Mummy?"

"It's just a way of showing someone that you love them, darling."

"Oh ho!" Oliver grinned. "That's a new one on me. I always thought it had to do with getting your rocks—"

"Shut up, you. You could at least let the children grow up a little before you taint them with your grubby perception of life."

"Is it like kissing?" Lily pressed.

"Yes; very much like kissing. That's part of it."

"Oh. Can I have some of the chocolate ones first, Mummy, and then the pink ones?" Lily's attention, unlike her father's, had not lingered on the subject of sex.

"Not that I'm against you doing a bit of extracurricular research, Mags. I'm all for it. You should do what Eddie suggests—I might even volunteer as a guinea-pig." He leered exaggeratedly, and Maggie laughed. A week ago this exchange might have erupted into a row, but ever since sleeping with Edward Maggie was bending over backwards to cooperate with Oliver.

"I'll think about it, Ol. I won't do anything *else*, you understand, but I *will* think about it. So, gang, what shall we do today?"

"I vote we go back to that supermarket for another four hours.

What was it called? Harris Tweeter." Lily's shrieks seconded Oliver's proposal.

"Harris Teeter, you idiot," Maggie corrected. "Anyway, we've got enough food to last the entire eight weeks." The previous day, their third in Lawrenceville, they had gone to the local supermarket recommended by Christy. It was the size of a football stadium—or bigger—aisles and aisles of exotic foods and junk foods, and about an acre or two of fresh fruit and vegetables, bathed in a perpetual mist of water to keep them looking just picked. Oliver and Lily had indulged in an orgiastic shopping bender, and spent two hours and $300 in the place. Maggie and Arthur had retired to stroll around the other shops and buy some guide books.

"I'm not suggesting we buy anything; we could just go and look; for entertainment."

"I quite fancy just hanging around the house—we could take the boat out on the lake, or play tennis, have a swim—God, it's so beautiful here!"

"When are we going to the beach, Mummy?"

"What do you think, Ol? We could spend today here, and then drive down tomorrow, maybe?"

"Whatever you like, my darling. I'm going to have to find some inspiration for my piece by Wednesday, though."

"Well, I could help you think of something."

"Oh no; you've got other things to occupy your sweet mind, Mags."

"What are you talking about?"

"Initiating sex," he said, pinching her bottom as he bit into a peach.

The Callahans had not known what to expect when Gabe and Christy had offered them the use of their beach house. Maggie envisioned a tiny, ramshackle hut on a deserted strip of sand where they could play at being Robinson Crusoe. She had even packed a case of mineral water, convinced that the shack would not be connected to the mains. Oliver expected an apartment in a seaside resort town chock-a-block with miniature golf courses, bungy jumping, and ice-cream parlours. They were both pleasantly surprised. Holden Beach was actually a small barrier island, connected to the mainland by a suspension bridge. The island was an eight-mile-long, one-mile-wide strip of upmarket real estate, flanked by the ocean on one side and the Intercoastal Waterway on the other. It was still light as they came over the bridge and saw the beach rolling out before them and the fleets of fishing boats bobbing out at sea. Pretty, pastel-coloured clapperboard houses lined the coastal road, and each and every house had a name-plate. Maggie, Oliver, and Leah shouted out the passing names to one another: "Southern Comfort"; "On Holden Pond"; "Final Resting Place"; "Tax Shelter"; "Wedidit"; "Life's A Beach"; "Inn Too Deep," and, worst of all, "C-D-C?" ... Oliver groaned at each new pun; a few were genuinely amusing, others too corny to be believable. But the houses themselves were lovely, positioned to catch the sea breezes, and appearing to grow out of the sand dunes. Three miles down from the bridge, Oliver pulled into the driveway of a pale yellow oceanfront house with a small and discreet plaque announcing "Ocean's Edge." The children considerately stayed asleep as they were transported from the car into the house and straight into their made-up beds. Leah unpacked the groceries, and within half an hour, the three adults were sitting on the back deck in their shorts, sipping a glass of wine, watching the sun set behind them over the Intercoastal Waterway and listening to the ocean breaking forty feet ahead of them.

"I think I've died. Pinch me, Leah, quick; I want to be sure this isn't a dream."

"I don't ever, ever want to leave this chair; I could stay here for the rest of my life and die happy. Screw the *Telegraph.*"

"This is the bloody business; this really is the business."

For once, all three of them were in perfect agreement.

Christy McCarthy was in the garden, Maggie's pruning shears in her hand, head cocked on one side as she selected which roses to cut for an arrangement for the drawing room. The tiny, pale pink buds of New Dawn on the trellis were tempting, but she had set her heart on the buff yellow climbing rose that fanned against the stone wall. If she snipped only the top blooms, she wouldn't spoil the display of the lower branches. She moved a tall ladder along the wall and positioned it gently so as not to disturb the rose. As she was about to climb the ladder, she heard Gabe shouting her name, and returned to the house.

"Christy, honey, have you seen any washcloths around?"

"No, I haven't, Gabe; I'll ask Mrs. Mason where Maggie keeps them when she comes in."

"Okay, no problem. Are you having a good time, honey?"

"Just grand."

When Christy returned to the garden, she found Jake at the very top of the ladder peeping over the wall.

"Jake McCarthy! You get down from there this instant! How many times do I have to tell you that stepladders are dangerous and you are not allowed to climb them unless there's an adult nearby?"

The little boy stood-stock still, gawking over the wall.

"Jake! Did you hear me? Get down this minute!"

Jake finally turned, and began to climb down the steps.

"But, Mom, there's a naked man over there."

"I don't care if there's a whole crowd of them; and don't you lie to me, young man; next thing you'll be telling me there's a pack of lions over there." She ruffled his curly black hair lovingly.

"Mommy, honest there is! He's as naked as a fish!"

"Jake McCarthy, if I climb up that ladder and find that you're not telling the truth, you will have some very serious explaining to do. You shouldn't be lookin' into other peoples' private gardens, and you *shouldn't* be lying."

"I'm not lying! Just go look!"

"You hush now." Christy climbed up the ladder and peeped over the top of the wall.

"Well, for heaven's sake . . ." she murmured.

The stone wall that surrounded the orchard of Bockhampton was the dividing line between *their* house, as Christy thought of it, and a neighbour's garden. On the far side of this garden, an elderly man was working the earth of what from a distance appeared to be a vegetable patch. He used one foot to drive the spade into the heavy soil. He was wearing a pair of green Wellington boots, and on his head was a Panama hat, which failed to cover his flowing grey locks. Otherwise he was as naked as a fish.

"Well, I declare . . ." Christy breathed.

A voice behind her startled her so badly that she almost fell off the ladder.

"Mrs. McCarthy? I'm so sorry to disturb you and barge in uninvited. I did ring the bell, but thought I'd take a look in the garden. I'm Edward Arabin," he said as he strode towards her and offered his hand to help her down. "A friend of the Callahans."

"I'm delighted to meet you." Christy blushed, sweeping her hair off her face. "Maggie told us about you, of course." She appraised

Edward. He was a very tall, elegant man with strong features set in a tanned and somewhat lined face. His eyes were emphasised by almost feminine long black lashes and heavy dark eyebrows with a distinct quirk in the left one that made him seem constantly amused.

"I meant to come by earlier and make sure you had settled in alright, but I'm afraid I haven't had a moment's peace until this morning. I'm an auctioneer in Salisbury, so I tend to be up to my neck in furniture most of the week."

They strolled towards the table, and Christy sat down on one of the benches.

"So, have you found everything alright? Has Mrs. Mason sorted things out for you?"

"Oh, she's been just perfect. So helpful. We're having the most lovely time, but it's so hard to tear ourselves away from the house, we've barely stuck our noses out of doors."

"What are your plans for the summer?"

"We really haven't made any yet. What would you recommend?"

"Oh, Lord; there are all sorts of summer events going on; horse shows, dog shows, bloody rabbit shows, probably. Bouncy castles. Dunking vicars."

"Dunking *vicars?*"

"Oh yes. A traditional English summer sport. Every village fête has its own dog-collared clergy man sitting under a barrel of water and patiently waiting for their frightfully keen parishioners to soak them. But that's a treat in store; I was just stopping by to ask you and your husband to pop over for a drink this evening. I'm having a few people round—just an impromptu thing. I live at the Old Barn. Just a mile or so down the main road to town on the left. You can't miss it. Shall we say six-thirty tonight?"

"That would be grand. We'd be delighted to come."

"And there's nothing I can do for you? Nothing you're lacking? No problems?"

"We-ell," Christy's eyes darted towards the orchard wall. "I am just a tad concerned about the man next door . . ."

"Next door? You mean at Compton Rising?"

"I guess. There's a man in that garden. I'm not sure that he should be there." She waved towards the wall.

"Yes. Well, that'll either be Sir Nigel Bavington, or it will be Fred, his gardener. Nothing to worry about in either case."

"You see, I don't know how to say this, but . . . he's in the nude."

"In the nude? You mean completely bare-arsed naked?" Edward raised his eyebrows.

"Not exactly. He's wearing boots and a hat. But his ass is definitely bare."

"In that case"—Edward winked at her—"it's definitely Sir Nigel." He tugged an imaginary forelock, repeated his invitation to the barn, and left her with Jake.

Christy abandoned the roses for the time being. She ushered Jake inside and into Mariella's waiting arms, and instructed the nanny to take him for a long walk with the dogs. She went into the kitchen to find the housekeeper.

"Good morning, madam," Joan greeted her.

"Oh please, Mrs. Mason. We are going to have to come to an agreement! I just can't stay here and be called madam! Please call me Christy."

Mrs. Mason smiled almost imperceptibly. "Alright, Mrs. M., I'll do my best."

"And could I call you . . . ?"

"Joan. Joan Mason. That's my name. You may call me what you please."

"Joan. What a very pretty name! I've been wanting to ask you something, Joan. Gabe and I have had trouble finding where Mrs. Callahan keeps her washcloths . . ."

"Mrs. C. doesn't 'keep' wash cloths. She doesn't *have* wash cloths. I keep *my* wash cloths under the kitchen sink," Joan pointed imperiously.

"Oh. Great. Well, we'll know where to look."

"If you have a need for them; I don't see why you should, myself, unless you're far more particular than Mrs. C."

Christy could only smile prettily and shrug. It was peculiar to keep washcloths in the kitchen, but far more peculiar not to use them; perhaps the Brits did things differently.

"I'll just take one up to my husband now, if that's okay with you."

She opened the cupboard door, and gazed at a pile of rather dirty floor rags.

"Joan. Are these really what my husband should use to wash his face?"

Mrs. Mason stared at her without speaking. Christy mimed washing her face. "A washcloth? You know?"

"Mrs. McCarthy. I believe the object to which you are referring is a flannel. They are kept in the linen press in the upstairs hall. I will find one for Mr. McCarthy directly."

Christy had thought it would be so easy to come to England; after all, there were no language barriers, and no significant cultural ones. After going to the village shop to find that the largest quantity of milk she could buy was a pint, when she had never bought less than a gallon in her life, after watching a man gardening naked, and hearing about dunking men of the cloth, and being offered a floor rag to clean her face, she was beginning to wonder if this holiday was going to be even more of a learning experience than she had anticipated. Now that Jake was out of her hair, and Gabe was occupied with his unpacking—and doubtless, phoning the office—Christy could do what she had been longing to do and explore Bockhampton alone. She needed to get a feel of the house, and its owners. As soon as she had crossed the threshold, she had had a strong sense of the house's character, which was presumably the character of those who lived in it, but she wanted to know every corner of it. All houses have faces, and Bockhampton had a particularly open and pleasant one, albeit one that had seen better days. Her most powerful feeling was that she would love the people who lived in this house. She got no further than the drawing room. She had been intrigued by the piano when she first saw it, and now examined the photographs arranged on the top. There were many of Oliver, who looked like a textbook English type—aquiline, a high and rather narrow brow, a dramatic sweep of fair hair, piercing blue eyes under lazy eyelids. He was really a very handsome man, Christy mused. The kids looked—nice. No mother ever thought somebody else's kids looked great, but these ones looked okay. The little girl clearly took after her dad, and the baby looked like a nice enough, plump baby. Not as pretty as Jake had been at nine months, but then Arthur was quite bald, whereas Jake had inherited his parents' dark, thick hair. There was only one picture of Maggie on the piano; it was a wedding snap. Maggie looked pretty, young, and bridal. But she was almost in the background and looking down at the ground rather submissively, and it was Oliver, in a flamboyant tapestried waistcoat, who stole the show. He was posing for the camera, bowing extravagantly, his arm outstretched, clearly inviting Maggie to dance, but his eyes were directed not at Maggie but at the camera lens. It was a great picture—of him. Christy looked at it for a long time. In some ways it was a pity that Maggie was in the photo at all. Of course, a bride *had* to be in a wedding snap, but from a purely aesthetic viewpoint, in terms of the artistic composition of the picture, it would have worked better as a sole portrait of Oliver. Christy held the frame up to the light, and studied it quizzically, one eye closed. She jumped as she felt Gabe's hand on her shoulder.

"I've been looking for you, kid . . ." He nuzzled her neck, and saw the photograph of the Callahans over her shoulder. "What a great photo! I hope you left our wedding snaps out . . ."

"I surely did. I always leave them out, honey." Christy thought of the ten-by-eights artfully displayed on her dressing table at Oak Ridge. It occurred to her that most of her own wedding photographs featured her and her huge white crinoline in the foreground of her parents' garden, with Gabe standing supportively behind her, all but obscured by her dress and veil.

"I've checked in with the office, darlin', so I'm all yours. What would you like to do today, Christy? I figured we could take Jake to Stonehenge—you've been hankering to see it."

Christy pulled away from his embrace. "I don't know, Gabe. Maybe not right now. Maybe later. I'd kind of like to see it at sunset, or sunrise . . ."

"But then we couldn't take Jake . . ."

"So? Maybe it would be more fun to leave him behind . . . Maybe we should do some things without him . . . Maybe we should pretend we were real young again, before we had a kid, and do something wild and adventurous. . . ." Christy was smiling, but there was the faintest thread of complaint running through her voice, and Gabe, with an ear ever cocked for his wife's dissatisfaction, heard it loud and clear.

"That sounds like a real good idea," he said tentatively. "So how should we do it? We could drive over at sunset tonight, take some wine, maybe, a picnic? We could take a rug and have that bottle of champagne? Maybe there's a nice place to have dinner? What do *you* think, darlin'?"

Christy's lips tightened fractionally. Having made one mistake, Gabe wasn't prepared to risk making another. The last thing that Christy wanted was to have to direct his every move, particularly when it came to something wild and carefree and romantic. She wanted him to take spontaneous decisions, yet she wanted them to be exactly the ones she would have taken for herself, without having to tell him so. She wanted something—but couldn't quite put her finger on what it was.

"Let's just leave it for today, okay? We're going to Edward Arabin's for drinks tonight, anyways. He's one of our neighbours—the auctioneer, remember? He seemed real nice. Till then, I just want to hang around the house and get to know it a bit." She squatted down to look at the lower bookshelves, and patted Gabe's leg to compensate for sounding sharp. "Don't you worry about me, darling, if you need to do some paperwork or something; I'm real happy just snooping around."

By late afternoon, Christy had learnt a great deal about the family who lived at Bockhampton, and almost everything was to her liking. She had spent most of the day looking at Oliver's books, her fingers trailing over their cracked spines, wondering why he had chosen each one, loving the fact that there were so many hardbacks, and that none of them looked new—they were almost all old copies, secondhand, probably, and much-thumbed. It was an eclectic collection, arranged haphazardly, unlike her own neatly alphabetised shelves. There were fine leather-bound editions of the complete works of Hardy, Eliot, Austen, Dickens, Conrad, the Brontës, all familiar to her, even if she hadn't quite read *all* of them. But scattered amongst them were books by someone called Wilkie Collins, and others she had never heard of—Charles Kingsley, George Meredith . . . She felt humbled by Oliver's erudition. He was an educated man; he was a cultured man; he was a man to respect.

Had Joan Mason not been such a diligent housekeeper, layers of dust on these books might have been a sufficient clue that they had not been touched, let alone thumbed, for many years. It might even have crossed Christy's mind that these were not Oliver's books at all, but were in fact the collection of his uncle Leo, and had simply "come with the house." But Joan Mason was a perfectionist, and Christy had never heard of Uncle Leo. She never considered that the books might belong to Maggie, because that one photograph had told her that Oliver was the dominant force in Bockhampton. This library contributed to her first impressions of Oliver Callahan, and first impressions, once they have taken hold, can be extremely difficult to uproot.

*   *   *

It was after ten when Maggie and Oliver woke to their first day at Holden Beach. Maggie wrapped a towel around her and stepped onto the deck, which faced the ocean, forgetting that they were literally surrounded by other houses, and that the beach, by that time in the morning, was already filling up. The sunlight was almost blinding, but she could see Lily and Leah playing at the water's edge in front of the house and Arthur digging happily in the sand. She returned to put on a swimsuit and get some fruit and coffee for breakfast on the porch. Oliver, sporting psychedelic trunks, leapt down the wooden stairs, swept up Arthur, and ran into the sea at full pelt, expecting the shock of cold water. Maggie heard him shout, "Brace yourself, Wart!" If Arthur did brace himself, he had no need to; the water was tepid, at least near the shore. Maggie watched them playing for a little while, Arthur untroubled by the waves, Lily nervous, skipping in and out at the edge, shrieking with excitement. It was going to be a wonderful summer. There was absolutely nothing to do but watch the water, swim, play in the sand, read a book or two, and sleep. Heaven. Maggie could cope with another seven weeks of this easily. Leah had discovered the McCarthys' hoard of beach chairs, coolers, towels, and rugs, and had pitched camp in between the house and the ocean. She had also found a huge selection of buckets and spades, and a very high-tech water wheel, which she was trying to demonstrate to Arthur. The baby rejected her efforts, preferring to use a pair of Leah's sneakers as both bucket and spade.

"Ol, you better put some cream on, you know. You'll be burnt to a crisp."

"Never. I never burn. How many times have you ever seen me burn, Mags? On any holiday?"

Maggie looked skeptical. "This is a much hotter sun, Ol. You'll be sorry."

The two children were smothered in white sunblock; even Leah, who had a permanent down-under tan, had taken the precaution of using factor 8. Maggie selected factor 15 from the huge assortment of bottles kindly left by the McCarthys, and chucked it at Oliver. He left it lying in the sand, and plunged back into the ocean, swimming out to sea. Lily had already befriended a little boy, and had imperiously taken over the architecture of his sandcastle; Maggie cringed as she heard her daughter's bell-like voice ordering him,

"Not like *that!* That's a stupid way to build it. You do it like *this . . .*"

Maggie picked up her book and began to read. When Leah took the children, much against their will, into the house for lunch, Maggie glanced at Oliver. He was lying asleep at her feet, face down on a towel, and his back was the colour of a tomato and roast red pepper purée. Maggie nudged him with her foot.

"Ol; you've got to go in. You're burning."

"Rubbish. I always go pink before I go brown."

"You're not pink. You're red, and turning purple in patches."

Oliver groaned long-sufferingly, and rolling onto his back, closed his eyes and went back to sleep. Maggie halfheartedly rubbed some cream onto his chest and stomach before going back to her book. If he hadn't been so stubborn, she might have made more of an effort, but there was only one way Oliver ever learnt a lesson. Painfully.

They were one of the last groups to pack up and leave the beach that afternoon. Leah had gone down to the pier to buy some fresh fish from Cap'n Pete—one of the McCarthys' recommendations— and Oliver and Maggie were trying to blast the sand off their children with a hose. Fine sand has an unrivalled ability to get into the crevices of a baby's bottom. Ol went to take a shower, and Maggie ran when she heard him shout. He was standing naked in the bathroom, staring at himself in the full-length mirror. As she looked at him, Maggie realised why *lobster-red* had become such a cliché. There was simply nothing other than freshly boiled lobster that could accurately describe the colour of his back and legs. His shoulders and chest had taken on a red marbled effect, with paler streaks marking the path of her fingers. Maggie knew better than to say "I told you so," but she was tempted to laugh. Oliver, however, had gone into crisis mode, and was rummaging through the bathroom cabinets for some sort of cure-all that would reverse the process. He had begun to groan with pain, and was muttering about heatstroke and dehydration. Maggie covered him in Noxema as gently as she could, but as he whimpered and shrank from her touch she became exasperated, and told him he was making more of a fuss than Lily would. Oliver closed his eyes and looked wounded as Maggie put him to bed with a pitcher of water and some salt tablets, switched on the fan, and switched off the light. As she crept from the room, she could hear him moaning quietly.

Oliver *was* in pain, and he did feel sick, but most of all he felt angry with Maggie for being so bloody unsympathetic. Maggie was the only woman of the many he had known whom he had wanted to share his life with, but at times like this she could have controlled her smirking and shown a bit of femininity. Women were always going on about bloody empathy and communication, for fuck's sake, and when it came to the crunch, they had no more natural empathy than your average newt. Oliver rolled over and winced. She should have been sitting beside him, cooling his fevered brow, and crooning a lullaby; instead, he could hear her laughing with Leah. They were probably laughing about him. At the back of his mind, he acknowledged that this might have been some sort of divine retribution for his treatment of Maggie before they had left England. He had dumped her in the shit, and while she'd been crawling her way out of it unaided, he'd bonked the all-too-available Sarah—not that Maggie knew about *that*—and she hadn't made much of a scene about it. In fact, she hadn't made a scene at all, had never even mentioned it. It wasn't like Maggie to forego her pound of flesh. Well, he could be magnanimous as well. She was being a bitch—in her own subtle way—but he would rise above it and suffer in silence. The misfortune of his sunburn would actually oblige him to stay inside for the next couple of days and write his piece for the *Telegraph,* and that would put his women back in their place. . . . His gaze roamed around the room restlessly, looking for something to send him to sleep. Last Thursday's edition of the *Independent* should do the trick.

Oliver winced and moaned exaggeratedly when Maggie slipped into bed next to him.

"I don't feel sorry for you, you know," she said crisply, "not a bit. It's your own silly fault."

"What on earth have I ever done to deserve you? I'm kind to dogs and babies, I help old women across the road—"

"Only if you fancy them."

"And what do I get for my pains? Some shrewish bitch of a wife who's got less sympathy than a house plant."

Maggie trailed her fingernails along his sore shoulder blades and licked his throat.

"What are you doing?"

"I would have thought it was obvious. Initiating sex."

"What?" Oliver sat up suddenly in bed and flinched as the sheet brushed against his skin.

"I just thought I might give it a whirl, that's all. Just to show I'm willing."

"You absolute cow. The one time I can't possibly move an inch, you decide you want to have sex."

"Forget it. I'm not all that keen. I was only being dutiful. It's not as if your lobster skin tone turns me on or anything." She casually raked her nails across his chest.

"Bitch, bitch, *bitch* . . ." Oliver was always most aroused by Maggie when she was either angry with him or being superior. "Come back here. I'll manage. Somehow." He gritted his teeth as Maggie, none too careful where she put her knees, climbed on top of him. "Did I ever tell you what an amazing wife you are?"

"No. As a matter of fact, you didn't."

"Ah. Well that's alright then. I'd hate to have given you the wrong impression."

He couldn't refuse sex with her. Sex was the only thing they shared.

Five

A postcard to Imogen and Curtis, Compton Stables, Wiltshire:

We're having a fantastic time, amazing house—both of them—amazing weather. I feel like a new woman. (Ol says he feels like a new woman, too). Hope you're all well. Kiss Bonny and Samson for me, okay? Tell them I'll be a lot fatter when I get home. Love and hugs, Maggie.

Pissing hot. I'll be as black as you when we come back, Curtis old boy. Can't get an English newspaper for love or money; no one reports on the cricket here. May have to fly home. Keep a straight bat—both of you. Cheers.

Oliver

EDWARD, EVER THE LADIES' MAN, TUCKED CHRISTY'S HAND INTO THE crook of his arm and kept her pinned tight to his side throughout most of his drinks party. Christy was having the time of her life. Other than her momentary concern about which dresses to pack for the trip, she had never expected the holiday in Bockhampton to be particularly sociable, and as she now did the rounds on her host's arm, she realised how much she had missed meeting new groups of people since her move to Lawrenceville. Within six months of arriving at Oak Ridge, Gabe and Christy had met anyone and everyone they were ever likely to want to meet in the area, and the past few years had just been seeing the same old, same old crowd. It wasn't that Christy didn't *like* their crowd, but it was stimulating to meet a whole new group of people, and she blossomed. Although she would never have admitted it, least of all to Gabe, she was delighted to realise that she was without a doubt the most attractive woman at the party. She had inspected the garden on arrival to check out the competition, and apart from a fragile and very pale blonde sitting on a bench and now talking to Gabe, Christy felt confident there were no other serious contenders to the belle of the ball title. Edward Arabin was also surprised by how much he was enjoying this little soirée. He had not expected to derive any satisfaction from acting as host to any woman other than Maggie Callahan. In fact, he found that being the official escort to the McCarthys served two purposes. First, it allowed him to fulfil an obligation to Maggie, and secondly it prevented him from wondering obsessively where Maggie was and what she was doing every minute of the day and night. If Maggie regretted sleeping with him, then it was far less painful spending a couple of months squiring Mrs. McCarthy while he licked his wounds than it would have been if Maggie and Oliver were in residence, and he had to witness their wedded "bliss." When the McCarthys had arrived at the garden gate of the barn, promptly at six-thirty, Edward had handed Gabe into Lucy Wickham-Edwardes' waiting arms, and whisked Christy away. Now he scanned the garden quickly, and led Christy to a tall, gaunt old man who stood stooped over talking to a small, round old man, both of them peering into the river that ran at the bottom of the lawn.

"Now, chaps, I'd like you to meet our lovely new neighbour— spending the summer at Bockhampton. Christy McCarthy, this is Major John Hangham, and this," he turned to the taller man, "is Sir Nigel Bavington. You may, perhaps, recognize Sir Nigel?"

Christy paused, smiling slightly and trying to be polite, but she didn't see how she could have met him before—unless ... Of course!

"I didn't recognise you in those clothes, Sir Nigel," she said sweetly.

"What! Seen an old snap of me in uniform, have you, missy? Haven't been in uniform for a long time now—almost before you were born, I dare say, young lady. . . . Enjoying your visit, are you? People treating you properly?"

"We've really only just arrived, but we're having a grand time, thank you, Sir Nigel. It's truly the most beautiful part of the country. . . ."

* * *

Lucy had spent about half an hour with Gabe, which was all she needed to find out most of his personal details. She knew when and where he was born, how many brothers and sisters he had, where he had been educated, what he did for a living, how he and Christy had met, when they married, the name and age of their son. . . . Gabe had accepted her interrogation graciously, but was beginning to wonder when she would arrive at the colour of his underwear. Lucy was the sort of woman who apologised endlessly for her brazenness and then used her self-confessed frankness as permission to ask ever more personal questions. When Christy appeared, she seized her hand. "I'm so thrilled to meet you. Your husband is being terribly naughty and won't tell me a single thing about you, much as I've pumped him"—she wagged her finger at Gabe—"but we all know how difficult men are, don't we? Now let's just leave them to talk about farming, or the economy, or whatever equally useless rubbish they randomly hit on." She led Christy back to a secluded bench, and virtually shoved her onto a cushion.

"Now tell me all. I'm quite agog."

Christy smiled. She had imagined English country ladies to be strapping, jolly women with broken-veined faces and mousy hair and sporting sensible tweeds and boots. Lucy Wickham-Edwardes didn't fit the bill at all. Lucy was very slim, very blond, with an alabaster complexion and big, baby blue eyes. The term *English rose* might have been coined for her. She was impeccably turned out for such an impromptu get-together in a pencil-thin grey wool skirt and light silk cardigan. Her legs, which might have looked like matchsticks had she worn high heels, had racehorse elegance in expensive, flat leather brogues. Although from the outside Lucy seemed perfectly composed, her hands fluttered whilst she talked, which meant that her hands fluttered constantly.

"You see, Christy, we're so isolated in our little valley that new blood is *enormously* exciting." Her eyes widened in emphasis. "You've finally given us something to talk about other than the blasted road extension or cattle-rustling, which is all I've heard about for the past month—and if you've heard one story about cattle-rustling, you've heard them all—and it probably bored you to death the first time, so we've been waiting with bated breath to find out *all* about you, and of course I was simply gutted that Maggie and Ol were going away for the whole summer—I thought, who on earth will I talk to? There'll be no one around with any spark, and no one to gossip with, because they are the only people with any real umph around here, apart from Eddie of course—and I'd re-signed myself to just *hibernating* all summer—I even thought I'd have to make a bolt for la belle France just to stop myself dying of boredom, except that the South of France has become so terribly tacky, but now you're here, and I can tell from your lovely hus-band—he does look terribly *young* for thirty-seven, my dear—what *do* you feed him? I shall have to put Charles on the same regimen *at once*—so now you're here, we can have some tremendous parties and do lots of lovely things together . . . I must introduce you to some fun people—if I can possibly think of any . . . Have you met Anne Vincey yet? She's related to the Pembrokes—at Wilton House, you know—she claims to be a cousin, but I think it's rather more distant than that, possibly a second or third cousin twenty times removed at best—but she's heaven, a great giggle, quite, quite mad, and you'll love her, and she'll simply *adore* you . . . Now what was it you were doing before you found that handsome specimen over there?" Lucy paused, less to wait for an answer to her question than to light her cigarette.

"I worked as a broker—a stockbroker, I guess you'd call it, in New York."

"Riveting." Lucy's innocent blue eyes widened again, but looked a little glazed. "Well, you must have been thrilled to find Gabe and leave all that nasty business behind, weren't you?"

"I was thrilled to find Gabe, but you know, I enjoyed working—"

"Oh, you sound just like Maggie! You *career* girls—" she said the word more with amusement than disdain, "you just don't realise what mistake you're making. All this rubbish about self-empowerment and independence and sufficiency. One day we'll just go back to realising that nothing, but *nothing* beats having a hard-working, successful husband who doesn't interfere and just keeps the old bank account well stocked. Provided he's hard-working enough not to be hanging around one's neck all the time. You'll see, when you're my age."

"I can't believe you're any older than I am, Lucy—"

"*Sweet*," Lucy cooed, and patted her hand. "I'm sure I am, though. Maybe just a year or two. Such a shame you didn't have a chance to meet Maggie. She's just like you."

Christy wondered how Lucy could have any idea what she was like, when she had only allowed her to utter about twenty words.

"What does your husband do, Lucy?"

Lucy looked contemplatively across the garden to where Charles stood with Edward and Gabe. "Do? I'm not exactly sure *what* he does. There's about a month around late March, April when he claims to be frantically busy with the lambing . . . That's also the end of the tax year, of course, so he gets a little fraught . . ." She concentrated hard. "There's the church; he reads the lesson from time to time, which at least gives his suit an airing. And some days, he reads the newspaper . . ." She flashed a brilliant smile at Christy. "As far as I'm concerned, he isn't nearly busy enough. I've always envied Maggie for being able to get Oliver out of the house so much."

"Do tell me about Maggie . . . And Oliver. It's so strange living in their house, and never having met them. In some ways, I feel like I know them—yet they're really complete strangers."

"Well, my *dear* . . . You've come to just the right person; they are simply my closest friends in the whole Valley. Ol is immensely glamorous and wonderfully good looking—great big, sleepy, sexy eyes, you know the type, I'm sure—positively straight to the bedroom, do not pass go, do not collect two hundred—and the wickedest, sneery smile—makes you think of some mad, bad, and heavenly to know pirate—and you haven't *lived* until you've seen him in jodhpurs. Charles looks like a buffoon in his—he wears those huge old-fashioned billowing ones, but Oliver's—well, they're tight enough to take his own blood pressure, and leave simply *nothing* to the imagination. And he's very clever, of course, and keeps us all in stitches with his stories, and he's revolutionised Bockhampton. Leo Callahan was a poppet, everyone says so, but he didn't entertain much—didn't get out at *all* in the last years—and Ol's just turned everything upside down—quite literally opened all the windows and let some fresh air in. And he's so very talented, and he has hundreds of glamorous people staying—he has journalists from Russia, and art critics, and once we met the most *extraordinary* man who had been a merchant banker—at Kleinworts, would you believe—and had thrown it all in and become a trapeze artist in a travelling circus. Well, that's the type of person Oliver attracts. He's like a magnet. I wouldn't be a bit surprised if he ends up editor of the *Telegraph*, y'know."

"His house is full of the most wonderful things—books, particularly."

Lucy cocked an eyebrow. "Is it? Books? Well, if you say so. I can't say I've ever noticed. God knows how he finds the time to read. He always seems to be rushing off somewhere. It leaves Maggie deliciously free."

"And what is Maggie like? What does she do in her free time, when Oliver's away?"

"Not enough in my opinion!" Lucy had a surprisingly deep laugh. "Talk about wasted opportunity . . . Maggie is a dear. A *dear*. Utterly and truly my best friend. She's a gem, and so pretty. Very bright to boot, makes me feel an awful dunce, although she's always very sweet about it. Maggie is *splendid*. No other word for her. It's a great shame you two aren't going to meet. You'd simply adore her. Everyone loves Maggie. She's very frank, you know. Quite outspoken, which I personally admire in a woman. I can't bear the types who sit there silently opening and shutting their mouths like fish. No, Maggie lets people know exactly what she thinks, particularly Oliver . . . I've heard her give him the most frightful bollocking—sometimes in public. Charles and I would never do that. I mean, the odd tiff in private, maybe, but in public? Never. Simply not done, is it? Oh, well. You know what they say. Opposites attract . . ." She carried on, and after twenty minutes, Christy was wondering not so much whether Lucy would open up as whether Lucy would ever shut up. Fortunately for Christy, Lucy's monologue was interrupted by a large woman in a starched blue shirtwaister dress and sensible shoes, her even more sensible handbag cradled in the crook of her arm in regal fashion, who sported a large cameo brooch on a shelf of a bosom that reached halfway to her stomach.

"Greetings, Lucy—I was hoping I'd see you here," she boomed. "We must have a chat about the wine and cheese next month. I can't quite decide whether Jules would be happier with a select little gathering—just our crowd, y'know—or whether we should have the whole blasted Valley, hoi polloi and all."

"Christy, may I introduce Marjorie Hangham? Marjorie, this is Christy McCarthy. She and her family are spending the summer at Bockhampton, while Maggie and Oliver are in America."

"Good Lord, have they gone to America? Why the blazes would they do a thing like that?" Marjorie pumped Christy's hand. "I'd say you have the best of the deal, young lady. Frightful place, America. Full of guns, they say. Drugs, too. And foreigners. Far better to keep on the civilised side of the pond and let them all shoot themselves over there."

"I come from America, Mrs. Hangham. From North Carolina. We exchanged houses for the summer with the Callahans."

Marjorie Hangham peered at her closely and rather suspiciously, as if she expected Christy to extract a large Kalashnikov from her handbag.

"Well, I'll be blowed. Don't know that I've ever met an American before. You don't *look* much like one."

Christy couldn't think of an appropriate reply, but smiled sweetly, deciding to take it as a compliment, and left Lucy to step into the breech while she looked past Marjorie and watched Major Hangham weaving drunkenly across the garden towards them. As he spotted his wife's broad rump placed firmly in between his path and Christy, he veered sharply to the left into a flower bed.

". . . So you must put the twenty-fifth of August in your diary, m'dear. Six-thirty sharp. At Chestnuts. Just a nibble of cheddar and a glass or two of plonk to set Jules up. You'll come, won't you, Edward? Help us get stuck in, don't you know?" Marjorie addressed herself to Edward Arabin, who had strolled up to stand behind Lucy and Christy.

"Without a doubt, Marj old girl. It looks to me like your husband's getting stuck in to my garden at the moment." They all turned to look at Major Hangham still struggling to extricate his trousers from the grip of Edward's rose thorns.

"Has he been at the gin again?" Marjorie muttered, and stomped away to release the major, braying at him as if he were an errant Jack Russell: "What are you doing in there, Major, you stupid old fool?"

Edward, Christy, and Lucy gazed after her, watching in silence as she tugged at her husband's trouser legs and dumped the remains of his pink gin over the flower bed.

"That'll do the peonies no end of good—nothing they like more than a slug of gin and Angostura . . ." Edward mused. "Now, I wanted to try to tempt you two ladies to stay on for a spot of supper—just a snack—when we've got rid of all these old soaks. Husbands invited, too, of course. Charles! Gabe!" he shouted, cheerily. "Come and join us!"

"It's grand of you to ask, Edward, but I think Christy and I should be getting back to our boy for dinner."

"Boy? Don't tell me you don't have a nanny?" Lucy looked horrified.

"We have an au pair—but we like to sit down and have a family dinner together, don't we, darlin'?"

"Oh, Gabe—I don't think he'd mind just this once—Mariella will be fine with him—he doesn't need to see us *every* night—"

"I should say not," Lucy said firmly. "Once a week is more than enough in my opinion. Both our boys are boarding at Summerfields, thank the Lord, so we only see them every other weekend. And that's only when I fail to bump them off to some little friends for the weekend. After ten years of unrelenting parenthood I feel I've earned some privacy and peace and quiet."

Gabe looked unhappy. "We don't have boarding schools like that back home. I was kind of enjoying spending so much time with Jake. I don't hanker after privacy that much."

Christy glanced at her watch. "Listen, darlin', I'm sure he's in bed already by now. If we go home, it will only get him all worked up. Why don't we go for a family picnic tomorrow to make it up to him? We could just call Mariella and tell her our plans have changed and we'll see her later."

"Phone's in the study, old man—help yourself." Edward turned back to Christy and Lucy as Gabe walked disconsolately across the garden to the house.

Gabe had meant what he said about wanting to spend his time with his son, but more than anything, he wanted to spend his time with his wife. It wasn't as if Gabe McCarthy was a jealous or possessive man. He believed that the good things in life—of which his wife was undoubtedly one—and his blessings—of which she was certainly the greatest—were meant to be shared, but he was beginning to suffer from withdrawal symptoms. In the past two hours, he had barely had a chance to look at her, let alone touch her or talk to her, and there was no one that Gabe enjoyed looking at, touching, or talking to as much as Christy. They had been married for nearly ten years, yet at least once a day, Christy would say something to him, or express an opinion, or an expression would come over her lovely face that would make Gabe feel he was meeting her for the first time. She had the gift of always surprising him, and yet never disappointing him. There was nobody else quite like her. He resigned himself with having to share her with the Brits for a just little bit longer.

* * *

By the time Gabe and Christy had returned to Bockhampton, and received a frenzied welcome from Boomer and Snuff—Lucius had, they knew, found new "sleeping accommodation" in Jake's arms, and wouldn't budge until Jake rose for breakfast—it was after eleven o'clock. Mariella had left the hall light on for them, but the rest of the house was pitch black, and, once the two dogs had returned snuffling to their baskets, utterly silent. Gabe was planning on heading straight for bed. He had been over-wined by Edward, and had been pumped for several hours by Charles on the intricacies of tobacco growing, and he longed for sleep. Christy was wound up like a spring coil by the party.

Gabe took off his jacket, and hung it on a hook in the hall. "Jeez, thank God we're home. Thank God we're alone. Let's go to bed."

"What's the matter? Didn't you enjoy the party?"

"The party was fine. It was the dinner I found rough. It's a real struggle to follow what they're talking about, and that Lucy never shuts her mouth. I'm tired, that's all, Christy. Let's go up." He embraced her, and started kissing her face. Christy twisted her head away.

"I thought you said you wanted to go to sleep?"

"Who said anything about sleep? I just said I was glad to be alone with you and that I wanted to go to bed." He lowered his big head to her neck and nuzzled her.

"Gabe. Please. I'm sorry, darling, but you're going to have to count me out. I've had a real bad headache for hours. I feel like my head's going to explode."

"You have? You seemed just fine at dinner—you were flying, honey."

"Are you sayin' I'm lying?" Christy snapped suddenly. "Are you calling me a liar?"

Gabe spread his arms wide in surprise at her tone, his hands palm up in the defensive position. Had he been a dog, he would have rolled on his back. "No, I believe you. I just didn't notice it before now."

"Well, maybe that's because I'm a good actress. Maybe it's because I'm too polite to show my true feelings all the time." She tried to find a reason to explain her sudden sense of irritation. She stood opposite him, arms folded across her chest, with one foot tapping on the flagstones.

"Unlike some people I know."

"What are you implying here, Christy?"

"Just that you didn't have to yawn all the way through dinner. These are real nice people, Gabe. Real interesting, too, and you could have made more of an effort, if only for my sake."

"Now that's not fair. You know I always make an effort for you." She wouldn't look at him. "I was tired, honey. I yawn when I'm tired. Most folks do."

"You should have gone home if you were that tired." She said the word witheringly.

"I tried, Christy. I said I didn't want to stay to dinner. You made it real clear you wanted to stay." He spoke mildly, without any reproach.

"You could have gone and left me there, rather than embarrassing me by nearly falling asleep at the table. You don't have to chaperone me, Gabe. You're not my shadow, for Chrissakes."

"Christy, sometimes I just don't understand you. You were in a great mood, and as soon as we get home, you turn ratty. Why?"

Christy saw the hurt in his eyes, and could have kicked herself for taking it out on him. She generally tried hard not to punish Gabe for things that had nothing to do with him.

"I'm sorry, Gabe, I've just got a headache."

"Okay. Let's forget it and get some sleep."

"I need to take a pill or something, maybe read for a bit to settle my mind, but you go on up."

Gabe shook his head slowly a couple of times, and turned to go towards the stairs. Christy laid a hand on his arm to halt him. "I'm real sorry for sounding like such a bitch, honey. You know what headaches do to me." She brushed her lips fleetingly against his cheek. She watched him walk slowly up the stairs, his shoulders slumped, and felt a surge of pure remorse. Headaches didn't turn her into a shrew. It was nothing but downright nastiness that made her take out her tension on Gabe. "I'll be up soon, darling!" she called.

When she heard Gabe's footsteps creaking above her, she went into the den. On the table to the left of the door six or seven bottles were arranged with a few glasses. Despite Maggie's instructions to help themselves to anything, Gabe had insisted that they shouldn't drain Oliver's cellars, and had gone out searching for bourbon their first afternoon in Wiltshire. As Christy looked at the assorted bottles—mainly blended whiskies and single malts—she decided to help herself. She rarely drank scotch, but sitting in Oliver's house it seemed appropriate. Wanting to go the whole hog, she didn't even bother to get any ice; she'd have it neat, as she'd seen Edward do. That was surely the local custom.

She wandered aimlessly through the dark house, glass in hand, glancing into different rooms and flicking on lights. When she came to the drawing room, she went immediately to the piano, and picked up the wedding photograph of Oliver and Maggie. Christy had the uncanny sense that she had met Oliver before. The question in his eyes and in his half-smile was so personal, so clearly directed at her. There was a knowing, suggestive look in his eyes, very different from the self-conscious but proud grin Gabe had worn throughout their wedding day. She replaced the photo and continued to prowl restlessly. She came at last to Oliver's office, and having closed the door behind her, sat down at his desk chair, and ran her fingers over the top of his computer. On the walls around her were stacks of files, and she pulled one down, which was labelled "Telegraph—Oct. '91–Oct. '92." She began to read Oliver's articles. They were very well written, sometimes funny, sometimes whimsical, but always with a sharp edge, a damning final line. By and large, he wrote in a direct and personal style about his own reaction to news and events: one article was about the local elections in Salisbury, another piece about the anti–blood sports league, another about the American vision of Britain as popularised by Merchant Ivory films, a fourth lambasting the coy advertising of feminine hygiene products. His interests were obviously eclectic, as she had deduced from his library, yet he brought to every subject the same flair and originality of tone. Christy wondered what on earth he would find of interest to describe in Lawrenceville. After an hour's dedicated reading, she snatched a piece of paper from his desk, marked her place in the file, and picked up the phone.

Oliver gingerly wrapped a towel around his waist, placed his hands firmly on the edge of the sink, and cleared his throat. He had spent most of the day either in bed or on the porch, working on his first article, and had had ample time to think about what he was going to say.

"Look, Maggie. We've had a few problems recently, and I think it's time to clear the air. It's not as if any of our differences are so major that they can't be sorted out. Let's address the trivial ones first. Your career is going down the plughole; mine is doing rather well, if I say so myself. What's the problem there? If you really want to work, go out and find a new career and grab it with both hands, as I did. If you *don't* want to work, and frankly, I don't see any reason why you should, then relax and stop getting worked up about what other people will think of you. Who cares if you're just a housewife? I don't. I make enough to support us, and as I see it, you should thank your lucky stars. So let's just cross that one off the agenda, shall we? Now. A slightly stickier subject. Your obsession that I am unfaithful to you." He frowned heavily, and raised a hand to silence her objections. "I admit, you have some just cause for suspicion, and I'm not going to stand here and pretend I am without sin. There *have* been other women—yes, more than one. Just hear me out. You don't mind if I shave while we talk, do you?" He took up his razor, acknowledging Maggie's silent agreement with a smile. "It started with Louise, and the last was Sarah. Last week. Just before we left England. God, it's a relief to have said it. I've been positive you suspected something, and I could feel it festering away inside you. I'm sorry, Maggie. I'm really sorry. If I could explain why I did it, I would, but I can't, and the most important thing is to make you understand that none of these women pose any threat to you." He shrugged. "Take a girl like Sarah, for example. She's not someone you'd have anything in common with, or want to talk to at length; Christ, I can't think what *I* talk to her about, other than talking about sex. We certainly didn't talk *after* sex, and I wouldn't do it with her again. No point. It was meant to be a one off. The thing is, Mags, these girls just don't matter. They're neither here nor there. They're certainly not worth your getting in a state about. That's why I haven't mentioned them before." He paused, the razor an inch from his cheek as he considered Maggie's expression. "I know women feel differently; I suppose you'd prefer to be betrayed for some grand, romantic affair rather than some meaningless one-night stand, but don't feel insulted by this. Men are different, Maggie my love. I'd never cheat on you with someone that really mattered to me. That's how much I care about you, don't you see? That's how I protect your dignity, and our marriage. Things will be much easier from now on if you can just remember that, put it somewhere in the back of your mind, and don't let these things affect us. Just treat it the same way you treat my playing cricket. If anything, it means less to me than cricket does. Come on, sweetheart. It never pays to bottle things up."

He stretched out a hand, and grinned at himself winningly in the mirror. All in all, he was pretty satisfied with his speech. The reasoning was good, perfectly logical, and his tone of voice had just the right balance between apologetic confession and authoritative superiority. Pity Mags hadn't been there to hear it. He whistled as he splashed cold water on his face and dried it. He spared himself the sting of aftershave. As he left the bathroom, the phone rang.

Christy had dialled her own number in Lawrenceville first, and heard Maggie's voice instructing callers to try the McCarthys in England on the Bockhampton number, or to call the Callahans in Holden Beach. Christy hung up without leaving a message, and immediately called the beach house. It would be early evening—they might be in, and she wanted to know how they were getting along.

" 'Lo, y'all . . ." drawled a strange male voice.

Christy hesitated for a moment, confused.

"Ahh . . . could I speak to Mr. or Mrs. Callahan, please?"

"This is Oliver Callahan speaking," the voice, now perfectly English, intoned.

"Oh, Oliver . . . this is Christy Moore McCarthy. I didn't recognise you for a moment. You sounded kind of weird."

Oliver laughed. "God, what rotten luck! I was practising my Southern accent—d'you mean to tell me I didn't sound Southern? Blast. I thought I was getting rather good. I hope you didn't think I was taking the piss?"

"Pardon me? Taking what? I just didn't know who was in the house."

"Well, don't worry—we haven't let it out to a bunch of weirdos; there's nobody here but us chickens. Only one rooster, actually. Mags and the dependents are still on the beach."

"Are y'all having a good time?" Christy asked, whilst wondering why Oliver bothered to imitate Southern accents when his own was so marrow-melting.

"Absolutely bloody marvelous. Wonderful place. Don't think you'll ever get us out of it. We can't get the infants out of the ocean—in fact I'd be there myself if I hadn't . . ." his voice trailed off.

"If you hadn't . . . ?"

"Well, just between you and me and the doorpost, and if you promise not to tell anyone: if I hadn't been such a bloody idiot and burnt myself half to death the other day." He spoke in a conspiratorial way, and ended with a deep chuckle. "Doesn't do much for my macho image to parade around the beach looking like a freshly boiled lobster." Christy laughed with him.

"I hope you're not too burned," she said with sudden concern. "Our sun can be real treacherous this time of year."

"Oh Lord, no! I've got a hide like a rhino—I'll be fine in a day or two. Gives me a good excuse to stay in and get some writing done."

"As you mention writing—I hope you don't mind—but I've been reading some of your work. I guess I should have asked first, but I accidentally came across one of your files of your column in the *Telegraph,* and I couldn't resist—"

"Help yourself! Be my guest! I just hope they don't bore the knickers—uh, bore you rigid." Oliver corrected himself. He had the impression that Christy was rather a proper young woman, and thought a reference to her underwear might be deemed unsuitable.

"I think they are absolutely riveting—wonderful—I could read them all night. . . ."

"Well, do me a favour and call my editor and tell him that, would you? You'll find his number in my address book under 'Bastards'— Peter Forbes." Oliver laughed again. "There's bound to be something more interesting lying around the house, if you sniff around."

"Well, I wouldn't wish to pry—"

"Go on, help yourself! Our house is your house. . . . Don't you know the first rule of writers—*anything* they write is for public consumption. Nothing brings you closer to a hack's heart than saying you accidentally came across some crap they wrote and thought it was brilliant. You carry on—help yourself. I hope you're not so bored in Compton Purlew that you're reduced to my old cuttings, though."

"No; we've actually just come home from a party at Edward Arabin's—we met so many nice folks there—your friends the Wickham-Edwardeses, and Sir Nigel, and Major Hangham and his wife—"

"Monstrous Marjorie? Well, no wonder you're reading my rubbish! I should think it *is* entertaining compared to listening to the Majorette. She's as thick as two pork chops. Salt of the earth, but as thick as two pork chops nonetheless. What was she banging on about this time?"

"She was talking about the Tory party wine and cheese party—"

Oliver guffawed. "And I suppose she invited you?"

"She did, very kindly."

"Whatever you do, don't go near it with a barge pole. Avoid her like she had a case of the clap—I mean, a case of bubonic plague. One of the best things about this house swap lark is that we have a legitimate reason to get out of it this year. If I can give you one bit of honest-to-God advice, don't go. Death would be preferable. Put your foot down and tell Eddie to stop introducing you to the Undead. The Wickham-Edwardes are good sorts, though. Is everything else alright?"

"It's grand. Simply grand."

Oliver's voice softened. "I love the way you say that."

"What?"

"Grand. 'Simply grand.' We've heard it a lot since we've been here, but no one says it as beautifully as you do." He sighed. "Simply grand. It sounds like an ocean breeze."

Christy blushed more than a thousand miles away.

"What a nice thing to say."

"I'm a nice man. A very, very nice man." Oliver had reverted to his flippant style.

"I'm sure you are. Well, if you have everything you need—"

"Now you mention it, Christy, there *is* one thing you could do for me—an enormous favour, but I'd be grateful till the day I die."

"Surely. I'd be only too happy," Christy replied earnestly.

"I left a diskette behind that I badly need. If you could dig it out and bung it in the post, I'll be indebted for life. I'd ask Mrs. Mason but she goes into paroxysms if I so much as ask her to go into my office. . . ."

"Of course. Where should I look?"

"Ah, there's the rub. I'm not very well organised—it's Mags' fault, really, she's always messing my stuff up when she's looking for something she wants. You'll find three boxes of diskettes on the shelf by the window; one says Blanks, one says Applications, and third is divided into *Telegraph* and Freelance. The diskette I need is labelled 'U.S. data '93', and it *ought* to be in the freelance section of the third box, but if you can't find it, it might have got chucked in somewhere else. Mags is always messing up my stuff. Bloody woman." Oliver laughed to show he didn't mean it. "Bet you'd never do that to Gabe's stuff."

"No, I wouldn't. I'm afraid that Gabe's the one who's disorganised in our house."

"Well, look, if you can find it, great—I'll kiss your feet when we meet. If you can't, no sweat, as your compatriots say. It won't be the first time I've invented statistics."

"I'll find it, Oliver. Shall I send it to the beach or Lawrenceville?"

"Oh, here, I guess. Maggie's working on her tan like most people work for a living."

"Tell her to be careful of the sun."

"Oh, she'll be fine. She's like me. Nothing gets under our skins."

"Okay. Well, you all take it easy. Let me know if you need anything else, and I'll get this out to you first thing tomorrow."

"You're an angel. It's been good talking to you, Christy. The big cock-up with this swap is that we don't get to spend time with *you*. We're being very well looked after, though."

"I'm real glad to hear it. Please give my warm wishes to Maggie, and don't forget to warn her about the sun. Goodbye, Oliver."

"Oh, Christy? Just one more thing before you go?"

"Yes?" she said eagerly.

"Say 'grand' just one more time."

"It's been grand talking to you, Oliver."

She heard him sigh with exaggerated pleasure as she gently put the phone back in its cradle.

Christy was determined to find Oliver's missing diskette before she went to bed. She pulled the three Perspex boxes off the shelf, and started to flip through the diskettes, looking for "U.S. Data." Oliver was right—they were in a terrible state. Some labels were typed, some hand-written, and the filing was diabolical—not even in chronological order, but shoved in haphazardly, so that *"Telegraph '90"* came well behind *"Telegraph '89"* and yet in front of *"Telegraph '87."* Instinctively she began to reorder them, first alphabetically, and then by date. The missing file was not to be found in the freelance box. She next flipped through the Application box, again reordering the files so that Excel came before MacWrite and MacWrite before Thunder 7. There was still no sign of "U.S. Data."

She pulled forward the Blanks box, which held around forty disk-ettes. Some were unlabelled, some had had their labels crossed out and rewritten four or five times, but she tried to put them in some meaningful order. Four disks were jammed in front of the divider. There was a diskette marked "Household Finances," a diskette marked "House Swap '93," a diskette with "Travel Pieces—Italy/France" scratched out and "Novel—A Sad Affair" scrawled under-neath in pencil, and, at last, a disk labelled "U.S. Data '93." Christy shoved it in an envelope, and wrote a note:

Dear Oliver,
    I hope this is the right disk, and solves your problem. Let me know if there's anything else—anything at *all*—you need or that I can do to help. Hope you're all having a grand time. We surely are. Your friend Edward is being the most perfect host and Lucy is delightful—such a gracious lady! I hope we'll be talking to you soon.

With warmest regards,
Christy

She addressed the envelope and put it in the front hall. She'd take it to the little post office in Compton Purlew personally first thing in the morning, so that Oliver would get it soonest. Before she went up to bed she carefully replaced the Perspex boxes on their shelf; she didn't know whether to put the "Travel Pieces/Novel: A Sad Affair" disk under T or under N, so she slipped it back into the very front of the box.

She meant to tell Gabe all about her conversation with Oliver, how charming he'd been, and how amusing it was that he liked her accent so much. But when she had turned all the lights out and tiptoed up to the big four-poster bedroom, Gabe was fast asleep, and the next morning, she was so busy making up to him for her bad temper that she didn't think to mention it.

Early one evening only four days later, Maggie stopped at the mailbox on her way back from the beach minimart with Lily. It seemed as if she went to the shop every day to restock three house-hold essentials—peanut butter, an ice-cream called "Peaches'n'-Cream" to which Lily, Arthur, and most of all Oliver had become seriously addicted, and suntan lotion. Oliver's burn had faded and, with the help of gallons of Noxema, had mellowed into a golden tan. Only his nose still looked as if it had been paint-stripped. As she pulled the relentless stack of catalogues out of the mailbox, she could see Oliver on the deck trying to teach Arthur how to shell enormous shrimp for their supper. Arthur was far more interested in cramming the discarded shells into his mouth.

"Christ, it's hot out there." Maggie groaned as she opened the screen door and dumped Lily and the brown bags onto the slatted floor of the porch.

"Hotter than hell," Oliver agreed. "Mags—I've finished my piece—would you have a look at it?"

"Hmm?" Maggie hadn't heard. She was distracted by an envelope in Christy McCarthy's handwriting addressed to Oliver.

"Read my piece, Mags love. It's on the dining-room table."

"Okay. Let me get a drink first—"

"I want a drink, Mummy—I want a drink—" Lily gabbled.

"No you don't, Lily. You don't *want* a drink, you say: Please may I have a drink, Mummy dearest, if it's not too much trouble—"

"But I *do* want a drink!" Lily shrieked.

"Okay, okay, hang on—Ol, there's a letter for you from Christy." She flipped it over to him and it landed in the shrimp bowl.

From the kitchen, she heard Oliver shriek "Hallelujah!" and took two glasses of lemonade out to the porch.

"What a star! Christy's found my disk and sent it express!"

"Did you call her?" Maggie asked, picking up the note from the floor.

"Hmm? No; she called me. A few nights ago. I asked her to try and dig it out, but I didn't think she had a snowflake's chance in hell of finding it. You must have stuffed it somewhere just before we left."

"You shouldn't have let her go through all the files—I mean, they're on holiday. It's a lot to ask of house guests."

"She didn't mind a bit."

"You didn't mention she's called."

"Didn't I? Must have forgot. You were on the beach. She just called to see if we were okay—nothing important."

"Oh. Fine. Were they alright?"

"Yeah. We didn't really talk. She said she was reading through my old cuttings—said she loved them."

"How nice of her."

"Yup. Very nice. She's got a great voice."

"Yes, I thought that, too." Maggie dropped the note. "No, Arthur, you can't have my ice—no, I said no, and I meant it—you can't, you'll choke. It's not good for you. No, Arthur! Absolutely not. Oh alright, then. One piece." It was preferable to give him a bit than have his fat, shrimp-flavoured little fingers paddling in her lemonade.

"Hey, y'all!" At the bottom of the steps down to the beach stood B.J. and Lindy Richards. "Mind if we come sit with y'all for a spell?"

"Delighted!" Oliver shouted, waving them up. "You'll have to excuse the mess—Arthur's preparing shrimp for dinner, and got a little bit carried away."

"Hell, that's what these houses are for, Oliver. When the deck gets too messy, you jest turn on the hose and sluish it all away. Hey, big fella." He picked Arthur up and for his pains had a lump of ice smashed into his eye.

"Lily, say hello to Mr. and Mrs. Richards—" Maggie prompted.

"Hello to Mr. and Mrs. Richards," Lily repeated mechanically, in a sing-song voice.

"My, you're looking as pretty as a picture, young lady, and we just stopped by to bring you a present."

"What is it? I hope it's a good one," Lily said bluntly.

"Lily! Mind your manners!" Oliver and Maggie scolded in unison.

"Don't you pay any heed to them, Lily. We had some kids to stay last weekend, and one of them left behind somethin' I thought you might kinda like—now don't you let Arthur ride him, 'cus he needs a firm hand on the reins—he's way too strong for the little fella . . ." From behind his back B.J. presented a large inflated rubber seahorse, and Lily's eyes shone with pleasure.

"Oh, Mr. Richards! Thank you awfully!" She stood on tiptoe as he bent down, and kissed him on a weather-beaten cheek. "How very kind of you!"

"You're right welcome, princess. Hey, Lily: Knock, knock."

"Who's there?"

"Butcher."

"Butcher who?"

"Butcher arms around me and give me a hug!" Lily giggled and flung her arms around his neck.

Maggie and Oliver looked on with proud parental smiles.

"Lindy, B.J., we didn't know you were coming down to the beach . . . d'you have a house here, too?"

"Not exactly. We come down here for a couple of weekends every summer, and either we stay here or we rent a place down the beach. . . ."

Maggie looked horrified. "Ohmigod, I hope we didn't kick you out of here?"

"Heck, no. We stay in lots of places at Holden—it's kind of neat to move around and check out new places."

"Sit down, sit down"—Oliver swept shrimp shells off the built-in bench—"and let me get you a drink. Lindy?"

"I'll take a glass of wine, something light and white. You sure we're not disturbin' you?"

"No, it's a treat. I was just wondering myself if the sun had gone over the yardarm."

Lindy and B.J. looked at him blankly.

"He means if it was time to open a bottle," Maggie interpreted.

"There's no time down here when it ain't time to open a bottle." B.J. and Lindy exchanged a glance as if to say that the sun had clearly got to the Brits' heads.

"Now, what can I get you, B.J.? Wine? A beer? A scotch, perhaps?"

"I'll take a bourbon, if you've got one, Oliver."

"Certainly. What with?"

"What with?"

"Yes. What do you drink it with? Water, soda, ice?"

"I figure just more bourbon. That's the way we drink it round here!"

"Then that's the way I'll drink it, too!"

As they talked, Leah, in a small bikini and soaking wet, came up the stairs. She greeted the Richards and scooped up Lily and Arthur, one under each arm, to give them their dinner.

"I don't know that I'd be comfortable having a girl like that lookin' after my kids," Lindy said thoughtfully.

"Leah? She's fantastic with them—they adore her. She can be entirely trusted with them."

"I'll bet she can, but I wasn't referring to whether you can trust *her* with them. I meant I wouldn't trust *them*"—she nodded meaningfully towards B.J. and Oliver, who were on the far side of the deck discussing taking a boat out to fish—"with her."

Maggie laughed. "Oh, I'd trust Oliver with Leah. He's much too scared of her to try anything on—she'd slap him round the chops if he did; but he wouldn't dare."

"Well, in my experience, Maggie, darlin', when they're young and good lookin' they dare anything with anyone. They only stop doin' it when they get so old and fat and tired you wouldn't care if they did try it on someone else." She spoke with a raspy, slow, Southern drawl that fell away at the end of every sentence, like a mechanical toy winding down. "But I guess you girls now have things better under control than we ever did. . . . Do you have a job, hon, or are your hands full with the babes?"

"Oh, I work. I do freelance articles for some of the papers and magazines back home; I write on women's issues, mainly; things about childbirth, or genetic screening. That sort of stuff. All very sporadically. More recently I've been trying to shift into travel writing; I thought I might do a piece on the Carolinas."

"Don't you go doing that, Maggie! We've got plenty much foreigners down here as it is . . . Oh, I don't mean people like you, hon; we like the *Brits*. Bless the Lord, you know North Carolina was the last state in the Confederacy, and the last to abandon the English King. No, we love the Brits; it's the Yankees we hate." She leant towards Maggie. "Do you know the difference between a Yankee and a damn Yankee?"

"No; tell me," Maggie said seriously.

"A Yankee is a Northerner who visits the South." A slow smile spread across Lindy's face. "And a damn Yankee is one who stays."

Maggie laughed. "I had no idea you still felt so strongly about all that Civil War stuff!" she said.

"Oh, hon, don't *ever* call it the Civil War. There weren't nothing civil about it. If you have to refer to it at all, you can call it the War of Northern Aggression. That's what it was sure enough. It weren't nothing to do with emancipation. It was to do with power, and envy, and taxes. Heck, everything's to do with taxes in the long run, ain't it? Beej"—she nodded towards her husband—*"he* calls it Our Recent Unpleasantness. People feel right strongly about it in these parts. Anyways, you were telling me about your writing."

"Well, I don't do that much any longer, maybe a couple of pieces a month, just to keep my hand in. To be honest, I don't think I'm very good at it any more. Maybe I never was any good, but I feel that since I've had the children my mind's only half on the job, and half on the kids and the house."

"And which half's for your husband?"

"Whatever's left over, I guess," Maggie replied with a laugh, but Lindy was no longer smiling. She was shaking her head sadly. "Christy says that when she and Gabe left New York they decided that each of them could only do one thing well at a time. So Gabe does the job and earns the money, and Christy makes the home for the family."

Maggie's tone sharpened a little. "Well, that's all very well for Christy, but everyone has to do what's right for them. When we left London, I didn't feel prepared to pack in everything I'd worked for. I need something that's just mine. Oliver and I didn't plan things like this—it's just the way things happened."

"Well ain't that the truth. Things never work out the way they're planned. I've told Christy that, 'cos she plans everything down to the last degree. I tell her to keep in the back of her mind what to do when the world turns upside down. You young things take your husbands for granted. I do, too, *now*, but then I've passed the danger point, wouldn't you say? I've told Christy to keep an eye on Gabe, and she always laughs at me. I guess you know what you're doing; you look like a smart cookie. Have you heard from Christy an' all yet?"

"Oliver spoke to her a few days ago. She said everything was fine. I hope they're coping with everything."

"Oh, Christy will cope just fine. Christy really belongs in a different era; she could have held back Sherman single-handed. These days she's wasted. She's a coper if ever there was one."

"Between our dogs, and our neighbours, and our cleaning lady, she's going to have an awful lot to cope with!"

"Don't you worry about her. She'll be having the time of her life. The bigger the challenge, the better Christy likes it. We've had some high old times down here, the four of us."

They were rejoined by Oliver and B. J.

"So d'you often meet the McCarthys down here?"

"Sure. Sometimes it's all four of us, and sometimes jes' the boys come on down, don't you, Beej?"

"Sure do. We have a regular thing once or twice a year when Gabe and I and a handful of the boys come on down for a fishing weekend. To get away from the wimmin—" he added with a wink to Oliver.

"Sounds like an admirable idea. What do you do?"

"Do? Well, mostly, we just sit on the porch, and drink licker, and tell lies. . . ." Maggie and Oliver burst out laughing. Lindy smiled patiently, as if she had heard this a thousand times. "I've bin doin' it for nigh on thirty years. . . . It's the Southern way." B.J. drained his glass, and held it out with a twinkle in his eye.

As Oliver went inside to get refills, the phone rang.

"Hello?"

"Oliver, it's Christy."

"Well, Christy, bless your heart! I owe you an enormous thank-you. I just got your letter today."

"Oh great! I wanted to make sure it had arrived. I was concerned."

"Sweet of you. We're just sittin' on the porch with B. J. drinking licker and tellin' lies."

"I surely hope he isn't telling any lies about me!"

"How could he? You're an angel!" Oliver said enthusiastically.

"Well, I don't want to keep you if you're busy, and I don't want to run up your phone bill. I was just calling to make sure it had arrived safely. And to say hey."

"Hey," Oliver said softly. "Thanks again."

"Talk to you soon."

The phone clicked. She really does have the most beautiful voice, Oliver thought as he slugged bourbon into two glasses, then tucked the wine bottle under his arm.

The Richardses ended up staying for dinner, as B.J. insisted that Oliver wouldn't know the first thing about barbecuing shrimp, and as Lindy wanted to show Maggie how to make corn bread. They were all in such high spirits that they relented and allowed Lily and Arthur to stay up, too, until Arthur fell asleep on Oliver's lap and Lily fell asleep on the floor—her head resting on her inflatable seahorse, which she had named Richard in honour of B.J. Soon after midnight, B.J. and Lindy tottered down the stairs, and began to stroll home along the beach. B.J. was singing "Dixie" at the top of his voice, and they could hear Lindy say, "Shut up, you silly old fool" a couple of times before joining in herself.

After putting the children in their beds, Maggie began to collect the clutter of dirty glasses and plates.

"Leave them, Mags. 'Come sit with me and be my love, and we will some new pleasures prove of golden sands' . . ."

"Are you pissed, Ol? It's not like you to be so slushy."

"You're such a cynic, Mags. What's the point of my having such a romantic soul if that's the response I get?" he grumbled. "Let's at least finish the bottle. You know how I hate leaving a bottle with anything in it."

Maggie sat down opposite him, and rested her bare feet on his lap.

"You really do have the most beautiful feet, Maggie. Extraordinarily beautiful . . ." He kissed one.

"Oh, Oliver . . ." Maggie covered her eyes for a moment, thinking again of Edward and awash with guilt. She quickly moved her feet off his lap as if they would incriminate her. "There's something I simply have to tell you . . ."

"What, my darling?"

"Oh . . ." Maggie looked out at the ocean. "Nothing. Just that I love you."

"Look who's being slushy now. But I'm not complaining, Mags, you lovely thing." Oliver murmured, making Maggie feel even worse. "You haven't got slushy with me for an age. Shall we go for a midnight beach stroll? Or a midnight beach roll . . . ?"

"You know how I hate getting sand in my knickers—"

"You could take them off—"

"What *would* the neighbours say?"

"With any luck, we wouldn't be able to understand what they were saying—and if anyone did catch us at it, we could pretend to be German—"

"I can't remember any German, except for *enschuldigung,* which would hardly be appropriate—"

"Just pretend you're reaching orgasm, and scream, *'Ich liebe dick!'* and they'll leave us alone."

"It's hardly fair on the Germans—"

"Since when were they fair on us? One minute it's air raids, the next they're pinching all the sodding loungers all over the Med. Anyway, you're just stalling for time. You don't really give a bugger about the Krauts." He pulled her to her feet. "Come on, Norwich."

"Norwich?"

"Nickers Off Ready When I Come Home."

"Oh, Ol; I haven't heard that since I was ten years old!"

"I'd like to know which blasted paedophile said it to you when you were ten years old," Oliver growled, and pulled her down the steps. "But it suits you as a nickname; I might add it to my repertoire."

As they meandered down the beach, the water lapping at their ankles and the moonlight spilling over the pier at the end of the island, Maggie tried to justify to herself once again why she had slept with Edward Arabin. At the moment—this moment—she felt drawn to Oliver, as she had the day they were married, and during the frivolous months of courtship before their wedding. When they were in bed, pissed, or joking together, they got on like the proverbial house on fire. She just wasn't sure that she loved him any longer. So many times she had read or heard warnings about not expecting sexual attraction to survive marriage; in her own case, the physical side of their relationship had survived very well, but everything else between them seemed well past its sell-by date. Much as she tried to block out the memory of sleeping with Eddie, she couldn't kid herself that it hadn't happened, and having a persistent and obstinate nature, she probed the sore spot as people apprehensively test a sensitive tooth with their tongues. She admitted she had been angry with Oliver for not coming home, and she knew that he'd been in the pub when he claimed to be in Pete's office, and she suspected that he was sleeping with somebody else, so she had more than enough motivation to get even. She also feared that it was prompted at least in part by his telling her about his chance of a TV show. Whatever she'd told Eddie about not being jealous of her own husband, her immediate reaction when she'd heard the news was: "Why him and not me?" Oliver had no idea how much it annoyed her that his career was rocketing when hers was about to sink without trace. There was a different scenario, which was simply that she trusted and cared more about Edward than she did about her husband. This was a far more frightening proposition, but it was the one that made increasing sense to her.

Oliver was now talking about where they should send the children to school, favouring his own alma mater for Arthur, but concerned by the fact that it was still single sex. As Maggie didn't seem to be in the mood to discuss it, they drifted into silence. Oliver was in the process of weighing up the advantages of light-hearted, romping sex against those of wild, uncontrolled erotic sex, when his musings were interrupted by Maggie's prodding him.

"Oliver? Are you listening to me or not?"

"Of course I am. I always listen to you, light of my life."

"Who called tonight?"

"Hmm?"

"Somebody rang when we were having drinks with the Richardses."

"Did they?"

"Yeah; you answered the phone."

"Oh yes; so I did." He paced slowly.

"So?" Maggie dug her elbow into his ribs. "Who was it?"

"A wrong number. Well, no, not a wrong number, exactly. I mean it wasn't for us. It was someone looking for Gabe. I just gave them the Bockhampton number. I had to chat for a bit—you know what they're like, they all say, 'Oh, you sound *English* ...' and then you have to explain the whole sodding story ..." His voice trailed away.

"I just thought it might be Patrick—he said he was coming to the States round about now, and that he'd call."

"No. It wasn't."

Oliver wished to Christ it had been Patrick, an old college friend of Maggie's. Even more, he wished to Christ he'd said it was Christy checking that he'd received the disk. There had been no reason to lie. There was nothing odd about Christy's calling, and nothing shameful about their conversation, and he'd never even *met* the woman. It was true he had got the faintest bit of a buzz from her voice, and had wondered what a woman who sounded like that would be like—in a one-to-one situation—but fantasising about a voice hardly constituted a felony. Maggie had talked to her far more than he had, and it was more than likely that Maggie would call her next week, and Christy would mention something about the Richardses' coming over to Ocean's Edge for a drink, and Maggie would put two and two together, and come up with eighteen, and he'd have a hell of a time digging himself out of a hole that he never should have buried himself in in the first place. . . . He worked out his escape strategy as he walked—he would say there had been *two* calls—one from Christy, which he'd forgotten, and one from someone looking for Gabe. He felt a sour taste in his mouth. When he really *had* to lie, as he had when Maggie had found out about

Louise, he was useless, botching it up every time, but when a lie was utterly pointless and unnecessary, it leapt boldly out of his mouth and caught him unawares, virtually punching him in the face. However much he liked the idea of telling Maggie the truth, however much he had justified his behaviour to himself, and however often he had rehearsed his speech in the mirror, a lie always seemed—well, *easier* to him than the truth. His worry about being found out over this one and jeopardising Maggie's current benevolence scared the pants off him and put all thoughts of sex clean out of his mind. He wheeled her round and headed for home, blaming a sudden thundering headache.

$\mathcal{S}ix$

A postcard to Mary-Jo Simton, Lawrenceville, North Carolina:

> *Hey, Mary-Jo! We're having the grandest of times here. You just wouldn't believe what it's like—like becoming a different person altogether. . . . You live somebody else's life, and it's real strange and real exciting. Some things about these people make my eyes stick out on stalks, and other things make me just fall in love with them. If we do an exchange next year, you and Frank will have to come with us for sure. Give Frank a special squeeze from me!*
>
> *Christy*

THE NEXT MORNING, MAGGIE READ OLIVER'S DRAFT ARTICLE OVER breakfast on the deck. Oliver sat opposite her, clipping his toenails and pretending not to be interested in her verdict.

"Nobody arrives anywhere—least of all in the Southern United States—without some sort of preconceptions. In the Deep South, one brings a bundle of them; all plantation houses, faded elegance and gentility, slaves preparing okra, and a redneck or two thrown in for colour. Television has a lot to answer for.

My wife and I decided to gear ourselves up for our summer in North Carolina by doing some preparatory research. In my wife's case, this consisted of renting three videos—*Gone with the Wind,* of course, *The Prince of Tides,* and finally *The Big Easy.* Much as I told her that New Orleans was culturally further from the Carolinas than Wiltshire is from the Caribbean, she insisted on the last video—probably something to do with the lead actor, whose name, Kincaid or something, escapes me, but whose physique is never far from her mind. My own preparations for our visit comprised a lengthy reading list, which enabled me to land with certain hard facts about this little known part of America: a) Following the Civil War, nowhere was the KKK as strong as in the upcountry region of North Carolina. b) The South remains, even after the many migrations north, the most African portion of America; slavery was not unique to the South, but it was most successful here, and more inextricably associated with race. c) North Carolina has the highest percentages of native-born residents in the United States. d) There still exists in Myrtle Beach, South Carolina, about forty miles from where I now sit, an association called S.O.S.—The Society of Shaggers. I hasten to point out that members are dedicated to the survival of the dance known as the Shag, rather than any other activity implied by the verb . . . and finally, e) North Carolina is known as the Tar Heel State; no Carolinian that I have so far met has been able to tell me why, but my research provided the answer. Jefferson Davis, the president of the Confederacy, said he would coat the heels of his soldiers with tar to help them stand their ground against the Yankees. There are many other legends about the origin of this nickname, and all of them refer to the Carolinians' legendary tenacity.

Armed with these five key facts, and assisted by my wife's learned research on cotton lawn crinolines and dancing the cotillion, I felt that nothing could surprise me. Boy, was I ever wrong. We arrived in North Carolina last week, and are still finding our feet, or "getting acclimatised" as our new neighbours would say, and I am so much the victim of sensory assault that I can only give you a stream of my first impressions of this glorious part of the world. So here we go, gentle reader, my first Postcard from North Carolina to whet your appetites:

The whirring of ceiling fans and the buzz of mosquitoes . . . Live oaks, crape myrtle, and palest plumbago, Spanish moss and kudzu . . . sweeping fields of soybean, corn, and tobacco . . . wrap-around porches, verandahs, hammocks, and joggling

boards . . . tales of piracy, slavery, and witchcraft cheek-to-cheek
with wealth, culture, and gentility . . . sweetgrass and palmetto
leaf baskets . . . littleneck clams, soft-shell crabs, pit barbecues,
sweetmarsh oyster stew, Wadmalaw vine-ripened tomatoes, egg-
plant, McClellanville crabcakes, fried Carolina quail with pecan
crumb and wild blackberry sauce. . . . The polygenetic South—
a paisley swirl of Europeans, Indians, and Africans . . .
oceanfront and creekside houses, barrier islands, tall dunes
sprinkled with sea oats, maritime forest, saltwater marshes,
thousands of acres of sandy beaches that, stripped of their
human occupants, would look like the West Coast of Africa. . . .
The courtesy and courtliness of the natives—deliciously soft-
spoken women, and children who still say ma'am and sir. . . .
This is heaven; a land of almost painful natural beauty, a world
of contrast and dichotomy; old-fashioned, exotic, redolent with
heat and summer and the well-rubbed, old gold colour of the
South.

Next week I will try to pull myself together and make a little
more sense of all of this. I have been invited to the open day
of the local junior high school. Maybe I'll go to the tobacco
auctions. Maybe I'll mosey on down to the pumpkin fest.
Maybe not. Maybe I'll just put my feet up on the porch, drink
liquor, and tell lies with my friend B.J. and the boys. . . ."

"So? What do you think?"

"I think it's crap." Maggie spoke with an audible shrug. She
didn't even need to move her shoulders. "But if that's the standard
you set yourself, who am I to question it?"

"Crap?" Oliver looked stunned.

"Well, the article isn't pure crap, but the references to me certainly
are—unadulterated crap, and lies to boot."

"Oh, Mags! Where's your sense of humour? Anyone who knows
you knows you don't sit around watching videos all day. Don't get
your knickers in a twist. It's a joke, for Chrissakes."

"It's not a very funny one. Did you see me splitting my sides
while I read it? The point is, Ol, as far as I'm personally concerned,
I'm not in the fortunate position of knowing most of your enormous
readership, so they *will* think I'm some sort of bimbo—"

"So what if they do? Who cares? Don't set off on another feminist
rant, Mags—it's just for a laugh—"

"And secondly, and more importantly, it's just such a cheap shot at women in general. You're painting a picture of a high-minded, erudite man against a dumb-bunny, superficial wife, and it makes me puke."

"Look, I deliberately made it light. It's the first piece—don't you know anything about wooing an audience? Don't any of you women have a sense of humour? What the hell do you want me to do? I'm meant to fax it through in the next hour."

"You can sodding well rewrite it. It can't have taken you more than half an hour to write that shit anyway."

"Sometimes your humourlessness is really tedious."

"Yeah? Well, sometimes your arrogance and insensitivity is really tedious." Maggie's eyes were blazing. The article had touched a sensitive spot, because she *did* feel that she was slipping into being a dumb-bunny, superficial wife; she'd done nothing for the past week except lie on the beach, read trash novels, and go to the supermarket, and it didn't amuse her at all to have this described in a national paper.

"You think you could write it better? Go on—you try. When the fuck did you last write anything worth printing? Christ, if we were holidaying on your salary, we wouldn't have got as far as fucking Salisbury. For fuck's sake, Maggie—"

"Daddy, stop swearing!" Lily ordered from the steps. "It's not nice."

Maggie and Oliver glared at each other. "You always have to put me down, don't you, Ol?"

"That's rich. Bloody women," Oliver said under his breath, but loud enough for Maggie to hear, "you're all the same—bloody stuck-up, sanctimonious cows. If there's one thing I can't stand it's this holier-than-thou attitude. . . ."

"It doesn't take much to be holier than you—"

"Talk about cheap shots . . ."

Maggie stomped down the steps, collecting Lily on the way, and Oliver watched them striding down the beach, refined noses in the air. You could never bloody tell with Maggie; one minute she was fantastically supportive, the best editor he'd ever had, and full of suggestions, and the next she had a hornet's nest in her bonnet and had no idea what sort of a strain it was producing a weekly column. It wasn't as if she'd ever tried it. Of course the article wasn't in his normal style, but there was a reason for that—he was thinking about the TV series, seeing the first five minutes of the film as an evocation of the beauties of the South—a stream of images that would set the agenda for a closer examination of the meatier issues. He had written it that way because he knew that Danny Bujevski, his potential producer, would be reading each and every piece with an eye on the camera angle. He dragged his portable pc out onto the deck, and began editing furiously. It occurred to Oliver that Maggie's outbursts grew out of her own insecurity, but right now he felt sorry for himself, and he was fed up with her. He was tired of pussy-footing around her. Even if she was worried about her career, she could have been grateful for all the things that he provided: the house of her dreams, money, freedom, shared child care, the best bloody cheese soufflé in Britain, not to mention great sex. . . .

Oliver's litany of his own skills and kindnesses bore an uncanny similarity to Christy's. The more time she spent in Bockhampton, the more golden her image of Oliver became. She had read all the files of clippings, and could have written a thesis on his opinions, almost all of which she agreed with. As she studied the family photo album, and noted shot after shot of Oliver clowning for his children's amusement, Oliver building a tree house for Lily, Oliver nearly submerged in Arthur's paddling pool, she built on her impression of him brick by brick. She rarely thought about Maggie. Her mind was focused on Oliver and on his house, and what she would do if she were in a position to change it. The garden, although pretty in an abandoned sort of way, could have done with a little more care and attention. The house could use a lick of paint at the very least, and as for the dogs—well, Christy, who liked dogs, believed in treating them as animals, and she was not amused by the way Boomer took his midday nap on the Georgian sofa, and treated the freezer as his private pantry, nor by the way Lucius had clearly been encouraged to impersonate a vacuum cleaner on the kitchen table. Joan Mason shared Christy's views, and had made various dark asides about the lack of a firm hand at Bockhampton. The more Christy learnt of Oliver, the more convinced she became that in some funny way, she already knew him.

Most people are curious about strangers. To some, it's no more than idle interest; to others it can reach pure voyeurism. Thank God for it. If you have no curiosity about other people, you might just as well wrap yourself in cotton wool and nail yourself into a coffin.

"Well, I suppose Mr. Callahan is too busy with his writing to train the dogs," Christy had said understandingly to Joan Mason. "And Mrs. Callahan must be busy, too."

"There's them that's busy and them that's busy," Joan had replied cryptically.

"He spends a lot of time in London, doesn't he?"

"His fair share." Christy had gingerly asked Mrs. Mason to clean all the glasses by hand, and had smoothed her feathers by staying in the kitchen to peel potatoes.

"It must be a terrible amount of work for you, running this enormous old house virtually single-handed."

"It's what I'm paid for."

"Nevertheless—it's a full-time job. I know how much there is that *I* have to do back home. Doesn't Mrs. Callahan have any time to spend on the house?"

Mrs. Mason pursed her lips, drying the last glass thoroughly. "She has the scamps to deal with, I suppose."

"But they do have a nanny, don't they?"

"They have a nanny of sorts." Joan Mason didn't hold with Australians. Her brother-in-law was Australian, and a bigger ne'er-do-well she had yet to meet, as she frequently told him.

"It's so important to find the right help, I always think, or you end up with more trouble than you started with."

"Mrs. C. seems perfectly happy with the girl. I believe they get on very well. She often stays to dinner," Mrs. Mason said with a sniff of disapproval. She didn't hold with staff staying to dinner.

"Well, I suppose Maggie has pretty good judgment if she hired *you*. You're worth your weight in gold. I only wish we could bottle you up and take you back home."

Mrs. Mason wasn't used to compliments, could barely recognise one, and certainly didn't know how to acknowledge them, but her normally rigid spine relaxed fractionally.

"Mrs. C. didn't hire me. *Mr.* Callahan hired me." Dear Mr. Leonard, Joan thought loyally.

"Oh, I *see* . . . that explains it." So Oliver not only worked his fingers to the bone, and cared for the children, but even had to find the domestic staff himself. Gabe would die if she'd ever asked him to be responsible for employing a cleaner. Christy went to dump the potato peel in the bin.

"Not in the bin, Mrs. M. I'll take them out to the compost heap. Waste not, want not." Joan Mason didn't hold with waste. She didn't hold with very much at all.

When she'd talked to Maggie on the phone from the States, Christy had liked her instinctively, but ever since she'd arrived at Bockhampton, she had stopped being curious about Maggie. Her preoccupation was entirely with Oliver. He was a really charismatic man, multitalented, dashing and witty, and he clearly understood how to handle women, whatever they were like—Lucy, or Marjorie Hangham, or even Joan Mason. As Christy and Mrs. Mason finished off in the kitchen, Christy felt with satisfaction that the pieces of the puzzle were beginning to come together like a huge jigsaw. She had experienced the same thrill watching an interior designer roll out a new bolt of fabric or wallpaper. The only thing that saddened Christy was that she wasn't going to have the chance to meet Oliver in the flesh. Oh well, she told herself philosophically: there was no harm in a little fantasy, so long as it didn't get in the way of one's obligations. This summer in England was the perfect opportunity for her to indulge in a private little game; it wouldn't have anything to do with real life back home at all.

Even the mere thought of speculating idly about Oliver left Christy feeling guilty towards Gabe, and she went in search of her husband, and found him asleep in Oliver's chair, contracts and spread sheets everywhere. She roused him gently and packed him off to bed, tucking him in with a teasingly unmaternal kiss. Her son was busy in the den building brick houses with Mariella, who had abandoned their daily walk owing to a sudden thunderstorm. Rain was now teeming off the roof and overflowing the dilapidated gutters, and even the dogs had retired to their baskets. Christy wasn't tired. The house felt cold, despite its being the end of July, and Christy didn't want to disturb Gabe by going back into the master bedroom. In the spare room across the hall, she found piles of sweaters and cardigans. They were all far too big for her—obviously Oliver's, but she couldn't seem to find anything of Maggie's. Anyway, with her narrow shoulders, men's clothes suited her rather well. Selecting a pale yellow cashmere sweater, she pulled it over her head and was surrounded by a faint, slightly bitter waft of citrusy aftershave. She inhaled deeply. She could see Oliver, and hear his voice . . . now, she could even smell him. She smiled at her own silliness, and returned to the office, darkened by the summer rainstorm, to clear up after Gabe. When all her husband's papers had been arranged in neat piles, she turned to the Perspex boxes of diskettes, with a mind to sorting them for the master of Bockhampton. The first one she came to was "Travel Pieces/Novel: A Sad Affair" and she slipped it into the computer to see what was actually on the disk, and where it should be correctly filed. She clicked the cursor on the icon labelled "Novel" and the monitor filled with text before her eyes:

I can tell you about that picnic by the river as if it had happened a couple of hours ago. In fact, it was thirteen months ago today. I can describe it in perfect detail, because even whilst we were there, sitting by the river, I knew it was a memory that would have to sustain me for the rest of my life. Somehow, I felt that if the details of the afternoon slipped, I would lose her forever. I couldn't risk that.

I sat a little to one side, on the grass, with my legs crossed, watching her. She was lying on her back on the tartan rug I had brought from the house. It was a black and green tartan—I think it's called Black Watch, but I've never really known, and I don't want to know now. Her eyes were closed, and her long pink skirt was a little rucked up over one knee. If I close my eyes now, I can see her perfectly, her left knee cap, slim, like a schoolboy's, a long calf with a tiny scar halfway down. I never knew what had caused that scar. I never asked her when I had the chance. Without taking my eyes off her I opened a second bottle of white wine. It was a bottle of Terre di Tufi—an Italian wine. I haven't tasted it since, but I can taste it now. There was an immense weight and drowsiness in the air. You might think it was because we had already finished one bottle, and because it was hot and close that day. But there was something else, too. The debris of our picnic was scattered about. She had pushed it off the rug before she lay back. I can't remember what we had eaten, and this upsets me enormously. I can describe everything else—the exact colour of her skirt, the texture of the rug, which wasn't as soft as it looked, how many sheep were grazing in the field on the other side of the river—but try as I do, I cannot remember what we ate. Perhaps we didn't eat anything—but I can see the plates, marked with food ... As I watched the sun on her face, one hand thrown up to shield her eyes, her wedding band glinted suddenly straight into my eyes. The sun was reddening her collarbone above the scooped neck of her white blouse. I wondered if I should wake her—if the sun was too strong. A bee hovered over her breast, and a stray phrase of Italian poetry sprang into my head—

Voler essere un ape, Donna ...

I can't remember the rest, or who wrote it, but it's a wonderful image of a man envying a bee for being allowed to hover so near his beloved's breast. The phrase nearly leapt out of my throat. I felt my voice break—an ugly noise—and I clapped my hand over my mouth to stop the words. She opened her eyes. I wanted to speak. I wanted to touch her—somehow, I even wanted to—to frighten her a little? I remember all this. But I looked away immediately. I couldn't look at her or speak, I couldn't risk losing that one moment, that moment as she opened her eyes and gazed at me. I chose to freeze it. So I, great coward that I was, and am, looked away. As I sit here and remember it now, thirteen months on, as I sit here at my desk and hear Helen upstairs calling to the children, I feel as if I am watching it all in slow motion: the skirt, her knee, the bee, her eyes opening, my head turning away. ...."

Christy felt bitterly cold despite the cashmere sweater. The room was gloomy from the overcast sky outside, and the grey-blue light of the screen was eerie. She shivered, hugging her arms, wrapped in Oliver's scent. She was freezing. Perfectly familiar with this word-processing system, she scrolled up to the beginning of the file. She knew she shouldn't be doing this. When Oliver had told her to feel free reading his articles, he couldn't have meant her to read this. It was almost like reading somebody's diary. The temptation, having read the last words, was irresistible. It was all a game, anyway. The very beginning of the file consisted simply of a title page, the words in stark bold lettering:

"A SAD AFFAIR"

A NOVEL

BY

ALEC BONES

Christy stared at the page. It was certainly written by Oliver; one of the travel pieces that hadn't been erased from the disk had been destined for the *Telegraph,* and she recognised Oliver's style in the brief account of weekending in Rome. Alec Bones was his pen-name. She scanned quickly through the file. The novel had been abandoned at page 123, in the middle of the twelfth chapter. She turned to the directory to see when he had last worked on the file—June 26th, 4.06pm. That would have been the week before he left for the States, so this was clearly work-in-progress. Oliver hadn't mentioned that he wrote fiction as well as journalism, but there was no doubt about the authorship of the book; Oliver was either publicly or secretly writing a novel. It was possible that Oliver had even wanted her to find it—he had said something about *writers,* not journalists, being thrilled by anyone coming across their work, and he had virtually instructed her to dig around. On impulse, she pulled an address book off the shelf, and looked up the *Telegraph.* There was a list of names under the *Telegraph*'s office, and one saying "Peter Forbes" with a direct number. She dialled it immediately.

"Forbes." A man answered brusquely.

"Mr. Forbes? I'm real sorry to bother you. My name's Christy Moore McCarthy," she said, in her lilting, liquid voice. "I'm calling on behalf of Oliver Callahan."

"Oh yes; I've just received a fax from him."

"Well, he's currently staying in our house in North Carolina, while we're visiting Wiltshire, and he asked me to make sure that you had his fax number over there."

"Right—you must be his swappers—or swappees—Let me just

check that—I know I have a couple of phone numbers for him—Oliver, Oliver, Oliver—yup, I have one—919,675,0902.''

"That's correct. I think he just wanted to double check. Oh, and Mr. Forbes—could I trouble you with one more thing?''

"Be my guest.'' Peter's voice had softened, as most male voices did, even those of short-tempered editors, when they talked to Christy.

"Oliver also asked me to find a number for someone called Alec—Alec Bones. I'm having some trouble tracking him down—I wonder if you knew how I could find him?''

"Alec Bones?'' Peter laughed. "No, doesn't ring a bell. Bloody ridiculous name. Hang on—now you mention it, I *have* heard the name—I've heard Oliver use it somewhere. Are you sure it's not one of his jokes? He's a terrible tease, you know. I'd say he was pulling your leg.''

"You're probably right. It's unkind to make fun of foreigners.''

"Well, from the piece he's just sent me, he's clearly fallen in love with your compatriots, so you shouldn't be worrying. It'll be in Saturday's paper if you want to have a look.''

"I surely will. I'll look forward to it. I've been reading some of his other articles—he writes real well.''

"When he meets his deadline, he does!'' Peter laughed again.

"Has Oliver ever published anything other than journalism? Has he ever written fiction, for instance?''

"No; not that I know of, at any rate. About a year ago, he told me he wanted to try to write a novel, and I told him to do it over my dead body.''

"Why ever was that?''

"As I said, Oliver has a deadline problem. The last thing I need is for one of my regular columnists to start pissing around with fiction.'' He said it disparagingly.

"I quite understand your point of view. Well, I mustn't keep you, Mr. Forbes. I'm sure you're a real busy man. You've been very kind to help.''

"Not a bit. Enjoy your stay. Pop in if you're in town, and I'll show you the office.''

"That's kind of you. Goodbye.''

"Cheers.''

So Oliver had started thinking about this book a year ago. It was probably his first novel. And first novels, Christy knew from her studies of comparative literature, nearly always had an autobiographical element, even if they claimed to be fiction. The last chapter he had written referred to a relationship thirteen months ago—that would be late May, 1992. The unhappiness and passion of the narrator was so strong, it just couldn't have been imagined. As Christy printed what there was of the manuscript, she wondered if Maggie had known about the book—and more to the point, had Maggie known about the love affair? Christy felt like a spy. There was nothing she wanted more than to sit down in some quiet place, protected from interruption, and read Oliver's book cover to cover, but it wasn't to be. Before the printer had finished its work, Jake had found her and dragged her into the kitchen to bake cookies. Bake *cookies . . . !* Christy, a dedicated wife and mother and guardienne of the home of ten years' standing, pummelled the dough to death in her resentment at being interrupted. As she pulled the misshapen cookies out of the Aga, Gabe came into the kitchen and grabbed her round the waist, and she made absolutely no effort to conceal her crossness. She blamed the burnt and broken batch on the combined factors of the wrong kind of flour, and her husband.

Gabe had no idea what was wrong with his wife. She was as jumpy as a cat, and was clearly longing to be rid of him and Jake. Not for the first time that summer, he wished he could read her mind the way she wanted him to. Generally, when Christy wanted him to guess what was going on in her perfect head, she fed him clues, pointers, really, so that when he cottoned on she could praise him for his astuteness. Now she was closing down the shutters on him in a way he'd never known her do.

"Did you have a good afternoon, honey?" he asked, sweeping up the cookie crumbs.

She looked at him blankly, and shrugged her shoulders.

"Would you like to go out to dinner tonight? We could go somewhere smart. Maybe Edward would recommend a place."

Christy yawned. "I'm real bushed, Gabe. I think I'll just have an early night."

Gabe put the broom aside, and stepped towards her, his arms outstretched. "Sounds like a grand idea to me, Christy." Christy ducked under his arm.

"You can't be tired, Gabe. You've slept half the day. I'm going to do some reading practise with Jake, and then I want to give Lucy a ring and see if she's around this weekend."

"I thought we could maybe go to Thomas Hardy's house in Dorset this weekend. I know you've been itching to see it."

"Not this weekend, Gabe. I don't have the energy. Anyway, I promised Edward he could come for lunch."

"Christy, am I doing something wrong? Have I done something to upset you?"

"Of course you haven't. You're just fine. But I've got some things on my mind." The look in her eye stopped him from asking what they were.

"Okay. I might just go on into town then. Anything you want?"

"Nothing in the world. Except—Gabe, there's a wine that Edward told me about; an Italian wine. It's called Terre di Tufi. I'd kind of like to try it."

In Salisbury, Gabe managed to find a shop that sold Christy's favourite perfume, and bought her the largest bottle they had in stock. He picked up an edition of Hardy's poetry in an antiquarian bookshop. He drove as far as Wichester to get a case of the Italian wine she hankered for. On his way back, he stopped at a pick-your-own berry farm, and paid a premium to have some picked for her. When he got home, he laid his trophies at her feet, and was rewarded with a small smile.

When you have lost someone's attention, and want it back, it is instinctive to jump up and down and wave your arms in the air. This often passes unnoticed. The wiser option is to walk away and leave the room. Most people sit up when they hear a door closing.

Christy read *A Sad Affair*—what there was of it—so many times that she could almost recite chunks of it. She suspected that there was more than a grain of truth in Oliver's story, but she was primarily gripped by the fantasy of sudden and overwhelming passion. The opening paragraph of the novel held particular appeal for her. It was almost as if it had been written for her.

> *I can no better explain why I have chosen this miserable day in this miserable month to write down my story than I can explain how or why it happened to me in the first place. All I can say is that about two years ago my life changed completely, almost overnight, and twelve months later it changed back to its former pat-*

tern. Before I met her, I was a happily married man, with a child, a decent job, and no serious complaints to make about the hand that Fate had dealt me. I am still married to Helen, and I now have two children, and I even have the same job, and I still have no complaints, but everything else about me has changed forever. Some people write in order to set the record straight, or to teach a moral lesson about the nature of life or love, or to achieve some kind of recognition from the public. I want none of these things. There is no record to set straight, because only two people really know what happened, and we share the same view. I do not wish to be seen as a moral man because I stayed with my wife; none of my actions were motivated by any kind of moral decision, and if my mission here is the truth, I cannot start off with a deception. I have lied too much to too many people already. I have certainly never desired public recognition in any form. I am writing this because I am frightened that in forty years' time age will have dulled me so much that I may forget, and if I forget what happened in that year, if I forget what I felt, and what she wore, and what we said, and the very scent of her, then I will have nothing to live for. When I met Louise I discovered—or she revealed—places in me that I didn't recognise and that I had never seen. This book is my attempt to build a wall around those places, to keep them green and fresh and secure. I do not believe that Louise will come back to me. I do not believe that anyone will enter those parts of my heart again. I do not believe that this book will provide a key to any reader to those parts of themselves, let alone mine. I guard them fiercely for myself alone. In all the time I have had, the endless tedious time since Louise went away, I haven't found an explanation for why these things happened to me, or why they happened right then. For a while, it bothered me. I felt I had to find the answer or I would lose my sanity. Perhaps I have lost my sanity, but now I tell myself, "things just happen."

As Christy read, she could not avoid the thought that perhaps, in all her efforts to perfect her life, to create the life that she believed she was destined for, she had missed the single most important thing—the experience of a true and perfect passion. This thought had occurred to her before, and she had dismissed it, believing pragmatically that the picture of perfect eternal union painted by romantic novelists was a falsity, a pleasant foray into fantasy, and no more meaningful than that. Until she read Oliver's book, she had thought that women's romantic ideal could never be fulfilled—had to remain fantasy—because of the uncrossable divide between men and women. Men don't talk; they are not intimate; they do not have the capacity for entering into somebody else's inner life. As she read Oliver's book, two things drummed away in her head; that she wasn't sure she wanted to enter into Gabe's inner life anymore, or let him into hers, and that Oliver Callahan felt the same way she did about the power of love.

Seven

A postcard to Billy Fairfield, Lawrenceville, North Carolina:

Dear Billy,
Hi how are you. I am fine. Dad and me catched a fish today.
It was big. It is nice here in England. Please go look at Jackson
to see hes doing OK for me. There are 3 dogs here. There fun.
See you.

Your frend Jake McCarthy

MAGGIE HAD AT LAST MADE CONTACT WITH HER FRIEND PATRICK. HE
was jetting around America on business, and was unable to come
to North Carolina, but they had agreed to meet in Orlando next
Saturday night. As Leah had gone down to Atlanta for a week to
stay with a chum from Australia who was waitressing there, Maggie
expected Oliver to kick up a fuss about being left with the children
for a night, but Oliver was surprisingly relaxed and simply said that
he knew how much Patrick meant to her, and she shouldn't miss
the chance of seeing him. "I'm perfectly capable of looking after
my own children for thirty-six hours, Mags. I'm not about to let
them starve, or send them out to play in the traffic. I'll miss you,
though." He spoke with sincerity. Since their tiff about his article,
they had been getting on reasonably well. At least, they weren't
fighting as often. Oliver was less frenetic than he was in England;
the holiday seemed to be doing him a world of good. They decided
to spend one last day on the beach, and then go out to dinner
alone; the next morning, Oliver would drop Maggie at the little
local airport at Wilmington, and then drive back to Oak Ridge with

the children. Lily and Arthur had made firm friends of the Braithwaite family who had taken a summer rental on the house next door
to Ocean's Edge, and spent most of each day playing in between
the two houses. Lily had ingratiated herself with Janice, the mother
next door, by her over-the-top manners and by complimenting her
on her delicious peanut butter sandwiches—*"Far* better than Mummy's, honestly, Mrs. Braithwaite; I wish I lived near you all the
time. . . ."

Maggie and Oliver lay on the sand, chatting about Patrick. He
was one of the few of Maggie's male friends that Oliver genuinely
liked—possibly because he was gay, but probably because he made
no attempt to hide the fact that he found Oliver intensely attractive.
Ol was never threatened by come-ons from other people, male or
female. He had had a long-standing joke with Patrick that if anything ever happened to his marriage with Maggie, Patrick would be
the first person he would turn to.

"I'm not sure that Patrick really thinks of it as a joke," Maggie
grumbled. "Every time I see him he asks in a very concerned tone
of voice if everything is 'okay' between us." Ol laughed, and Maggie
continued. "What I really resent is that if we ever *did* have problems,
I wouldn't be able to confide in Patrick. He'd be round like a shot
with a bottle of chilled champagne."

"Well, you'll just have to make sure we never do have any
problems."

"That's a pretty tall order."

"You're a very big person, you can handle it."

"I don't appreciate the word *big.*"

"It was metaphorical, my darling, and you know it." He kissed
her flat stomach through her swimsuit. "Mags, d'you remember
when we first met?"

"Do I remember! You were a total bastard."

"I wasn't. I just fancied you rotten."

"Well, you didn't show it. You made lots of rude comments about
women reporters, and how if I wanted to write about politics I
should have stayed on a provincial paper, and that women were
incapable of interviewing . . . Everyone told me you were the office
Lothario. You weren't. You were just a complete sexist pig."

"And all the time all I could think about was how Pete didn't
allow interoffice 'relationships,' and that if I couldn't move you onto
another paper, I'd never be able to get you into bed."

"Pete's opinions didn't seem to carry that much weight. They certainly didn't stop you having an affair with Louise."

"Mags, let's not go over her again. I've told you a hundred times she was just an act of madness—fear." Oliver hurried quickly over the reference to Louise. "When it came to you, I was serious, and Pete's opinions carried a lot of weight. I was scared shitless. But I couldn't resist you. You were such a challenge; so bright, and so difficult, and so sexy—"

"Ah, the rose-tinted glasses of memory!"

"You still are."

"Only to you."

"I should bloody well hope so."

Maggie rolled onto her stomach, nursing the secret of Edward. She lifted her hair off her shoulders. "Could you do my back, Ol?"

"With pleasure."

Oliver spilled oil into the palm of his hand, and began to caress her shoulders. His hands ran down the backs of her thighs, and stroked the place behind her knees where two pale green veins rose beneath her golden skin.

"Mags?"

"Hmm?"

"What are these?"

Maggie craned her head round to look at the backs of her legs, where Oliver's finger traced the path of the vein.

"*Those*, Oliver, are what we in the business of having children call varicose veins. I got the one on the left when I was pregnant with Lily, and Wart gave me the one on the right. Not a pretty sight, are they?"

Ol kissed each one tenderly. "They're beautiful. The most beautiful of battle scars." He stroked them again, and Maggie saw his eyes moisten with tears.

"Ol! I can't believe that you, of all people, would be moved by a pair of varicose veins." Maggie didn't really like it when Oliver was sweet. She never trusted it to last long.

"Oh but I am, Maggie. More moved than I can tell you." He slipped his hands under her, cupping her breasts for a moment, and then sat up suddenly.

"Janice!" he shouted. "Is it okay if we leave the children with you for an hour? I know you're having them tonight, but is it okay if we go in for a bit?"

"Sure! I'll give them all lunch—we're grilling hot-dogs." She peered over the railings of the deck.

"You burning again, Oliver?"

"You could say that."

Maggie and Oliver retreated to their bedroom, angled on the corner of the house so that the salty breeze blew straight through the room.

Christy had decided to host a party for all her new neighbours, and enlisted Edward's help to draw up an invitation list.

"Cocktails? Compton Purlew won't know what's hit it, Christy. You'll spoil them rotten."

"I just want to make sure I ask all the right people, Edward. I thought I'd ask all the people we've met, but I don't know if they all get along with one another."

"So long as they don't all get *off* with one another, it'll be fine. On second thoughts, it would probably be even more of a success if they *do* get off with one another," Edward mused. "It could be a legendary occasion. Now. A guest list. Let's see. Myself, of course."

"Of *course*."

"Loopy Lucy and Charles Wickham-Edwardes."

"Why do you call her Loopy, Edward? She seems perfectly normal to me."

"Appearances can be deceiving, you know, Christy, particularly with English people. They're masters of disguise. To be honest, Oliver coined the phrase. He has a passion for nicknames. You better ask Sir Nigel, and the Hanghams—Hang'em High, as Ol calls him— and you ought to ask Imogen and Curtis."

"What's their last name?"

"Imogen Berkeley and Curtis Abrams—but they're not formal. Just put Imogen and Curtis."

"You mean they are not married?"

Edward's voice dropped to a conspiratorial whisper. "They are *living in sin,* but don't tell anyone I told you. Then you better ask Bill and Sarah Trencher, from the Manor."

"Isn't he the oil millionaire you introduced me to? The man with the big chestnut hunter?" Edward had introduced Christy to Bill, who was riding down the lane on his enormous horse while talking on his mobile phone.

"Scrap metal millionaire, Christy, but he doesn't like anyone to

141

talk about it. Since he bought the Manor he's retired from commerce, and the less said about it the better. Lucy never misses an opportunity to ask him if he can advise her on some old pile of junk she's got in the stables, but he doesn't like it very much."

"Back home we really respect self-made men."

"I prefer self-made women myself. Now you'd better ask the vicar and his wife—"

"Won't they disapprove of the ah—unmarried couple?"

"Good God, no! He's not that sort of vicar, and anyway, he plays cricket with Curtis, and one's batting average overrides all other moral considerations in this part of the country. You'll have to ask the Brig—Brigadier Newton-Bowles—he was very big in the Gulf war—has a poor little mousy wife that he bullies constantly—she's called Martha, appropriately—and if you want to get some younger people along, ask Georgie Lamington and her husband. They always have a houseful of people staying. I'll give her a call and tell her about it. I'm sure she'd be delighted. Now let me see . . . who else would make it go with a swing? Of course, Oliver's the man to have at a party; shame he's not around."

"Isn't it?" Christy echoed with feeling.

"Life and soul, is old Oliver . . . You could try a couple of the farmers, they're good for a laugh—some of them, that is. Arthur Crombey, at Crombey's House, for example—he's got a couple of thousand acres. He's the bugger that has all those fields planted with rape—makes the countryside look like some sort of hideous cheap Spanish painting, but that's the price of membership of the EEC, I suppose. I'll bring Hillary from the salesroom, if you'll allow me. That might amuse you."

"You're most welcome."

"Talking of the salesroom, Christy, you haven't forgotten you're coming to the auction with me tomorrow, have you?"

"I'm really looking forward to it."

"Excellent. Well, that will give you about twenty bods for your bash, and I'll pick you up at Bockhampton at nine-thirty tomorrow morning. Okay?"

"Grand. Thank you, Edward, I'll get the invitations out today."

"Invitations? Frightfully posh. They *will* be impressed. At home with Mrs. McCarthy . . . Goodbye, Christy."

*   *   *

At home at Bockhampton House! What a divine idea! If it *was* her own house, she'd make a few subtle alterations, of course. She'd open up the kitchen into the pantry, and she'd redecorate the drawing room so that it wasn't quite so oppressive on grey days—and she'd turn the den into a proper playroom for the children, maybe extend it out onto the terrace. . . . Even without doing anything radical, she could improve things just a little for the sake of the party. If it was a fine evening, she'd open all the doors into the garden, so that the terrace and lawn could become an "outdoor room"—if she could find some nice material in Salisbury she'd fling it over the settees that Boomer had ruined—maybe she'd be able to pick it up at tomorrow's auction; Edward had said there would be a textile section.

Christy had invited herself to the Bishop & Moodey antique sale. She had only ever been to a Sotheby's sale in New York, and thought it would be quaint to see a country auction. Edward himself would be acting as auctioneer, and had said the sale had some good lots. The salesroom was full by the time they arrived at five to ten, and after ensuring that Christy was allocated a paddle number, in case she wanted to bid, Edward installed Christy at the ringside of the carpet section. He greeted some of the regular dealers, before taking his place on the auctioneer's dais. Edward surveyed the room, and tapped the desk gently with the gavel to get the punters' attention.

"Good morning, ladies and gentlemen. I think we're ready for the off." He cleared his throat and smiled at an ancient porter who had brought him a glass of water. "Thanks, Derek, but I prefer a slice of lemon with it. Not too heavy with the tonic, were you?" The crowd chuckled good-naturedly, and two white-coated porters carried the first lot, a large Kazak rug, and laid it ceremoniously in the middle of the central clearing.

"I have a bid of seventy pounds with me." Edward's eyes swept the room, noting those punters who nodded, those who raised a finger, those who smiled, and those who waved their paddle numbers flamboyantly. "Seventy-five, and eighty; eighty-five and ninety. Ninety with me . . . Ninety-five, one hundred. And five. And ten. Fifteen. And twenty. Twenty-five. One hundred and twenty-five . . ." The gavel tapped the desk. By the tenth lot, Edward was well into his stride, and beginning to give the crowd a hard time. He peered over the podium at an Afshar rug that had been delivered in two pieces, described in the catalogue as "two parts; one repaired."

"Lot eleven. An Afshar rug. Pretty thing. In two bits, so much easier to carry. Ah, isn't that nice! Make of it what you will. Come on, Peter, here's one crying out for your needle and thread. I have eighty pounds. Eighty-five. Ninety . . . Come on! You're all half asleep. Wakey-wakey. Two lovely bits of Afshar. Could be his and hers, if you like. Ninety-five . . ."

Christy gazed round the shabby salesroom, curious to see who attended. There were the eastern carpet regulars, all of whom Edward knew by name, and some of whom looked Iranian. Whenever a particularly interesting carpet came up, they would stampede the central reservation en masse, obliterating everyone else's view, and kick up the corners of the carpet with their shoes to look at the knotting on the back. There was a collection of nicely dressed housewives, hoping to pick up something cheap for their teenage son's school study. Milling around the room were seven or eight white-coated porters, ranging in age from about fourteen to about a hundred and five. Christy eavesdropped on the people immediately next to her, clearly local dealers, who chatted to one another about the problems of buying in the grand bazaar in Istanbul. She heard a camp voice behind her, and turned to see a pencil-thin man in a dark navy suit worn with a collarless shirt, with slicked back hair, and obviously capped teeth. When he grinned, which he did a great deal, he showed his full set of dentistry, and wrinkled his nose. "Darling!" he greeted the woman leaning on the rail next to Christy, and kissing the air about her cheeks, said, "I haven't missed twenty-eight, have I? I simply couldn't drag myself out of bed this morning."

"Late night, Michael?"

"Wickedly late." He wrinkled his nose again. "But my, it was worth it."

"Now everybody, pay attention. Lot twenty-six. Camel dressings. Qashqa'i, by the look of them, or so I'm reliably informed. I saw plenty of you arriving by camel this morning, and a very sorry picture you made indeed. Need dressing up, that's the problem. Who'll start me at eighty? Peter? Thank you. Eighty. Eighty-five. Ninety. Five. Hundred. And five. And ten. Fifteen. A hundred and fifteen. A hundred and fifteen?" Tap.

"Now here's a lovely Mahal, with a few honourable battle scars—"

"Meshed."

"Sorry, Mr. D.?"

"Meshed. Not Mahal."

"It says Mahal in the catalogue."

"It's a Meshed," the elderly Iranian insisted.

Edward cleared his throat. "In that case, here's a lovely Meshed. If Mr. D. says it's a Meshed, a Meshed it is. . . ."

Watching Edward effortlessly wooing his audience, Christy realised that this was what he was born to do. He clearly enjoyed teasing the buyers, and had established a rapport over the years with at least half the regulars in the room. Out of a total of perhaps two hundred and fifty rugs, ten to fifteen were of significant value or interest, with guide prices over the thousand-pound marker, but Edward made just as much effort, and in fact seemed to enjoy himself more, over the extremely worn and holed scraps of carpet, faded to an indeterminate colour and no distinguishable pattern. Whenever a particularly shabby specimen turned up, Edward bullied the dealers: "You know what they say—if you buy them worn out, then they can't wear out on you, can they? No denying the logic in that!"

"Lot eighty-two. A tribal bedcover. Jolly nice medallions and things. Pretty little birds up in that corner. Just the sort of thing to slip under on a cold night, wouldn't you say, Mr. D.? I have fifty with me." Christy saw that the queen behind her was bidding for it. He didn't gesture or wave, simply wrinkled his nose hard whenever Edward looked at him. The bidding reached a hundred and twenty, and then faltered.

"Any advance on a hundred and twenty? Mr. D? Thank you. One twenty-five." The Nose wrinkled again. "Thirty behind you. Thirty-five. Forty at the back of the room. Forty-five." The Nose made a little mark in his Filofax, tossed his head back, turned his disdainful profile away from Edward, and closed his eyes. "Sold for one hundred and forty-five." Edward took a sip of water.

"Lot one seventy-nine. Afghan runner, with octagons and all sorts of things that Afghans are fond of. There appears to be an Afghan hole in the middle as well. No need to worry about where to put the tent pole, at least. Afghan plus hole. A bargain. Peter? Fifty. Thank you. Fifty-five, sixty. And five. Seventy. And five. Bid's with me here at eighty. That's an awful lot of carpet for the price of decent underfelt. It's a long runner, too. What I'd call a bit of a marathon." His joke was met with a deep groan from the punters. "Heard that before, have you? No need to be uncharitable . . . Eighty. Lot one eighty. A Heriz. No one should go home today without a Heriz, and that's one on the floor . . ."

Edward kept up the pace for two and a half hours, selling the last lot just after twelve-thirty. The punters either left or shuffled into the other salesroom to bid in the furniture auction. Edward rejoined Christy, wiping his forehead with a large linen handkerchief.

"Lord, it's hot in here. Look, d'you fancy a pub lunch? Hillary's taking over the afternoon sale, so we could slip off."

Edward pulled his dark blue Mercedes out of the car park, and headed towards the village of Pitton.

"I hope you won't mind a pub; there aren't many places to lunch in Salisbury, and I'm in no rush to get back. Are you sure you don't mind missing the rest of the sale?"

"Not at all. I've had quite enough excitement for one day. I'm real hungry, to tell the truth. Shopping always gives me an appetite; even window-shopping."

"Really? Selling gives me one; shopping makes me lose my appetite completely. The Silver Plough's a decent place—does a bit more than chicken Kiev and chips, if you know what I mean."

"It sounds grand," said Christy, looking sideways at Edward in the mirror.

"So. Did you enjoy that? Was it what you expected?"

"No way! I didn't expect all the pros—I thought it was just goin' to be sweet little old ladies picking up bits and bobs for their cottages."

"It's the sweet little old ladies we have to watch out for—they're far tougher than the dealers."

They continued in silence down the A36.

"You know, I often think that the best way of appreciating the beauty of the Wiltshire countryside is through a rearview mirror," Edward said suddenly. "It sounds a strange thing to say, but you actually get a sense of this great space"—he stabbed at the mirror with a finger—"the way the land suddenly drops off, the fields—the roughness of it all. You get the feeling that the houses have just grown out of the landscape—you can see all the colours of the stone palette—honey-coloured limestone, blue lias, that greenish-grey, mildewed look, and the glow of brick and flint when the sun hits it right. D'you see that bonfire smoke hanging like a haze over the copse? There's something wild about this part of the country—something prehistoric—none of the namby-pamby, ladylike little rolling hills of the Cotswolds—here—" he stabbed the mirror—"you can see the *scale* of the whole thing."

Christy nodded, a little perturbed that Edward used his mirror purely to appreciate the view.

Once they were settled next to the fire of the Silver Plough, which was burning merrily despite the warm weather, and after they had been brought a bottle of claret, and placed an order for lunch, Edward removed his jacket, loosened his tie, and leant back, ruffling his sleek greying hair with his hand.

"What a treat to have lunch with a beautiful woman."

"But you seem to have so many lady friends—and some of them very beautiful, and I bet very flirtatious—Lucy, Maggie—"

Edward smiled, and removed his tie completely. "Lucy flirts with every man between the ages of seventeen and one hundred and twelve. I get no special attention. And Maggie—well, Maggie's a different case. Anyway, you've never seen Maggie and me together. What makes you think she flirts with me?"

"Feminine intuition?" Christy suggested sweetly. "You speak very fondly of her."

"I do, and deservedly so. I am very, *very* fond of Maggie Callahan. She has a special place in my heart."

"I knew it. I may not have been here for very long, but I've always been considered a quick learner." Christy toyed with her salad. "And is it reciprocated?"

"Funny you should ask that. I've been rather wondering myself." His tone, initially jocular, softened perceptibly. "When she's here, I feel like I've known her all my life, as if there's nothing I couldn't say to her. She's a good friend. Now that she's gone—well, I feel at a bit of a loss to tell you the truth. Damn it, I miss her. And Oliver, too, of course. I've grown accustomed to seeing them. To-gether, separately, whatever. I suppose I've grown closer to Maggie because Oliver spends quite a bit of time in London, and Maggie and I cheer each other up—you know, I in my lonely bachelorhood, and Maggie when she's feeling like a single mother."

"I can quite imagine. That must be real nice for you both," Christy encouraged.

"Yes; one of those happy twists of fate. Don't know why I'm

telling you all this. I suppose it's easier confessing to a stranger. Must be one of the reasons those Catholic johnnies do so well." He emptied the bottle—most of which he had consumed—into Christy's glass, and signalled for another.

"And d'you think that maybe Oliver has some friend—some bachelor girl—that *he* gets close to when he's in London, and playing at being a bachelor?"

Edward looked amused. "I don't know what it is with you ladies. Maggie asked me something very similar shortly before she left. You are all clearly obsessed with the notion of infidelity. Reminds me of George Bernard Shaw—'What is virtue but the Trade Unionism of the married?' Nice thought, isn't it? Sadly untrue. But, back to your question, I haven't the foggiest. If Oliver does have a bit on the side, and I'd wring his neck if I ever heard about it, he certainly hasn't told me."

"Perhaps he doesn't like the idea of having his neck wrung."

"He'd be a bloody idiot if he ever strayed from Maggie. But then, sometimes he *is* a bloody idiot."

"I'm only asking because I'm reading a book at the moment—a book I found in Bockhampton, and it's all about a great passion that's doomed to fail. I mean, it's requited love and all, but for various reasons, the two people have to forget their love, and part. I guess it's been on my mind."

For a moment, Edward Arabin looked terribly sad. "Sometimes these things happen; you can't go around messing up somebody's life just because you get the notion that you love them. No one has that right."

"Don't they?" Christy prompted innocently. "Isn't all fair in love and war?"

"No, it's not. In war maybe; but you can't play poker and bet the roof over your head if you're in love. You can't. Not when there are other people—children, whatever—around. That's been my experience, at least."

Christy took a sip of wine. Her thoughts turned not to the Callahan children, but to Jake. She would never do anything that might jeopardise his happiness, not if her own life depended on it. "So you don't think Oliver ever had some secret lost love? Some *grand passion*"—she smiled, so that Edward wouldn't think she was being entirely serious—"that he abandoned for Maggie?"

"You never know the truth about a marriage unless you're on the

148

inside—unless you're one of the two people concerned, I mean. Some of them that look great on the surface of the skin are rotten to the core, and some of the mouldy old bruised ones have the sweetest flavour. But to answer your question"—he pushed his plate aside virtually untouched—"no, I don't think Ol has a secret lost love. If he does, it's for Maggie."

"How do you mean that?" Christy was gripped. This espionage business was becoming addictive.

"I mean that maybe familiarity breeds contempt. Maybe Oliver doesn't realise how much he depends on Maggie—how much he loves her. In that way, it could be described as secret, and if he once knew, and doesn't now, then you could say it was lost. But the key thing is that in her heart of hearts, Maggie knows. So she'll hold them together."

He spoke rapidly, with a tinge of bitterness that Christy construed as envy. So Edward Arabin was in love with Maggie—and at some point had at least hoped that Maggie was in love with him—and he couldn't hide his jealousy. Because of his own infatuation, he was incapable of believing that Oliver could have loved somebody other than Maggie. Edward clearly hadn't been allowed a sneak preview of *A Sad Affair* and had no inkling of the way that Oliver had portrayed Maggie—or Helen, as he called her in the book, as "a perfectly decent, ordinary woman who should have married anybody but me." Christy liked Edward; he was a nice guy at heart, but Christy was looking for a lot more than niceness. Christy was looking for an emotion that would hit her like a tidal wave, that was dangerous and awful. Lunch with Edward was far too pleasant for her current appetite. Thinking about the way Oliver had described the experience of love, she smiled to herself.

"Does that amuse you?"

Christy had to think hard to remember what Edward had last said.

"No—it's just such a nice romantic idea. I love romance—don't you? Living in England is far more romantic than living in li'l ol' Lawrenceville, N.C."

"What a funny idea. Romance is where you find it."

"You're not wrong there." And Christy ducked her chin again, looking up at him through her lashes. If Edward Arabin was a middle-aged, cynical man who had had more passes made at him by women young and old than he could remember, he gave nothing away.

"If you look hard enough, you can find romance wherever you want it. Even in Compton Purlew."

"You think?" Christy asked pensively.

"Oh, I more than think; I know," Edward acknowledged with a smile.

"Are you looking, Edward?"

"Me? Heaven forbid. It was just a general observation."

Christy was the sort of woman who liked to be desired by every man she met; she had never questioned her attractiveness—but she believed in *exercising* her natural appeal. Every time she met a man, she set out to court him. Not to bed him, but just enough so that he'd walk away wanting, at least a little, to be in Gabe's shoes. It was a way of flexing her muscles. It was something she had never taken very seriously—it was just a game. Now she found herself not really caring whether Edward Arabin desired her or not. She didn't want him; she wanted, however briefly, something quite, quite different.

Maggie and Oliver argued about where to eat the night before Maggie's departure. Oliver was particularly keen on a small Thai restaurant they had discovered about ten miles away from Holden Beach in the town of Shallotte. He liked the idea that a small immigrant family had had the nerve to open a Thai restaurant in this Southern backwater, and he loved the fact that, as the restaurant had no liquor license, at the bottom of their menu they graciously offered "$2 charge for cockage." As Oliver had said, "It's not the first time I've seen that, but it's the first time in a restaurant. And such a bargain!" That evening, Maggie finally persuaded him to try a new place, "Bad Bob's," which boasted real "homestyle" cooking. Although it was Friday night, and only nine o'clock, the restaurant was deserted when they arrived.

"Are we too early for dinner?" He addressed a waitress in a short pink dress with a little white apron.

"No, hon; most of our regular crowd have bin and gone. Yew all aren't from around heah, are yew?"

"No. We're from England."

"Wel-come!" She pointed to the name tag pinned on her left breast. "I'm Wendy, jest like it says heah, and I'm real happy to be serving yew tonight."

"Why thank you, Wendy," Oliver said formally. "I'm Oliver, and this is Maggie." He always got a kick out of this bizarre American habit of restaurant introduction.

"Well, we're right glad to have yew with us. Is there anything I can be gittin' yew while y'all are looking at the menu? Some hush puppies, m'be?"

"What are hush puppies, Wendy—other than shoes advertised by a basset hound?"

"Heah, on the menu. They're real good. It's another way of ordering bypass surgery—double bypass for a straight order, or triple bypass if you take them with honey butter."

"Which do you recommend, Wendy?"

"Oh, I'll bring you the triple. You might jest as well go whole hog." She winked, and Oliver watched her retreating legs and bottom.

"You love that, don't you, Ol?"

"What? Looking at the waitress's bum?"

"No; I know you love *that*, but I meant introducing yourself."

"I'm just a well brought up gentleman, Mags. If a lady tells me her name, it would be discourteous not to tell her mine."

"That was no lady—"

"All the more reason!" They laughed together.

"Ol, would you ever consider moving to the States?"

"Well, hon, I sure like it real well aroun' heah." Ol attempted a Southern accent, and butchered it miserably.

"Seriously."

"*Seriously,* no I wouldn't. There's nowhere I'd rather be on holiday, but people like us don't belong here, Mags. We'd never survive. I'd degenerate into an old soak within a year—"

"—month—"

"—Thank you—and you'd start eating hot-dogs and collecting sand dollars and the kids would call me sir, and I'd have to get a boat and go shrimping and you'd never sunbathe topless again and we'd give up being sophisticated and superior and get all "neighbourly" and life would be too goddamn nice and comfortable, and we'd lose our cynicism and then where the hell would we be without that?" Ol was still teasing, but Maggie knew he was serious beneath the playfulness.

"Maybe the steadiness would be good for us."

"Steadiness isn't good for anyone. Living on the edge is good for us. Discomfort is good for us. Struggle is good for the soul. Just compare contemporary Russian and British art if you don't believe me."

"I'm not sure about that any longer. I used to think so. Now I think wouldn't it be nice to wake up and know exactly what was going to happen every day?"

"Mags, that's one of the only benefits of your stubbornness. You *always* go to sleep knowing exactly what you're going to think the next day."

"Ha ha. What I mean is, it's civilised around here—more civilised than England. If you try to pull the car out into traffic, you *know* people are going to wave you in, with a smile. In England, they just *might*, but they're as likely to scream 'you fucking bitch' and accelerate."

"Mags, we're just here on holiday. When you visit a country like this, you don't know what it's like to *live* here, any more than the McCarthys really know what goes on in Compton Purlew. We're all just playing at this, looking through a little porthole—you've got tunnel vision at the moment."

Maggie shook her head stubbornly. "I know what you're saying, but there is something *nicer* about people here. They trust one another. They actually *like* one another. Do you know what I mean?"

"No." Oliver finished the last hush puppy—a little ball of deep-fried dough like the holes punched out of doughnuts. "I don't believe people really *like* one another anywhere. People just know that they need other people to survive and to ward off loneliness, and so they compromise, and pretend they like one another because it's easier that way. It's part of civilisation, socialisation." He waved a barbecue rib in the direction of Wendy. "D'you think Wendy likes us? Do you think she really thinks it's 'grand' to serve us for five lousy bucks an hour? Like hell. She just thinks she's got a better chance of a bigger tip if she's nice to us."

"It's still different," Maggie insisted. "Both a British waitress and an American waitress know they ought to be trying to get a bigger tip, but the American one is instinctively nice, and the English one is instinctively surly, and resents the fact that she has to serve you at all."

"All that tells you is that the American is either more commercial, or just plain smarter."

"You are a cynical old bugger, Ol, aren't you?"

"It's got me where I am today," he acknowledged, with a smug smile. "Anyway, Mags, that's not what you said this afternoon. This afternoon, you said I was passionate and hot and made you feel like a teenager."

"I also said you shouldn't let it go to your head."

"As if I would . . ." He rubbed her leg with his foot under the table, and then stuck his fork in the salad bowl. "Hey, look at this, Mags. I ordered a house side salad, and they've brought me half the world's natural reserves of raw vegetables. This is a truly remarkable country." He chomped through two lettuces and half a bushel of tomatoes, lightly sprinkled with twelve ounces of Parmesan. "I'm going to miss you, Mags."

"I'm only going to be away for thirty-six hours."

"Thirty-six miserably long hours as far as I'm concerned."

"You and the kids could always come, too."

"What, and spoil your gossip session? Stop you having the chance to slander me? I wouldn't dream of it. I don't want to get in the way of your friendships, and I know you're always happier seeing Patrick alone. Just like you like seeing Eddie alone. And I trust the two of you."

"Me and Patrick?"

"Uh-huh."

"Because he's gay?"

"Absolutely because he's gay. I wouldn't let you go alone if he wasn't." Oliver spoke simply.

"You don't mean that, do you, Ol?"

"Well, of course I'd let you go see some straight male friend, but I wouldn't be happy about it. I'd lie awake all night wondering if anything was going on." Whatever Oliver said, he had never once seriously considered the possibility that Maggie might be unfaithful to him.

"So what do you think I feel when you're off in London alone?"

Oliver didn't reply.

"Ol?" She pressed him. "D'you expect me to trust you?"

"Don't you?"

"Sometimes. I could have reasons not to. Sometimes when you tell me something, or tell me who you're with, I don't know whether to believe you or not. I suppose it still goes back to Louise."

"Christ, Maggie! When are you going to let go of this? I told you about it, I confessed everything, and I said I was sorry. We agreed not to talk about it." He sounded exasperated.

"Not talking about it doesn't mean not thinking about it. Perhaps we were wrong to agree not to talk about it."

"Mags, we talked nonstop about Louise for two whole weeks. We spent far longer talking about her than I ever spent thinking about her—let alone sleeping with her. If she hadn't bored me to begin with, analysing her with you for two weeks would have slaughtered any interest I had in her. I told you what was behind it; I was frightened. I was frightened of having made a lifetime commitment to another person. Louise was a kind of involuntary, reflex action. The last salute of a dying soldier. No more than that. The point is, Mags, that that wasn't love. That was just sex."

Maggie felt her stomach rise. "And just sex doesn't count? You feel free to have sex with anyone you want so long as you don't love them?"

"Of course I don't."

"Have you slept with anyone else, Ol? Since Louise? Have you had any other affairs?" There. She'd said it.

"No, Maggie, for the last time, no. Why can't you believe me? You know, your watching me the whole time, your not trusting me does more harm to our marriage than if I *were* having an affair. Which I'm not," he added hurriedly. "God, you can't resist dragging up these old ghosts! All I meant was that it's different being jealous about a sexual fling and being jealous because your wife is falling in love with someone. One's a minor cock-up, if you'll excuse the pun, a misdemeanour, if you will, and the other's a betrayal."

"So you wouldn't be jealous if I had a sexual fling? With Patrick, or someone?"

Oliver roared with laughter. "If you had a sexual fling with Patrick I'd eat my hat long before I got jealous, I promise you that. I'd slap you on the back. That's what I call going from the sublime to the ridiculous. What I mean, Mags, is that you just aren't the type of woman to have a meaningless sexual fling. If *you* ever had an affair, it would be because you really loved somebody."

"And then you'd be jealous?"

"Jealous? I'd kill the bastard. After I'd killed you. Maybe him first. I don't know."

"So your bottom line is that if you're unfaithful, it's just a bonk, so it doesn't mean anything, so there's no point in my getting jealous, but if *I'm* unfaithful, then it's emotional, and that's not on, and you'd kill me for it?"

"Apart from the fact that with the sole exception of Louise I haven't been unfaithful, I would say that's succinct, accurate—that's it, in a nutshell." Oliver beamed.

"Bloody convenient system, isn't it, Ol? Your affair with Louise meant nothing, you get to confess it all to me—after I've discovered it, let's not forget—and the slate is wiped clean, whereas if *I* had an affair, it would be summary execution, right?"

"Who are you thinking of having an affair with, Mags? That would be a factor. Give me some names, as a hypothesis."

"Hell, I don't know, just anyone . . . Bob Braithwaite next door, Patrick, Charles Wickham-Edwardes, Edward Arabin . . . It's irrelevant—it's just for the sake of argument."

"Alright. Just for the sake of argument—something you are remarkably adept at, my darling, let's consider them . . ." He ran through the contenders, counting them off on his fingers. "Bob next door is out of the question. He's a fat, lazy slob who does nothing except follow the baseball results, and Janice would pay you to take him away from her. I'd section you into the nearest loony bin. Patrick, as I've said, is a ludicrous notion, and I'd eat my hat. *I'm* the one Patrick wants, not you. Charles is even more ridiculous, he's so wrapped around Lucy's finger you'd never disentangle him, and Edward is just as ridiculous as Charles."

"Why?"

"Why? Because he just is, that's why! He's my closest mate at home, for God's sake, he's old enough to be your father, he's close enough to be your brother, he doesn't believe in romance, and if he did, you're not his type, and anyway, you're my wife. It's ridiculous. End of story."

"He's not old enough to be my father—not unless he fathered me at the age of twelve, and how the hell do you know I'm not his type? Anyway, that's neither here nor there. The thing is, Ol, that as far as you're concerned, the relevant factor is always the nature of the man involved, not the woman. You ask yourself, 'Would they sleep with Maggie?' not 'Would Maggie sleep with them?' and that's bloody insulting. Do you think the whole story of the human race is about men's choices? D'you think women just sit there waiting to get picked up and then waiting to get dumped or passed over, while they cling on for dear life?"

"I admit this may not be a particularly fashionable view, Mags, it may not be quite p.c., but *yes,* I do think that when it comes to sex the male drive is stronger, and that men do the fighting and the picking. They do the impregnating, after all, and the women do the rearing and nurturing. That's why when we use the word *mothering* we all know the connotations—caring, comforting, protecting, wiping tears away, looking after and all that crap, and when we say a man 'fathered' someone, it just means that his sperm fertilised some goddamn egg. Ba-ba-boom. That's it. Wham, bam, sperm meets egg. I've heard some bonkers theory that the primary carer selects the sexual mate, but I say that's crap. I say all women are the objects of all men's lust, to put it bluntly. That is the full extent of our responsibility, when push comes to shove—that's what we're expected to do, and that's all we get the credit for. When somebody says what a delightful child Lily is, do I get any credit? Like hell I do. It's: 'what a wonderful mother Maggie must be . . .' So don't deprive us of the only responsibility we can honestly claim. Right down at the nitty-gritty, right down at the fundamental level, down at the bottom, sex is a man's world. That's why if you set up this ludicrous proposition of your potential lovers, I'm going to analyse the men and their motives, not yours. You are secondary in that instance." He paused, and patted her hand. "No disrespect intended."

"None taken, I assure you. I was just curious."

"Are yew folks jest about done here?" Wendy asked, wiping the table around them.

"We surely are, Wendy. Real done. You must be longing to get off home." Oliver winked at her.

"Nope. You take jest as long as yew like, Oliver. You're on vacation. Yew have a real good time now."

When they finally left "Bad Bob's," leaving Wendy 20 percent of the tab, Maggie made a few decisions. She decided not to tell Oliver anything, ever, about what had happened with Edward. She decided that Oliver probably hadn't had an affair since the one with Louise, but there was no reason to suppose he wouldn't have others in the future, and she decided that the males of the human race could definitely be divided into two clear-cut types. The Australian desert mouse, or "A" type of man, was naturally polygamous, naturally aggressive, and had three dominant characteristics—he had an eye for the ladies, an instinct for weighing up his rival males, and a complete lack of responsibility for his actions. The baboon man, or type "B," was a long-term thinker and planner—he was in it for the long haul. He made his choice, knew what the outcome of that was going to be, good and bad, and stuck with it through thick and thin. She wondered if it was possible to fit women into the same categories, but she came to the conclusion that it wasn't. Perhaps a few women began their mating careers as mice, but by the time they hit forty, they had all, whether by choice or physical inevitability, transformed into greater or lesser baboons. There was no doubt in Maggie's mind that she had married a desert mouse; an appealing one, and an entertaining one, but a mouse nonetheless. The mouse had proved to be an acceptable partner in the playing and mating days of their relationship, but had certain drawbacks as a lifetime companion. The remaining question that teased her was whether she had made the wisest choice of the two possible options.

Eight

An invitation on vellum:

Mrs. Gabriel McCarthy
At Home

Bockhampton House
Compton Purlew

Saturday August 6th, 1993

Cocktails 6.30pm
RSVP: 0873 655381

SATURDAY, AUGUST 6TH, DAWNED BRIGHT AND CLEAR, MUCH TO
Christy's relief. By four in the afternoon she had set out some
small, linen-draped tables in the garden, each with its own indi-
vidual arrangement of sweet peas, roses, and foliage, each with an
ashtray, and each with two to four pretty, ironwork chairs that
she had hired for the occasion. Trays of truly spectacular canapés
were arranged on the kitchen table, ready to be warmed through
by Joan Mason, who had put the boat out so far as to don a
white apron. In the drawing room, Christy had set up a large
table as a makeshift bar, and ran a third check to be sure she
hadn't forgotten anything; she couldn't think of a drink she
hadn't catered for, and she knew she could rely on Gabe to con-
coct any request—except her own house special, which she had

named the "Oak Ridge"—she would do that herself, and had already prepared the base. She hoped her guests would be a little adventurous and step away from the glass of white wine, gin-and-tonic routine. If she could persuade half of them to try an Oak Ridge, or a Seabreeze, or an Old-Fashioned, she'd be content. Everyone she had invited had accepted, and her guest list had expanded to twenty-seven thanks to two late additions—Lucy had asked if she could bring Anne Vincey from Wilton, who was simply "dying" to meet Christy, and Marjorie Hangham had called and said in a tone dripping with self-satisfaction that she would be bringing Julian Pargitter, "our honourable member, m'dear," who was booked to dine with Marjorie later that night.

After Christy had bathed, she lay on the four-poster with her now much-thumbed copy of Oliver's novel. She had marked various sections in the text, people or places she wanted to try to identify. She knew that she was becoming a little bit obsessed with the book, and with Oliver himself, and hoped that this party might be a fun way of unlocking a few more doors around him. She reread the picnic scene, and then flipped back to the first meeting of Oliver and Louise. They had met at the house of a friend—a friend that Christy liked to think was modelled on Lucy Wickham-Edwardes—and Christy wanted to make a few mental notes to see whether Lucy—if prompted—would inadvertently identify Louise.

By chance, Helen had not come with me to Megan's for drinks that day. The baby was not well, and she had chosen to stay home. There was nothing unusual about this. Helen frequently backed out of arrangements at the last minute on one pretext or another, and I no longer minded. Although Helen herself would never admit it, she didn't like Megan very much anyway, so I wasn't surprised. There is no reason to tell you all this. Helen and Megan's friendship—or lack of it—has nothing to do with my story, and nothing to do with what happened. I couldn't be less interested in it. I mention it only to stress that there was nothing irregular about the day, nothing to alert me to the upheaval that all our lives were about to suffer. Not least, mine. Not least, Louise's. Maybe things would have worked out differently if Helen had come. I don't know. I've never really thought about it, and to be honest, and I'm meant to be being honest, aren't I?—I don't care.

I parked on the road, so that I wouldn't blocked in by cars if Megan and her guests were particularly boring and I needed to make a bolt for it. There were already six or seven cars parked in the drive as I walked down, and I congratulated myself on my foresight. By one o'clock, I would have been trapped. Megan had opened one of the doors to the terrace, although it was blustery, and no one in their right minds would want to go outside. I knew most of the people there, and the ones I didn't know, I felt that I had at least met somewhere, sometime. They had those sorts of faces. I mean that they weren't in any way out of place sitting on Megan's nicely upholstered armchairs, and gazing at her collection of Chinese prints and Burmese wood blocks. I chatted to a couple that I hadn't seen for a long time, who asked after Helen. They didn't know we had had a baby, so I told the story about the birth again, about how the hospital said we weren't registered. I've heard Helen tell the story so many times. She loads it with drama and self-pity, and people listen open-mouthed, and then express horror at the NHS. I tell it as a joke, as a funny story, which is what it was, and this couple—I can't remember just now who they were, but it will come back to me—laughed and laughed. If Helen had been there, I probably wouldn't have told the story. Or not like that, anyhow.

As I said, it was an ordinary March day, drizzling a bit, and blowing a gale, so no one was on the terrace. I went out there for a breather, and also because I saw Isobel waving at me from across the room, and I didn't feel like talking to the old trout. Once I was on the terrace, I saw that there was a woman sitting out there, on the steps that go down to the croquet lawn, right on the far side of the terrace so that you can't see them from the drawing room. From the back, I could tell she was cold. She had one arm wrapped around her, hugging herself, and she was wearing a flimsy little cardigan, not the sort of thing for March at all. With her other hand, she was stubbing out a cigarette on the stone step. I had two simultaneous thoughts: "Uh-oh; Megan wouldn't like that at all" and "Oh-ho! Another smoker!" I walked towards her and said, "Come out for a quiet smoke, have you?" She didn't jump, or even turn her head to look at me. She just said, "No; I've given up, actually" and sat staring out across the valley, without moving. She had black hair, really black black hair, and it was looped up on her neck in a sort of old-fashioned, haphazard way. I squatted down next to her and said, "I'm Peter. Peter Fletcher." She ignored my hand, so I had to pretend it was only stuck out there to scratch my knee. "Are you a friend of Megan's?" She still didn't look at me, but she said "Sort of" in a really quiet voice. "D'you live around here?" I don't know why I persisted, I don't normally bother with strangers, and she made it perfectly obvious she didn't want to chat. I also knew she couldn't live around us—I would have met her before if she did. It's an incestuous sort of place we live in. She ignored my question anyway, and so I cleared my throat a couple of times, and I was about to shuffle off, but she turned and looked straight at me, and said slowly, "Do you have a cigarette you could lend me?" I stared at her. She was incredibly beautiful, fine-boned and delicate, with huge sad eyes and her whole soul in them and I kept on looking at her and thinking, "Lend you? Lend you? How can I lend you one? Are you going to give me the butt-end back when you've finished with it? Are you going to pop one in the post—get my address from Megan—and send one back with a little thank-you note? 'Thank you for the cigarette, which I now return'; lend you?" And I kept on staring at her, and all the time my mind was spewing rubbish out I was looking at her and thinking, how lovely and delicate she is, and then a man came out onto the terrace, a big burly oaf of a man, and he said, "Come on, Louise, we've got to go. Chop-chop." Like that. Chop-chop. And she stood up very smoothly and slowly, like a dancer, and she left. That's when I met her. That's when I first learned her name. Louise. Now, when people mention her, I can barely speak her name. I stammer and stutter over it. Even when I say it alone, it catches in my throat. Yet I'm an eloquent man. My work—my life— depends on eloquence and control.

"Mom? Mommy?" Jake climbed up on the bed next to her, having to hang on to the bedpost to lever his short little body up. "Dad says I can't come to your party, and I want to come 'cos you came to mine and Daddy did, too. It's not fair that I don't get to come to yours."

Christy hugged him tight. "Darling, if Daddy says no then I'm afraid that means the answer's no; what Daddy says, goes." Jake's eyes filled with tears that spilled over his eyelids like an overflowing sink, and Christy relented a little. "Okay. Now listen. You can come for a little bit—just when the guests arrive. You can stay with us for half an hour if you promise to be as good as gold, and go to bed lickety-split when Mariella tells you. Is that a deal?" She held out her hand, and Jake, solemn but no longer crying, shook it formally. "Yeah, that's a deal."

"What did you say, Jake? I didn't hear you correctly."

"I said, 'Yes, ma'am, that's a deal.'"

"That's better. Now you skedaddle out of here and put on some civilised clothes so everyone can see what a handsome young man you are, and not a ragamuffin. Off you go."

Christy would have quite happily stayed on the bed rereading *A Sad Affair*, but she wanted to look her best for the party. She was certain that Megan was in reality Lucy—although Megan herself didn't play a big role in the story, the description of her house, a very faithful portrait of Lucy's. The drive—the terrace—and all that Oriental stuff that Christy had noted when she went to tea at the Wickham-Edwardeses'. In the book, Megan wasn't married, but it was Oliver's poetic license to delete Charles. Christy did her face and perfume before slipping on the pale lilac lace dress that Gabe had insisted she bring. She would have packed it anyway because it was one of the most flattering things in her wardrobe, and set off her hair and her eyes to perfection. She brushed her hair out, spraying the roots to lift them, and gave her neck a last extra squirt of scent. As they were likely to spend the evening outside, she wasn't at risk of overpowering anyone with her perfume. She was looking at her rear view in the mirror when Gabe came into the room.

"My, oh my . . . My favourite dress on my favourite lady," he murmured, kissing her just above the ear.

"My hair, Gabe, don't muss my hair!" Her hands flew to protect her head.

"Not just a little?" he teased.

"Not an inch, buster. It's taken me hours to achieve this carefree effect. Paws off. I went to that funny little salon in the town—you know, the one called 'Maurice of Paris' and Lucy told me the guy is probably Morris from Swindon—and the girl who set it for me told me that if I really wanted to keep the set—as if I would—I ought to sleep with a pair of elasticized *underpants* on my head.

In fact, she said knickers, and I had to get her to explain what she meant."

Gabe laughed. "Maybe that explains why they say that Englishmen are lousy lovers—I mean, if their women go to bed wearing their pants over their heads, it wouldn't do much for the system of any red-blooded male. . . ."

"Maybe I should it try it one night, and see if it does anything for you." For about half an hour, Christy and Gabe were back to their happily married, at-home state, Christy in high spirits because she was excited about the party and because she knew she looked wonderful, and Gabe because she was teasing him, and being playful . . . and because she looked wonderful.

At six-fifteen, the McCarthy family was assembled in the drawing room of Bockhampton, Christy in her lilac lace, Gabe in a mushroom-coloured linen suit, selected by Christy and just sufficiently crumpled to prove it was pure linen, and Mariella in a neat black dress with a struggling but presentable Jake gripped by one hand. Jake was attired in navy, with his beloved baseball cap worn backwards, and his curls tumbling out of the gap in the band. They could have been posing for a family portrait. Christy looked at her husband, trying to see him objectively, trying to guess how others might see him. She studied his face carefully. It was not a face anyone could dislike; it was a pleasant face, wearing a habitual expression of benign tolerance mingled with faint surprise. He had regular features, a nice mouth, perhaps a touch on the full side, a strong chin, and that great crest of springy dark hair. Yes, it was a face that anyone would like. But it wasn't a face you could love passionately. Not really. As Gabe mixed a drink for his wife, and pressed a glass of wine on Mariella, Edward Arabin strode across the garden accompanied by a tall, thin young man with an aloof expression who reminded Christy of a heron.

"Christy, Gabriel; allow me to introduce my friend and colleague, Hillary Knowles."

Christy, who had assumed that when Edward had said he would be bringing a colleague called Hillary he had meant a woman, recovered her poise immediately.

"How kind of you both to come. Now what can Gabe fix you? A Manhattan, a gin fizz—a mint julep? Or perhaps our house special?"

"I'll take a house special, thanks, Christy. Hillary is one of these ghastly teetotal bores, he's a New Ager, or a Buddhist or some such rubbish. Just give him an empty glass to meditate on and a cherry to suck."

Hillary glided to the table and asked Gabe for a small glass of orange juice without ice. As Christy ushered Edward into the garden, where other guests were approaching, Hillary lingered behind, looking at the Persian carpets on the drawing-room floor, and kicking the corners over with his toe. Edward groaned audibly, marched back into the house, and dragged his colleague out. "We haven't been asked here to do a bloody valuation, Hill; behave yourself, for God's sake. The house doesn't even belong to these people."

"That's precisely why I'm taking the opportunity to see what the real owners have got," Hillary drawled. "No risk of offending a sensitive owner by telling her her prized Regency padouk chiffonnier is a piece of repro crap."

"I happen to know this particular owner very well, and she wouldn't care if you told her her chiffonier was a piece of piss. Get out there and mix."

Within half an hour, all the guests had arrived, and Gabe was glued to the bar mixing a variety of exotic cocktails while Christy circulated. Everyone—except Hillary of course—complimented her on the house special, and begged to know the ingredients.

"I can't really take credit for it myself; it was the invention of one of our American writers—E. B. White; perhaps you've heard of him?" Charles Wickham-Edwardes nodded enthusiastically, although he knew less about Evie Whatsit than he knew about Sanskrit verse structures. "It's a jigger each of lime juice, honey, dry vermouth, and apricot brandy topped up with eight ounces of Bombay gin."

"You Southerners certainly believe in drinking, don't you?"

"Honey, where we come from, people take martinis the way normal people take aspirin."

"Well, I'm very glad to hear it. I have a feeling this concoction might get adopted all over the Valley. What do you call it?"

"We've never had a name for it."

"We'll get the vicar over to christen it—maybe something local— maybe the Bockhampton . . . or the Purlew?" Charles suggested.

"How about the Callahan?" Christy said innocently. "In memory of absent friends?"

"God, yes! Oliver would love that! That would be a true lifetime achievement to him, to have a cocktail named in his honour. I might just see if Gabe could fix me up with a refill so that we can propose a toast."

Everyone had dressed up for the occasion, although Christy would never know how much conferring had gone on among the ladies of the Valley as to correct cocktail party attire. The evening was still and sultry, the air redolent with an old-fashioned exoticism, English rose gardens fusing with the gold tones of the American South. Pretty and ugly women alike skittered in high heels on the stone steps up to the house, and punched stiletto holes in the Callahans' far from manicured lawn. As the evening went on, voices became louder, drinks went faster—now self-service, as Lucy had insisted on Gabe joining the party—and laughter rang out, none more melodic than Christy's. Christy drifted from group to group, with Gabe following a few minutes later in the slipstream of her perfume. Once Christy had done the rounds and had greeted everyone in person, with a different gracious comment to each guest, she stood still, and let people come to her. People always came to Christy; she drew people magnetically, whether they were complete strangers or people she had come to know relatively well over the course of the past month. The marmalade-haired Georgie Lamington told her all about the best picnic spots around Bockhampton; Curtis, Imogen Berkeley's frighteningly sexy black lover, confided in her his fears about the lack of an emerging bowling attack amongst the West Indian cricket team; Sir Nigel Bavington asked her advice about the sudden outbreak of blackspot on his prize rose, Souvenir de la Malmaison; Brigadier Newton-Bowles told her in specific detail exactly how England had won the war before the Americans ever arrived, and then, with one look into her sympathetic violet eyes, said they could never have done it without the bravery of the Yanks. Even the vicar, a young and earnest man who was possessed of a true missionary zeal, was drawn to Christy, despite the fact that he could hardly recruit for his flock from North Carolina. Christy, who restricted her church involvement in Lawrenceville to twice-monthly attendance, inclined her head and commiserated about the difficulties of setting up a church-cleaning rota, and gently suggested a couple of advantages to the Church of the ordination of women priests. The Reverend Martin Worth, who was wholly opposed to women in the church doing anything other than the flowers, listened to her seriously, and admitted that she had a point.

At around nine, most of the guests had drifted away reluctantly. A hard core remained scattered around the garden. Poor Martha Newton-Bowles had been backed into a corner by Major Hangham, who had cunningly persuaded Marjorie to go home before him. Lucy and Edward sat on a bench on the terrace, teasing Charles about his fishing failures, Georgie Lamington could be seen flirting recklessly with the aquiline Hillary Knowles, and the vicar wandered around the kitchen garden calling for his wife. Christy, with Gabe at her elbow, surveyed the scene. The party had been a resounding success, but she had made no progress in identifying the woman in Oliver's novel.

"Excuse me, darling, I just need to have a quick word with Lucy."

"I'll come with you. I haven't spoken to her tonight."

"No, Gabe." Christy took a deep breath, and swallowed the urge to tell him that he might have spoken to Lucy if he hadn't been trailing after her like a dog on a lead. "It's private, darlin'. Girls' talk. You're needed as a host, anyways. Why don't you go rescue Mrs. Newton-Bowles? She surely looks like she could use some rescuing."

Christy stepped quickly across to the bench. "Lucy, could I trouble you for a moment, honey? I need to ask your advice about something in the garden. Don't any the rest of you move an inch; I'll be real cross if I find you've left."

"You see, Charles?" Lucy said, rising, "You see how many people value my opinion?" She looped her arm through Christy's, and allowed her hostess to lead her through the gate to the orchard.

"You shouldn't be bothering with the garden when you're on holiday, Christy; Maggie never does, and Mr. Gordon has it all in hand."

"Well," Christy drawled, "it isn't exactly the *garden* I wanted to discuss." She halted, sighed, ran a hand through her hair, and looked uncomfortable.

"What's the matter?" Lucy asked.

"I don't want to speak out of place; I'm sure it's none of my business . . . I just wanted to ask you something about the Callahans . . . There was something I heard this evening. . . ."

"Go on," Lucy urged, her curiosity heightened. "I'm all ears."

"I don't want you to think I'm a gossip . . ." Christy stalled. "Maybe I just shouldn't say anything, being a stranger here. Maybe I should just button my lip."

"You can trust me to tell you if there's any truth in it or not. I've heard all the gossip there is to hear about anyone and everyone. And I *never* tell." Lucy zipped up her mouth in the gesture of an eight-year-old.

"Are the Callahans happy? Somebody here tonight kind of suggested that maybe they weren't."

Lucy gave a peal of laughter. "Is that what's been worrying you? Of course they're not!" She continued to stroll through the orchard. Christy felt a frisson of something—exoneration, pleasure, anticipation all mixed up—tremble through her body, and then Lucy continued. "Nobody here is *happy*, Christy. It's such a simply dreadful thing to be. Desperately unfashionable. It's all very well for you new Americans to be happy and satisfied with your lot, but not for us. My God! If we were happy, there'd be nothing to complain about, and we'd all be in a dreadful pickle. No; the preferred range of emotions in England runs from the dismally discontented to the dementedly depressed. That's the way we like it. Born cynics can't ever be just *happy*." She giggled again, and Christy almost stamped her foot in irritation.

"Lucy, I'm serious. You know, I feel like I know them, that I really care about them, and I'm worried. Maybe they have marital problems?"

"Oh my God, Christy, everyone has marital problems! It's an inevitable conclusion of getting married. I mean, I'm not suggesting that you and the Gorgeous Gabe have marital problems, because you are clearly the perfect couple, but for the rest of us poor mortals, it's all par for the course. Do you know the single biggest thing that a woman has to give up when she decides to marry?"

"Her independence?"

"No—her brain." Lucy's laughter rang across the orchard. "Oliver told me that."

"Well, if you say there's nothing to worry about, then I guess that means everything's fine. I wanted to ask you something else. Oliver mentioned a friend of his he thought I might look up. I think her name was Louise, but I'm not sure. Do you know anybody called Louise?"

"Certainly. Louise O'Dougherty—she was captain of lacrosse at school, we all idolised her, simply worshipped her, and then I saw her at a wedding last year and my dear, you could have knocked me down with a feather—a frump through and through and broad as a row of terraced houses. Could it be her?"

"No. Any other Louises?"

"Let me think. I know a bonkers woman called Louise Sharp. Dog mad. Breeds Jack Russells. I think Ol and Maggie bought Snuff from her. But she's not what I would call a friend; she smells dreadfully—eau de pedigree chum, I imagine. I can't believe that Ol would have wanted you to meet her."

"Maybe it wasn't Louise. Maybe I've just got the name wrong. I thought Oliver said that you had introduced him to her—maybe last year," Christy said cunningly, and played her joker, "and he said she was very pretty, and married. Any ideas? I feel so dumb having forgotten her name."

Lucy thought for a while. "I've introduced so many people to Mags and Ol—God, who do I know who's really good looking? Natasha, maybe, but she's never been married—and Ol took a violent dislike to her . . . I have a sweet Italian friend called Leonora; her husband is one of the thrillingest, dashingest men I know, barring Oliver; she married very well, as they say—but I don't think Oliver was here the last time they came to stay. She only met Maggie. Did Ol say anything about this woman's husband?"

"Not much. I got the feeling he didn't like him real well. He said he was a bit of an oaf."

"Isn't this exciting—just like playing twenty questions: Animal, vegetable, or mineral? I just love games, don't you? No, I'll be serious—just let me think. No, my dear, I can't for the life of me—" She snapped her fingers. "Yes I can! I've got it! You mean Jenny! You're thinking of Jenny Campbell!"

"That could be the name; what does she look like?"

"Oh Lord—simply horribly lovely. I think she was a model before she married. She has a great lion's-mane of blond hair—highlighted I'm sure, immensely tall, *huge* knockers for which I personally *loathed* her, and an absolute berk of a husband. Oliver said that three-quarters of Steven Campbell were despicable, and the last quarter was pitiful. He *is* jolly well off, though. They've gone to their villa in France for the summer, or I would have introduced you."

"I'm sure Oliver said this lady was dark haired. And I don't think she lives locally."

"Not Jenny then." Lucy tapped a finger against her forehead. "Think, think . . . Susie? Not really what I would call a beauty. Bit of a nose problem, poor girl. Ginny, *perhaps,* but Ol plays cricket with her husband. . . . Christy, I'll simply have to go home and scour my address book. I just can't think of anyone offhand who fits the bill."

"Please, don't go to any trouble. Forget I mentioned it. It really isn't important, and it's probably too late for me to get in touch with her."

"No, it's intriguing. Beautiful, dark, married to an oaf, and not from around here, and I introduced them. Why don't you just call Ol and ask him?"

"Oh, I feel bad about leaving it so late in the day, and if she's in London or something, I don't want to feel obliged to have to go visit with her, and I'd have to if I asked Oliver again."

"That's true. I could always call Ol for you?"

"Please don't do that, Lucy. Then I'd feel even more obliged to follow it up, and I really don't have the time. I'd rather spend our last month with our friends right here."

"Aren't you sweet? Well, I won't call, but I'll have a look in the little black book anyway, just for the fun of it. Now I must go scrape Charles off your lawn."

Christy really didn't mind at all that she hadn't identified Louise. As she had told Lucy, it really wasn't important who Louise was, if she was anyone at all. The only thing that was important was that Oliver had felt about Louise the way Christy longed for a man to feel about her.

#

A postcard of Holden Beach, to Peter Forbes, the *Daily Telegraph:*

> *This is the life, eh Peter? Sun, sand, and stunning six-foot blondes, and the odd bouncing brunette. Any news from Bujev-ski? I haven't heard a word from him, and think we should go for this. Give him a shove, could you? Love to Sarah—she's doing a bloody good job on my copy—doesn't cut a word. Give her a pat on the back from me, would you?*
>
> *Cheers,*
> *Oliver*

THIS WAS THE WORST VACATION THAT GABE MCCARTHY HAD EVER spent. It was far, far worse than that nightmare summer when he and half his football team at Wharton had rented a house down on the Florida Keys and got mindlessly trashed every night for a month, smashed up two cars, and then faced the humiliation of having to ask his parents to drive down and bail them all out of prison. When Christy had coaxed him and cajoled him into taking extended leave from the office to come to England, he had fully expected it to be a second honeymoon. Okay, so a holiday with a five-year-old and a nanny in tow wasn't exactly a conventional honeymoon, but he had had a vision of leisurely family picnics, and Christy looking like something from a Merchant Ivory film, and family games, and frolics, and romance. . . . Right up until last night's party, he'd been hopeful. He'd even listened to Christy asking the lady with the orange hair about the best picnic spots in the area, but when he'd reminded her about it in bed that night, saying what a great idea it would be to go and explore a different location with Jake each day, Christy had rolled over onto her side, turning her back on him, and said that she hated picnics. She'd said it in a voice that meant he ought to *know* she hated picnics, a really deadpan, bored voice, and when he'd remonstrated that she'd organised hundreds of the darn things back home in Lawrenceville and at the beach, she'd just snapped his head off, and said that they weren't at home *now*, and she was damn glad they weren't, and that it was precisely because she did it all the time at home that she didn't want to do it here, and finally she wouldn't give a hoot if they never went on a picnic again. Gabe had never before had to deal with Christy being really short-tempered, and his inexperience led him to make a fatal error.

If Gabe had told her to stop acting like a spoiled baby, if he had told her to snap out of it and stop ruining their holiday, and if he had told her she was behaving like a bitch, and that he wasn't going to stand for it, there might have been a way back. But he followed his regular path, straight ahead, not looking to the sides or behind him. He put out one hesitant hand, stroked her hair with the most gentle of caresses, and laid his other hand tentatively on her thigh. When she made no acknowledgement of his approach, he slipped his hand between her legs.

"What are you doing, Gabe?" She looked at him, and although she forced herself to smile, her eyes were cold enough to skate on.

Gabe didn't say anything; he found it impossible to state the obvious, and was surprised by her blatant rejection. Normally when Christy didn't want to make love, she said she had a headache, or she fell fast asleep as soon as she climbed into bed. He removed his hand as if he'd been burnt. "You must be exhausted, darling. It was a swell party." Maybe she just needed a good night's sleep. He reached up to turn off the overhead light. Christy flicked it back on at once.

"D'you mind?" she said. "I'm not tired. I just want to read for a while."

The next-to-last thing Christy wanted to do was sleep, at least not tucked up all neat and cosy with Gabe. She had been flying after the party, elated and full of excitement, but when they had finally closed the door on Edward, who was the last to leave, and Gabe had put his arms around her, her mood had collapsed like a spoiled soufflé. She had undressed and brushed her hair, spoiling for a fight, while Gabe had just padded softly around saying what a great party it had been. She scowled at him in the mirror. It could have been a whole hell of a lot greater if he hadn't dogged her every step. Christy felt tight and wound up and ready to explode, and every move Gabe made pushed her closer to that point. Then she scowled at herself. She didn't like what she saw in the mirror. She had spent the holiday trying to be good to Gabe, really trying, but over the last few days he had become a source of constant and intense irritation. Every word he said, every expression on his kind, familiar face infuriated her. She couldn't take a step without his asking if she was okay, and had everything she wanted. Christy knew what the problem was; she was tired of maintaining her performance as the perfect, happy wife; the strain of pretending that life was just dandy was becoming unbearable. All she really wanted was some time out—a chance, maybe just the remaining few weeks of their trip, to have some fun, and play at being young and free again. She wanted to be with a different kind of man—at least in her imagination—a dangerous, mysterious man, a man who could make her lose her reason. Gabe was never going to be that sort of man; he would always be solid and immutable. Years ago, that had given her great security, but at this moment it drove her to an extreme of frustration. She remembered her mama saying that the mark of a true lady was that she'd make sure her drapes were spring-cleaned even if she were on her deathbed. If a real lady was going to go mad, then she went mad discreetly, and with spotless linen. Christy was prepared to summon up every last ounce of discipline she possessed to keep up appearances, but in the privacy of their bedroom, she could no longer stand it. All the time she knew that this was her problem, Gabe was blameless, and innocent, and she didn't want to hurt him. Nonetheless, she couldn't bear Gabe to touch her. In less than four weeks they would be getting on the plane, and she would resume her normal life, and she was prepared to do all in her power to please him once they got back home, if only he could understand that she needed the next four weeks for herself. Four weeks of being wild and reckless would sustain her for life. But if Gabe wasn't even aware of her fantasies, it was unlikely that he would be able to give her the chance to indulge them. And there was no way she could tell him what was in her heart. It was like hearing a judge sentence you to life, and it was going to take all her nerve to win a successful appeal. She reached under the bed to find her copy of *A Sad Affair*, and tried to forget about Gabe:

I suppose you are waiting for me to describe what making love to Louise was like? Readers seem to expect to be told the nitty gritty of sex these days. I suppose you want to know what it was like that first time; to know the texture of her skin, the way she smelt, exactly where we touched each other and how long it lasted and exactly how many degrees the earth moved? Well, I'm sorry to disappoint you, but I'm not going to do it. I'm not saying you're all a bunch of prurient voyeurs, you understand—I mean no offence, and it makes no difference to me how you get your kicks. But it's a private business, isn't it? All I am prepared to say is that it was very different from the other sexual encounters I have had. You see, without boasting, I know that I'm a good lover, and it doesn't have anything to do with being good looking or having a large cock or finding G-spots or any of that crap. What I offer is something a little more simple, but much more unusual. I listen to women. Up until Louise, this was the one tactic I religiously employed, and believe me, it always worked. You could say I'm a manipulative bastard, you could say that I do this deliberately to make women emotionally and physically dependent on me, and you wouldn't be far wrong. Anyway, if you want to improve your pulling power, it's something to bear in mind. Give it a whirl, and let me know if it works for you. I can't do it any longer.

Louise was different, because I wasn't in control of myself, let alone her. I wasn't conscious of what I was doing. All I was aware of was that it was bliss being with her, even if it was only for a moment, and if you asked me what the sex was like, I wouldn't know, and I wouldn't give a hoot if it was bad so long as it carried on forever. Loving Louise made me feel alive. If you are not in love with the woman you are in bed with, then however active and busy and technically proficient your sex life, it doesn't mean anything. It will just slide off you without leaving a mark. Making love to Louise was like being hit by a cyclone, or a storm surge, or some other sort of natural catastrophe from which you can't emerge unscathed.

That's why I'm not going to tell you more about it. It is too frightening. Anyway, you've all got imaginations, haven't you? You've all had sex at least once when it's been so good that you

*can't describe it. Just dig deep into your memory and find that
time, and slot it in here. I'll leave a few blank lines for you to
fill in. And if you haven't any idea of the kind of experience that
I'm talking about, then I pity you, you poor bastard, but you're
not going to share mine. Understood?*

Christy wanted to faint with love, die for love, be hurt by love;
to be overwhelmed by the combined force of love and sex. Love
and sex with Gabe left her standing all too firmly on her feet. Oliver
was right. It should be chronic. It should be fatal.

The next day Christy began a campaign to keep Gabe away from
her. She stopped talking to him. She blamed herself for her feelings
far more than she blamed him and told herself that this was all for
Gabe's own good. She knew that she was becoming obsessed with
Oliver Callahan to the point where she feared for her sanity. If Gabe
was driving her crazy, then she had to avoid him for his own sake.
She could just about maintain everything on an even keel so long
as she kept him at an isolated distance until they returned home.
Her dissatisfaction was inspired by her musing on the way things
might have been if she had married a different kind of man—a man
like Oliver Callahan, for example. Oliver was a man who would have
taken the lead, who would have stood up to her, and matched her
dynamism with his own. Life with Oliver would certainly never be
dull, and on top of that, he was a man who clearly understood a
woman's needs. He was that rare combination of a man who knew
how women thought and felt, and remained wholly masculine. He
listened to women, but he remained a lad. It was a lethal combination. All the chaps bemoaned Oliver's absence at the forthcoming
village cricket match. Everyone at the party had talked about him
with fondness and admiration, chuckling at the pranks he had pulled,
respectful of his career achievements, grateful for the role he played
in the local community. In addition to all these tributes, Christy
knew something about Oliver that all his closest friends and
neighbours didn't. That he had been passionately in love, that despite his written denials of nobility, he had sacrificed his own happiness for the good of his family, and had spent the last year in a state
of loss. If anything, it was the nobility of his sacrifice that drew
Christy to him.

Christy hoped she, too, would be able to make that sacrifice, for her husband and child, if called on. Right now, all she was doing was playing a game, and there was no way it could step out of the novel and into her real life. She looked again at the last page of *A Sad Affair*:

Last night I went alone to see Ballo in Maschera. *I had never seen it before, and God knows what made me go. I hate opera. I always have. If you're not familiar with the plot, the hero, Riccardo, is in love with his best friend's wife, and she with him. At the end of the opera he is shot at a masked ball because he cannot stop himself from talking to the woman of his life. I think he is a lucky man. In some ways I have died, too, because Louise was the thing that let me live—she was my oxygen, and without her I am gasping, dried up at the very gills. I have been thinking about her a great deal this week, partly because it is her birthday, and partly because I think about her a great deal all the time. Sometimes I feel so haunted by her that I think I am going a little mad. There are so many things about her I still see—sitting in my office I can smell the talc she used after a bath, I can still see her footprints clear in the white powder on the bathroom floor, I can see the colour of the lipstick she wore imprinted on cigarette ends. Clearing up and throwing away the debris of our relationship was the hardest thing I ever did—harder even than saying goodbye to her. I wanted to keep those footprints forever, that thin, fragile line between the ball and the heel ... Everything about Louise is vibrant and packed with life. I see her as a radiant young girl, and I see her when she's forty, and I see her when she's sixty, and in all these magical encounters I am beside her, with her, and then I tell myself that I will never actually see her again, and it hurts so much that I don't think I can survive it. And then I remind myself that I'm not really alive anyway, so I can survive anything so long as I stay half-asleep. I have never known anybody else who can instil the spirit of importance, or occasion, or vitality or beauty or sheer hell to any situation the way Louise does so effortlessly. When I took her to Rome, she changed everything about it for me, and we were only there for two days, and I had lived there for six years. I don't know if the vision I possessed when I was with her was because of her, or because of being in love. I believe that her gift for bringing life to dead things—to me most of all—is something unique to her, and maybe everybody recognises it, but I hope not; I hope it was my private and secret discovery, something I will never have to share with some stranger. Love made me feel ecstatic and exhilarated—I saw everything in heightened colours, and now, not with her, however busy and active I am, I can't seem to see anything anymore, I don't seem to react to anything. The whole of life, all of it, the family and the work and the world, seem to take place around me without making any impact at all.*

I have been reading Proust this week, and he seems a sorry excuse for a man to me. His vision of love is completely self-interested. The selfish aspects of love tower above anything self-denying, and I can see no links between his experience of love and my own. But who am I to talk of self-denial? When Louise made her final offer, I had no sense of choice. I couldn't distinguish between what I should allow myself to accept and what I should force myself to leave—they were one and the same, and inseparable, so Louise made the choice for me. Most of the time, I think about what Louise denied herself. In my blackest moments, I could vomit with fear at the thought that perhaps she wasn't denying herself—perhaps she really wanted to leave me. Perhaps it was just a game to her, and she tired of it. I dread that feeling most of all, because it means that in just a few months my trust in her has weakened and has been corrupted by my own jealousy, just as Louise predicted it would. Now I just sit here like a disabled fool, not thinking at all, tapping away at the keyboard, and writing rubbish that I don't want anybody to read anyway.

I want someone to tell me what love is, but whatever they tell me, I know it will not do for me, or for you either.

Maggie had spent a wonderful day in Orlando with Patrick. They had decided to book rooms at the Hyatt Orlando, which sat in the middle of the airport terminal, to minimise the risk of either of them missing their early-morning flights. As they really just wanted to be with each other, rather than seeing the sights, it made sense to stay at the airport. In practise, it turned out to be a wonderful if eccentric choice. After dinner, they retired to the hotel's swimming-pool, which was open air and on the tenth floor. They spent two hours sitting in the whirlpool section, occasionally managing a length or

two, and admiring the night sky, lit by the runway lights so that it
ranged between hues of orangey-pink to dark aubergine. Every few
minutes they could hear the roar of a plane taking off or landing,
but they couldn't see them. It created a surreal effect—the hot pool,
the slightly cooler but still balmy air, the palm trees surrounding
them, and the incredible noise. They had had an indulgent time
catching up on news and gossiping about old friends.

Patrick, as always, was keen to have news of Oliver.

"So how is His Gorgeousness, Maggie sweet? Has he slithered
his way out of the closet yet?"

"You'll never give up hope, will you, Patrick? It's not exactly
flattering to me, is it? The idea that being married to me could turn
Ol gay."

"Oh, I don't know about that—I meant it as flattering . . . I
mean, if I were married to you, I bet you'd be able to turn me
straight, and that would be much more difficult than doing the
reverse to Oliver."

"You say the sweetest things." Maggie pushed his head under
the water.

"Seriously though," Patrick said, spluttering, "how is the dear
man?"

"He's fine. He's written some quite good stuff since we've been
here, and it looks like he's in the running for a telly series, a travel
doc on the Southern States—"

"—the cameras will *love* him. They'll just lap him up. He'll be
God."

"C'mon, Patrick! Don't insult him! He sees himself as the whole
damn Trinity in one. Ol the Father, Ol the Son—"

"And Ol the Holy Ghost—or Host," Patrick finished, crossing
himself.

"And won't he just revel in it. He's not the most modest of men."

"Praise the Lord. I hate modest men. There are so many of them
who have every reason to be modest, and aren't, I can't stand it
when the yummy ones are modest. It's such a waste."

"Have no fears about Ol."

"And are you two thinking of producing any more little Callahans? Spreading the seed, so to speak?"

"God, Patrick! I'm bogged down enough as it is. If I have any
more children I'll turn into a zombie. You know, sometimes, in the
middle of when I'm meant to be working, when I'm supposed to

be concentrating on some serious topic, or as serious as I ever get to do, I find myself singing 'Piggy on the Railway.' It's that bad."

"Can't say I know that one."

"I'm not surprised." Only those who have lived in close proximity to a toddler *would* know it, Maggie mused. "You're not missing much. It's a piece of crap. Anyway, it's part of the inescapable face of parenthood. It begins the slow but ceaseless process of decline during which your brain and stomach muscles turn to mush, and your most pressing decision is whether to buy first- or second-class stamps. Sometimes I go shopping and spend half an hour staring at the cereal shelves wondering if Lily will have a seizure if I only buy bran flakes rather than buying Coco-Pops." Patrick began to laugh, and Maggie grinned, but continued vehemently. "It's not a joke, Pat! It's the absolute truth. Nobody tells you about it when you first get pregnant, because it's one of those enormous conspiracies. . . . Every mother in the world wants to see every other woman in the same mindless boat."

"And what about the fathers? I can't see Ol getting in a state about cornflakes."

"No. Parenthood affects fathers differently. If at all. They either regress and become children themselves, or they become masters of the art of discreetly sloping off. I have to admit, Ol's not too bad—in fact, he's pretty good, though don't ever tell him I said that, but even with Ol the children come second. I mean, he loves them madly—he dotes on them—but he still sees himself as a single entity, and he still measures himself in terms of his career, and not his family."

"You sound the faintest touch bitter, Maggie."

"Do I?" Maggie pulled herself out of the pool and sat on the edge, kicking her feet in the water. "How very unattractive of me. I don't know, Pat. We've had problems. Big ones. I guess everybody does. It's nothing I can't handle—I think. It's probably just that my whole idea of marriage was based on something out of a teen magazine, and I didn't anticipate any bad bits. That's what Edward says, at least."

"Edward? Who's he? Your therapist?"

"No—Edward Arabin. You know? Our neighbour? You've met him."

"Oh yeah, the really tall auctioneer. I quite fancied him."

"You did? What a coincidence. We clearly have exactly the same taste in men."

"I've always thought you had good taste, Mags. It's just a shame when you get there first. So tell me about these hiccups in the Garden of Eden."

"I can't, Patrick. The more I think about it, the more terrified I get that we're just not going to make it. I think it's better right now just to pretend there's nothing wrong, and concentrate on the good times. There really isn't that much wrong, I guess. Honest."

"Fair enough. So. Does Oliver want more kids?"

"He wants about ten." Maggie's face was a portrait of dread.

"What are you going to settle on?"

"I guess three. Four if pushed. But first, I'm going to get my career back on the rails, and then we'll do about something about it."

"Have you got any idea what to do?"

"To get pregnant? I think I've got the hang of it now, thank you, Patrick. . . ."

"Still the same old smart arse, aren't you, Mags? No, you berk—work. I'm talking about work."

"I've got a couple of ideas, but nothing I want to talk about right now. So. Tell me. The new man. Tall, dark, and handsome? A lawyer? Spill."

"He's blond. And gorgeous. He's an advertising executive—originally from Glasgow, so he's got the most heavenly voice, and he really melts my butter as they say over here. . . ."

"He sounds fantastic. Would you introduce me to him?"

"No I would not. It's not that I don't trust him, you understand, but I don't trust you."

"Beast! *You're* one of the very few people that I do trust. . . ."

Maggie landed at Fayetteville Airport, where Oliver was due to pick her up, feeling rejuvenated and happy to be coming back to her family. She hung around at the gate with her bag, but there was no sign of Oliver. This didn't surprise Maggie—if there was anything one could rely on with Oliver, it was that he would be late. Just as she had ordered a coffee, she heard an announcement play over the public address system:

*　　*　　*

"Could arriving passenger Alec Bones please meet their party at Door C on the departures level?"

Maggie smiled. She hadn't heard that name in an age. As she approached the meeting place, she saw Lily hurtling towards her, arms outstretched, and behind her came Oliver, Arthur in his arms, running nearly as quickly and shouting nearly as loudly as his daughter. At that moment, as Maggie saw her children's delight and Oliver's characteristic lopsided grin, she silenced her gnawing fear about her marriage and began to count her blessings. She came up with the grand total of two. One of them, Lily, leapt into her arms.

"Mummy, Mummy—how did you know where we were? I thought you'd never find us! You came home—and we missed you, and Arthur's been so dreadfully naughty, but *I* haven't, because I'm a girl and girls aren't naughty, are they . . ." Oliver kissed Maggie over their children's heads at the very moment that Arthur began to wail, for the first time aware, now that his mother was back, that she had in fact left him. "And Daddy's got a surprise for you at home—but it's a secret, so I can't tell . . . But, Mummy, how did you know we were here? You didn't tell me."

"Come on, everyone, into the car or we'll get towed. Maggie, look a little bit crippled, could you? I told the big cop outside that you were in a wheelchair, and if he's still hanging around you are going to have to fake a miraculous recovery. . . ." Oliver ushered his family outside, while Maggie tried simultaneously to comfort Arthur, answer Lily, and limp convincingly.

"I knew where you were because Daddy had them read out a message for me—they announced it on a loudspeaker, darling—"

"But Daddy said that, and then they didn't say your name. I was listening all the time, and they didn't say it. Your name's Callahan, like mine."

"I know, darling, but Daddy used a different name—he used his secret name, just for fun."

"What name? I didn't hear it." Lily was becoming petulant as Oliver chucked her into the car seat and wrestled her arms through the straps.

"The lady read out a message for Alec Bones, sweetheart."

"I've never heard anybody call you *that*. *That's* a silly name. Alec Bones. It's silly."

"Only Daddy uses it, darling. He used to call me that before you were born. It *is* a silly name, you're right. . . ."

Maggie's face relaxed as the car pulled out of the airport. There was something about having all her family within the close confines of a car on an open road that comforted her, and Oliver's spontaneous use of the old nickname had raised her spirits. Oliver, removed from his habitual circle of friends and cronies and detached from his professional life, was rather more attentive than she had seen him for years. Oliver's "surprise" was a dining room full of flowers and dinner for two in the oven, and you could have knocked Maggie down with much less than a feather. Oliver had very rarely cooked dinner for her, other than an annual cheese soufflé, which he was inclined to overcook. He occasionally stretched to getting an Indian take-away and keeping it warm if Maggie was coming home late, but to walk into a kitchen and find it spotlessly clean, a table laid, and a three-course meal catered and the kids out of sight had the same disorienting effect as walking into the Hall of Mirrors. And after dinner . . . Well. Oliver had always been "good in bed," he'd always worked hard at it, but that night he made love to Maggie with a hunger that had by no means been sated by his culinary endeavours. Maggie wondered what it was all about. She would have liked to believe that it was appreciation, but thought that guilt was a far more probable motive.

If it hadn't been for a stray cat, or rather, if it hadn't been for the freak combination of a stray cat, a milk bottle, and a prank doorbell-ringer, Maggie and Oliver might just have returned home with a new sense of commitment to each other. Maggie might have come back to Bockhampton determined not to dwell on the past. Oliver might have come back to Bockhampton with a new sense of commitment in his life, and might have decided to stick to the written word rather than risk a foray onto the small screen. Christy and Gabe might have arrived back at Oak Ridge to find a scratch or two on their pine kitchen table, and a broken plate, but otherwise unchanged lives. Christy might have recorded the Wiltshire venture as a broadening experience, or just a bit of a lark, and might have sent Christmas cards to the Callahans and the Wickham-Edwardeses for three, even four years to come. Christy might have filled her time organising voluntary work at the local hospital, and that might have filled the gap in her life. Perhaps Lindy Richards would have given Christy a good talking to, and maybe Christy would have listened, and perhaps Gabe would have been made senior partner at Winkler Barrows, senior partner at Winkler, Barrows & McCarthy even, and perhaps Christy would have been satisfied. Perhaps Christy would have arranged another house swap—this time in Italy with a retired Tuscan couple, or perhaps they would have bought a third home in Maine, and avoided the summer heat there. But there *was* a ring at a doorbell, and a cat, and a bottle of semi-skimmed milk. . . .

On the morning of Wednesday, August 10th, Gillian Bujevski was halfway though getting dressed when the doorbell rang. Her bedroom window overlooked the street entrance to their Hampstead house, but when she looked out, she couldn't see anyone except a couple of young layabouts on the other side of the road. She sat at a prettily draped dressing table in her underwear and began her makeup, which she always did before putting her clothes on. The doorbell rang again. Again, she could see no one, unless they were screened by the porch. She could, however, see a courier bike parked slightly down the road. When the bell rang a third time, she put down her lipstick, with only her lower lip painted, cursed her husband's constant courier deliveries, flung a dressing gown over her bra and pants, and ran downstairs in her new Charles Jourdan high heels. As she opened the front door, a cat with some godawful contraption tied to its tail shot across the doorstep, overturning the two milk bottles that Gillian hadn't yet brought inside. She heard a tinkling of broken glass and a high-pitched laughter coming from the kids across the road, and she stepped forward to give them a piece of her mind. Her first step took her virgin leather-soled shoe into a puddle of milk and she skidded, fell heavily and awkwardly, and fractured her left tibia in two places and the fibula in one. A shaft of bone came through her Elbeo stockings, and there was an awful lot of blood amongst the pool of milk.

Danny Bujevski got a call while filming that his wife was at the Princess Grace Hospital and feeling extremely sorry for herself. He spoke to her orthopaedic consultant, who confirmed that her leg injuries were serious, and that the Bujevskis would, regrettably, be forced to postpone their three-week holiday in Corfu, scheduled to start next Monday. Danny Bujevski didn't like having his arrangements altered whatever the reason, and he didn't like having his production schedule mucked around, and he didn't like the idea of having three weeks' booked holiday stuck in Hampstead tending to his bedridden and doubly plastered wife. He had proposed to Gillian what seemed like a lifetime ago, when her uncle just happened to be on the BBC board of governors. By the time they got back from honeymoon, Uncle Robert had retired to the South of France. Sod's law. He was about to wrap this shoot, and if he could bring forward his next project scheduled for mid-September, he would still be left with a gap in his books for October and November. On the spur of the moment, he rang a number for Oliver Callahan in Squitsville, North Carolina. If he could get the blasted hack back in time to put forward a detailed proposal to the suits at Channel Four, there was a chance that he wouldn't be assigned to some dog-drivel travel series to keep him busy. He left a warm and heartfelt message for Oliver asking him if there was any chance of his nipping back to England pronto pronto, as they had a chance—a slim one—at getting the show an early slot, and he wanted to run with it.

A postcard of Disney World, Orlando, Florida, to Edward Arabin, the Old Barn, Compton Purlew:

Darling Eddie,
  Here I am in ultimate fantasy land. Came to Florida to meet up with Patrick Steeple—remember him? He says he fancies you. Back home tomorrow to the family. The holiday's flown—we've only got three weeks left, and then it's back to humdrum old Wiltshire. Not that you're humdrum, my friend. Hope you're well . . . Thinking of you.

  Love,
  Mags

  P.S. I hate writing postcards, don't you?

IT WILL COME AS NO SURPRISE THAT OLIVER WANTED TO RUN WITH it as well, and that Maggie was persuaded to stagger alongisde. As Bujevski had agreed to stump up the cost of a return ticket from North Carolina to London, Oliver had no earthly reason to delay his departure, and, as he explained to Maggie, the sooner he went, the sooner he would be back. He'd be gone five days at the outside, which would still leave them nearly two weeks of frolicking on the beaches of North Carolina.

Thirty-six hours after Bujevski's phone call, Oliver found himself sitting in the producer's Hampstead sitting room, drinking coffee laced with whisky, and arguing about the programme concept.

"I think it would be catchy if you travelled with some kind of gimmick—you know, went round the Southeast coast on a bicycle,

184

or a horse or something; if we're going to sell this, it's got to be different. I don't want any BBC2 talking heads crap about the history of how Charleston was built, or race riots or crap like that. Maybe a bicycle is the answer. It would make you a kind of *personality;* a sort of semi-political, semi-travel show, free-wheeling kind of guy. It has a nineties feel about it."

"I don't ride bicycles. I haven't been on a bicycle since I was eight years old." Oliver closed his eyes, his forehead wrinkled in pain. "It's a big country, you know, Danny. We're talking about roughly a thousand miles if we just stick to the coastal Carolinas and don't touch Georgia. Do you realise how long it would take me to cycle that distance? I'd qualify for my bus pass if it didn't kill me first."

"Okay, okay; maybe a motorbike then." Oliver winced. "A Harley?" Oliver blanched. "You've got to help me out here, Oliver. You've got a lot riding on this, and so have I. We've got to package you as a kind of Keith Floyd of the travel world, you see what I'm saying?"

Oliver leant close to the producer, his hands spread wide in appeal. "The thing is, Danny; the thing *is,* I'm a serious *journalist.* I write *serious* copy; I am a serious political and social *commentator.* Are you telling me that what you envision is my riding around the Southern states with a cameraman riding pillion, and when we find some poor black down-and-out lying in the gutter in Savannah, my saying, 'Now, Clive, let's have a nice big juicy mouth-watering close-up of this product of Southern racism' whilst I sit back and chug a Coors Lite?"

"Not exactly that, Oliver, but you're getting the picture. We need an angle. We need to see a personality on screen, or you're not going to get the viewing figures after the first episode. We're talking about four—maybe, if we're lucky, six—half-hour episodes. Two to three hours is a hell of a long time to expect Sharon in Bromsgrove to watch *serious social commentary* about a place she's never going to bloody visit."

"Then we're going to have to think of something else, aren't we, Danny?"

"You're going to have to think of something else, or I'm going to have to think of *someone* else. . . . In fact, Floyd's no bad idea. That way we can get the personality, the travel, and the cooking viewers all in one bag. . . ."

"Give me a break, for Christ's sake, Bujevski. I got off a plane eight hours ago, after a fucking nightmare flight—I notice your enthusiasm for this project didn't stretch to a business-class seat—and after six hours' talk you're telling me you want to replace me with Keith Floyd? *Floyd*, for fuck's sake? Just let me sleep on it and I'll come up with something. Okay?"

Danny Bujevski looked smug. Dealing with the talent was just like dealing with a clapped-out mule. It required a combination of carrot and stick, and in his opinion, Oliver Callahan had had more than his fair share of carrot.

"Sleep on it, Oliver, by all means. But I want you to dream big, okay? Dream Cadillacs, horse-drawn carriages, skateboards for all I care, but come up with something good. Something different. Come back here tomorrow with an idea, okay? Or I'm going to have to pull the plug."

"Fan-bloody-tastic."

Oliver went back to his studio flat in Notting Hill Gate and collapsed into bed. Just before his eyes closed, he managed to thump out Edward Arabin's telephone number.

"Eddie? It's Oliver."

"Oliver! Enjoying the sunshine?"

"No. It's pissing down. I'm in London."

"What the hell are you doing there?"

"Something's come up about this TV idea; they begged me to drop everything and rush back for a production meeting." Whatever his current crisis, Oliver wasn't going to let on to Edward that there might not even be a TV series. If Bujevski dumped him, Oliver could always say he'd withdrawn because the concept was too shallow.

"Any chance of you coming down here, Ol? It's the big match tomorrow."

"Big match?" Oliver's brain was battling with exhaustion, depression, hangover, and jet lag.

"Come on, Ol! Compton Purlew versus the West Indies?"

"What the hell are you talking about?"

"Thwack of leather on willow? The cricket, man! We're up against Curtis' eleven tomorrow at two-thirty."

"Oh, God, yes, I remember. Cricket. I don't know. I'm meant to be meeting my producer tomorrow, but it's tempting . . . Could I get a game?"

"Of course you could—either for the village or you could be the only white man on Curtis' side. I think you should play for the village, though; it might improve our odds a bit."

"Not the way I'm feeling, it won't."

"Look; just go to sleep now, catch the train up in the morning, I'll pick you up at the station, we'll pop into The Fox for a pint and a bite, and then pad up. What d'you say, old man?"

"You're on. I wouldn't mind meeting the McCarthys, anyway, and I always get my best ideas on the train. I'll be on the ten forty-five from Waterloo, okay?"

"Excellent. I'll let the troops know that the cavalry's coming."

As sleep overcame him, Oliver was still working on the lie he would tell Bujevski to explain his no-show. It was going to have to be a good one.

Edward dropped in on Christy on his way home, to check that she hadn't regretted her offer to make the team tea for the match. Compton Purlew normally paid Mrs. Mason two pounds fifty a head for rolling out stale jam sandwiches and a couple of sponge cakes from Tesco's, so they had leapt at Christy's offer to do it all for free. Edward found Christy in the kitchen baking batches of corn bread and making a minted chicken and watercress salad.

"Hello, fair lady. Excuse me for barging in, but the door was open and the fearsome hounds seem to be off duty."

Boomer raised his head a good inch off the kitchen floor on the off chance that the newcomer just happened to be carrying a plate of roast beef sandwiches. Boomer dedicated his life to the pursuit of food rather than the pursuit of love. He managed an act of grand larceny every two to three days—a chicken here, a lamb chop there. When he saw Edward he farted in greeting; he was a magnanimous dog, and bore no lasting grudge against Edward for being empty-handed.

"Edward! How grand of you to come by! I'm just finishing things off for tomorrow—I'll do most of it in the morning, the strawberry shortcake and all, so it's real fresh, but I thought I'd get these done now."

"Smells delicious. Divine. I just hope we get to field first."

"Pardon me?"

"Field first. It's bloody hard to field after eating the sort of tea you're laying on."

Christy laughed, and continued stirring. "Oh, it's nothing special; just good, old-fashioned homestyle cooking."

"You can come and cook in my home anytime you like." Edward tasted a sliver of chicken. "Anytime. Oh, Christy? Guess who just phoned me?"

"Tell me! Someone exciting?" Her eyes sparkled.

"Oliver. Oliver Callahan."

Christy blushed faintly. She had been thinking about Oliver just as Edward walked into the kitchen. This was no great coincidence, seeing as she thought about him most of the time these days.

"How are they all doing?" Christy murmured.

"Fine, I suppose. I didn't really have a chance to ask about Mags and the vermin. Ol was exhausted." Edward stole another piece of chicken. "He's in London. He's coming down tomorrow—for the match."

The blood left Christy's cheeks, and she turned to Edward with her violet eyes wide in shock. "He's coming *here? Tomorrow?*"

"Yes. He's coming here, tomorrow, to play cricket," Edward repeated patiently. "Why on earth are you looking so dismayed? He doesn't bite."

Christy's hands were trembling as she took off her apron. "No, that's fine; I mean, I understand and all, and it's his house. I'm just surprised. I mean, we can move out, we can go to a hotel for the weekend; I'll just have to tidy things up a little. I mean, if I'd known before—"

"Relax!" Edward laughed. "He's not going to turn you out of Bockhampton. He's literally just coming to play cricket and say hello. If he wants to stay the night he can stay with me. I've got plenty of room."

"Well now, that just wouldn't be right. I mean, he'll want to be in his own house—I must get on with things, Edward, if you'll excuse me—I have so much to do to get ready for him—"

Edward took her arm and pulled her onto a seat. "Christy, believe me, you have nothing to do. It's all arranged. Oliver will stay with me, he wants to come and say hello to you, and then he's back to London and off to your house. Besides, Bockhampton's never looked better. He'll be utterly delighted."

Christy couldn't sit still. She really did have an awful lot of things to sort out, the biggest of them being getting rid of Gabe, and the least of them being getting her hair fixed.

"Edward, I must insist—I hate to be so inhospitable, but with the cooking and all . . ." Her voice died away, but her eyes beseeched him to leave, and so he did, amused by her domestic panic.

Christy was not a procrastinator; when she *had* to do something, she did it there and then without any fuss, however unpleasant it was and however badly she felt about it. Besides, she had rehearsed this particular scene in her fantasies often enough, although she had never expected to have the opportunity to play it for real. Over the past few weeks she had toyed with various ideas of how to get Oliver back to England—she had considered sending him a note, something dramatic about his novel, which might bring him running—she had even considered setting fire to Bockhampton, but she expected that would bring both the Callahans running, and she had no desire to meet Maggie. Never in her wildest dreams had she expected Oliver to turn up of his own accord, to turn up for a cricket match. She knew one thing for certain: she was never going to get another chance to meet him; she was never going to get another chance to meet a man like him. She was going to seize this chance with both hands, and nothing was going to be allowed to get in her way. She wiped her hands, steeled herself, and went into the garden to find Gabe.

Her husband was in the process of being buried in the sandpit by Jake; he was even helping to fill the buckets.

"Gabe, honey; where's Mariella?"

"I gave her the rest of the day off, darling."

"Gabe McCarthy, why on earth do we bring the girl to England and pay her to look after Jake if you're always sending her away and doing it yourself?"

"It's no trouble; I like looking after him. And you were busy in the kitchen, darling, and he should have one of us around."

"You look like a fool," Christy commented, but she was smiling.

"Hell, it feels good to be a fool sometimes, and if you can't do it in your own backyard, in front of your own family, when can you do it?"

Christy squatted down beside him, brushing the sand off his face.

"Gabe. I've had a real good idea."

"Shoot."

"You know how you were saying about taking Jake to Devon, to see where your great granddaddy came from? You mentioned it a couple of weeks ago that you'd like for him to see it."

"Sure. He came from a place called Monkokehampton, after he left Scotland, that is."

"Well, why don't you go? With Jake?"

"Sure, we could go next week. I thought you didn't feel like driving around."

"I've been thinking it about it, sweetheart"—she stroked his hair—"and I just don't think it's fair of me to get in the way of what you want to do. So I think you should go. Right away. Tomorrow."

"Christy, darlin', that's real sweet, but we can't go tomorrow. You're doing the food for this cricket thing—"

"I wasn't planning on coming with y'all, Gabe. I'll stay here and do the tea, and you and Jake can go off for a couple of days, and do your own thing. You can take Mariella to help if you like. Then I won't get in your way, and I won't feel guilty about spoiling your fun."

"But I wanted you to see the place as well as Jake."

"It's *your* heritage, Gabe. It's all about family. It's what a daddy should show to his son. I mean, he's a real McCarthy and all."

"Well, maybe. But we'll go next week, okay? Would you like that, Jake? To go on an adventure?" Jake replied by jumping up and down on his father, shrieking with excitement. Christy waited for him to settle down.

"No, Gabe. I think you should go first thing tomorrow. Then you can be back on Monday. I have other plans for next week, and then it'll be nearabout time to go home. We're running out of time here!" It was Christy who was running out of time. If her plan was to work, she had to get Gabe to agree, pack for him and Jake, finish the preparations for tea, and start preparing herself.

"I don't know, honey. We've still got at least two weeks before we go home, and anyway, we're all planning on watching the cricket game together."

"Now, Gabe. Don't you try and be nice to me. You *hate* cricket—you've said so a thousand times—you made me promise before we came that I wouldn't make you watch any darn cricket, and it's only because I got myself roped into this crazy tea thing that we said we'd go at all. Now I'm not going to let you martyr yourself just because of my behaviour. You know real well that you and Jake would be bored senseless, and it's just a waste of a perfect weekend. It's a real shame I can't come, too, but it's my own hare-brained fault."

"We could go next trip . . ."

"No. I absolutely insist." She spoke firmly yet sweetly, and shook her head vehemently so that her dark hair tumbled around her face. "I will not, I repeat, will not have my family's entire weekend ruined due to my own damn fool behaviour." She stood up, and brushed the sand off her skirt. "Now I'm going to go find a nice place for you all to stay in one of Maggie's guide books. Then I'll pack for you. I don't want you to do a thing. I'll make all the arrangements, and you could fix us a nice drink to have while I get dinner ready."

She walked quickly away before Gabe could open his mouth. She was trembling with the effort of her artifice. She hated herself for causing that hurt expression in her husband's face. She'd make it up to him later. Gabe would have a good time, so would Jake, and neither of them would ever know why she was so keen for them to leave. All she wanted was to have a chance to have fun for a change—a chance to have a little bit of magic back in her life. And it might give her a memory to take home with her, a memory of what might have been that would keep her going over the years to come. In the long run, that would have to be good for Gabe and Jake, too. It was almost in their interests.

Having fallen asleep at five in the afternoon, Oliver woke up in the middle of the night. It gave him a chance to phone Maggie and catch her at home. He didn't tell her quite how badly his meeting with Bujevski had gone, but he gave her the gist of it.

"So his whole line is that they want to turn me into a real celebrity—a kind of star turn—you know, maybe like Jeremy Paxman, or something."

"But you can't be that, Ol; you've never been on the telly, and Paxman's never been off it. I mean, maybe there's a chance that if this series is a smash hit, *then* you'd be a household name, but you're not going to start as one, are you?"

"Well, no," Oliver admitted, "but they're very confident. Very committed. I just have to come up with my own theme—my own U.S.P."

"U.S.P."

"Unique Selling Point."

"Oh, for God's sake, Ol, don't do anything gimmicky. They're not going to make you drive around in a pink Cadillac, are they?" Oliver winced, grateful that Maggie didn't know how close she'd come to the truth.

"God no. Nothing like that, I'm sure. I just need to think of something that would make it different—a new style of programme—"

"How about making it thoughtful and intelligent? *That* would be kind of different." He could hear her laughing.

"Thank you, Maggie, that's very helpful. I can see I'm going to have to come up with this all by myself."

"You're the talent, darling; you're the writer; you're the one with all the ideas. I'm just the little homebody."

"Mags, stop taking the piss."

"Okay. What you *don't* want to do is end up looking like some second-class Keith Floyd rabbiting on in a silly hat and trying to be funny. I mean, personally I like Floyd, and he carries it off, but you couldn't. You'd be crap at that. Real crap."

For a moment, Oliver wondered how the hell she knew about Floyd—and then realised it was just a stab in the dark. Amazingly accurate, though.

"You really know how to make a man feel good. Such refreshing honesty."

"It's just one of those things that even your best friends won't tell you. I'm not your best friend—I'm your wife, so I will. Anyway, if you don't want my advice, don't ask for it."

"I do, Mags, my sweet, I do, but I think I'm looking for something else—I can't quite put my finger on it. Look. I'm going home tomorrow—just to watch the cricket. I'll meet up with Bujevski Sunday or Monday at the latest, so I'll be back with you Tuesday at the latest."

"Can't wait."

"D'you miss me?"

"Like a dose of the clap."

"Ha ha. Come on, Mags. D'you miss me?"

"Of course I do, silly. I shouldn't. My mother told me not to get mixed up with men like you, but it's too late now."

"Way too late."

"Water under the bridge."

"Your mother's always been an idiot anyway. How's she coping in that home for distressed canines she went to?"

"Are you calling my mother a bitch or a dog?"

"I dunno. She's a subtle mixture of the two."

"She speaks very well of you."

"Like hell she does. She'd like to dance on my grave."

"She *did* offer to pay for a band."

"How are the kids?"

"Fine. We've found a way to get Arthur to sleep."

"Oh yeah?"

"Yes. Leah soaked a cork in gin and gave it to him to suck. It worked like a charm."

"Maggie!" Oliver's voice became grave. "You can't possibly do that to the child. Do you have any idea how bad gin is for a baby?" He paused for effect, his timing perfect. "Give him a decent whisky, for God's sake."

Maggie chuckled. "Will do. Hey, Ol; I realised something. If this TV series is a hit, you know you'll have to leave the *Telegraph*, don't you?"

"Why should I do that?"

"Well, you'll get so conceited that you'll want your photo by-line to be in colour, so you'll have to move to the *Times*. Maybe you'll have to get your hair highlighted." She laughed. He didn't. "Good night, Ol. Give my love to everyone at home. Good luck tomorrow. Don't drop any catches. Don't be out for a duck."

"Good night, Alec."

"Quack, quack."

Maggie was suffering from the conventional mixed emotions when she put the phone down, and love and jealousy are two emotions that don't mix at all, however frequently they are asked to. She did miss Oliver, and she did love him in a way, and it had been great talking to him—she always liked him best when they were joking at the opposite ends of a telephone line—and she wished him well, and she knew he'd be great on the blasted television, and it would benefit the whole family if he got the series approved, and he was always at his best when he was feeling enthusiastic about work— but. Some small yet vicious worm twisted in her gut. Oliver always had it so damned easy. He had been brought up, as so many boys are, as her own Arthur was being, to believe that life was an enormous, fixed-price smorgasbord. Men just sat down, and made their choices, ticking off their selection on the menu, as much or as little as they felt like. It wasn't like that for Maggie, or any of the women she knew. When the tray of patisseries comes round, and you're the last in line, and all that's left is a stale custard tart, you take it, because you're a good little girl, a nicely brought up little girl. You take it, you eat it, and you damn well like it, and if you don't, you damn well shut up. Here was Oliver, with no greater talent than her own, as she tried to convince herself, having a great journalistic career, then being offered telly on a platter, then being told to choose what kind of a programme he wanted to make, and then asking her to help him.

What of all the feminist crap about women having it all? About the new age of womanhood? About a woman's right to choose? And what about the anti-feminists, the banner-wavers of men's liberation, who said that men had had a simply *terrible* time having to share their triumphs with their wives, having to be the breadwinner *and* be sensitive, having the intolerable pressure of being successful enough for two? It isn't like that. Women don't really have acceptable choices, and if you don't get to choose, you aren't worth anything. Your preferences just don't count. It is pretty much a set menu as far as women were concerned.

Maggie's greatest dilemma was that even if she had had the whole range of options before her, she wasn't sure what it was she wanted from life. She wanted to be with a man she loved and trusted, and who loved her completely. She wanted Lily and Arthur to grow up safely and happily with their parents, and be protected from all the disappointments of life. She wanted to be able to express herself, and have some part of the world that was hers alone, and yet to be supported in that. She wanted to be a good person. She wanted to feel that there was still a perfect, magical future lying out there, waiting for her to seize it. She wanted to be convinced that she hadn't stepped over it, let it pass her by when she wasn't looking. There was nothing unique or even unusual about Maggie's desires. She just wanted to be—happy. It sounds like such an easy thing, but Maggie couldn't think of a person that she knew, outside of the movies, who was completely happy. Movies and books were obliged to depict two extremes of life—tragedy and joy, or, most popular of all, joy overcoming tragedy. Nobody wanted to watch a film about ordinary, interminable day-to-day discontent. It was comforting to watch the lives of people who were far happier than yourself, because it gave you something to aspire to, and it was even more comforting to watch lives that were far worse, because it let you feel advantaged. Fiction, whether on the screen or on the page, provided an escape from the numbing mediocrity of real life, where most people settled for a system of compromise. This view was what allowed Maggie to tolerate her situation. If she could have had Edward, she would have had to give up one of her other wants, and if the sacrifice was either her children or the sense of her own morality, that was too much of a price to pay. Before Edward, she had been more content with her life, because she hadn't been able to see an alternative to Oliver. Oliver was just a problem; now Edward had become a very real, tangible choice, but one she simply couldn't elect.

Maggie went into the children's room to tuck Lily in. She squatted down by the bed to kiss her daughter, who was reading *Peter Rabbit*.

"Lily? Lily, darling, what do you want to be when you grow up?"

Her daughter's big green eyes blinked at her. "I don't know, Mummy. What do you think I should be?"

"It's not for me to say, sweetheart. It's *your* choice. You can be whatever you want—whatever you think would make you happy."

"Daddy says Arthur's either going to be Prime Minister, or he's going to bat for England."

"Does he? Would you like to be Prime Minister, or bat for England?"

"No, Mummy. I don't think so."

"What would you really, really like to be? Most in the whole wide world? The best thing you can possibly think of?"

"I think I'd like to be like you, Mummy."

"That's a nice thing to say. Good night, my pudding. Sleep tight."

Maggie left the room quickly so that Lily wouldn't see the tears in her eyes.

Oliver was lucky the next morning. Danny Bujevski was cursing as he cooked his wife a full English breakfast—she had been even more petulant than usual since leaving hospital and couldn't be bothered to pick up the telephone. So Oliver was able to leave a short message on the answering machine without being interrupted:

Danny: Oliver Callahan here. I have had a superb idea for the series, and am just going off to put the finishing touches to it, but it's in the bag. I will call you Sunday night or Monday morning, and am confident of roughing out a format by Monday. Cheers.

Oliver got on the train at Waterloo with barely an idea in his head; he got off at Salisbury with less of one, but he didn't care. What could possibly be more important than cricket? Who was it who had so wisely said that cricket was the greatest thing God ever created on Earth, even greater than sex, though sex wasn't too bad either? Oliver couldn't remember, but he could always pretend he had thought of it himself. After a couple of bracing pints at The Fox in Garters, he and Edward strolled down to the cricket ground to join the rest of the team. Steve Makepiece, captain of the Compton Purlew eleven and familiarly known as Steve the Papers (because he did the paper delivery for the Valley), was secretly overjoyed to see Oliver arrive in his whites, but in his normal laconic style gave nothing away.

"Afternoon, Oliver. Fancy a game, do you?"

"Good afternoon, Steve. I flew all the way from America just to play."

"Well, you could have done me the favour of letting me know you'd be available—we've sorted out the side already—don't think it would be on for me to dump one of the chaps just because you've graced us with your presence at this late stage. . . ."

"Come on, Steve! You know Ol's our best bat—we can't possibly not play him!"

"I'm the captain, so I'll be the judge of who plays and who watches, thank you, Mr. Arabin." Steve studied his batting order, shaking his head, and sucking the air in over his teeth. "Seeing as you've come all this way, I could just possibly squeeze you in. Are you fit?"

"Fit? What is this, the bloody England Selectors Committee? Of course I'm not bloody fit! I haven't been fit since I was eighteen years old!" Oliver laughed. Steve took his captaincy extremely seriously, and scowled at Oliver. He pointed in the direction of Curtis, who was lying on his back bicycling with his legs, and talking to an enormously tall black man. Oliver gazed at them in awe.

"Bloody hell. He's brought Joel Garner. Curtis has actually roped Big Bird in to play against Compton Purlew. What a bastard."

"Couldn't put it better myself, Oliver. You'll understand now why I asked if you were fit." Steve's jaw was clenched. "Right. This is what we're going to do. I'll open the batting with Mike, Edward, you go in at three, Roberts at four, Oliver five, Martin at six, the general bats seven, the youngster at eight, the vicar . . ." Steve continued mapping out his order, but both Edward and Oliver had strolled away to greet Curtis, and beg an introduction to the legendary West Indian bowler.

"Oliver! My man!" Curtis grasped Oliver's forearm. "Glad you're playing today!"

"I'm not, Curtis. Not now I've seen your new recruits . . ."

"Joel, this is Oliver Callahan, Edward Arabin . . . My brother, Cardigan, my cousin, Malcolm, my brother-in-law Nelson . . ." Curtis introduced his team, and Oliver paled beneath his North Carolinian tan. There were eleven extremely tall, extremely fit, extremely handsome smiling West Indians looking down at him—Curtis, at around six two, was one of the shortest.

"Well, Curtis. It looks like we're going to have a match to remember. Is Joel going to lead the bowling?"

Curtis laughed. "Would I do that to you, man? No, that wouldn't be cricket. Joel is going to bat. I'm going to open the bowling."

"Ah. Well then. That makes all the difference, wouldn't you say, Eddie? I think I might just nip off and have another pint. Dutch courage, as they say." Oliver and Edward walked back towards their team mates, who sat on the pavilion benches holding their middle-aged paunches on their laps. Oliver crossed himself. Out of the corner of his eye he saw the rear view of a young woman, her torso disappearing into the back of a familiar estate car. She was wearing white shorts, and had, even to the eye of a connoisseur like Oliver, fantastic legs.

"Now that, Eddie, is what I call an uplifting sight."

Edward Arabin followed the direction of Oliver's finger. "D'you think so?" Edward sounded unconvinced. "That's your house guest, Ol. That uplifting sight is Christy McCarthy."

Oliver brightened up, and ambled off to greet her, ruffling his hair and swinging his bat nonchalantly. When he was about twenty feet away, Christy straightened up in lifting a crate of food from the car to the grass. Oliver halted. He could see the curve of her breast in profile beneath her pink shirt as she bent to put the food down. When she stood up again, she turned her head to face him, and ran a hand through her hair as she gazed at him quite calmly. Oliver was about to wave, or to speak, when she slowly turned her head away, back to the car. Oliver would never forget the impact of that steady look, and the fact that she had turned away. Something inside him, whether his stomach or his heart, turned over. He wasn't accustomed to women turning away from him. Generally when he looked at a woman, he made a rapid assessment of her sexual potential, and gauged his own interest. These women did not really *exist* as individuals for him, but were merely the amalgamation of his own energy and appetite. Christy was quite different; she was immediately real. He felt nervous as he drew near.

"Mrs. McCarthy? Christy?" he said hesitantly to her back. "I'm Oliver Callahan."

Christy turned again. It was a hot, airless August afternoon, and she had worked hard finishing off the preparations and loading the car. Perspiration had dampened her brow, and small tendrils of hair clung to her forehead. She again swept her hair back, and her violet eyes once more rested on Oliver.

"Why, Oliver. I thought it might be you. Edward told me last night that you might be coming for the game. I've been hoping we'd meet."

"I wouldn't have missed it for the world." Oliver stared at her, tongue-tied. She was even more beautiful than she sounded on the phone—more beautiful than she looked in her photographs. She was wearing a sleeveless pink chambray shirt, tucked into a pair of white shorts. A glistening line of sweat trickled from her throat and disappeared into the swell of her cleavage, but Oliver couldn't take his eyes away from her face. She sat down on the tailgate of Oliver's Volvo, and crossed her slim brown legs.

"You'll have to excuse me—I must look a terrible mess. I volunteered to do the tea." She gestured towards the mountains of food in the car.

"So I see. Are you, um . . . a cricket fan?" He listened to himself sounding like an idiot.

"I'd hardly describe myself as a fan—this will be the first game I've ever seen, but I'm sure looking forward to it. I'm a tad nervous that I won't understand the rules."

"Don't be nervous. With any luck we'll win the toss and bat first, and then I can sit next to you and talk you through the first few overs so you understand everything. How would that be?"

"That would be grand. Simply grand." She smiled at him, and

he melted completely. He began to speak, sighed, tongue-tied by her beauty, and tried to cover up by clearing his throat.

"Pardon me? I didn't hear?" Christy said politely.

"Nothing. Ticklish throat, that's all. Let me help you with all these things—they're far too heavy for you to carry. Tell you what— I'll get some of the chaps to unload, and then we can sit down and have a cool drink and meet properly." He picked up a small thermos in one hand, and held the other out to her. She slipped her fingers through his without any hesitation, and walked with him back to the pavilion. As she had expected, Oliver was a man who always took the initiative. She was completely happy to leave everything up to him.

As Oliver had hoped, Compton Purlew won the toss, and Steve bravely elected to bat first. As Mike took his guard, Oliver began his lesson.

"You shouldn't have too much trouble today because you can at least tell the difference between the two teams. All the good-looking, muscular black men are the visitors, and the home team, Compton Purlew, is the sorry collection of ageing, pasty-faced white men sur-rounding you on the bench." Oliver struggled to keep his tone light. He found Christy's closeness disconcerting. "Mike and Steve are opening the batting, so they are the two chaps whose knees are knocking together out there. Sitting down on the grass are our regular throng of devoted spectators." Oliver pointed towards an old man and a dog, and a teenage girl with a toddler. "We always pack the crowd in at Compton Purlew."

"So Curtis is the pitcher?"

"The bowler. That's right. You see what a fast learner you are!"

"So Curtis throws the ball at Mike, and Mike hits it?"

"Unlikely, although possible. If pigs can fly. It's more probable that Curtis bowls the ball at Mike and either takes his head off or Mike swings wildly and misses it, but we'll see. Watch."

Curtis walked back about three miles, and delivered a thunderbolt. A great cry went up from the West Indians, who threw their arms in the air. Somebody wearing a doctor's white coat shook his head. Curtis threw the ball again, and looked really cross when Mike hit it. Then he threw a third ball, and Mike didn't even try to hit it— he just walked back to the pavilion.

"I'm not sure I understand what happened then." Christy had no interest whatsoever in what was happening on the pitch.

"Quite simple. Curtis had a loud lbw decision turned down, glared when Mike edged a boundary, and then pointed him to the pavilion with a perfect inswinger that uprooted leg stump."

"Pardon me?"

Oliver beamed at her. "He's out, Christy. He's just out. We've lost our first wicket for four."

"You mean he doesn't get three chances?"

Oliver smiled at her again, an amused light in his eye. "D'you know, Christy, it's far too hot to talk about cricket. Why don't we have a glass of wine, and then you tell me how you've been getting on at Bockhampton. Forget about the field. If you hear anybody clapping in a halfhearted sort of way, join in. If you see one of the white men walk off the field, and slump miserably by himself behind the pavilion, then clap a little more forcibly, but for God's sake don't speak to him directly. That's all you really have to know about cricket etiquette." He poured a glass for her. His hand was trembling, and a little wine spilt on the grass.

"So. How do you like our little place?"

"Bockhampton? It's grand. I simply love it. I feel like I could spend my whole life here—we've had the most perfect vacation, and I just can't believe how lucky we were to find you."

"I feel exactly the same. I'm working on an idea at the moment that might just mean I spend more time in North Carolina." Oliver desperately wanted Christy to know about his new triumph.

"Really?" Christy's eyes sparkled. "Tell me all about it."

"I'm working with a TV producer on an idea for a series—six episodes—that would be a sort of guide to the Southern states—maybe just the coastal Carolinas—we haven't yet decided where to limit ourselves—but I want to give people in England a real *flavour* of what it means to be in the South. We want to cover a bit of the history, the culture, the society of the Old South, but I'm not interested in making a *Gone with the Wind* cliché about plantation houses. I want to show it like it is, the good and the bad, the reality of being a Southerner. There's something that sets it apart from the rest of the States, something I can't quite put my finger on—"

"—I know exactly what you mean—"

"I knew you would—you see, most English people think that the States is either New York, a kind of drug-crazed, frenzied outlaw town, or they think it's all great desert plains and illiterate hicks, or they think of California and alfalfa sprouts and movie stars. I want to show them the truth. If I can just work out what it is about the South that's so different—"

"Roots."

"Sorry?"

"The Southern states having a feeling of having roots. The people are rooted there. We're not like itinerant Northerners. We know precisely where we come from, and what we are, and wherever we go, we take our home and our tradition and our roots with us. Southerners are never really *content* far away from their homes. Not for long, at least." Strangely enough, Christy didn't care how far from home she was.

"That's what the programme should be about. Maybe I could just ask people what they felt about the South—about their homes and traditions. It has all sorts of possibilities." Why the hell was he sounding so mindless? "I just need to work out a format. Maybe I should have a co-presenter—an important Southern figure—the Governor of North Carolina or something, who could talk about it all as I asked questions. . . ."

"Oh, Oliver, it sounds like a grand idea, but don't use a politician! We don't really like them all that well, and you won't find an honest one. What you need is a real Southerner. Why not, given your own, ah, background, I mean, being a writer and all, why not use a more literary figure?"

"What do you mean? Who, for example?"

"Well, for instance, maybe a novelist, maybe someone who really writes about the South and conveys the spirit of it. Someone like Pat Conroy, or maybe Reynolds Price. They're all marvellous writers, and you could discuss the literary tradition of the South, and you could compare it with your own style and all . . ." She trailed off rather lamely. She wanted to let Oliver know that she *knew*—that she knew what a great writer he was, that she'd read his book, that she knew all about Louise, and understood what he said about love. She wanted to tell him that everything would be okay. But she couldn't say anything. Oliver was staring hard at her, sitting very close so that she could see lines on his face and how his light blue eyes crinkled at the corners when he smiled, how his dead straight hair flopped over his brow, and how he habitually swept it back off his high forehead. Unconsciously she imitated him, raising her hand to her own hair whenever he did. "Well, here I am shooting my mouth off and I don't know the first thing about books or TV, and you are a real expert. I better just concentrate on the game and stop trying to tell you what to do. I guess I better hush up, right?"

"Christy, don't ever hush up. I think you understand *instinctively* what I'm looking for, and I can't tell you how much I value that—"

"Oliver! Pad up!" Oliver turned round. He had been so absorbed in Christy that he had forgotten about the cricket. Steve was out, clean-bowled by Curtis, and was now stomping towards him. Edward had gone to take Mike's place, so Oliver would be in after Roberts. The score was fourteen for two.

"Blast. I'm going to have to pay attention, damn it, and I'd far rather talk to you. Don't forget a single thought in your head, and we can talk about it all after the match. Or rather, when I'm out, which shouldn't put too great a strain on your memory. Well played, Steve." He clapped loudly, so Christy followed his lead.

"Bloody black bastard," Steve grumbled. "He did that deliberately."

"I'm sure he did, Steve," Oliver agreed mildly. "It's what a bowler's meant to do after all."

It took Curtis three more balls to get Gavin Roberts out, caught behind.

"Wish me luck," Oliver whispered to Christy. "If I'm really lucky, I'll be back here within ten minutes. Keep my seat warm." He strolled out onto the pitch, waving his hat in Ian Botham style, and saluted Edward Arabin. At least he and Eddie had a bit of height between them, which might even things up. He wanted to perform well. The score stood at sixteen for three; the West Indians were taking it easy, and were justifiably complacent. Joel Garner, fielding at fine leg, was sufficiently relaxed to be lying flat on his back on the grass, and was giving a convincing impersonation of a man in a deep sleep.

Curtis pulled his fielders in closer, so that Oliver was surrounded by three slips, a short leg, and a silly point. Only Joel stayed way in the deep, too far out for anyone to hear whether he was snoring or not. Oliver snatched a quick single, and Edward faced the bowling. Curtis walked back another five miles, rubbing the ball on his lean thigh. The ball clipped the edge of Edward's bat and flew into the gloves of the grinning wicket keeper. A groan went up from the pavilion, and Edward exited gracefully to take Oliver's place on the grass next to Christy.

"Well done, Edward. That looked great."

"I played bloody awfully, but thanks all the same, Christy. I think we're all counting on Ol now."

"He's very good, isn't he?"

"He cuts a fine figure. Lovely left foot driver. He could be a little more defensive, though. Just until he's got his fifty."

"Wouldn't that be dull? I mean, surely he might just as well go for it?"

"Oh he will, he will. And Curtis knows it. Christ, it's hot. I'm bloody glad I was out; I might have had a heart attack out there."

Christy was mesmerized by Oliver. The sun glinted off his dark gold hair, and he looked supremely elegant as he waited for each delivery. Edward opened a can of beer, and refilled Christy's glass with wine.

"It is sporting of you to do the tea and sit and watch the blasted game. Well beyond the call of duty. Maggie never comes, or if she does, she brings a pile of books and has to be prodded when the match is over."

"I can't imagine why—it's a fascinating game, and just so incredibly . . . English."

"Are Gabe and your little lad coming?"

Christy looked at him in surprise. "Didn't Gabe tell you that he wasn't coming? He told me he'd phone you. No; he and Jake have gone to Devon to the see the town where his family came from. He said it was the only weekend he could go, but just between you and me, Edward, I don't think he's very interested in cricket. He's more of a baseball man."

"Then it's even more noble of you to have foregone the family outing and stayed behind to support us."

"I wouldn't have missed this for the world, believe me." There was such a fervent note in her tone of voice that Edward glanced at her curiously, but Christy was watching the match intently. Her eyes rarely strayed from the batsman. She had all the makings of a passionate fan.

As the afternoon passed, Compton Purlew's batsmen fell under the assault of Curtis and his brother's pace attack. By four forty-five, the score was ninety-seven for nine, with Oliver and Charles Wickham-Edwardes at the crease. Lucy had arrived and was furious to find that her husband was still batting. "I thought I had timed it perfectly to arrive for tea and find them all out. I make it a point of principle never to watch Charles make an ass of himself. Blast. His batting's no better than an average hamster's would be. Now I'm going to have to witness the whole sorry spectacle." But Lucy worried needlessly. The next ball was directed at Oliver, and it was a bouncer. Oliver hoicked it clean over the heads of the close fielders, and it sailed towards the boundary in the direction of deep square leg. Just as Compton Purlew prepared to celebrate a score edging over one hundred, a long black arm snaked up from the grass, and Joel Garner caught Oliver without moving from his supine position. Oliver didn't even see the catch; his eyes were on Christy. It was time for tea.

Christy, although a newcomer to village cricket, took the serving of tea in her confident stride. She was very nervous in Oliver's company, but no one would have guessed it. Recently, she'd had a lot of experience in hiding her true feelings. All the players with the exception of Steve Makepiece were clearly more involved in stuffing chicken salad and chatting up Christy than they were in the game. Steve bustled around trying to stop his own side from drinking beer and encouraging the opposition to drink up and have another one, but the rest of them knew that Curtis' eleven would wipe the floor with them even if the West Indians were totally inebriated. Oliver stood apart, watching Christy perform. She had the aura of a great heroine—beautiful and bright, gracious yet alluring. From time to time she would raise her head slowly, like a watchful gazelle, and gaze across the pavilion, and when her eyes caught Oliver's, she smiled a shy sweet smile, as if apologising for her intrusion in his privacy.

"She is absolutely stunning," Oliver commented emphatically to Edward.

"I thought you were only interested in her rear view?"

"Don't be ridiculous," Oliver snapped. He bitterly regretted the comment he had made to Edward before Christy had looked at him. He didn't think he could ever look at her like that again.

"There's no question that she's an improvement on Joan Mason," Edward concurred.

"What's her husband like?"

"Gabe? He's a decent bloke, I think. I'm not sure that I know. He's somewhat in her shadow, as you might expect. He looks the part, though. When you see the two of them together, you'd think they'd stepped out of some up-market mail-order catalogue. It's all perfectly honed bodies and coiffed hair, and sparkling white teeth. You know the sort."

"She's not only beautiful; she just gave me quite a lecture on the South and its literary stars."

"Oh, she's no bimbo. I have a feeling that Christy McCarthy knows exactly what she wants, and probably gets it. Great shame Mags can't be here to meet her."

"Isn't it?" Oliver watched Christy talking to Curtis. He had never before seen a woman that lovely, who knew it, and yet didn't flirt. "How do the McCarthys get on with the Valley crowd?"

"Pretty well I'd say. Christy has made a great effort to acclimatise herself, as she puts it. Leaves no stone unturned. Look at her now with the vicar. He's positively lapping her up."

"She's fascinating. She combines seeming available with being untouchable. A real challenge. As if somewhere she's a real vamp, but too much of a lady to let it go."

"Oliver, you sound smitten."

"I'm just intrigued, Ed. All writers are curious about strangers. I think I'll just pop across and have a word with her."

"To ask if she's a vamp or a lady?"

Oliver looked disdainful. "Give me a bit of credit, old man. I wasn't born yesterday."

Christy wouldn't have been surprised to learn that the two men were discussing her. She knew that they were from the way they kept looking at her, but she would have been shocked to the core to know the nature of their discussion.

"My compliments to the cook," Oliver murmured, stepping up behind her. Christy could feel his warm breath on the back of her neck.

"Why, thank you, Oliver. It's nothing special—just ordinary home cooking."

"Where I come from, home cooking is a couple of burnt sausages or a ham sandwich."

"Now, Oliver, d'you think Maggie would like to hear you say that?" she scolded.

"Maggie wouldn't care. Her idea of a perfect meal is getting somebody else to cook it."

"I enjoy cooking. I think it can be a creative experience—not creative the way you are, of course, but it's still a creative expression in a way. I think when people cook with love, you can taste it in the food."

"What a charming idea. When Maggie cooks I taste boredom. Or impatience."

"I hope Gabe doesn't talk like that about me when my back's turned."

"I'm quite sure he doesn't. Now look, tell me more about your ideas for my programme. Maybe I could get you a credit—'original concept by Christy Moore McCarthy,' something like that."

"I don't need to get any credit, Oliver. It's just a real pleasure to be able to help."

"Clever, beautiful, and modest, too—is there no end to your talents?"

"Is there no end to your flattery?" She looked at him boldly, a half smile on her lips.

"Touché. I stand corrected. Now please, leave the mob and come and sit with me."

They retired to a grassy verge.

"You were saying something about John Reynolds . . ."

"Reynolds Price. He's one of several contemporary Southern writers that I admire, and he happens to come from North Carolina. I think maybe you should meet some of them, sound them out. The way I see it, the programme could be Reynolds, or several different writers in turn, escorting you to locations in the South that are real significant to them—places that sum up the essence of Southern life. That way it wouldn't be just another tourist-trap tour of the conventional sites, do you know what I mean?"

"Absolutely."

"It's just that with your being a serious writer and all, and having a feeling for real life and real people, you know—what *really* happens in people's lives, beneath the surface—it might be a nice idea to explore some old Southern characters—get out to Daufuskie Island, maybe some of the old Gullah settlements that surely haven't changed in a hundred years. Then while you walked around, you and the other writer could debate—discuss things about England and the way of life in the South, what the differences are, what the similarities are . . ." As she talked, her fingers tugged at the daisies in the grass, her eyes were downcast, but occasionally flicked up at him through her black lashes.

"So there are similarities?"

"Why certainly! There are so many things here, in Compton Purlew, that put me in mind of home . . . the way village life works, the way you all know one another, a sense of history, things going way back, then back some . . . And moral standards, and family, and values . . . That sense of trying to live the life you're intended to . . . You of all people know what I'm saying, Oliver. You're part of all this." Her outstretched arms encompassed the village green.

"Christy, do you have plans for tomorrow?" Oliver asked quietly.

"Plans? Well, nothing fixed, I suppose. Nothing I couldn't rearrange if you needed me—or is it the house? Did you need me to move out for a bit?"

"Good God, no! I thought I might buy you a spot of lunch. I thought I'd like to talk some more, see which places you think we could go to, just knock ideas around. Would you mind doing that?"

"It would be a real honour," she said sincerely. "But why don't we have a picnic? I could throw something together . . . you know I love cooking . . . We could go to that little spot next to the river at Great Wishford—you know, just over the bridge and down the footpath?"

Oliver looked puzzled for a moment, and looked away from her. Christy could have kicked herself for mentioning it. She had wanted to stretch the rules of the game out a little but she had gone too far—she was treading on very thin ice. For a moment neither of them spoke, and then Oliver's face cleared.

"I know exactly the spot you mean. It's one of my favourites. How very clever of you to find it. It's so roman . . . bucolic. *Bucolic,* that's the word I was searching for."

"Isn't it just? I often go there, just to wander and to think."

The players were making their way back to the field, and Oliver held out his hand to Christy to help her to her feet.

"If you don't want to hang around for the end of the game and the dreaded postmortem at the pub, then I will pick you up at Bockhampton at twelve-thirty sharp tomorrow. You bring the food, I'll bring some wine."

"Oh please don't, Oliver—I have wine in the icebox at home—I mean, at your house—and you'll be tired after your game. I'll get everything ready and see you tomorrow. I hope the rest of the afternoon goes well—I thought you played . . . beautifully."

"You are a very gracious lady, Mrs. McCarthy. I'm very glad I came back today to play, and not just for the cricket. It was a stroke of fate." He touched his lips to her hand, then sauntered off to take up his position at extra cover.

Christy didn't stay to see the end of the game. She had no real understanding of or interest in cricket, but it was pretty clear even to her what the match result would be. There was only one thing on her mind, and that was tomorrow's impromptu picnic. There was only one thing she wanted to do that evening, and that was to prepare herself for it. There was only one thing that she knew with certainty, and that was that at long last she was in love. She had just fallen in love with Oliver Callahan, as easily as falling off a barrel.

Oliver, in the covers, was also preoccupied. Christy had given him an idea that might just save his bacon with Danny Bujevski. His interpretation of the idea was a little bit different from Christy's. The last thing he wanted to do was to plod around the tobacco fields of North Carolina with some quasi-academic American literary bore in tow. But the thing that would give the show character, that would give it a different angle, would be to tour the South with someone who really knew it and really loved it, someone who epitomised the South itself. There should be a lighthearted, bantering relationship between Oliver and his co-presenter, and the two of them should embody the differences between English and American culture. Sometimes they'd argue, sometimes they'd joke, sometimes they'd explain things to each other, and if the co-presenter happened to be an extremely beautiful and charming woman, that would be no bad thing for the ratings. Oliver planned to make himself a star, and spend a lot more time with Christy McCarthy into the bargain.

Steve Makepiece's temper shortened with the length of the late afternoon sun. The score was seventy for none, and Steve didn't know who to bawl out next, his bowlers or his fielders. As the Reverend Martin Worth stomped back at the end of another expensive over, and said to his captain, "I really had him flummoxed that time," Steve forgot that he was addressing a man of the cloth, and remarked bitterly, "Course you did, Martin; he didn't know whether to hit you for six or for four."

Finally, the game was over, with the faintest of whimpers. Oliver, thinking about Christy, and toying with what he would choose as

his favourite item on his mantelpiece when it came to celebrity inter-
views, dropped a catch that his son Arthur could have caught.

"I'm sorry, Steve." He shrugged. "I think that with the change
in climates, I must have caught a summer cold."

"You couldn't catch a dose of the clap, Oliver," Steve said in
disgust, and went behind the pavilion to wipe his eyes. He was
inclined to take things a little too seriously, and Oliver suspected
that approximately ten people in Compton Purlew wouldn't be re-
ceiving their newspapers the next morning.

After the booze up in The Fox in Garters, fortunately funded by
the winning side, Edward and Oliver returned to the barn for a bit
of bread and cheese and a nightcap. Oliver had no intention of
discussing his plans for Christy until she had agreed, and Edward
was more interested in asking about Maggie than talking about the
American visitors.

"Is Mags having a good time?"

"Certainly is. She does nothing except lie on her back in the sun
and insult my column. It's her favourite occupation."

"You shouldn't be so hard on her, Oliver. She's had a tough time
recently—she needs a break."

"I'm not bloody hard on her! She's hard on me—I can't even
blow my nose without getting some waspish comment about how
I could do it better."

"She's a wonderful woman. I'm not sure that you really appreciate
how wonderful she is."

"Oh, stop talking as if you were my father. Mags is fine, and we
get along perfectly well. She's just an old cow sometimes and she
doesn't realise how much strain I'm under about this TV idea. I
need a little support, too, you know. I'm the one who's working
full time and trying to support the family."

"My heart bleeds."

"It's alright for you, Eddie. Here you are in splendid isolation,
with not a care in the world; you're a free agent: if you want to
stay out all night, you just do it; if you want to chat up some bird,
no one's going to interfere. If you want to play cricket all weekend
and every weekend, who's going to grumble? You have no idea what
pressure it is having a wife and family."

"What utter balls. You have no idea what it's like coming home
alone to an empty house, having no one to care about your minor

triumphs or petty tragedies. What does it matter if I play cricket all the time if there's nobody there to cheer when I score a century?"

"Well, Maggie wouldn't bloody cheer. She'd be far more likely to say, 'Century? You look like a bloody century.' That's the sort of wifely support and encouragement I get."

"She's just trying to keep you on your toes, old man, and she does a very good job at it."

"Alec Bones."

"What?"

"That's what I call her. Alec Bones."

"Rather an odd term of endearment, isn't it?"

"Not at all. It's very apt. Smart Alec, Lazy Bones. Those are Maggie's two dominant characteristics."

"You know how fond I am of Maggie, Oliver. She's a precious girl, and I won't hear a word said against her."

"As if I'd ever say one. Any more in that bottle, old man?"

Eleven

**A postcard of a horse, to Maggie Callahan,
Holden Beach, North Carolina:**

Here's the latest bulletin from the Valley:

Compton Purlew:	*97 all out (O. Callahan 63)*
Windies:	*99 for 0*
Man of the Match:	*Joel Garner*
Happy as a sandboy:	*Curtis Abrams*
Sick as a parrot:	*Steve the Papers*

Shame you missed it—bloody good laugh.

Love,
Mog

CHRISTY WAS UNABLE TO SLEEP THE NIGHT AFTER THE CRICKET match. She paced the house restlessly, trying to decide what to do. She had read and reread the picnic scene in Oliver's book, and couldn't decide how to play it. As she saw it, she had three choices. She could be direct and honest, and simply tell him as soon as he arrived that she had read his book, and knew the significance of the spot for him. Or, she could ignore the book and everything she had discovered about him, and simply treat the lunch as a straightforward discussion about his TV programme. If he wanted to raise other subjects, that would be his decision. Or, she could say and do enough to let him know that she *knew*, and if he chose to unburden himself, that she'd be there for him. Rationally, she thought honesty was the best policy, but Christy was in a far from rational state. Since meeting Oliver the day before, her feelings were more than ever confused. She was still intrigued by the author of the book, and she wanted to hear him talk about the choices he had made, and why he had chosen to remain locked into his miserable marriage, but beyond that, she was now in love with the flesh-and-blood man, and longing to indulge a passion she hadn't felt for years—if ever. When she came home she was unable to sit still and called her friend Julie in Boston. Even as she dialed the number, she was uncertain what she would tell her.

"Hey, Julie. It's Christy."

"Christy Moore, I haven't heard from you in an age! Talk about a coincidence—Greg and I were just talking about you."

"I guess my ears were burning."

"So what's new?"

"I'm in England. On vacation. We did a house exchange."

"That sounds great! Lucky you. I wish I could get to Europe, but what with the business, and Greg's surgery and all—"

"How is he?"

"He's doing fine. The left knee's okay—"

"Julie, I'm in love."

"I should hope you are after ten years. Jesus, has it taken you that long to fall in love with Gabe? I told you the night before your wedding that was the way the best marriages work. Just like your mama always said: marry a good man and ease yourself into loving him. I didn't think it would take this long, though—"

"Julie. I'm not in love with Gabe."

"Oh." There was a long pause on the phone. Then another flat "Oh."

"I'm in love with a man over here. I just met him."

Christy could hear her friend dragging on a cigarette, and then Julie replied, speaking carefully. "That's just not the way it's meant to be, Christy Moore. The way it's *meant* to be is that you meet a nice guy, a good guy, like Gabe, you marry him, you fall in love and you have babies and live happily ever after. You don't do all the rest of that shit and then go fall in love with somebody else."

"What about the other way? What about falling in love—really in love—first, and then marrying the guy?"

"That only happens in books, sweetie."

"Tell me something, Julie. Would you have fallen in love with Gabe?"

"If I can remember that far back, honey, I wasn't the one he proposed to. I probably would have married him if he'd asked."

"No kidding?"

"No kidding. I'm not saying he stole my heart, you hear me, but at that time, before Greg came on the scene, sure I might have married him. He had good . . . prospects."

"But would you have fallen in *love* with him?"

"I know I would have tried to real hard. If he'd given me what he's given you. He does everything to please you."

"How? By buying me dresses and bringing me flowers, and choosing jewellery I don't want? By arranging intimate little outings when I want to stay at home? Why should I be grateful to him for that?" Christy sighed. "Oh, Julie. What a bitch I am, and what fools we were. Remember how we talked? The night before my wedding? Sitting up all night together in Mamma's house? We planned my dining room, and the dinner parties I'd have, and how you'd be godmother to my kids and I'd be godmother to yours?"

"Sure I do. And it's all worked out just like we planned."

"No it hasn't."

"That's up to you, my friend."

"You mean, you don't approve?"

"Approve? Hell, Christy Moore, you've gone way past approval. You spent the first twenty-six years of your life worrying about your mother's approval. Don't ask for mine—I wouldn't give it anyway. Don't fall back in that trap."

Christy groaned. "Julie, do you ever think about what we might have been, you and I, if we hadn't had to live up to Blanche and Helena's expectations? If they'd never existed?"

"If they'd never existed, we wouldn't have either," Julie finished abruptly. "What are you going to do now, Christy?"

"Nothing. There's nothing I can do. I mean, this man is married, and nothing's going to happen. I just haven't ever been in love before, and now I am, and I had to tell someone because it feels so good. I wanted to tell you just so I'd know it was real, that it was true. I'm just glad to feel like this once—even if this is the only night of my life I ever feel really in love. I feel like I've risen from the dead."

"Christy, I've gotta go. I'm not saying I approve, and I'm not saying I don't. You just keep me posted, okay?"

"Okay."

Christy was glad she'd called Julie, but it hadn't helped her make a decision. This might be her only chance of ever being alone with Oliver, and Christy wasn't going to let the opportunity pass her by. She didn't have a long pink skirt, but she had a blue one, and she did have a white, scooped-neck blouse. She left her hair loose, packed the picnic, and put two bottles of Terre di Tufi wine in the cooler. She found the Black Watch rug and laid it neatly on top of the picnic hamper. She was about to play a very dangerous game that could go hideously wrong or wonderfully right. It would be Oliver's choice. She was ready for Oliver well before twelve-thirty.

He gave no sign of surprise or recognition when she opened the door to him, simply commenting on how pretty she looked. As they drove to Great Wishford and parked the car he chatted about the cricket and what a lucky innings he had had. They left the car at the pub car park, and strolled down to the river, Oliver carrying the rug and hamper, and Christy carrying the wine.

"You know, when I was fielding yesterday, I was trying to think how I could really explain the essence of cricket to you, I mean to someone who knows nothing about it. It really is such a part of English life. So many cricketing expressions have been absorbed into our day-to-day language, you see? Even people who don't understand cricket use them: I'm completely stumped; knocked or hit for six; I'm on a bit of a sticky wicket . . ." It amused him that those particular expressions, which so neatly described his current state, had sprung to mind.

"I guess I still have a great deal to learn—you might as well be talking a foreign language as far as I'm concerned."

Oliver looked at her keenly. "You're not really interested in it, are you? You are probably bored to death by it all. I'll shut up. I'm glad you found this place. I think it was Georgie Lamington who first told me about it; she lives near here."

"What a coincidence! She was the lady who told me about it. . . ."

"Eddie mentioned you'd had all the locals over for a drink. It sounds like the party of the season . . . Made you quite the talk of the town." He winked at her, and helped her over the stile. He continued to chat as they chose a spot and laid out the picnic. Christy could hardly bring herself to speak.

"You are amazing, Christy." Oliver looked at their lunch. "One glorious spread after another. Crab, smoked salmon, terrine . . . It's a feast. Are you a believer in the theory that the way to a man's heart is through his stomach?"

"All Southern girls believe that, Oliver, at least if we're dealing with Southern men. We're brought up on it with our mother's milk. It's the best way to trap your man." Christy smiled, then added hurriedly, "If you're trying to trap a man, that is."

"God, I'm being crass. I didn't mean you were looking for a way to *my* heart . . ." Oliver blustered. There was something about the straightness with which Christy replied to his flippancies that disempowered him. He had never felt quite so shallow and transparent as he did with her. "It was just a figure of speech. Now. Let's have a glass of wine, and then we can get down to business." He opened a bottle of Terre di Tufi without even looking at the label, and poured two glasses. Christy watched him carefully as he tasted it. He took two sips, and then picked the bottle up and studied the label. Christy saw his mouth tighten slightly.

"I have the strangest sensation," Oliver began quietly. "I can't really put it into words." He so wanted to impress her, to be witty and confident and sophisticated, and instead, he heard himself uttering idiocies.

"Try," Christy encouraged in a whisper.

"I feel as if I've known you rather a long time. I can't really describe it. This just feels very familiar. Being here with you. It seems fitting."

"Maybe it's just that in a way we *do* know each other—from living in each other's houses. I feel as if I've known you for a long time, too. I guess it's just a result of living some stranger's life—so intimately, I mean." She lowered her eyes in an uncharacteristically shy gesture. She had no doubt that Oliver remembered everything that had happened in this spot—that she had subjected him to a wave of possibly very unhappy memories—but he wasn't going to talk about it to a stranger.

"You're probably right. I think it's just meeting you on my own home ground, and talking about the TV series so much yesterday, and coming here—I haven't actually been here for a year or so. It's a very strange sensation." Oliver sidestepped from his normal pattern of seduction. Christy would not fall for the same ploys as Louise, or Sarah, or countless other easy conquests.

"I hope it's not an unpleasant one?"

"Christ no; it's great. I wouldn't have missed it for the world. I said that yesterday, didn't I? You must think I'm a clichéd old hack."

"Oliver, I think you are a wonderful writer." Christy leant towards him, her face earnest, her eyes fervent. "I mean it. I think you write about everything so evocatively. When I read what you write, I just feel like I'm *there*, like I'm seeing it with you, it's so personal. It's so honest."

"You'll have me blushing in a minute. And you think all that just from reading my stuff from the States?"

"No, I did read some other things . . . Things I found in your office."

"I forgot you'd read through some of my files. It's music to my ears, Christy. I haven't been so flattered since I won the journalism prize at school."

"It's not flattery, Oliver. I mean it. I'm sure you'll win lots of prizes . . . You deserve to." Oliver lay back on the grass with his hands beneath his head, leaving Christy the rug.

"You know, I've been thinking about what you said about similarities between the States and England—" If he didn't get onto safer ground he'd do something really stupid—like make a pass at her, or something worse.

"Between the South and England. I don't think there are so many similarities between the Yankees and the English."

"I stand corrected. One of the things I really love about the States—the *South*—is that you people aren't afraid to praise. You're not uncomfortable about paying compliments. You'd never catch an Englishman—or -woman—doing that. If I ask a friend, or even my own wife, what they think of my writing, the closest I'll get to approval is 'well, it's not bad as far as that sort of crap goes.' "

"But that's a crying shame! Back home, we just tell it like we see it, and if it's good, then you say so."

"I could see myself settling quite easily in America."

"You could? I can't imagine you anywhere other than Bockhampton. You seem to belong here so naturally." Christy passed him a plate of crab remoulade. "What about Maggie? Would she like to live in the States?"

"I don't know what Maggie wants. She's got a touch of the feminist vapours at the moment, so I guess she wants it all." Oliver didn't see Christy wrinkle her nose at the word *feminist;* he had his eyes closed. He was thinking that discussing Maggie was closer to quicksand than safe ground.

"There are plenty of women back home who talk about having it all. In my opinion . . ." She didn't finish the sentence, and Oliver sat up sharply.

"In your opinion? In your opinion, what?"

She tossed her head dramatically. "In my humble opinion, there are a sight too many women going round like spoilt children who are old enough to know better. There ought to be less having, and more giving. I think life is just too short to wail around feeling sorry for yourself all the time. I think you should just fish or cut bait."

"Fish or cut bait?" Oliver smiled. "What a good expression. I'll have to remember to tell Maggie that next time she starts whinging about how awful life is."

"But she must have a wonderful life here."

"Oh, she does, but you know what it's like, it's always about her not being fulfilled, and about her career, and about how the kids take all her time, and all her energy, and about how she's stuck out in the country, and doesn't have any choice in the matter."

"That's just plain ridiculous! Everyone has choices, man or woman. We all have to make choices, sometimes real unpleasant ones, and it doesn't help to complain about them. Anyways, with a nice home, and a husband, and two children, she should feel lucky. Plenty of folks would be real envious of her. I could be myself—for having two kids, I mean." Her eyes gazed away towards the distant fields across the river. Oliver watched her. Everything was right about her—her spirit, her appearance, her accent, her strong views. She had a sort of forthright stridency that was very sexy, and quite different from Maggie's temperamental tantrums. He edged closer to her.

"Christy, I have to say something. It's going to sound very peculiar as we've only just met, but I can't help myself. I have to ask you something."

A shiver ran through her, and Oliver was close enough to feel it. Instinctively, he put his arm around her shoulders. She felt so soft as her body relaxed against his. She had such confidence, and he, surprisingly, had none.

"Are you cold? Do you want my sweater?"

She turned to him, her mouth inches from his own.

"No. Someone just walked over my grave, that's all." Oliver left his arm where it was.

"I want to make a proposition to you. Proposition? Proposal. I don't know. I've been thinking about this all yesterday afternoon, and I can't get it out of my head." He flicked his hair back off his forehead and looked at her intently. "I don't want to do my programme with Reynolds Price. Or with Pat Conroy. Or with the other bloke you mentioned."

Christy looked crestfallen. "I see. I'm sure there's somebody else who would be suitable that I could think of. Maybe a lady writer . . ."

"That's more what I had in mind . . ."

"Let me see, maybe Kaye Gibbons . . ."

"I was thinking of Christy Moore McCarthy . . ."

She looked at him blankly. "But, Oliver, you surely have misunderstood; *I'm* not a writer, I'm not anything really."

"You are. You're everything. You're a genuine Southern lady, and you'd be perfect. You know the country, you know all about how people feel, you have strong, original opinions, you're very beautiful, and you'd look great on camera—you *are* the contemporary South, don't you see?" He didn't need to convince himself, but it mattered desperately to him that she believed what he said, and didn't think he was just making up to her. He couldn't imagine flirting with Christy. He couldn't see himself treating any woman like that again. He tried to concentrate on the programme. "Everything would be just as you suggested. We'd travel around, you'd take me to places, and I'd ask questions, and maybe we'd argue or agree. Come on, Christy, what do you say? Let's give it a whirl. You've got nothing to lose. How would you like a career on British television?"

Christy shook her head numbly. She couldn't believe what Oliver was saying.

"I think the heat must have got to you, Oliver; or maybe to me, and I didn't hear you right. I'm a little surprised."

"Aren't all the best things in life surprises? Inspirations? Come on, Christy! I was meant to come back here and meet you. It was all laid out like this—it's fate. Destiny. There I was, with no good idea how to make this work, and I come back to play a village cricket game, and who's at the pavilion but the solution to all my problems. Let's drink to it."

Oliver filled their glasses to the brim, and clinked his against hers. "To us. Say yes."

"I don't know what to say. You've taken my breath away."

"Say yes. You don't need much breath for that."

"But I wouldn't know what to do—I wouldn't know what to say—"

"Nor would I. We'd both be beginners, hand in hand. That's the beauty of it. It's just two people chatting intimately, not some boring old professional celebrity or dull as ditchwater travel hack. Just ordinary people talking about the South just the way you do to me. It'll be great. Trust me. Say yes."

"But . . . but . . ."

"Christy, my dear girl, there are no buts." She seemed desperately dear to him at that moment, with confusion and reluctance in her face. He had to persuade her whatever her reservations. The programme seemed suddenly worthless if she wouldn't be there with him. Floyd could have it. "We'll film entirely in the Carolinas; you won't even have to go far from home. Gabe can't possibly object. This was meant to happen. Things *do* just happen, don't you see? Say yes. Please."

"Yes, please," she whispered.

Impulsively, Oliver pulled her towards him and kissed her on the mouth, and she kissed him back. He had intended it to be a smacking great kiss of celebration, of exultation, a kiss to seal a deal. At least, he *thought* that was what he had intended . . . The honey flavour of the wine lingered on her tongue. He pushed her back on the black and green rug, so that her skirt rode up over her knees, and kissed her again and again, holding her head gently between both his hands. After a time, he drew back, ashamed of how he had treated her. For all his noble intentions, he had behaved like an animal. Christy lay motionless on the rug, her eyes closed. He had no excuses. He, the man who had always said that any man who made excuses had no self-respect, that excuses were for wimps, struggled to think of one. His eyes stung, and instead of speaking, he groaned. Christy opened her melting violet eyes, and smiled enigmatically. He rolled onto his elbow, not taking his eyes away from hers.

"Shit. I owe you an apology."

"You do?" Her eyes widened.

"I'm afraid I do. I don't know what came over me. There's no excuse." He gestured randomly. "The heat, the wine, relief that you said yes . . . I don't know. I don't normally behave like that. Believe me." He wished with all his heart that he never had behaved like that.

"You don't?"

"Never. Well, almost never."

"That's a crying shame." She spoke so softly that Oliver thought he had misheard.

"What did you say?"

"I said it's a shame you don't behave like that more often. I kind of liked it."

"My God, Christy, my God." He kissed her again, more roughly this time, holding her shoulders pinioned to the rug, and she responded with equal passion.

She could see herself as they kissed, lying on her back, one leg bent, her skirt baring her knee, her collarbone reddened by the sun, her hair tangled by Oliver's searching fingers. This was no time to mention Louise, and all at once Louise was utterly irrelevant. Whether Oliver wanted her because she reminded him of Louise or whether Oliver wanted her for herself didn't matter. All that mattered was that for some reason he wanted her, and she wanted to make every second of these few solitary hours last. They kissed like teenage lovers, content just to kiss in the grass, oblivious to their surroundings. Finally, with a long sigh, Oliver sat up and put his head in his hands.

"Christy, you know I have to go back to London? I have to go back—probably tonight." She nodded calmly, her expression grave. "I'm meant to go back to Lawrenceville tomorrow night." She nodded again, although she barely heard him. "I have to go." He repeated himself angrily.

"I know that you do."

"I don't want to go."

"I know."

"I have to. I don't know what to say. I don't know what to do."

"It's okay." She began to clear away the picnic. "We didn't really eat anything."

"I'll have to leave tonight. Maybe at the crack of dawn tomorrow. I ought to leave tonight."

"I hear you."

"It's just that I need to sort out everything before I fly back. Everything about the programme, I mean."

She nodded.

"Everything. Sort it out."

She nodded again. "Of course you do."

"You see, Maggie . . ." He swallowed hard. "Maggie will be expecting me to call and say when I'm coming—that I've sorted things. Maggie will be waiting."

"You shouldn't make her wait."

"No, of course not."

"It's getting late. Would you like to come home and freshen up before your journey? I could offer you another drink?"

She had cleared away all the debris of their picnic. The empty bottles were in the cooler, the tartan rug neatly folded through the handles of the hamper. She stood watching him, smiling sweetly. Oliver, still kneeling on the grass, buried his face in her stomach and clung to her for dear life.

They drove back to Bockhampton. The garden was at its loveliest at twilight, when the scent of honeysuckle wafted through the French windows. They sat in the drawing room, avoiding the garden in case it encouraged a neighbour to join them. Oliver had even taken the precaution of locking the front door to protect their privacy. They sat in semi-darkness and talked. Oliver found it easy to talk to Christy about his wife, how he loved Maggie, and how he didn't *love* Maggie, and Christy made no demands of him, but just held his hand and listened. When he in turn asked her how she felt about Gabe, she said simply that she no longer knew, and that she didn't want to think about it for the moment, not that day, not while Oliver was in the house. Oliver didn't press her. He had forgotten what it was like to talk properly to a woman who wanted to listen to him, to have a woman's undivided attention, to have no interruption from the children, to have her eyes tirelessly on him and not half-reading a newspaper or looking for a missing piece of Duplo. Oliver talked and talked, but made no mention of Louise, or any woman other than Maggie.

At eight, Christy looked at her watch.

"Oliver, what time do you have to leave?"

"It doesn't matter. I can get the train, or I can stay at Eddie's and leave in the morning."

"You don't have to stay at Eddie's. You know that."

"Yes, I know."

Christy brought another bottle of wine into the drawing room.

She found Oliver looking at the wedding photograph on top of the piano.

"Oliver, I don't want to do anything that would put you in a difficult position."

"Difficult position? You don't want to compromise me?" Oliver laughed hollowly. "God, we've somehow got ourselves upside down here, haven't we? I've never wanted to be a gentleman in my whole life, never given a toss about it, and here I am, wishing to God I was one. Lord knows who's in the more difficult position, or how we got ourselves there."

"You know what I mean. I don't want you to suffer for my sake—I don't want anyone to suffer for my sake. That's the only thing we have to avoid."

Oliver slammed his fist on the piano, sending the keys jangling, and the photographs crashing to the floor. "I didn't come over here to make love to you, Christy. The thought never crossed my mind. I mean, I thought you were sexy as hell as soon as I saw you, but I never intended to do anything about it, I swear to God. I didn't want to treat you like—other women. I've only known you for twenty-four hours, for God's sake. I cannot for the life of me understand why I feel like this, or what's happening, or why I find myself so unable to leave. I feel like a child."

"As you said, Oliver, things just happen. All we can do is decide how to react to them. There's nothing here that we can't reverse. You can go away now, and no one's hurt. How can a kiss hurt anyone?"

"I know what I ought to do . . . I know how I ought to react . . . But it's not what I want to do."

"What do you want to do?"

"I want to make love to you and forget about everything else and everyone else in the world. I want to draw a curtain over everything else and just have you to myself right now."

"Then let's do just as you say. Let's go upstairs, and forget about everything."

"Are you sure you mean that?"

"I most certainly do. I don't rightly know when I've ever meant anything more."

Christy seemed very calm. Oliver followed her up the curving staircase, and into his own bedroom at the top of the stairs. He watched while she undressed slowly, placing her grass-stained skirt and shirt neatly on the chair. When she was in her bra and pants, she came to him and sat on his lap, and undid the buttons of his shirt. Her cool fingers played across his chest, massaged his neck, stroked back his hair. Christy hadn't touched a man other than Gabe for ten years. Oliver felt shockingly different. Her own body felt shockingly different, as far as she could distinguish between the two. Her fingers were far more sensitive touching his skin than Gabe's. His body was much smoother and leaner than Gabe's, and his skin was burning. He removed her bra, stroking her breasts as her back arched to welcome him. Oliver carried her across to his bed, and laid her gently on the top of the sheets, and drew the heavy, tapestried curtains around the four-poster. He would never forget the black and white and pinkness of her, those simple colours so stark and pure against the ornate tapestry of the bedcover. Her vulnerability made him feel protective and almost fatherly. He kissed and caressed her, thrilled by her responsiveness, and by the pulse he could see beating above her collarbone. Christy was an artful lover, knowing that whatever the books claimed, no man appreciated step-by-step instruction on how to make love to a woman. All Oliver needed was encouragement, and she gave it unself-consciously. Even if Oliver hadn't taken such pains to arouse her, she would have reached orgasm, because her dreaming of his touch had already brought her more than halfway there. The touch itself simply hardened her desire, and triggered the release of years of frustration. In many ways, it was better than she had anticipated, because in all her fantasies, she had never believed that she would love him like this. They didn't speak at all. Now, mingled with her intensifying passion, she felt an overwhelming surge of gratitude towards the man next to her. And it was an extraordinary moment for him, utterly specific, that moment's possession of the body of that woman.

Christy lay in the crook of his elbow, sideways across the bed, her hair spilling over the edge of the four-poster. Their time was over.

"Oliver," she whispered. "Oliver. There's one thing I have to tell you. I feel so guilty."

"How could you possibly feel guilty about anything? You are a blessed angel." He stroked her cheek tenderly, and laid his hand across her mouth, kissing her damp breasts in turn. She twisted out from under his arm, and struggled out of bed, draping his discarded shirt over her shoulders. She began to pace the room, while Oliver, still in a haze of contentment, admired the firm swell of her buttock

223

showing beneath his shirt-tails. She bit at her lip, frightened of both what she might say and what she might not say. She poured herself a glass of wine.

"Well, ma'am; I'm waiting already." Oliver had another bash at a Southern accent, just to see her smile again. He was propped up on an elbow, stretched out naked on the bed, the curtains drawn back to admire her.

"I have a confession to make. It's a bad one, and I'm frightened you'll be angry with me."

"Christy, after what we've just done there is *nothing* in the world that could make me angry with you. Nothing in the whole sweet world."

"You better wait and hear me out before you make any rash promises." She stopped anxiously at Maggie's dressing table, and put a band round her hair—anything to stall for time. "I feel like a cigarette."

"Well, have one! Have whatever your dear heart desires!"

"I don't smoke." She resumed her pacing.

"For the love of God, Christy, stop prowling around like an expectant tigress and tell me what's on your mind. You're making me think you're about to tell me you're a transsexual or something." He was grinning at her, amused by her discomfort. To his mind, her post-coital confusion and embarrassment made her even more entrancing than if she had been confident and assured. "Pass me a glass of wine and tell all. Come on. I won't bite. Did you break a piece of china or something?"

"No; I wouldn't be upset by *that.*"

"You shouldn't be upset by anything. Look, Christy, we're pretty much stuck in a black hole of deception and betrayal, you and I. We're in this together, slap bang in the murky depths of the same boat, and at the moment, I couldn't give a damn about the rest of them. We might as well come clean with each other."

She stopped dead still and looked at him, her resolution weakened by his crooked grin and the dangerous glint in his blue eyes, and the way he lay naked so confidently across his wife's bed. He frightened her, and she had so longed to be frightened.

"Oliver, have you ever done this before?"

"This?" He gestured expansively. "This? You mean sex? I must admit that I have. Is that what's bothering you, ma'am? That I'm not a virgin? I'm sorry to disappoint, but like your George Washington, I cannot tell a lie." He laid one hand flat against his heart, and looked at her solemnly.

"Oliver, have you ever been unfaithful to Maggie before?"

It was Oliver's turn to look uncomfortable. He sighed, and moved to the edge of the bed, his arms folded across his chest.

"We're going to have *that* conversation, are we, Christy? Already?"

"I'm not being possessive or jealous or any of that shit. I wouldn't think less of you if you'd had a thousand affairs. And I don't think I'm capable of thinking more of you than I already do. I just need to know. Before you go."

He scratched his head. "Then the answer is yes. I have. I'm not proud of it. I wish I could say no. I can say it has never happened quite like this before—it's never been quite so impulsive, so—*shattering*—but yes, it has happened. There it is." He held out his hands, wrists towards her, offering them for handcuffs. "Do I get a last meal before my execution? A last kiss, maybe?"

Christy shook her head, and resumed pacing.

"I'm not judging you for being unfaithful. That would be a tad hypocritical of me, don't you think? Just for the record, I have never been unfaithful to Gabe until today." Saying her husband's name out loud made her flinch. "But that doesn't warrant any prizes. I don't regret what happened, and I surely hope you don't."

"I don't. So what's the problem?"

"The problem is . . . the problem is . . . That I know all about Louise. I mean, I know what happened, and I'm real ashamed I didn't say anything before we—you know—and I just felt I had to say something. So that when I think back on this—all this—I can feel that in some way I was honest. There. I said it. I'm sorrier than I know how to admit."

"I don't know what on earth you are babbling about. Louise. Alright. I admit Louise. Mea culpa, mea maxima culpa." Christy couldn't bring herself to look at Oliver, or she would have seen the half-amused, half-bewildered look on his face change to one of suspicion. "But how the hell did you find out about Louise? Which bastard told you about her?" The volume of his voice rose slightly as his thoughts shifted from Christy to Maggie. Maggie couldn't have told Christy, but she might just have told Edward Arabin. . . .

"I've said I'm sorry—please don't shout at me! Look, Oliver, I just *know*. If you want to pretend that Louise never really existed, then that's your prerogative—you don't owe me anything—but I feel like I have to tell you the truth. I know it was none of my business, and now, with what's happened and all—I never for a moment thought I would actually meet you—I never imagined *this,* not in my wildest dreams—I can't tell you how much I regret it, but I *do* know . . ." She collapsed on the chair at the dressing table. Oliver could see from her heaving shoulders that she was crying, and the mirror reflected her tear-streaked face half shielded by her fingers.

"Louise has absolutely nothing to do with this. Nothing. What gave you that impression? Who mentioned her to you in the first place?" His voice was deathly calm, almost expressionless. His one wish was to reassure Christy that whatever she had been told, there was no similarity between the casual flings he had had in the past, and what he felt for her now. He knew that someone had been gossiping—either Edward or maybe Lucy; Maggie must have told one of them about Louise. This was all very straightforward. This was all about Maggie's being a bitch. He was angry now, but he certainly wasn't angry with Christy. He was angry with his wife.

Christy saw that she had made a fatal mistake. Oliver had wanted to make love to her, maybe just to snatch some brief interlude of distraction, but he had worked manfully to put his love for Louise behind him, out of his mind forever. Now she had reopened painful wounds, terrible old scars that had taken a year to heal. Rather than setting herself outside Oliver's past, as something belonging to the present, she had fixed herself forever as part of his pain. He would surely resent her now as much as he resented Maggie. She sank into misery and regret that she had ever mentioned it.

"Who told you, Christy?" Oliver asked again, his voice ominously quiet.

"You told me. You told me yourself."

"What are you talking about?"

"Your book. Your novel—so-called novel. *A Sad Affair.* I read it, Oliver. I'm sorry. It was an accident. I didn't mean to. It was so wonderful, it broke my heart, and I feel for you so much not being with the person you loved, I mean, I *know* how you feel, do you understand that? Like when you say you just feel half dead, and everything's such an effort, and you're just kind of disconnected. I mean, because I don't love Gabe, and I've been telling myself that

I just *have* to, I felt kind of stunned into apathy, you see? I've felt what you feel. I felt dead. Up till tonight. That's my punishment, I guess. I'm just so sorry, and I don't blame you if you hate me, I surely don't. I deserve that for being so foolish and having all these silly romantic notions." Sobs overcame her.

"Christy, what are you talking about? Give me the book."

Christy took the manuscript of the novella out of the bottom drawer of the dressing table, and threw it across the room. It landed on the bed. The only sound in the room was Christy's broken weeping as Oliver looked at the frontispiece:

"A SAD AFFAIR"

A NOVEL

BY

ALEC BONES

Oliver looked at the beginning of the book, his eyes skimming the first five pages. He flipped to the end, read for a moment, and closed it. He listened to Christy's sobbing. He put the manuscript on the floor on top of his trousers, and thought quickly. He half carried and half dragged Christy back to the bed, then wiped the tears off her cheeks.

"Christy, listen to me." He spoke very quietly and seriously. "This book isn't finished."

"I know."

"So you don't know how it ends."

"I know."

"Well, nor do I."

"What do you mean?"

"I just mean it isn't finished, and it isn't going to be. And that's all there is to say about it."

"But, Oliver! You *must* finish it! It's a wonderful book—it's the most moving thing I have ever read. I read it, oh, God knows how many times, and there is no one who understands love and unhappiness like you do, and it made me fall for you before I ever met you, understanding how women feel and all—well, it's just wonderful."

"Is it?"

"You know it is."

"Maybe you're right, but we're not going to talk about it. I want to tell you one thing, and I want you to remember it for a long time. All your life. Look at me."

She turned her tear-stained face towards him.

"Louise was a lifetime ago. An age. She was a silly little girl. She meant nothing to me. Nothing. I haven't thought about her for well over a year, and I mean that honestly. The only thing that's bothering me is what to do about you, and what to do about Maggie. And at this very moment, I'm not even bothered about Maggie. At this moment, nothing—d'you hear me—nothing, exists for me except this room, and this bed, and you in it. So do you know what I'm going to do?"

She shook her head mutely.

"I'm going to screw you like you've never been screwed before. Excuse the lack of sentiment, but right at this moment I don't feel like making love, however much I do love you. I feel like screwing. I think it will add to the chemistry of our on-screen relationship. Our off-screen relationship doesn't need any assistance."

Within the ardour of Oliver's technique, far more dominant this time round, Christy felt his anger. She didn't object to it; in fact it heightened her desire. It was dangerous, and she was tired of Gabe's oh-so-gentlemanly sexual manners. She also felt that she deserved it. If the only price she had to pay for opening his wounds was a little rough foreplay, she'd pay it willingly. She'd even enjoy it. He had implied that this wasn't to be the end of their relationship, but she didn't care to think about the future. She'd accept whatever terms he offered now, because he had given her something that she believed existed only in books and dreams.

At three in the morning, Oliver rose and dressed.

"Christy," he whispered, "I'm going to London. I'll see if I can borrow Edward's car."

She murmured, half asleep, and he shook her gently by the shoulder.

"Christy, I have to leave now." She wrapped her arms and legs around him to keep him with her.

"My darling, I have to leave."

"I know. Just kiss me. Once more, and then you can go forever."

He kissed her lovingly. "But I *am* coming back. I promise you that. And we *are* going to do this series together. And things *are* going to change."

His words brought Christy fully awake. "But, Oliver—what should I do? I don't know what to do—Gabe's coming back today. What should I do?"

"You're a very intelligent and resourceful woman, Christy, so you'll work something out. If I were you . . ."

"Yes?"

"I'd tell him the truth. I'd tell him you've found someone else."

Christy lay awake in bed until dawn. She had grown up in a conformist society in which illicit yearning, let alone its fulfilment, could not be tolerated. She dreaded seeing Gabe. If it had been unpleasant deceiving him and sending him off to Devon, this would be far, far worse. She knew she had been betraying him ever since they had set foot in Bockhampton. Christy knew that she could have handled telling Gabe she'd cheated on him, but she didn't know if she could bring herself to look at his face when she told him that she had fallen in love with Oliver. All her protective instincts told her to be a coward and a liar, to settle for what she had already, pack her bags and go home with her husband, but when it came to the point, she knew she'd have to tell the truth. It was bad enough admitting the truth to herself. She had entered into a game without believing she would face any consequences, and now she had lost control of it. It was easy to say that she didn't want Gabe to get hurt, but it was going to be far harder to protect him from her actions. She couldn't bear to even think about Jake. And yet beneath a surge of guilt, she acknowledged a steady stream of joy.

Few relationships break up on a Tuesday morning in October at the family breakfast table. The cracks may be there, but the crisis occurs in a foreign setting. It may be on holiday, it may be moving to a new house, it may be the birth of a baby; at the least it will come at an unreal hour in the middle of the night. These are the dangerous times in a relationship, when the normal order and routine of things have been taken away, and all is unfamiliar.

Oliver let himself into the barn without disturbing Edward. He poured himself a large whisky, and took the glass and the bottle into Edward's study. He sat down and read *A Sad Affair* from cover to unfinished cover, and drank half the bottle of whisky doing so. He felt no remorse about finishing Edward's premium malt. He felt no remorse about sleeping with Christy. He felt no remorse about anything. He had no shadow of a doubt in his mind that Maggie had written *A Sad Affair* and he had no shadow of a doubt that Christy's judgment was right. It was a wonderful book, and his wife had written it, and she had never mentioned it to him, and she'd used him and he wanted to kill her. In common with most people, Oliver found it far easier to live with anger than guilt.

$\mathcal{T}welve$

A postcard of a watercolour to Mrs. Christy Moore McCarthy, Bockhampton House, Wiltshire:

My Dear Christy,

I'm so happy that you and Gabe are having such a pleasant vacation together. Your father and I have many happy memories of trips we made to Europe. I hope Mariella is looking after Jake—may I remind you again that before you spend quality time with your children, you should spend it with your husband! Could you be a darling and stop by Harrods—I hope you're not too far away—and pick me out a new Burberry's raincoat? The traditional style—size 8 (American size)—if you've forgotten. I'm sure your father would appreciate a new scarf; maybe for Christmas?

Your ever loving mother,
Blanche Hewlett Moore

AT SEVEN-THIRTY IN THE MORNING, OLIVER PHONED DANNY BUJEVski, who was livid that Oliver had done a disappearing act all weekend.

"This isn't the way programmes get sold, Callahan. It's not the way we do things for the screen."

"Oh yeah? Well, it's the way I do things."

"That's just not good enough—"

"Listen to me carefully, Danny, because I've got three things to say to you. Number one, I'll spend my weekends how I goddamn please. Number two, what we're going to do for the series is that I'm going to travel down the Southeast coast of the States accompanied by a woman called Christy Moore McCarthy who knocks the socks off Scarlett O'Hara."

"Is she sexy?"

"She's on a different plane from anything you've ever come across, and she's a real Southern belle to boot. She was born for the job. Number three, I'm not coming into London today, and I'm not going to see you, because I've got to get back to the States. Family business. I will be back in three to four days' time—let me correct that; I'll be back when I'm goddamn back, but I'll be back with an outline, and we'll take it from there. Is that okay by you?"

"That sounds fine, Oliver. That's sounds great. Glad to see you're behaving professionally and getting your priorities right. Tickety-boo."

"Tickety-boo? You're an asshole, Bujevski. A real asshole. I guess that's what television does to people."

"Arsehole, Oliver. We say arsehole over here. Don't get too Americanised—I want to keep the dramatic distinction between you and the skirt. You see, if an American calls you an ass, you have no idea if they're calling you a donkey or an anus. The British are more specific; an ass is an ass, and an arse is an anus. It's a nice subtlety. Don't miss your flight."

"Arsehole."

Oliver's raised voice had woken Edward, who came downstairs looking rather the worse for wear, glanced at Oliver's packed bag and the empty whisky bottle, and without commenting went into the kitchen to make some coffee. He overheard Oliver leaving a very clipped message for Maggie.

"Maggie, this is Oliver. It's Monday morning my time. I'm going to try and get on the noon flight for Raleigh-Durham, but I don't have a reservation. Don't bother to come to the airport—I'll make my own way home. If you're at home, I'll see you, but don't do anything radical like changing your plans on my account."

"Early start, old man?"

"Yes. That is, I need you to take me to Heathrow. I won't make the flight if I get the train."

"No problem, if you give me a chance to put some clothes on." Edward poured coffee. "You seem a little—unsettled, Oliver? Did you have a pleasant day yesterday? I'm afraid I didn't wait up."

"It was fine. Very informative. Eye-opening, in fact. Look, Edward, I'm really pressed for time. I'm sorry to have to ask you this, but can we leave?"

"Go wait in the car. I'll be down in a moment."

They set off for Heathrow. Oliver talked nonstop, in the drunken yet lucid way that people do when they've been drinking steadily all night and haven't gone to bed. He talked mainly about Christy and Maggie.

"Christy McCarthy is an incredible woman. Truly incredible. I feel like I've known her all my life. Funny thing, that. I've spent a day and a half talking to her and I feel I know her backwards." Edward cocked a quizzical eyebrow, but Oliver didn't notice. "It's amazing how little you can know about a person even when you've been married to them for seven years, isn't it, Edward? Well, I suppose you wouldn't know, would you, never having taken the leap yourself. I find myself almost open-mouthed in wonder at each stage when I learn another side of my beloved wife's infinitely complex character. What do you think? Do you think Maggie is complicated? Our dear old, sweet old Mags? What do you think, hmm?"

"Oliver, I have no idea what you're talking about."

"No, you wouldn't, would you? You're not married to her. You can't begin to know what she's like, can you, Eddie old man? You probably think she's a lovely girl, just like I did. You wouldn't know any better, would you? You've only seen her best side. Well, when you know Maggie like I know Maggie . . ." He broke into song, and as suddenly broke off. "What do you think, Edward?"

"I think you're drunk."

"You're damn right I'm drunk. I started getting drunk with the delectable Mrs. McCarthy and ended up finishing the job all by myself. And if you knew all that I now know—*not to say that you don't*—you'd be drunk, too. Isn't that what men do, Edward? Isn't that what upstanding men do to comfort themselves when their wives betray them?"

"I wouldn't know."

"Ah, no, of course not! What a blessed state bachelorhood must be! Such freedom from responsibility. I've left it so long ago I can barely remember it . . . Not like Maggie, of course. Maggie remembers *everything*. Photographic memory, our dear Mags. Never forgets anything—just squirrels it all away somewhere—and never tells anything." He zipped his lips. "Zzzzppp. 'My lips are sealed.' That's

Maggie's motto. On second thoughts, I bet she breaks the rule for you, Eddie. I bet she tells *you* private things, hmm?"

Edward had no doubt now that someone had told Oliver about his and Maggie's very briefest of affairs. He drove on in silence down the M3.

"What do you think about this, Edward? Let me try it on you for size. You see, I have a theory. I have this theory that says all women think they understand all men better than any man understands any woman. That's the first premise. The second premise is that all women are intrinsically jealous of all men, and seek to destroy them, particularly if they happen to be married to said man. The third premise is that no man can possibly aspire to being as sensitive and perceptive and puke-makingly *intuitive* as any woman, because women are to a man cheating bitches, and mad to boot. And you can't be perceptive about madness, can you? No you bloody well can't. You see, the thing about madness is that it's irrational, and we men are, after all, rational creatures, so how can we be expected to perceive the insanity that governs their tiny lives?"

Edward turned onto the M25 and headed for the airport.

"You know, Edward, it's taken me all night, but I've finally twigged it. This is what Maggie's all about: she pretends to be all sweetness and light just to give you the false confidence that she's on your side, so that you won't see her take the knife out. If I hadn't heard something last night, I probably wouldn't have even noticed as she wriggled it into my ribs. I would have just quietly bled to death on the carpet, like a dutiful husband. What do you think of that idea? Don't you see? Don't you see what I'm saying about her? You, of all people? I mean, you're far more intimate with her than anybody else, me included. Has she got you in her little book?"

"I don't know what you're talking about."

"Ah well, lucky you. But then, you don't know her quite the way I know her, do you, Ed? Not that you don't *know* her, if you see what I mean—"

"I think you are raving. I don't agree with a single thing you're saying about Maggie. You ought to shut up now. I have something to say."

Edward drove up the departure ramp, stopped the car, turned off the engine, and turned to face his passenger.

"Oliver, you and I are old friends. We are also both grown men.

As you seem determined to trap me into a lie, I would rather pre-empt you. I don't appreciate your playing cat and mouse with me for an hour on the M3 any more than you presumably appreciate my sleeping with your wife. If you wanted to know how I came to go to bed with Maggie, or why, you had only to ask me directly and I would have told you. As I'm sure she would have. I make no excuses for my own behaviour, but yours is uncivilised, and I would guess, deeply hypocritical. I would suggest that your anger with Maggie is triggered by your own guilt. I sincerely hope you don't approach Maggie in the same way that you have me, and if you do, then my most fervent wish is that she tells you where to put it. You don't own Maggie, Oliver; you owe her understanding, and you haven't paid your dues for a long time. Now would you kindly get out of my car?"

Oliver sat frozen in his seat, staring at Edward. He felt his scalp tighten in an odd, rippling manner, as if he had a series of tight rubber bands creeping inch by inch over his head. Edward leant across him and opened his door, and Oliver climbed out without saying a word. He was too stunned to speak. Edward watched Oliver walk through the terminal doors and then drove to the first petrol station and made a long-distance call to North Carolina. He also got the answering machine. He cursed the invention of the damn thing, wishing he could have relied on Maggie eventually to stumble out of bed and answer the phone. But you can't halt progress, or turn back the clock. He left a message warning Maggie that Oliver knew they had slept together, and that Oliver was on his way home, angry and drunk as a skunk, but would no doubt sober up on the plane.

Oliver managed to sweet-talk his way onto the direct flight to the Raleigh-Durham airport. He even upgraded himself to business class, paying a whacking premium, in the hope that he wouldn't sit next to some boring creep who banged on about their holiday in England for the entire flight. He was lucky. He sat by himself at the back of the business-class section and was brought a glass of champagne before take-off. A celebratory glass; Oliver lifted it in a cynical toast to Maggie. Edward was mistaken about the likelihood of Oliver sobering up. He was also mistaken in thinking that Oliver had known about him and Maggie. He'd been right that Oliver was drunk, and that the combination of alcohol and guilt had prompted his tirade. Oliver had really registered only one thing that Edward had said: that Edward had gone to bed with Maggie. The knowledge that his wife and Edward had been having an affair left him speechless. He had a thumping headache.

The flight to Raleigh-Durham took eight hours. He rejected the flight attendant's offer of newspapers and read *A Sad Affair* twice. He had been angry with Maggie the first time he'd read it, but on each rereading it irked him more. Oliver was bothered by the book for three reasons. First because it was good—a lot better than he could have done. Secondly because she had used bits of him—she had borrowed things he had told her, even the name of his first extra-marital fling, and that annoyed him. She was mocking him, and it was humiliating. Thirdly, he was disturbed by the fact that she never told him about it, and that made him wonder how many other times he had been kept in the dark.

As he had been about Edward. It would take Oliver a lot more than eight hours to take on board the fact that Maggie had been unfaithful to him. His frequent and minor infidelities could not be compared to Maggie's. Up until now, Oliver had suffered from a particular type of male vanity that said that although *he* could not be satisfied by one woman alone, any of his women, and certainly the primary one, should be entirely satisfied by him. The thought of Maggie in bed with Edward—Edward of all people—was intolerable. It was so unacceptable to him that he almost talked himself into believing that Edward had lied about it. In his heart of hearts, Oliver knew that Edward hadn't lied; Edward would never see infidelity as a joking matter. If Oliver had believed for one moment that Maggie might have slept with Edward for a sexual thrill, or in the casual manner that he himself had screwed the gap-toothed Sarah, he might have been able to live with it. It might even have added a certain piquancy to their own sexual relationship. But the thought that made Oliver's stomach seize up and rise to his throat was the thought that Maggie must have really *wanted* to screw Edward—that she thought it would be—or, worse, was—better with Edward than with him. It was grim that his wife had written a book and not told him about it; that was a form of betrayal. The fact that the book was good was another betrayal; it meant that she didn't share everything with him, had kept a part of herself back. Wasn't satisfied by him. The fact that she had written a book about love and infidelity and sexual betrayal while having an affair with his friend and neighbour felt far worse than betrayal. Oliver felt physically battered.

It was no bad thing that the flight to Raleigh-Durham was a long one. Had Oliver been making a short hop to Paris there was a serious chance that he would have assaulted Maggie on his arrival. Although he continued to drink throughout the flight, and although his manners towards the flight attendants became increasingly surly, he had time to calm his initial rage. He realised that for him his marriage was over, because he could never live with a woman he couldn't trust. He had been privately proud that Maggie was so talented and bright, so long as he was the only person who recognised it. He had been comfortable when she was discreetly subsumed by him. Most of all, he had been happy to know that her passion was for him alone; what he had seen as her sexual devotion to him had given him the confidence to seduce others. The idea of adultery had always been tempting, even when he was a carefree bachelor. In some ways it was one of the great hidden benefits of marriage— almost a *purpose* of marriage—being able to conduct short affairs without any of the nasty complications about commitment single men had thrust upon them. If Maggie had been satisfied with what he gave her, he might have stayed with her forever. He had genuinely never doubted the strength of their marriage. He could even have been faithful to her, if that was the final quid pro quo. But she hadn't been satisfied. Perhaps she never had been. Perhaps Eddie was simply the latest in a long string of men that she used to compensate for Oliver's shortcomings. She had gone behind his back, feeling she didn't need him, or needed more than him. She'd made her choice, and now he would be forced to make his. And this wasn't the way he wanted to play the game. This was changing the rules midstream. It wasn't cricket.

Oliver stepped off the plane in a daze. He passed through Immigration, and started for the car rental desk before he had second thoughts: automatic pilot could land him in more trouble than he was in already. He turned and headed back to the airport bar, and ordered a double scotch. The problem was, he still cared about Maggie. There was a chance that if she cried, if she said that she had slept with Edward because she was drunk, and lonely, and frightened she was losing him, if she said that her book was crap, if she said all she wanted to do was go back home and have another baby, if she said she couldn't live without him, if the whole awful business was swept under the carpet and never repeated, then he might, *just might,* take her back. He had no desire to leave his children. He had no desire to live alone; he didn't envy Edward his bachelor state. At the back of his mind, Oliver saw Christy, which was a very comforting thought. Christy really believed in him. Christy asked nothing other than to be allowed to continue in a state of romantic and sexual intoxication. The risk was that if he saw Maggie and she didn't apologise, if she turned on him and said that it was her right to have affairs and do what she wanted, then he could lose it all. He could lose his pride.

He walked to a telephone, and tapped out the Oak Ridge number.

"G'day?" It was Leah's voice.

"Leah, it's Oliver."

"Hi, Ol. How you doing?"

"I'm fine. I've just landed at the airport. Is Maggie there?"

"Dunno. I'll see if I can track her down. She *was* down the beach. Hang on a tick."

Oliver hung on for an eternity.

"Oliver?" Maggie's voice sounded tentative.

"Yes. I'm here."

"Leah says you're at the airport?"

"That's right."

"Did everything go okay?"

"What do you think?" he asked tersely.

"I guess not, as you're back early, and as you sound cross. I'm really sorry, Oliver."

"Are you? What do you have to be sorry about?"

She didn't reply.

"Maggie, did you sleep with Edward Arabin?"

Again there was a long silence. Finally, "You know I did, so why ask the question?"

"So you don't deny it?"

"No, I don't." She sounded composed.

"And what do you have to say for yourself?" Oliver winced as he heard himself—he sounded like a Victorian headmaster—not how he meant to sound at all.

"I think we should talk about it when you get home."

"I'm on my way. I thought I'd do the decent thing and let you know—that I knew."

"Edward's already called me. He left a message."

"What a great set-up you've got, Maggie. A decent husband and a loyal lover. However do you pull it off?"

"Ol, let's leave this till you get home, okay? We need to talk."

"I'm not at all sure that I feel like talking to you, Maggie." She made no reply. "I feel like getting straight back on the next plane to London." Still no reply. "Are you there, Maggie?"

"Yes."

"It will take me a couple of hours to drive back. Can you wait that long? You won't feel the need to rush off and screw somebody else?"

"I'll see you later, Oliver." Maggie hung up the phone.

Christy jumped when she heard the scrunch of the car tires on the gravel path. She felt as if she had aged ten years waiting for Gabe to come home. After Oliver had gone early that morning, she had risen herself, stripped and changed the bed linen, and opened all the windows in the room; it had reeked of sex, the sweet smell seeming to linger in the folds of the four-poster curtains. Not long after dawn, she had gone to work in the garden, and had come inside to look through the mail. After she read her mother's post-card, she finally decided what she would say to Gabe. She made up her face with even more care than usual, and spent two hours sitting at the kitchen table, waiting for them to come home. She heard the car at noon, and went to greet them, hunkering down to hug Jake, and tilting her face for Gabe's kiss.

"Did you all have a grand time?"

"Mommy, it was fantastic—Dad took me to see the ponies on Dartmoor, and we went fishing, and we had ice-cream for *breakfast,* but I dropped mine on the sidewalk . . ." he ended plaintively.

"Sounds like a real good thing I didn't come along with you all; what was Daddy doing giving you ice-cream for breakfast?" She glanced up at Gabe, who looked suitably shame-faced.

"It was *wicked.*"

"You can say that again. Did you enjoy yourself, Mariella?"

"Yes, ma'am, thank you. It was very pretty."

"Well now, you all run along inside and get some lunch—and Jake? No more ice-cream, okay?"

As Jake galloped into the house to greet the dogs, Christy looked at her husband nervously, and struggled to keep control of her voice. When she spoke, she sounded cool and professional.

"Could we just go into the drawing room for a moment, Gabe?

I need to share something with you." Gabe felt like a trainee being summoned into the boss's office for a real dressing-down—and all on account of a couple of lousy ice-cream cones. . . .

Christy stood at the window, looking out over the terrace with her back to Gabe.

"How was the cricket game?"

"It was fine. Gabe, Oliver Callahan came by this weekend."

"No kidding? I didn't know he was coming over—I'm sorry I missed him. What's he like?"

"A perfect gentleman. He came to play cricket."

"Great. Tell me about the game."

"It was fine, just fine. I think they all liked the food." She folded her arms tightly across her chest. "Gabe? Oliver wants me to work with him on a television series he's planning on the South."

"Well wha'd'you know? That sounds like it could be fun. Are you going to do the research, or what?"

"I don't know for sure—we didn't have time to work out the details. He thinks, more like a presenter."

"Terrific, honey! My wife the movie star! You'll be great, Christy. You don't look all that excited about it."

She turned to face him, her face expressionless. "You see, this kind of changes everything."

"Why, when are you going to start filming? D'you need to get back home early or something?"

"No; the thing is, Gabe, that I'm not going home."

"You're gonna film it here? And waste all those camera angles over our glorious beaches?"

"No; I mean I'm not going home with you at all. I mean, our marriage is over."

Gabe roared with laughter. "Christy Moore McCarthy, you were born to be on the screen! To think how close you came to missing your true vocation! How long have you been rehearsing your lines? Honey, I had a long drive. I'm gonna go upstairs and freshen up some, and then we can talk about this whole TV thing."

"Gabe—don't go now, please. Hear me out. The thing is, when I say our marriage is over, I mean just that. This is going to be real hard for me to explain, and I don't expect you'll understand, but I'm going to try." She swallowed hard. "I'm going to stay here with Jake for a while, and I think it's for the best if you go home. Maybe just for the time being."

Gabe chuckled. "You know, for a moment you had me fooled. I guess there's one born every minute. For a moment I thought you were so goddamn mad about the ice-cream you really wanted to send me off to the doghouse. Come here, sugar, and give me a big hug."

Christy stood her ground, and drew in a deep breath. "Gabe, I am in love with Oliver Callahan." She felt a surge of exhilaration just saying his name out loud. "I can't explain it, but I love him hopelessly, and I can't bring myself to pretend that nothing's happened. I thought about it—about saying nothing—but it wouldn't be fair to you."

"Christy, darling—have you gone mad? You don't even know the man."

"Yes I do. I've known him for a long time—I've been waiting for him for a long time."

There was an honesty and sadness in her voice that made Gabe's blood run cold, but he chose not to acknowledge it.

"Christy, you are talking through your sweet ass, if you'll pardon the expression. Have you been at the booze? Are you lit? I've had a long journey with Jake bawling all the way, and I don't need to hear this. This is downright ridiculous, you hear me?"

"I don't think you are listening to me, Gabe. Let me try saying this again. I love Oliver Callahan. I am going to work with him. I would give just about anything I have to spend the rest of my life with him, not that I can do that. I spent last night with him upstairs in our bed. In his bed, I guess I should say. I am real sorry for you, and I feel read bad and real guilty and all, and I'm prepared to pay the price for what I've done, but I just can't help feeling happy for me, and I just can't hide it." Her eyes were full of tears.

Gabe slumped into a chair next to the fireplace, staring at her. He still didn't understand what she was saying. It was too incredible that he could come home from a weekend and find his beloved Christy in love with a man she didn't know. A hundred thoughts flashed through his head—how he'd have to get her home, whether she was well enough to travel, whether he should call their doctor in Lawrenceville; he knew of a psychiatrist in New York, but not at home; he remembered reading something about HRT, that maybe younger women should start having it to keep in balance; he wondered if it was okay for Christy to be around Jake—there was no telling what she might say to him—even do to him. There were stories about mothers losing it and hurting their own adored children. He had heard about women believing their fantasies, and she had been acting mighty strange lately. She was young for a midlife crisis, but then that's what crisis is—something that catches you unprepared. Gabe had not previously wasted much of his time thinking about what went on in people's heads; he thought that if someone got sick, you called in an expert, just like you called in a mechanic to fix your car. He was not one for sticking his head under the hood and dabbling around. Nonetheless, if this was what was required of him, he would look after her—she'd have the best care and want for nothing. All the time he stared at her as if she might collapse or implode at any minute. Christy stood perfectly still.

"Gabe, don't look at me like I've grown horns or something. I realise this must be a real shock for you, and I've had all day to think things through. You don't know what to say. We both need time to get our heads screwed on, and come to an arrangement about the future. I think we can do that best apart. I want to stay here, and you should go back home for the time being." Gabe, who had never understood his wife all that well, couldn't see the effort Christy was making. Her apparent calm drove Gabe to fury, and he couldn't stop himself from jumping up and shaking her.

"You just snap out of it now, Christy! You just come to your senses and listen to the crap you're talking! We're not going anywhere—not until you pull yourself together. I know you haven't been happy, I know you've got problems, I know you were more upset by not having another baby than you ever let on, even to yourself, and we'll sort it all out, but we've got to do it *together,* Christy. I'll stand by you—we'll see this through whatever the hell this is really about."

Christy shook her head slowly, and touched his cheek with one hand. It was the first gesture of genuine, if hesitant affection she had shown him for a long time.

"I'm sorry, Gabe. I'm so truly sorry; I can't find any words to tell you how sorry I am for what I've done to you. It won't make it any better, but believe me, I never meant this to happen. Even up till this morning, I thought we could just go home, and you could never know about him, and you and Jake wouldn't be any the worse off. I thought I could just do something spontaneous and walk away with nothing changed. If there was any way I could do this without hurting you, believe me, I would. But it *is* over. You *must* believe me. I'm sure of that more than I've ever been sure of anything. I know it in here." She touched her lower stomach. "I'm not sick, or drunk, or anything else. I'm just deliriously in love—so much I can't rightly describe how it feels. I don't even know if he loves *me*, but I don't care." Her voice rose elatedly as she was unable to control her happiness in simply talking about Oliver. "I love him. If he doesn't want me, I just can't pretend any longer that I can be happy with you. I just want to be with him. I've never lied to you, Gabe; I've never had to. I won't start now."

"I don't believe you."

Christy stamped her foot in sheer frustration. "You just ain't listening to me, Gabe! What do I have to do to make you hear me?" She chewed at her lower lip, staring at him. Her chin trembled. "Come closer, Gabe; come real close; that's right." She stood on tiptoe, just under his chin, and raised the collar of her shirt. "You can smell him on me, Gabe. I just couldn't bear to take a bath. Does that make you believe me?"

He hit her, lashing out hard against the side of her head, and sent her reeling against the fireplace. "Christy, darling, my darling girl, what have I done? Christy I'm so sorry, my darling . . ." He helped her up, stroking her hair, cradling her cheek in his hand, immediately repentant. Christy was relieved that he had hit her; as her love for Oliver had developed, it had become inextricably meshed in her misery at her own marriage, however much she had tried to keep them separate. Now that Gabe had at last reacted spontaneously, she was no longer angry with him; she felt nothing for him but remorse and pity, and a strange new tenderness.

"It's okay, Gabe, I'm okay, it's not your fault, it's okay, baby . . . You see, now, you *see* why we have to part for a while. I'm so sorry I had to tell you that way, but you see, I'm certain. I *know*. Nothing's going to change my mind."

Gabe believed her. He at least believed that in some nightmare she had slept with Oliver, and talked herself into being in love with him. Whether she really was, or whether it was an excuse to get away from him, he didn't know. It didn't seem to matter much. It was the same outcome for him either way. His only option was to do what he had always done—to do what she wanted, to go along with her, to hold back and shut up, and pray to God that things sorted themselves out. When she came to her senses, he'd be there to take her back.

They sat at opposite ends of the sofa, Christy tentatively nursing her cheek, which was already turning a deep purple.

"This room always seems kind of dark and gloomy in the afternoon, doesn't it?" Christy sighed.

"You talking about a separation, Christy?"

"It's the only way, Gabe. For a couple of months. Let's see how it goes."

"And you plan to stay put here?"

"I don't know about that. It's up to Oliver."

"I see. And what about Mrs. Callahan? How does she fit into the picture? Does she have any say in this?"

"I haven't even thought about her," Christy admitted. "I don't want her to get hurt—not for me. That's up to Oliver, too. I don't know. We didn't talk about her."

"You didn't, huh? I guess you didn't have much time for talking."

"Gabe, can we try and be calm about this? I know I've betrayed you, but what I'm trying to explain is that I think I've been betraying myself for a long time. You're not the only one who has been deceived—I have, too, by *myself,* trying to pretend I could live like that. I want you to understand me. Let's talk, be civilised . . ."

"Sure. Civilised." His tone was ironic. "We'll just pretend we're talking about somebody else, okay? Okay. D'you want to tell me how it all happened?"

"Not really. Not just now, that is."

"Am I ever to be told? Just idle curiosity, you know, sugar. I'm a tad curious how we can be married—happily, I thought—for ten years, and then you go to bed with some complete stranger."

"The thing is, that even before I met him, I've had the oddest sensation—like *you've* been the stranger, and not him. Gabe, all I can tell you is that ever since we set foot in this house I've been falling in love with him—it's felt like an irresistible magnet, everything I see and touch and hear drawing me closer to him. Then I read a book he wrote, and it was like he was talking to me, face to face. He wrote everything I've ever felt and not let myself think about. Then I met him, and he said he felt he'd known me forever, and I felt the same way, and we made love."

"That simple, huh? Was it good, Christy?" She didn't reply, but he read her answer in her eyes.

"Shit. And then you live happily ever after? You guys gonna get married, or what?" Every word he uttered dripped with bitterness.

"It hadn't occurred to me. We didn't plan any of this, Gabe."

"Get real, Christy. Maybe this guy will stay hot for a month or two, but this kind of story doesn't have a happy ending. It's just a holiday romance—you're from different places, you have different roots, different ideas about life. You can't make a match that way. He'll have enough, he'll want his own wife back, or someone new, and you'll have messed up all our lives for nothing." He tried a new tack as Christy shook her head sadly. "What about your parents? What do you think your mother will say? You'll shame them."

"I know. That doesn't bother me a jot."

He tried again. "An affair doesn't have to end a marriage. We made a bond for life. I'm happy to keep to that whatever you've done."

"I know you are, Gabe; I really respect that. But I can't keep to it; I surely wish I could, but I can't."

"Christy, you've got to. That's what life's all about. You make a decision, you choose something, and you stick to it. You don't run away when things get tough." Christy just shook her head. "I see. So we're back to doing things your way. What about Jake?"

"He'll stay with me."

"No way; you better just think again. You want to leave home, okay. I can't stop you. You chose this, Christy; you pay the price."

"No. Not Jake. I'm not paying that price."

"You said you'd pay the price; you said you'd give everything you had. You should have thought about him before; if you were any kind of a mother, you would have thought about him before you hopped into bed with a stranger."

"Gabe, you're entitled to call me every name under the sun. I will crawl, or beat myself or do whatever you please, but don't tell me I haven't thought about Jake. I've done nothing but think about him, and what he needs, and what this'll do to him. We owe it to Jake to think about him together. You can't take him away from me. You're not thinking about him—you're just thinking of the one way you can hurt me back as bad as I've hurt you. I already know what price I'm going to pay, and I'll never be able to forgive myself for hurting you, but don't make Jake pay—not twice over—don't make him suffer more than he has to! I won't allow it, you hear? If you love him, really love him, you'll leave him with me."

"Shit, Christy; you've even given yourself all the good lines, huh? You want to walk away looking like the noble mother, too. Well, you ain't. It just ain't right to split up a boy and his father—it's no good for me, and no good for him."

"You're right. I agree. It shouldn't have to happen. But if I *can't* live with you anymore, are you saying that it's better to split up a little boy and his mother? Not just any little boy, but Jake? Are you really considering your son's best interests?"

"Are you?" Gabe tried his damnedest to resist her arguments, but she'd left him no real alternatives. "What about school? What about his friends? What about his home?"

"They have schools in England, Gabe. Good schools. His home is with me; houses don't matter. He'll make new friends; he's young enough." Suddenly this separation had nothing temporary or trial about it. As Christy said the words, she realised for the first time just how far she was prepared to go; her home and her friends and her roots didn't matter so long as she could be with Oliver. And keep Jake.

"He may be, but I don't know that I am. Have you thought about what we're going to tell him?"

"For the time being I'll just say that I have a new job, and I need to be in England, so he's going to have the chance of a semester or two here. He'll understand that you have to go back to the office."

"He will, will he? It's more than I do."

"I think so. If he's told the right way."

"You're gonna be travelling a lot. I thought you didn't hold with mothers working when their kids are little?"

"I've changed my mind. I think that if I'm happy, that will be the best thing for Jake."

"Well, that's real convenient, ain't it? Looks to me like you've thought of everything, Christy darling; just like I knew you would. Have you thought about money?"

"I don't care about money."

"You don't, huh? I wonder what your new lover will say to that." He stood up.

"Where are you going, Gabe?"

"I'm going to pack. Unless, of course, you've already done that for me?"

She shook her head. "There's no hurry."

"No hurry? Oh, Christy . . ." His eyes were brimming with tears as he looked at her. "Oh, Christy . . . I don't think you even hear what you're sayin' . . ."

Gabe repacked everything Christy had packed for him seven weeks earlier, and left his suitcase and his briefcase in the hall. He called the airport, called the number of a local taxi, and went into the kitchen.

"Hey, big fella! How are you doing, guy?" He ruffled Jake's hair. "Mariella, would you mind leaving us alone for just a minute? I need to talk to my main man."

"Sure, Mr. McCarthy."

"Now, Jake; we need to have a man-to-man chat, okay? I've got to go back home. Your mother told me when we got back that my stinky old office had called, and I've got to dash back and sort something out." Jake immediately shuffled off his seat, and started collecting toys scattered all over the kitchen floor.

"I'm coming with you, Daddy—I'm coming, too! I want to see Jackson, and you've gotta wait for me—"

"Now just slow down a minute, son! If you come along with me, who's going to look after Lucius?"

"He can come, too. I know what—he can sit with us on the plane! He can sit on my lap. He won't take up much room."

"No, Jake; we can't do that, I'm afraid. He belongs here. And anyway, who's going to look after your mom? I was kind of counting on you to take my place and be the man of the house, you know?"

"But aren't we *all* going home, Dad?"

"Soon, son; but not yet. We're all going to be together soon, just like always. I'm never going to leave you for long, come hell or high water."

"But I don't like it when you go away!"

"C'mon, Jake! I've always told you that's a daddy's job: we're only put here to make your life miserable—your mom gets to do all the good stuff, and I get to be the real stinker. That's the way I like it." His son rewarded him with a smile. "Now you take good care of her for me, and take care of all the dogs." Jake clambered onto him, and snuggled onto his father's lap. Gabe held him so tight that the little boy wriggled to get free. "It won't be long before we're all back home, or maybe I'll come fetch you, okay? Is that a deal?" Jake solemnly held his hand out to shake on it, but Gabe squeezed him in another bear hug as he heard a taxi pull up outside.

"Okay, son—scoot. I'm going to have to run or I'll miss my plane and be in big trouble. I'll just say hey to your mom."

Christy was still sitting motionless in the drawing room.

247

"I'm leaving now. I told Jake I was going back to work, and I'd see him in a while. I didn't know what else to say. You're going to have to tell him the rest. And don't think there's any chance of my giving him up, Christy; you can get that idea right out of your head."

She half turned in her seat, looking at him over the back of the sofa, with her eyes like headlights switched onto full beam.

"Gabe? Do you hate me? Please don't hate me."

"Jesus Christ, Christy . . . Dear God, please not this. Don't do this to me. You tell me that you love—excuse me, that you are really *in love* with—another man. I think *deliriously* was the word you used. You make me smell him on you, for Christ's sake. You kick me out of the house faster than goose shit. And now you turn those big innocent eyes on me and ask me in that little voice not to hate you? Isn't it a bit late for all that? What the hell do you really want, Christy? You don't want me, you don't want me to love you, and you won't even allow me the comfort of hating you? Spare me that, if you ever cared shit about me. Do I hate you? What do you think, Christy?"

"I guess you do."

"You're darn right I hate you. But that doesn't mean I don't love you. I've never stopped loving you from the day I laid eyes on you. I want you. You are all I *ever* wanted. My tragedy isn't that I hate you, it's that I love you. I want you to be my wife again, and for us to be just like we always were. If you want me to be different— I'll be different. I'll turn cartwheels or shave my head. I'll do any darn fool thing you want, so long as you tell me what and why. But you're going to have to make your own way back, Christy, because I'm not going to have you back under my roof and in my bed with this English asshole still in your head. You clear it up. Then you call me at the apartment. If it was just Oliver I was dealing with, I'd kick the little shit clean out of my house, but I'm not going to turn Mrs. Callahan out. This ain't her fault. So you can find me at the apartment. But don't call till you're good and ready and done with this all this crap."

He slammed the door behind him.

Thirteen

A postcard of Stonehenge, to Lindy and B. J. Richards:

Hey, Guys!

 This is where we're staying. They said it was a bit run down, but I never thought it would be this bad . . . No heating, no running water. Take me back south of the Mason-Dixon line! Seriously, folks, this is the big tourist attraction. I say it's a heap of rubble, but Christy says it has mystical significance. . . . Having a grand time. Catch you later.

               Gabe

MAGGIE WAS WAITING FOR OLIVER IN THE KITCHEN. SHE LOOKED TER-rible, tired and pale beneath her tan, and she hadn't bothered to put on any makeup. She rarely did, and there was little point in changing her habits now just for Oliver's sake. The table was still littered with boxes of cereal and bowls from the children's breakfast that Maggie hadn't bothered to clear up. When Oliver walked in, she noticed that he looked even worse than she did. She had prom-ised herself that the one thing she wouldn't do was feel sorry for him.

Oliver sat stiffly at the table.

"Oliver. I want to try to explain things to you."

"I don't think there's anything you can say that would explain how you have been having an affair with my best friend under my nose."

"We haven't been having an affair, Ol. We slept together, once."

"Is that supposed to make me feel better?"

"No," she agreed reasonably, "I just think you should know the facts before we fight about it."

"Why should I believe you? Why should I believe anything you say?"

"Because I don't lie. Look, it doesn't make any difference if we did it once or a hundred times. What I want to tell you is that I slept with Eddie because I've been really unhappy, for ages—"

"Oh, I see. It's a new version of the old story. My husband doesn't understand me."

Maggie bit her lip. "Actually, I don't think you *do* understand me. But that's just one of the reasons for my being unhappy."

"You stagger me, Maggie. You're still just thinking about yourself; you haven't given a moment's thought to what you have done to me—how you have humiliated me. Do you have any idea how I feel?"

"So that's the problem, is it, Ol?" Maggie said quietly. "It isn't about Eddie; it's about you losing face?"

"Is that what you'd call it? My losing face? I can think of a much cruder and more truthful expression for what you've done to me."

"I just bet you can. You're such a hypocrite, Oliver. You've had plenty of experience in describing these situations, haven't you? How would you describe your relationship with Louise?"

"You can't compare that to this. You didn't even know Louise. If you hadn't been so nosy you would never have known about her, and it would never have affected you. I did everything I could to protect you from it. I wasn't taking anything away from you."

"I don't believe you can have just said what I think you did." Maggie put her head in her hands. "You surely can't expect me to buy the crappy old excuse that because I didn't know about it, your screwing Louise wasn't taking anything from me?"

"It wasn't. It didn't change how I felt about you; it had nothing to do with our marriage."

"Then you're right. It can't be compared to what happened between me and Eddie. That had *everything* to do with our marriage, and I *knew* it was taking something away from you."

"My respect."

"No!" Maggie shouted. "Me. It was taking me from you."

"I have never, in any affair, withdrawn myself from you."

"Precisely. Because you've never put anything of yourself *into* a

250

relationship. So. It wasn't just Louise then. You admit you've had other affairs? Other women?"

"Yes, I do. I've got nothing to lose now."

"Oh, fine. You've got nothing to lose *now*. But all the times you've lied to me, all the times you've called me neurotic and paranoid, you lied because you felt you did have something to lose?" Oliver shrugged noncommittally. "So when you actually did have something to lose—me—that didn't stop you climbing into bed with them, did it? It was enough to make you lie, but not enough to stop you doing it?"

"You can interpret it any way you like, Maggie. I just don't care anymore."

Maggie stared at him. However much she had told herself that she simply didn't love Oliver, and that he had treated her abominably, listening to her husband's confirmation that he didn't care about her hurt more than she had anticipated. Oliver studied the back of a cereal packet.

"By the way, Maggie, I wanted to mention that I picked up a really interesting little book at Bockhampton this weekend."

"Oh yes?"

"Yes. *A Sad Affair,* it was called. Not the punchiest of titles, I'll admit. What made you use Alec Bones as a nom de plume? I don't think you'll get very far with that. It doesn't have the right ring to it, if you know what I mean."

"Just don't, Oliver."

"Why didn't you tell me about the book, Maggie? It's clearly based on me. You even used Louise's name. You should have told me about it."

Maggie shook her head in disbelief. "It isn't about you, Ol. Maybe you prompted it, but only in that you were making me so unhappy. It's about *me*, Oliver. Can't you understand that? It's all about *me*, and *my* fantasies. If it's about anyone else, then it's about Eddie. Just a fantasy. It's all about how I wanted to be loved."

"That explains why it's such . . ." Oliver paused.

"Such what? Such crap? Is that what you were going to say? That it is just sentimental, drivelling crap? Alright, I admit it. Maybe it *is* crap. But at least I was doing something for me—at least it came from me, and was mine alone." Maggie was so accustomed to Oliver's putting her down, the only way she could protect herself was to get there before him.

Unlike the McCarthys, who had rarely ever disagreed, the Callahans had developed a private, customised code of warfare. They both favoured the pre-emptive strike technique, to disarm the opposition. Oliver was inclined to lie before there was a need to lie; Maggie either attacked before she herself was attacked, or pretended to drop the barriers that she was in fact fortifying.

"It *is* crap, isn't it, Oliver?" Maggie prayed that there was still enough charity left in Oliver to give her some reassurance. Even though she had most irrevocably withdrawn her love from him, his opinion still mattered to her. No one else had read the book, after all.

"Yes, it's crap, Maggie," Oliver said wearily. "But I don't give a fuck about your book. It's a bit late for a literary critique, wouldn't you say? I don't even want to speak to you any longer. I don't want to hear any more. I'm going back to England. I've got a lot of work—a lot of things to sort out. By myself. I can't stand the thought of you."

Maggie's nerves snapped. "That's impressive, Oliver. When you fucked Louise, repeatedly, and God knows who else, I carried on loving you and trying to understand you for six years, but it's only taken you twenty-four hours to get over me and just walk away. Fast work."

Oliver stood up unsteadily. He couldn't stand the sneer in her voice. "You have no idea how much you've hurt me."

"Think about someone else for a change, Oliver. What about the children? Don't you want to see them before you go? They're at the lake."

He bent over the table, pushing his face close to hers. His expression was so angry that Maggie drew back in alarm.

"Don't, just *don't* mention the children to me, Maggie. I can't see them now. It might make me feel I had to stay with you."

"What do you expect me to do? You can't run away from this. You can't leave us sitting here in a foreign country in some stranger's house . . . Should I just pack up? Go home? What? What do you want me to do?"

"You'll sort it out, Maggie. You'll do what you want to do. You don't need me, do you? You're a big girl. If you're really that desperate for someone to lean on, call Eddie."

"You can't be so irresponsible. We have to make plans. What happens now?"

"In the immortal lines of your hero, Maggie: Frankly, I don't give a damn."

Maggie listened to his car pull away down the drive.

Maybe marriage was never intended to be about togetherness, but it damn well meant foreverness, and Oliver was walking away from their problems like a little boy sulking about football. The thing that really riled her was his totally uncalled for mockery of *A Sad Affair;* Maggie was sufficiently self-critical to know that it wasn't very good, but it had been her first attempt to do something she really wanted, to do something independently, and Ol should have supported it. He would have, if he hadn't been sulking so badly. After her initial anger, Maggie found a new sense of calm, a sense of genuine relief. She resolved to carry on as if nothing had happened. As far as Lily was concerned, her daughter knew that Daddy was working in London, and would be home as soon as he could. Arthur had not yet reached the age of demanding explanations. The only person who did need an explanation was Leah, and Leah knew Oliver well enough for that to be a brief one. Maggie joined her family at the lake.

"Leah, Oliver's gone back to London."

"But he just bloody got here!"

"He did, but we had a row and he decided to get on a plane back to England."

"What the hell d'y'say? Sure must have put his bloody nose out of joint."

"You could say that."

"Men. You can't bloody live *with* them . . ."

"You can't bloody live with them. Exactly."

"You 'right, Maggie?"

"Never better."

That evening the Callahans were expected at a barbecue at the Richardses. Maggie had explained that Oliver might or might not be back in time, and they had told her to go ahead and bring anyone or no one as she chose. They were a very informal couple. She was in no mood for a party, but sitting home alone would somehow give Oliver the moral victory, and he'd been winning long enough. She made more of an effort than usual to dress for the Richardses. They had said "pool wear," real casual, so Maggie wore shorts and a shirt, but the shorts were silk and the shirt linen. She even had her hair set by Christy's hairdresser, and she couldn't remember how long ago it was that she'd had her hair done. She took Christy's little run-around to the Richardses' house; they lived about four miles away from Oak Ridge, out in the country. The front yards of the neighbouring houses were full of pumpkins lined up in regimental rows, ready for storing for the fall. There were already plenty of cars, signifying that however informal the party, the Richardses could count on a big turnout.

"Maggie, child, come and meet all these folks!" B.J. came out to greet her. "I guess Oliver didn't make it back in time?"

"No—he was tied up, I'm afraid. You'll have to make do with me."

"That'd be our pleasure, honey. C'mon on in. Did you bring your swimsuit? You're welcome to have a dip in the pool. But let's get you fixed up with something long and cold first." As he poured her a drink, he continued. "Hey, Maggie—we've got a surprise house guest . . . He just came from the airport an hour back." His eyes twinkled at her. For an awful moment Maggie thought he meant Oliver. Surely Oliver wouldn't have gone to the Richardses' rather than the airport? It was possible. He had done equally embarrassing things in the past.

"Is it anyone I know?" she asked nervously.

"I wouldn't say you know him, exactly, but you're pretty close." He shouted across the patio that surrounded the pool.

"Gabe, I'd like you to meet my eh-min-nent neighbour, Maggie Callahan. Maggie, this is my old buddy, Gabe McCarthy, recently arrived from England."

"Why, Mr. McCarthy, I had no idea you were coming back early! You should have told us."

"It's an honour to meet you, Mrs. Callahan. I didn't know myself I'd be coming back until just this morning. I called Beej here and asked him to pick me up and give me a bunk for a night or two."

"But you must come back to Oak Ridge—there's plenty of room—well, you know that, and I could take the children back to the beach house—unless you wanted to go there?"

"No, I would surely hate to disturb your holiday. I've just come back to do some work, so I'll be spending most of my time in Charlotte. We keep an apartment there. I may need to get a few things from the house—if I may, that is."

"Of course! Absolutely. Look, I really feel terrible about this. We can easily move. Has Christy come back with you?"

Gabe looked away for a moment, and then answered, "No; I think she's going to finish her vacation over there; unless you and Oliver have made other plans?"

"We haven't made any plans at all. I mean, Oliver's actually in England at the moment—"

"I know that."

"You do? Of course you do! He mentioned he was going to drop in to Bockhampton at the weekend to say hello."

"He did that alright."

"So you met him?"

Before Gabe could answer, Lindy had dragged Maggie away to meet a friend of hers from Charleston. Lindy was very keen for Maggie to see Charleston before she left the States, and had roped in her friend for support. "You can hitch up with Gabe later, child; he'll be hanging around for some time. You're our guest of honour, so he's just gonna have to stand in line."

Maggie could feel Gabe watching her as she was led away. She was dying to corner him and find out what had happened over the weekend, and whether Oliver had given anything away to the McCarthys about the row.

Maggie enjoyed the party in spite of herself. The Richardses were good and generous hosts, and barring the odd politically incorrect racist comment that would have brought a New York or London party to a stunned standstill, their friends were the soul of charm and hospitality. Maggie pondered on what made the people in this part of the world so very different from the rest of the human race that she had encountered. In part, it was that the men evidenced a genuine spirit of chivalry. Had she attended a party in London, or even in Compton Purlew, alone, Maggie would either have been left unattended, or she would have been hit on. Here on the outskirts of Lawrenceville, she was not abandoned for a moment. It was a little like being thrown into the middle of a Jane Austen novel, just dumped at a reception in the Upper Rooms of Bath. She never had fewer than three men tending to her needs—one insisting on refreshing her drink, one on getting her something to eat, and a third inquiring on how she was enjoying her stay. And all of them without a hint of impropriety. They inhabited a very gracious world, a society that had in many ways stood still for a century, and Maggie found herself envying them. The women, long accustomed to this sort of attention, were strong yet tender ladies, whose speech was like a bolt of silk unrolling, giving the entirely false impression that they were soft as silk inside. Maggie was glad to see that Gabe had rejoined the small group at her side.

"Mrs. Callahan, I do hope you're being properly looked after?"

"Perfectly, thank you. But please call me Maggie." He inclined his dark head.

"You never told me if you'd met my husband last weekend."

"I didn't. I was away at the time, and unaware he was coming, or I would surely have stayed behind. My wife met him."

"Oh good! I'm expecting him back—maybe later this week."

Gabe took her arm and led her slightly away from the crowd.

"Have you spoken to him recently, Maggie? To Oliver?"

Maggie moistened her lips. "Only very briefly. He's been desperately busy working on a TV project."

"Yes, I believe Christy mentioned that."

"He probably wanted to pick her brains. It's meant to be all about the South."

"It would be interesting to see it through his eyes."

"Oh, you know how tourists never get the real story—they tend to go home with all the wrong impressions."

"If they go home at all."

Maggie raised her eyebrows. "I hope you don't think we're never going to get out of your house and leave you in peace? I promise you we will."

"I was thinking more of my own wife; she's become very attached to your Valley."

"And did *you* enjoy your stay?"

"It's a very pleasant part of the world," Gabe replied noncommittally. His face looked rather grim, and Maggie suspected that Bockhampton hadn't lived up to expectations—had been a little too shabby, or the dogs had been a nuisance, or something else had put him off.

"I hope our neighbours have been helpful—they're not quite as hospitable to strangers as your friends are, but they do grow on you."

"They have been perfectly delightful."

"Good." Maggie was finding it hard to keep the conversation

going; Gabe McCarthy seemed slightly distracted, although he seemed in no hurry to leave her company.

"Maggie . . . I find myself in very difficult circumstances. I feel as if I may be the bearer of bad news, and it's not easy to do that as a stranger."

"Is it something about the house? The dogs? It's not Snuff, is it? He's fearfully old—I told Oliver we shouldn't leave him."

"No, they're all just fine. It's more to do with your husband."

"Don't say he was out for a duck? That would explain a lot," she said cynically, before taking in the blank expression on Gabe's face. "The cricket? They lost? He was disgraced?"

"I'm afraid I know nothing about that."

"Oh. Well, what?"

He drew her still further away from the party, his head bent towards hers.

"Did Oliver mention anything about my wife? About Christy?"

Maggie thought for a moment. "I don't think so. No, I don't think he mentioned her at all. But as I said, he was in a hurry. She's alright, isn't she? Nothing's happened?"

"Maggie, my wife told me that she is having an affair with your husband. At least that's what she claimed. It may not be the truth."

"That's impossible." Maggie shook her head nervously, and tried a tight little smile that didn't quite work. Damn Oliver for washing their dirty linen in public. "I'm afraid you've got the wrong end of the stick. She must have been talking about Edward."

"No. She told me very simply that she was in love with Oliver, and that they had . . . uh, spent the night together, Sunday night, I believe, and she told me that she didn't want me in the house. That's why I'm here. Maybe I shouldn't have said anything. I'm not really thinking straight."

"But this is crazy! They don't even know each other! There's been an awful misunderstanding—you must feel terrible, but this really isn't anything to do with you and Christy. I know what it's about; it's all my fault. . . ."

"I don't believe it's your fault or mine, Maggie. I believe we are what the courts describe as the injured parties. It is perfectly possible that Christy"—he swallowed hard—"that my wife has somehow imagined all this, and that your husband is in no way implicated, but I have to admit that whatever else has happened, I do believe that they . . . that they . . ."

"Screwed?" Maggie's eyes glittered as she struggled to keep her face composed.

"Yes. I have reasons to believe—"

"What reasons? How do you know?"

"I can't bring myself to tell you that, Maggie. That's between you and your husband, and I'm sure it meant nothing to him, although my wife, Christy, well, she hopes to God it did."

"I see. Well. It's strange to hear this at such a pleasant little evening, but I wouldn't be all that surprised. It fills in a few of the gaps, in fact. Thank you for—for *sharing* this with me, Gabe. We clearly have more in common than we realised. Now, if you'll excuse me, I think I'll call it a night." Maggie turned on her heel, too outraged to make any farewells. Oliver must have found out about her and Eddie and slept with Christy in an act of completely childish and irresponsible retaliation.

As Gabe led her to her car—to Christy's car—B.J. spotted them, and physically hauled them back to a small table laid out under the patio lights.

"No way! You ain't leaving till you've tasted Lindy's chowder, and Gabe, you ain't gonna monopolise the prettiest lady here. Now you two sit yourselves down right here with Maybelle and Jerry, and I'll just finish up the barbecue. I won't take no for an answer."

So Maggie and Gabe were trapped and sat, grim-faced, listening to Maybelle gossip. Gabe was controlled and fed Maybelle with questions, but Maggie made no effort. When spoken to, she replied monosyllabically or not at all. A sudden howl went up from the grill where B.J. was turning the ribs:

"Shit! Oh, shit! Oh, Jesus, Mary, and Joseph!" B.J. had burned himself and was surrounded by concerned guests, the women suggesting the best salves for burns and the men slightly smugly offering to take over the barbecue.

"You can sure get terrible injuries from barbecuing," Maybelle commented. "Ah always make sure Jerry wears gloves. He plays the piano, near about professional standard, you know, so his hands are real important to him. Ah protect them like Ah protect my babies. Ah mean, they're his livelihood." She turned to Maggie. "You must feel just the same about Oliver, with him being a writer and all. Ah guess his hands are just as important to him."

Maggie looked up from her untouched salad bowl, an innocent

expression in her green eyes. "You mean because he's a professional wanker, Maybelle?"

Oliver, back in London, spelt out his idea for the series to Danny Bujevski, who immediately suggested a coproduction with an American channel. All they would have to do was screen test Oliver and Christy together, but Oliver could see that Bujevski had it all mapped out: Keith Floyd meets Vivien Leigh down on the bayou. While Bujevski met the suits and put the wheels in motion, there was little for Oliver to do except return to Bockhampton and wait. Christy was on the doorstep to greet him with open arms if not lips; she had no intention of ever upsetting Jake.

Oliver spent the rest of the week at Bockhampton, officially staying in the spare bedroom. After Jake and Mariella had gone to bed, he would sneak down the corridor into his own room and make love to Christy, and then sneak back down the corridor at dawn. On the third night, he bumped into Jake as he was closing the door of the master bedroom, but he persuaded the little boy that he'd just gone for a pee and had forgotten which room he was staying in. He avoided Edward, dreading a further confrontation, and told everyone he met in the village that it was ironic that he had had to come home to Bockhampton at exactly the same time that Gabe had been summoned back to the States. Privately, he revelled in his relationship with Christy. She made no demands on him at all. He was more than happy to sleep with her whenever he got the chance, and settled comfortably into her ordered domestic routine. She went to great lengths to keep him outside the tedium of domestic life, so there were none of the squabbles about who should take the garbage out or who had forgotten to lock the front door that had so characterized his marriage. Christy wouldn't let anything normal or boring intrude on their love affair. He was beginning to believe that she was the best thing that had ever happened to him, but he chose not to dwell on the thought. On his fifth night back at Bockhampton, Christy took him by surprise. They were lying in bed, Oliver half asleep, Christy wide awake.

"Oliver, we have to talk."

"In the morning, hmm?"

"No. We can't really talk when Jake and Mariella are about."

Oliver pretended that he had fallen asleep again, but Christy wasn't fooled, and her next words made him sit up sharp.

"I don't want to talk about *us*. You know where I stand; I'm happy with things just the way they are until you want something different. And I don't want to talk about Louise, or any other woman. You've told me all you want to say, and that's good enough for me. I want to talk about you and your future."

"My future?"

"Your future career, Oliver. Your career as an author. You just *have* to publish *A Sad Affair*. You know you do."

Oliver hadn't mentioned the book since his return; he had no intention of ever telling her that Maggie had written it. Christy seemed content with the idea that it was simply too painful for Oliver to talk about. The fact that Christy hadn't referred to *A Sad Affair* in five days had led him to hope that she'd forgotten all about it, too. Little did Oliver know then that Christy would never forget about it; she would always see it as the path that had brought her to him. This was one lie that was going to weigh heavily on him for some time to come.

"It's just too good to keep in a bottom drawer, Oliver; believe me. I know."

"I can't publish it, Christy. I just can't. It's too . . ."

"Personal? Painful? I understand that, darling, but maybe it would exorcise your ghosts. Maybe it would help you put the past behind you." She spoke to him so gently, so seductively, just whispering in his ear. Oliver's nerves tingled. He had been in a hole in so many lies to Maggie, and he swore by Callahan's First Law: when you've really dug yourself in deep, you might just as well dig faster in the hope of getting out the other side. He had hoped to wipe the slate clean with Christy, and never lie to her, but Maggie's blasted book remained a stumbling block.

"It's just that I feel I've already put it behind me, but it's something I'm not ready to share yet. I can't even talk about it to you, Christy. How can I tell the whole world what it felt like?"

"You just need time, Oliver. There'll come a time when you're ready, when you'll see that it's not about you—it's about everyone and anyone."

"It's not just that. It's Maggie."

"But Maggie knows all about it, doesn't she? She knows what happened."

"Oh yes, she certainly knows all that."

"Then it won't be any surprise to her."

"No . . . it wouldn't *surprise* her, exactly. . . . But I don't feel that I can hurt her anymore."

"Oliver . . . You are a wonderful man. I admire your loyalty to Maggie, I surely do, but now it's time to look after *you*. You've protected Maggie for so long, you sacrificed everything for her sake, and you need somebody else to look out for your needs. Just maybe I'm that person? I can see things as an outsider—I can see what you've gone through, and I want to do everything in my power to make sure you're happy from here on. You deserve a little happiness, Oliver."

"Thank you, sweetheart. Nobody's said that to me for a very long time." Nobody had *ever* said that to him.

"I know. I can just feel it; you've been denied everything, Oliver—you've denied yourself everything, and now it's time to put that old life behind you, and look ahead."

"Perhaps you're right. But I still can't publish the book. I just can't do that to Maggie. Please don't mention it again."

"Okay, okay, hush, darling; let's take it step by step. Let's do your TV thing—though it's beyond me why you want my help—and then see how you feel. But one day, you're going to wake up and find yourself a very famous and respected writer."

Oliver was desperate to move the conversation away from the book. "And are you going to wake up next to me, Christy?"

"I don't know, my darling; I'm content to leave that choice up to you. Whatever you decide, this time will be enough for me for the rest of my life." She lowered her head, and began to kiss his chest with feathery, butterfly kisses. Some time later, they were both asleep. Unlike Maggie, Christy actually slept with Oliver, their limbs tumbled together like a warm nest of puppies.

Lucius normally woke before Jake and licked the boy's face until he rose to serve breakfast. That morning, as boy and dog trotted onto the first-floor landing, Lucius caught a waft of a familiar scent, and snuffled at the door of the master bedroom, scratching at it with a paw and whining.

"No, Lucius, down boy! Mom's asleep. She'll come down later. Let's go get Mariella and have breakfast." But Lucius was determined, and Jake decided it was better to let him in than have him start barking and wake Mr. Callahan. He opened the door, and Lucius bolted straight towards the bed. The curtains were drawn around the four-poster. Jake walked up to one side, and drew back the curtain. His mother was fast asleep, the sheets drawn up under her nose, and her hair spilling out across the bare chest of Mr. Callahan. Jake stared at them in silence, but Lucius jumped on the bed and began to lick Mr. Callahan's face, whimpering.

"Fuck off, dog. It's the middle of the night. Just fuck off back to your basket." Oliver kept his eyes clamped shut, trying to shove Lucius off with an arm, and simultaneously throwing off the bedcovers. The dog persisted, and Oliver opened his eyes and looked straight into the serious grey ones of the little boy standing inches away from him.

"What are you doing in my daddy's bed? Why haven't you got your clothes on?" Jake's high-pitched voice woke Christy immediately.

"Jake! What are you doing in here? You shouldn't walk into other people's bedrooms without knocking."

"What's he doing in here, Mom? What's he doing in Daddy's bed? Why hasn't he got any clothes on? I can see his pee-wee." Oliver dragged the duvet up, while Christy reached for her dressing gown and pulled it round her as she scrambled out of bed.

"Jake. Leave Mr. Callahan alone, and come downstairs with me this instant. We'll talk about it downstairs." She grabbed Jake by the shoulder and hustled him through the door. Oliver could hear Jake all the way down the stairs, asking plaintively, *"Why* didn't he have his jammies on, Mommy? Why don't any of these English folk wear clothes? He was as naked as a fish—just like that man in the garden. I *did* see his pee-wee—honest I did." Oliver couldn't help smiling at the boy's persistence and directness. If you want to get right to the nub of something, always ask a five-year-old.

Christy wasn't smiling at all. She had dreaded this happening. She sat Jake down at the kitchen table, and fixed his cornflakes before saying anything. Then she sat opposite him, her arms folded on the table.

"Jake, you and I need to talk, honey."

"You didn't answer my question, Mom."

"Jake, darling, that's because you asked such a difficult question. You're going to have to try real hard to understand. You see, sometimes grown-ups do things that you *can't* understand, and you just have to accept that they're doing it for the right reason."

"But why was that man in Daddy's bed?"

"Don't call him 'that man,' darling. You call him Mr. Callahan, or 'sir' if you're talking to him face to face."

"Why was Mr. Callahan in your bed?" Jake was a well-mannered little boy, but he was also a determined one.

"Because he's my friend, darling."

"Isn't Daddy your friend?"

"Yes, Daddy's my friend, too, and he's your daddy, which is the most important thing of all. He'll always be your daddy. But Mr. Callahan is a real good friend of Mommy's. Do you understand the difference?"

"I guess." The little boy shrugged. "But I don't get why he was in your bed."

"He's my friend, darling, that's why. You like him, don't you, Jake?"

"No. I don't like him. I don't want him to be here. I want Daddy to be here."

"Darling, this is Mr. Callahan's house, and he's letting us stay here. Daddy's at our house."

"Then *I* want to go to our house! I want to be where Daddy is!" He was working his mouth to hold back the tears, but his chin wobbled with the tell-tale tremor.

"Jake, darling, you know I can't go home now; I'm doing some work here—I have to stay here for a while. You want to be with me, don't you, Jake? You don't want to leave me behind?"

"I want to be with you *and* Daddy! I want to be with you *and* Daddy! I want to be with you *and* Daddy!" Jake was in full flood now, repeating his plea like a mantra. Christy knelt down beside him and wrapped her arms around his skinny frame. "I know, I know, hush now, baby, it'll be okay, hush now, my baby, Mama'll make everything okay . . ."

"Mommy, I want to be with Daddy. I want to go home." Christy resolved then to put things right, for Jake's sake.

"Jake, listen to me real hard, 'cos this is going to be difficult

263

for you to understand. Sometimes, grown-ups do things that seem wrong—sometimes they do things that *are* wrong . . . We're not always right, even if we tell you kids that. Sometimes grown-ups are bad, or naughty. . . ."

"Has Daddy done something naughty? Is he in prison?" Christy smiled.

"No; no, darling, and he hasn't done anything naughty. Not ever."

"So why can't we be with him? Doesn't he like us?"

"Sure he does! It's my fault, Jake. Daddy's angry with me. I guess, if anyone's been naughty, it's me. And I'm going to try real hard to put everything right, I promise you that. What you have to remember is that Daddy really loves you, and that I really love you, and in a little while, everything will be fine again, okay?" For the first time, Christy wondered whether she would be able to keep Jake all to herself. She dreaded what she might have to give up in order to have Oliver.

She rocked the little boy in her arms. One way or another, she would have to make everything okay.

Oliver, now in a track suit, leant against the kitchen door watching them. Absorbed in each other, they didn't notice him before he slipped into the garden. Hearing the anguish in Christy's voice, he missed his own children, and wondered if they missed him as much as Jake missed his father, and what Maggie had told them. He had gone through the past week without looking at the consequences of his actions. Now, as he jogged down the footpath that led to the farm, he forced himself to think seriously about what was going to happen to all their lives. He mentally listed the points of his argument, his feet pounding a rhythm that paced his thoughts. Snuff and Boomer ran with him, the little Jack Russell racing to keep up, Boomer easily distracted by the faintest of rabbit smells. Point one, he was still very angry with Maggie, and he had no intention of taking her back, even if she pleaded. Point two, he knew Maggie wasn't going to plead with him; she hadn't even attempted to phone him the whole week. Point three, if he didn't have Maggie, he was unlikely to have Lily and Arthur. He didn't want to deal with that point at the moment. Point four; he needed Christy. Not only did he need her for the TV series, but he needed her for himself. She made him feel that it wasn't too late for him to rule the world. She had such boundless confidence in him and his talent that it removed any cancerous fear he had of his own failure. Christy would be a loving, supportive, and nurturing partner; for all Maggie's banging on about communication and sharing, she hadn't been prepared to share anything of herself with him, whereas Christy had no fear of saying her happiness depended on him. If Oliver was ever going to make it to the big time, he could do it with Christy at his side; Maggie was only going to drag him down. Point five; Christy stood up to him. She made him try harder, because he felt she deserved so much, and made him feel lucky. In just a week, she had changed the way he looked at women. When he passed a pretty girl in the street, his thoughts now immediately turned to Christy. Point six; Christy was really in love with him; he could see it in her eyes, he could feel it in the way her body responded to his touch, he could tell it most of all by the way she was prepared to turn her life upside down for his sake. That alone was enough to make him love her, even if she didn't have so many other attributes. When he had met Maggie, Maggie and he had talked at length about how she saw marriage, what compromises he would have to make, what she was prepared and not prepared to do; if their agreement had lapsed somewhat over the years, that was Maggie's fault for trying to lay down the law in the first place. Maggie had gone into marriage with all her guards up. Christy made no demands, conducted no negotiation; she wanted to make him happy. End of story. Point seven; other than when he himself had seduced her—Oliver was convinced he had been the seducer—she had never been unfaithful to her husband; Christy was not the sort of woman to bonk her husband's best friend casually. Point eight. There wasn't a point eight. Yes, there was. It was hard for him to admit it, because it amazed him, and it frightened him, and he hated feeling frightened, but he forced himself to admit it, to say it out loud. "Point eight. I've fallen in love with Christy McCarthy." The scales were massively tipped in Christy's favour, whichever way you looked at it. So long as you didn't happen to glance in the direction of Lily and Arthur. As he ran, Oliver found himself making deals with some divine authority the way a child does; if he could just jog as far as the farm, if he could just keep going until the last oak tree, if he could just complete the whole circuit in less than forty-five minutes, then everything would be alright.

*　　*　　*

Oliver headed for home, and found what he was looking for in the sandpit.

"Jake? Are you having a good time, old chap?"

"I'm not old. I'm only five. You're old. Sir." Jake carried on digging after one resentful glance.

"You don't have to call me 'sir.' You make me feel ancient. I'm not even forty yet. I'm exactly the same age as your mum. I wanted to talk to you about this morning."

"Mommy talked to me. She told me to call you sir. She didn't tell me why you had no clothes on."

"Maybe it was hot. Don't you sometimes want to take your jammies off when it's really hot?"

"Nope."

"Well, doesn't your daddy sometimes take his jammies off?"

Jake shrugged. "Sometimes, I guess. When he's in the shower."

"Listen, old fellow, I know how you must feel. I know you must be missing your dad. I have a little boy, and a little girl, too, and I know how much I miss them. I want us to be really good friends."

"Does that mean I have to sleep in your bed?"

"Not if you don't want to."

"I don't. I don't want for you to sleep in my mommy's bed, either."

"I see. Well, I'm glad you're a man who knows his own mind. I respect that in a chap. Now I suggest we come to an arrangement."

"You mean we make a deal?"

"That's right. I'll do my best to respect your wishes concerning your mother, if you do something for me."

"What?" Jake looked at him suspiciously.

"Promise me that for one hour a day, you'll play cricket with me."

"I don't know how to play cricket."

"Then it's high time you learned. Why don't we start right now? Lily's got a bat inside that would be just about right for you—I'll bowl to you, and let's see how you get on. It's a gentleman's game, Jake. You'll like it. Have we got a deal?" He held his hand out to the little boy, and Jake shook it solemnly, and left his hand in Oliver's as they walked back to the house.

Lucy Wickham-Edwardes was curious why Oliver hadn't phoned her, let alone dropped in. She'd heard from Steve the Papers that he was back in residence at Bockhampton, and had expected him to pop in and tell her and Charles about the holiday as soon as he had unpacked. Oliver hadn't even been to see Edward Arabin; Lucy had called him first to get the lowdown on the TV show, and Edward had simply said that Oliver must be working very hard or lying low. Lucy had a perfectly good excuse for a visit to Bockhampton; she had promised Christy her recipe for plum and hazelnut crumble.

On arriving at Bockhampton that afternoon, Lucy found the house empty, and wandered into the orchard. There appeared to be no one there. On the point of leaving separate notes for Oliver and Christy, Lucy noticed that the old hammock under the apple tree was swaying, and walked towards it. Oliver and Christy were lying in the hammock. Together. Side by side. It may be that there is no *essential* impropriety in sharing a hammock with somebody, but it certainly struck Lucy as a very bizarre and intimate activity for two total strangers. It wasn't as if she herself had ever been invited to share Oliver's hammock, and she'd known him for the best part of her life. They were talking to each other quietly, and didn't notice her approach. When she was about twenty feet away from them, Lucy stopped, put her hands on her hips, and said, "My, you two certainly look very . . . cosy." Oliver nearly tipped Christy out of the hammock in his rush to get his feet on the ground.

"Lucy! You surprised us!"

"I can see that," Lucy replied, her eyes narrow.

"I was just on my way round to see you—say hello, whatever." Oliver shook his hair out of his eyes, and gave a boyish grin.

"It didn't look like you were on your way anywhere. It looked like you were settled for the duration."

Oliver laughed rather nervously, and waved around at the orchard. "You know, sunshine, late summer, good lunch, apple trees—I'd just nodded off, I suppose."

"Oh, I see. Hello, Christy." The two women appraised each other coolly. For some weeks they had shown every sign of being the best of friends. In a split second, their relationship changed to one of open hostility.

"Hey, Lucy. How did you get in? I thought I'd locked the front door."

"I never use the front door here, Christy. Maggie always tells me to come round the back door, or straight into the garden."

Christy shrugged, and began to rock the hammock again, pulling on an old rope tied to a tree. "I guess, being American, I'm always a bit concerned about security."

"I guess, being American, you should be." One of Lucy's feet tapped the ground nervously. She looked hard at Oliver, who was shifting his weight uncomfortably from foot to foot. "Well, I won't disturb you two any longer. I just came by to ask how Maggie is, Oliver. I guess I'll phone her."

"She's fine—just fine—I couldn't tear her away from the beach. But she's tip top—on cracking form."

"Good. As I said, I'll give her a call." As she turned to go, she continued, as an afterthought, "Oh, Christy?" Christy's eyes were closed, one leg thrown over the side of the hammock. "I'll leave that crumble recipe you asked for on the kitchen table, okay?"

"Sure. I'll try it, so long as the fat content isn't too high. I can't abide all the butter you English use in food."

"Really? You surprise me. I would have guessed you had something of an insatiable sweet tooth." Lucy bared her teeth for an instant and left.

Oliver stomped in a circle around the hammock, muttering swear words under his breath.

"Don't fret yourself about her, Oliver, she's just a noisy old gossip out sniffing for trouble."

"That's exactly what I'm worried about. Anyway, I thought you two got on like a house on fire. You told me you thought she was terrific."

"I did? Well, I guess I thought so at first. She was real friendly and all. Like a snake tries to make friends with its prey. When I first met her, I thought she was real nice, and real pretty in that English rose kind of way. But when you look at her up close, she's not pretty one bit. Maybe she *is* a natural blonde, but she's had her hair so highlighted and lowlighted, and bleached and glossed and colour-rinsed, it looks like dried-out straw. You know what it reminds me of?" She opened her eyes, and Oliver saw a wicked sparkle in them. "It reminds me of those lamp shades we used to make at kindergarten when I was a little girl—you know, when you'd wind bits of nylon raffia round and round an ugly metal frame. That's what her hair looks like. I mean, her face is okay, she's got a good classic shape, but Jesus!" She rolled her eyes dramatically. "When she smiles—ugh! It's like the grimace of a death mask. The corners of her mouth draw down tight, the top lip pulls flat and thin—near about disappears—and all you can see are her little animal-like lower incisors and canines. The sinews in her neck stand out all taut and thin from her collarbone to her jaw, and her skin's pretty dried up, too." Christy mimicked one of Lucy's habitual forced smiles, and the exaggerated impersonation was so good that Oliver laughed in spite of himself. "No, I'll tell you what Lucy Wickham-Edwardes needs: she needs to be seen only in a certain flattering light, and if I were her, I'd be darn sure I carried it around with me."

Oliver knew that Christy's portrayal of his old friend was unfair, but he had enjoyed it. She amused him. He had once feared that Christy was almost too ladylike and charming to be any fun, but the better he knew her, the more her sharpness intrigued him. She was a great deal tougher than he had perceived, and the realisation fascinated him. He also couldn't keep his hands off her. He climbed back into the hammock, and tugged the rope again.

When the phone rang, Maggie was still asleep. She had had a bad night with the children, and had ended up at three in the morning with both Lily and Arthur in bed with her. Arthur was teething, and had whimpered and moaned most of the night, and Lily was not prepared to be excluded from the chance of sleeping in her parents' bed whenever there was a window of opportunity. Maggie reached across her sleeping daughter and fumbled for the phone. It might be Oliver. It might, of course, be a wrong number, but she hoped it was Oliver.

"Hullo?" she groaned.

"Maggie? Mags? Is that you? You sound very peculiar. It's Lucy."

"*Lucy!* How fantastic to hear you!"

"What's the matter with your voice? Are you ill? Why are you whispering?"

"I just woke up. I'm in bed with the kids, and I don't want to wake them up. I'm fine. It's just very early."

"I'm sorry—I can't ever work out this time difference business. I can't for the life of me understand why everyone in the world can't be on the same time as we are. It would make life so much simpler."

"You sound like something out of the last days of the Raj, Luce. How are you? How is everyone back home?"

"We're all fine. You know Compton Purlew—nothing ever changes."

"Good. I'd hate it to change when I'm away and miss all the action."

"Look, Maggie—now you mention it, there's is something just the faintest bit *odd* . . ."

Maggie waited for a moment, both longing for and dreading what Lucy was going to say. Finally, after a pause that could have produced full-term triplets, Maggie had to prompt her.

"What, Luce? What's odd? Don't keep me in suspense."

"It's about Oliver." Lucy was now whispering as well, although she was home alone. Nonetheless, she felt conspiratorial, so she dropped her tone to match Maggie's. "I've just been to see him."

"Oh yes?" Maggie eased her arm, which was going dead, from under Arthur's head.

"There's something very strange going on between Oliver and that Christy McCarthy woman."

"D'you mean something very strange like an affair?"

"*Maggie!* How can you suggest that! Heaven forbid! I wasn't implying anything of the kind! What on *earth* made you think that?"

"Just something somebody told me. A little bird. Sort of an American eagle, to tell the truth."

"Please, darling, do me a favour and speak English. I have simply not the faintest idea what you are talking about."

"Tell me first what you thought was odd about Oliver."

"Well. Just between you and me . . ."

"Who else do you think is listening, Luce? The CIA?"

"He was lying in the hammock, Mags."

"Seems pretty inoffensive to me, Luce."

"With *her*. He was lying in the hammock next to her, Mags."

"Oh." Maggie was silent for such a long time, Lucy began to worry that she had fainted or something.

"Maggie? Maggie? *Maggie!* Are you still there? Can you hear me, Maggie? What are you doing?"

"I'm thinking that at least she managed to get Oliver to put the hammock up. It's more than I ever did." She mused. "I suppose she might have done it herself . . . what do you think?"

"Maggie, you don't even sound surprised. How on earth can you be so calm about this? It's simply dreadful. Disgusting, in fact. It's a scandal."

"As I said, Luce, I was forewarned. By Christy's husband. He's over here at the moment. So it's not really a bolt from the blue. They're having an affair. So what? Big deal. More power to them."

"Maggie, what is the matter with you? Are you sure you're not ill? I'm talking about Oliver. Your husband, Oliver."

"I know who you're talking about. I know who I'm married to, Luce. More's the pity."

"Why aren't you more upset?"

"Oh for God's sake, Lucy, don't you understand? I *am* upset in a way, but it's not the first time Oliver's been unfaithful. It's just the first time there's been hard-core evidence—objective witnesses. I'm not surprised, or shocked, or destroyed or anything else. I'm just fed up with him. He's a low-lying, lily-livered, selfish bastard and I'm not in the mood to cry over him."

"Why haven't you told me any of this before?"

"Lucy. Dear Lucy. Two reasons. One, you've got the biggest mouth in the Southern counties, and you'd have told the whole parish by the time I'd put down the phone, and two, I cared at some level about Oliver's reputation. Now I don't care about your gossiping or Oliver's reputation."

"That hurts, Maggie. That really hurts. You don't honestly think I'd gossip about you, do you?"

Maggie laughed. "Not intentionally, Luce. But it's like a disease with you. You can't stop yourself, any more than Oliver can stop himself lying and cheating."

"I won't say a word about this to anyone. Cross my heart."

"And hope to die?"

"And hope to—you *are* horrid, Maggie!" Lucy grumbled, suddenly realising that Maggie was pulling her leg. "Now, look; what do you want me to do about it? Shall I have a word directly with Oliver? Or ask the vicar to? Perhaps Edward would be the best person to take him aside?"

"No!" Maggie shouted, waking her children. "Leave Edward out of it! Don't say a word to anyone, promise me, Luce. Certainly not Edward. I don't want any sympathy—I don't want everyone in the Valley whispering about poor little Maggie, and I don't want to be put on the roster for special prayers at Matins. If anybody else brings it up, then just say I know what's going on, I don't give a bugger, and I fully intend to finish my holiday in peace. Alright?"

"Whatever you say," Lucy agreed meekly.

"And now, just to satisfy my curiosity, tell me about Christy. Is she really so beautiful?"

"More than you can imagine," Lucy groaned. "She's positively gorgeous. But it's not just her looks, it's the way she does everything so perfectly. She never really slips up, she's incredibly elegant, she's clever, she draws people towards her—I even thought Charles was falling for her at her party, and I'm sure Edward has gone hook, line, and sinker—"

"Edward?"

"You know what he's like with pretty women. Anyway, she's just Miss—or Mrs.—Perfect. Looks like she's stepped out of a Dior fashion shoot, cooks like one of the Roux brothers, most amazing voice, and she talks about literature, and the stock market, and agricultural policy, and architecture . . . That reminds me, Maggie; she asked me a lot of questions about some friend of Ol's called Louise. Do you have any idea who she was talking about?"

"Louise? Yes. I do as a matter of fact, and I've got a pretty good idea of how Christy heard about her. How funny. I'm almost tempted to call her and ask her what she thinks. Did I ever tell you, Luce, that I'd started writing a novel?"

"Maggie, how thrilling! You never mentioned it."

"I said it before, Luce. Your mouth—you know, being the size of the Channel Tunnel . . ."

"I'm never going to tell you anything again, Maggie Callahan, seeing as you don't trust me."

"Tell me one more thing, Lucy: how's Eddie?"

"Eddie? He's fine, I think. I haven't seen him for about a week or two. Not since the cricket match, in fact. Maybe he's gone away. Maybe he's having an affair with Christy, too; I wouldn't put it past her. Why do you ask?"

"Oh, no reason. I just miss all of you."

"When are you coming home?"

"I don't know. Maybe ten days or so. I haven't really decided."

"We'll have a real chin-wag when you get back, Maggie. You must tell me *everything*."

"Never." Maggie laughed.

"You're such a bitch . . ."

As Lucy was finishing her conversation with Maggie, Charles strolled into the drawing room, put his arms around her waist, and hugged her. When she hung up the telephone, he asked casually, "Who was that on the blower?"

"None of your bloody business!" Lucy snapped.

"Pardon me for breathing. I just heard you call someone a bitch, and I thought you might have been talking to my dear mother-in-law."

"I don't have to tell you everything, you know. I'm entitled to my own thoughts! What do you think I am, the Channel Tunnel?" Lucy stormed from the room, and paused in the doorway to shout, bristling with female solidarity, "And you can leave my mother out of it!"

Charles stared after her in utter bewilderment.

Fourteen

A rose-covered postcard to Maggie Callahan,
Holden Beach, North Carolina:

*Just to say this business is absolutely disgusting—I won't ever
speak to Oliver again, until he makes amends. Men. You can't
trust any of them, can you? We're all behind you, darling—I
happened to bump into Imogen in town and had a quick
word—about your situation—knew you wouldn't mind. Now
be brave and don't worry. He'll come round to his senses.*

All love,
Lucy

DESPITE MAGGIE'S ACT OF BRAVADO ON THE TELEPHONE TO LUCY,
she was feeling far less phlegmatic about Oliver than she pretended.
At one time her biggest problem had been that she thought she was
just mediocre—she had an okay marriage and an okay career and an
okay life. Overnight, that had all been wiped out. Now she had
nothing. She forced herself to face the facts; she had no job, no
husband as such, probably no home, no money of her own in the
bank, and she was sitting in a stranger's kitchen in a foreign country
with her two small children and a nanny who was asking no questions, but obviously knew something was up. She'd talked big to
Lucy about having had enough of Oliver, and being fed up with
him, but the fact was she was now completely stranded, and terrified
by the thought of being really alone. If Oliver didn't call her by the
end of next week, when they were scheduled to end the swap anyway, she would have to call him. Her only other option was to pack

up the kids, get on the plane home, and turn up at Bockhampton as the pitiful betrayed wife with her babes in arms. Maggie gagged at the thought of it. She didn't want to beg Oliver to come back to her—because she didn't want Oliver back, and right now she wouldn't have asked him for a postage stamp—but she felt overwhelmed by the sheer practical difficulties of dealing with the situation alone. She longed to pour her heart out to Edward, but not until she had pulled herself together. She didn't want anyone's sympathy, or anyone's help. Lucy's comment that Edward was besotted with Christy had thrown her; however much she trusted Edward, her experience with Oliver had taught her to be wary, and Eddie didn't owe her anything after all. Independence was much on her mind when she picked up the phone to find Edward on the end of the line. She briefly summarised her last conversation with Oliver for Edward's benefit.

"Maggie, just come back home and everything will be sorted out. I really feel this is all my fault."

"It's not your fault, and it's not mine. Oliver and I have had problems for far longer than you know, Eddie—it really isn't to do with my sleeping with you. It's a point of principle. He thinks he controls me, and I've let him, because I was too pathetic to put up a fight. If he storms off like this, if he's going to be so childish, do you really think I have any respect left for him? Do you really want me to go crawling back moaning that I'm sorry? No; I've had it. I'm damn well staying put until our agreement's over, and then I'll decide what to do. Then I'll talk to Oliver myself, and we'll sort things out."

"Isn't there anything I can do to help you? Can I fly out? Can I go talk to Oliver? Do you need money? Anything, lovely. Please. Indulge me. Let me try to help you."

"The only thing you can do for me is let me know if Oliver screwed Christy before or after he found out about us." She would have liked to ask him if there was anything going on between him and the American woman, as Lucy had suggested, but she couldn't begin to phrase the question.

"I didn't even know he *had* screwed Christy."

"Then the jungle telephone serves me better than it does you. I'll find out for myself. Eddie, don't think I don't appreciate what you're saying, but listen. I'm okay. I'll come back when I'm ready to. If I'm ready to. Maybe I'll just stay put and get a job here. I don't know yet. I told you that my problems with Oliver were because I was too frightened to stand on my own feet, so I let him walk all over me. I'm just not going to do that ever again. I suddenly feel like I understand everything. It's been a road to Damascus experience, and I'm converted. I know why I fell in love with Oliver, and now, at last, I know how to handle him."

Edward's stomach heaved. "You're not too depressed?"

"I feel fine. I feel a bit homesick—I mean, I'm really surprised how much I miss home." Maggie was longing to tell him that she missed him, but he hadn't said anything about missing her; he was just being a loyal friend, supportive, dependable, but detached.

"Home is where the heart is, Mags."

"The cliché to end all clichés."

"Don't knock clichés; there's plenty of truth in them, mark my words. So there's really nothing I can do? It would make me feel better."

"No, dear Eddie. Just keep calling once in a while, and don't . . . completely forget about me."

Edward made a strange, choking snort, and said goodbye.

Other than chatting to Edward and Lucy, and waiting for Oliver to ring while pretending that she wasn't expecting Oliver to ring, Maggie didn't have very much to do. She had seen nothing of Gabe since the Richardses' party, and although she knew that the two of them would have to sit down and talk about what had happened, she couldn't quite bring herself to pick up the phone and suggest that they meet. Maggie really tried to be methodical, to approach her problems logically and work out a solution. She jotted down a list of the things that were bothering her:

a) Marital breakdown.
b) Lily and Arthur.
c) Eddie.
d) Due to leave USA; nowhere to go to.
e) An unknown woman appears to be living in my house, and sleeping with my husband.
f) If you can call it my house, and him my husband.
g) Only $1,800 left in traveller's cheques.
h) No call from Ol.
i) Arthur and Lily.

k) Lily due to start school in three weeks' time.
l) Gabe McCarthy.

Maggie stared at the list and then crumpled it into a ball. She felt that the least difficult of her problems was Gabe, and the fact that she probably had to get out of his house. Lindy Richards gave Maggie his office number, and she steeled herself to dial it, feeling sick to the stomach. Gabe's voice, when she was put through, was reassuringly calm and steady.

"Maggie? I've been meaning to ring you."

"Yes, well, I just thought, you know, that maybe we should talk about things and try to sort something out, make some plans, or do something. . . ." Maggie's incoherence didn't conceal the desperate note in her voice.

"I couldn't agree more. I was going to call to ask if you minded if I came to Oak Ridge this weekend. I'd use the guest quarters, naturally—I don't want to inconvenience you further."

"Inconvenience me? Of course not! It's your house, after all. When do you think you'll get here?"

"I can probably leave early Friday. As you know, I wasn't planning on being in the office this week, so I don't have that much to do. I've been trying to keep busy." Maggie couldn't think of anything to say. "I should be with you around seven, seven-thirty. Would that suit?"

"Of course. Maybe we could . . . have a drink . . . or dinner?"

"Surely. See you Friday."

"Bye."

That Friday evening, Gabe went through the motions that had become his routine every Thursday for the last five years. He spent half an hour with his assistant, Lilah, running through his schedule for the following week. He got a taxi from his office to the airport, dropping Lilah off at her condo on the way, flew the short hop to Fayetteville, picked up his car, drove forty minutes to Lawrenceville, drove up his own driveway, parked carefully, locked the car, loosened his tie, grabbed his briefcase and overnight bag, and slung his jacket over his shoulder as he walked towards the back porch. This time, he hadn't brought a bunch of flowers, although he had actually considered it for a moment. He could almost believe that nothing at all had happened, and that Christy, cool and collected, would be waiting to greet him with a pitcher of something refreshing on the porch. As he rounded the curve of the garden path, quite a different sight met his eyes.

Maggie was sitting scrunched up in a chair, wearing cut-off jeans and a T-shirt that was way too big for her, making her look like a teenager. The porch was littered with mangled-up bits of paper and scribble pads. At her elbow was a bottle of cheap white wine and a single glass. A little girl and a tall young woman he didn't recognise were galloping around his pristine tennis court. A baby played with some tennis balls at the bottom of the porch steps.

"Maggie?" He cleared his throat.

"Christ! Is it seven o'clock already?" Maggie scrambled to her feet, and raced down the stairs, swooping up Arthur in her path, and holding her hand out shyly to Gabe. He pressed it briefly.

"Seven-thirty. If you'll excuse me—I'll just go freshen up."

"Of course—the bathroom's—" She gestured hesitantly, and he gave a slight smile.

"I remember what it is. I'll use the guest wing and be with you in a minute."

Maggie dumped Arthur with Leah, and begged her to put the children to bed. "If they don't go to sleep right away, just drug them or knock them out cold or something, but don't let them come downstairs or scream, okay?" Leah winked her understanding, and shuffled the protesting children out of sight and earshot. Maggie just had time to fling on a clean shirt, drag a comb through her hair, and clear away her papers before Gabe strode purposefully back onto the porch.

"Now. How about that drink?"

"I'm afraid I started without you." Maggie blushed a little. She had opened the bottle sometime between three and four in the afternoon, and the wine was now lukewarm and two-thirds empty.

"Let me get you something else. A gin and tonic? That's what everyone seemed to drink in your neck of the woods."

"Please. That would be lovely. Thanks."

As Gabe fixed the drinks, Maggie paced nervously along the terrace. This meeting with Gabe felt intensely artificial. They were both on their best behaviour, full of pleases and thank-yous and nervous smiles—as if they had been set up on a blind date. Yet how else could they behave? It wasn't as if Gabe could roll his sleeves up and say, "Right. Your bastard of a husband is screwing my bitch of a wife. What are we going to do about it then?" Some men might have adopted that approach, but not Gabe. Maggie wondered how long it would take them to get round to the key question of the day. Maybe they'd just discuss the weather for an hour or so, and then Gabe would retire to bed? She braced herself to take the bit between her teeth and face up to realities, however determined Gabe was to be formal. He handed her a long glass, and sank heavily onto the little rattan sofa.

"Right, Maggie. I don't believe in beating around the bush. Your husband is sleeping with my wife in your house." Maggie's eyes widened in surprise. "I thought we'd established that?"

"Ah, yes. Yes, we did."

"Good. Then we're starting from the same point. Have you talked to Oliver yet?"

"Not about Christy, I haven't. I've been waiting for him to call."

Gabe's mouth twitched in irritation. "Damn. I hoped you'd at least have made *some* progress."

Maggie almost giggled in embarrassment. The situation was so bizarre, and Gabe was talking as if he and she were running some sort of campaign.

"Did I say something funny?" Gabe's eyebrows were drawn together in a dark frown.

"Not a bit. I just find it a little difficult discussing my husband's infidelity and my marriage with a man I don't really know." Gabe stared hard at her for a minute, the frown fixed on his face and his jaw clenched. After a moment, he rubbed his eyes and his face relaxed.

"Okay. My mistake. I'm sorry, I just feel a little bit . . . tense. Let's start again, okay?" He smiled this time, and Maggie nodded as he continued. "You see, I'm finding it mighty hard to believe what's happened, and I just don't how to proceed. I had thought— I'd hoped, kind of wildly, I guess—that maybe you and Oliver would have fixed everything between you, and you were going to tell me that Christy and my son were on their way home."

Maggie shook her head sadly, and saw the hope in Gabe's eyes die. He slumped forward, elbows on his knees, his glass clenched in both hands.

"Then I don't know what to do. I've talked to Christy at least once a day this week. She says she wants to keep things as they are now. She says she hasn't had enough time to sort out the way she feels. She says she needs to be alone. She said she needed to be alone with *Oliver.*" He glanced up at her, his eyes haunted. "How can she take time to decide what she feels about a man she doesn't *know?*"

"Maybe she's trying to decide what she feels about you?" Maggie suggested tentatively.

"Hell, no! Christy and I have never had any problems! Never!" Gabe was vehement. "If anything has changed, it's because of your husband. There was never anything wrong with our marriage. She always had everything she ever wanted. There's nothing I wouldn't give her!"

It crossed Maggie's mind to say that maybe what Christy wanted wasn't in Gabe's gift, but she bit her tongue. She had the impression that Gabe was asking her to take some responsibility for the fact that her husband was an arsehole.

"I wish I could say the same about me and Oliver, but I'm afraid I can't. I'm as shocked as you are about what's happened with your wife, but I can't say that Oliver and I have never had any problems. I think you've been pretty lucky if you've been married so long and you haven't had any problems before."

"It's not a question of luck, Maggie. I've worked damn hard at my marriage—Christy, too. It's something we take very seriously— at least, I thought she did. I married for *life;* d'you think I'm about to blow it all on some cock-eyed vacation romance?"

When Maggie saw how desperate he was, she felt truly sorry for him, far sorrier for him than for herself, and she instinctively reached out a hand to touch his arm.

"I'm really sorry, Gabe. I'm sorry we're both in this position. I just can't believe it's all Oliver's fault. He may be a shit—to me— he may not be anyone's idea of a faithful, loyal husband, but he's not a demon, and he's never forced his attentions on any woman, to my knowledge. He's never had to. If he and Christy really *are* in love—and we've only got Christy's word for it—then I don't see what we can do."

"Christy keeps going on about some book or other—something your husband wrote—I think she fell in love with him over a god-damn book, for Chrissakes . . . That's why she went to bed with him that Sunday night."

Maggie was puzzled. When Gabe had first told her that his wife had slept with Ol, she had imagined that Oliver had found out about her and Eddie and had seduced Christy in retaliation. It was possible, given how upset he had been. Now it occurred to her that it was just as possible, and much more plausible, that Ol had screwed Christy before he'd found out about her and Eddie. It also sounded like he was passing her book off as his own, despite the disparaging comments he'd made about it.

"Bastard."

"What the hell have *I* done?"

"Not you, Gabe. Sorry, I was thinking about something else."

"So you think we should let them make the decision?"

Maggie shook her head hard.

"No. I intend to take some decisions myself, but they don't concern Christy."

"What are you going to do?"

"I'm going to leave Oliver. Before he officially leaves me. Whatever happens. I've had enough. I've had enough of making do, and trying to believe that everything's going to be okay in the long run, and that he really does love me, and that it's all worth it, and that everybody's marriage is like this. I mean, yours certainly isn't. Or, wasn't. I'm sick of settling for six out of ten." Gabe looked at her bleakly. "I'm going back to England."

"To Bockhampton?" There was a renewed note of hope in his voice.

"No. That's Oliver's house. I'll go to the studio flat, or to my parents, or friends—I haven't thought that far. But I'm not going to fight for Oliver. D'you see, Gabe, I just don't have the heart."

"Then it's finished."

"What do you mean?"

"My best chance was that you'd go back and kick Christy out of your house. Then she'd come back here, and I could glue everything back together. I'm not saying we could just forget all about it, but in time, with effort, it could have worked. . . ." Gabe wasn't crying. He didn't seem to be a crying sort of man, but his eyes were rimmed with red.

"Oh, Gabe! The fact that I've given up on my marriage doesn't imply anything about yours. Christy's an intelligent woman, from all I've heard. D'you think she's going to throw it all away—all of *this*"—she gestured broadly—"for the sake of *Oliver?* For the sake of a *whim?*"

"Yeah. I think she just might. I always thought all this mattered to her—that's why I did it, but now I think she was just filling in her time till something she really wanted came along."

"You don't know that. Maybe she just needed a bit of excitement . . . a thrill. Lots of married women with children feel like that. They just want to know they're still attractive—to someone, anyone, for God's sake. Women adore that sense of enchantment when you first fall in love. Believe me. It's true. But somebody fancying you—even the sex—doesn't compare to the fulfilment of a good relationship. She'll tire of it soon enough."

"Do you really think so?"

"I know so." Maggie knew nothing of the kind, but her instincts were to comfort, not to challenge. For all Maggie's good intentions, Gabe McCarthy was no fool, and he knew his wife was perfectly capable of turning a whim into a will, and he knew that despite all his efforts to satisfy her—perhaps because of them—he had made the fatal mistake of boring her.

"You see, Maggie, when I met Christy, I always felt she was real special. Maybe a cut above me—you know, something in a different class. I thought that if I could just give her whatever she wanted, and just be there for her, then even if she wandered off and did her own thing, she'd always come back to me. You know, like I was her rock." He spoke with a tinge of bitterness, but no self-pity.

"Maybe she will come back to you."

"Nope. I mean, I'll wait and all. But she won't come back. She's set her sights on something new, and there's no room for me in it."

"I'm going to get you another drink. Maybe I'll bring the bottles out. It saves time."

"Maggie, one thing you and me have surely both got is time."

It is possible, although not very common, for two people to connect so immediately that they talk as if they have known each other all their lives. Christy had felt this with Oliver; she had felt it, because for the six weeks before she met him, she had felt that she lived inside of him, and that meeting him was simply the cementing of everything she had come to believe about him. Maggie and Gabe bonded on a different level, the way you might bond to someone you'd been shipwrecked with, or met through some other form of natural disaster.

* * *

"How're your kids, Maggie?"

"They're fine. They've had a great holiday—they love it here, and at the beach. They're upstairs at the moment, in bed."

"Asleep?"

"Oh, certainly," Maggie said with a smile. She had a vision of Leah sitting between their beds, with a hand clamped over each little mouth.

"Would you give up Oliver if it meant giving up on your children?"

"Never." She spoke the word simply and matter-of-factly, as if it was something she had considered long and hard, and reached a decision over. The idea had never crossed her mind.

"D'you think Christy would give me custody, if it came to that?"

"If it comes to that . . . I don't know, Gabe. I hope it doesn't come to that. For your sake. And hers. And your son's. But if I were her, I'd never give my kid up."

"She wouldn't either. If it came to that. And if she had a choice about it. But I'm not giving him up either—any court in the land would grant me custody after what she's done."

They sat in silence for a while, watching the light fade and night approach.

"When are you going back to England?"

"Our tickets are booked for next week. I'm not sure where to go then, but we've got to get out of your hair, and I'll have to face up to things back home."

"You can stay here as long as you like. A month, six months, whatever suits you. I don't even want to move into the house, to be frank with you. I'm happy in the guest quarters. I won't get in your way. I'll only use it some weekends." He spoke almost apologetically.

"Thanks, Gabe, but I couldn't do that. I can't hang around like some sort of a waif or stray. You need your house back."

"I don't. I mean it. I don't feel that comfortable being in the house, if you see what I mean. I'll hardly be here, and it's good to have kids around, using the place. We designed it for kids. A whole pack of them. There's something else that wasn't meant to be. Please stay as long as you feel like. I mean it."

Maggie looked at him, and wondered if she was looking at the baboon man incarnate. A man who devoted himself to the ceaseless care and companionship of his mate, a loyal, dependable, family man. How was it that she hadn't come across one of them seven years ago?

"Maybe it would be nice to stay a bit longer. For the children's sake, at least. Until I can work out what to tell them. D'you mind if I think about it for a bit?"

"Think about it as long as you like. I got no plans." Gabe drained his glass, and poured the remains of the bourbon bottle into the tumbler. "Your daughter sure is pretty, Maggie. Takes after her mother. You're a lovely lady."

"Thank you, Gabe." Maggie felt uncomfortable. Although she had had a head start, she hadn't had nearly as much to drink as Gabe, and the effect of alcohol was evident in his slightly slurred speech. Not that she was blaming him for drinking himself out of his misery. Not that she'd blame him for anything. The more he drank and the more he lost his inhibitions, the more he reminded her of a little boy struggling to behave like a grown-up.

"And why does a lovely lady decide to up and walk out on her husband? Must be because he ain't worthy of her. Must be because way down somewhere, he's just worthless. That's what I'm thinking, anyways."

"Gabe, don't say that. I mean, if you're saying it about Oliver, then heck, it's true. But it's not true of you. People just do things. Things just happen. It doesn't necessarily mean anyone's in the wrong, or anyone's a shit. Bad things happen. And good ones."

"Only to the deserving."

"No, you're wrong. It's got nothing to do with what you deserve. It's just to do with your attitude."

"Maggie, I never had any attitude. I played my marriage the only way I knew how. I played it like it was for life, and like she thought so, too. I wanted to do everything that would make her happy. That's what made me happy. It didn't work. I lost. I don't know how to play it any different way."

"Do you ever lie, Gabe?" Maggie asked the question bluntly, and he looked confused.

"Lie?"

"Yes; do you ever tell lies?"

"Well, only when I'm paid to; in the legal profession, we call it being frugal with the truth."

"But you don't lie to Christy?"

"Why should I ever do that? I got nothing to hide from my own wife."

"Have you ever cheated on her? Been unfaithful?"

Gabe closed his eyes and kept them closed when he asked her a question instead of replying.

"Have you ever seen Christy?"

"No; not in the flesh."

"Then I understand your question. If you'd ever laid eyes on her, you wouldn't even think to ask that."

Gabe eventually went to bed. He took with him another bottle of bourbon, and shuffled along the wrap-around porch to the guest quarters with the gait of an idle browser in a book shop. Maggie was left alone with the mosquitoes on the back porch.

By midday the next day, Gabe hadn't appeared. Maggie had half expected him at breakfast, had even poured a glass of juice for him, but he hadn't shown. When playing with the children in the garden, she had seen his white face watching them from the window a couple of times, but he didn't emerge. It worried her. From the little she knew of him, she didn't take him for a heavy drinker, and doubted that he was the depressive type. The sight of somebody else's misery allowed her to forget about her own problems. There had still been no word from Oliver. Lindy Richards had called, to say that, seeing as the last party had been such a success, they were having another one that night, and would Maggie come, and did Maggie by any chance know where Gabe was? When Maggie admitted that he was holed up in Oak Ridge's guest wing, she had had to promise Lindy that she would do her best to bring him along. By three in the afternoon, Gabe still hadn't come out, and had ignored Maggie's tentative knock at the door. She resolved on a plan that she was sure would rout him if anything could.

Maggie hated tennis. She hadn't played since she'd left school, when she and her best friend used to bag the court furthest away from the tennis coach, Mrs. Shepherd, and play with an imaginary ball, shouting encouragement to each other, such as "Good shot, Jo!" "Lovely volley, Mags! Whizzo!" and hope that their enthusiasm would persuade the coach to leave them alone. That day, Maggie selected one of Gabe's racquets, a particularly heavy one, and strode purposefully out onto the court. She set the ball practice machine at top speed, filled it with a hundred tennis balls, and went into the opposite court with the remote control. Pressing "start," she swung wildly. With one eye, she watched the window of the guest wing. Sure enough, the rhythmic thwack of the machine brought Gabe to the window. She deliberately missed even those balls that she might have been able to hit. By the time the machine had emptied its reserve of balls, the full hundred, of which Maggie had hit eight, and five of those out of the court, Gabe was standing at the court gate.

"Are you having trouble with that machine? It's on a pretty fast setting."

"Is it? I didn't notice. I'm just lousy at tennis, that's all. Don't blame the machine!" Maggie laughed.

"That racquet's too big for you, that's the problem. Let me get you one of Christy's, and we'll see if that helps."

Gabe strode into the house, and emerged with another racquet.

"Give me that one, and you try this." Maggie took the lighter racquet he held out, and clenched it.

"No, you see, your grip's all wrong. You'll get blisters holding it like that, and it gives you no control. Here. Let me show you." He wrapped his hand over hers around the handle, shifting her thumb, and standing behind her, swung her arm back in a gentle arc. "It's all in the action, Maggie, just smooth and steady, and watch the ball. Let me send you a few before you try the machine again."

For fifteen minutes, Gabe sent her balls that a one-armed bandit could have returned, and Maggie managed to hit at least five. She saw Gabe grin, and shake his head in disbelief.

"You see? Now do you believe that I'm useless?"

"Nothing we can't fix, so long as you're prepared to try, Maggie. I've seen worse."

"Well, that's a relief! D'you think I've got a chance at Wimbledon then?"

Okay, it wasn't that great as jokes go, but it was an attempt, and it brought another flash of a grin to Gabe's lips, which was all Maggie had intended.

As they played, Lily wandered along the tall wire fence that surrounded the court. She came through the gate, and ran towards her mother.

"Watch out you don't get hit, sugar!" Gabe shouted.

"Mummy, who is that man?"

"His name is Gabe, sweetheart. He is the man who owns this house. He lives here."

"With us?"

"Well, not exactly."

"What do you mean then?"

"I can't explain. He's staying here while we're here. We're sharing things at the moment. Like you and Arthur share."

Lily looked darkly at Gabe.

"Why are you playing with him and not me, Mummy?" she asked bluntly. "You should be playing with me."

"I will a bit later, darling. When I'm through here."

"Daddy always plays with me. When's Daddy coming back?"

"I can't answer that, Lily. I don't know." Maggie shifted from foot to foot, her racquet hanging limp at her side. Gabe stood waiting on the other side of the net, examining the strings of his.

"Why don't you know?"

"Because I just don't. Now run along and play, sweetheart."

"I don't want to play. I want to stay with you." Lily wound her arms around Maggie's legs.

"Pudding, don't be silly and don't be difficult. Gabe's teaching me to play tennis. I'll play with you later."

"That's not fair."

"It's perfectly fair. This is grown-up time."

"I didn't mean that. I mean it's not fair that you do things you can't explain. It's not fair you do things I can't understand. You're not fair to me." She began to walk off the court, kicking the clay up around her.

"Lily? I'll come and play with you later, alright? We'll read some stories."

"I don't want to play with you, Mummy. I want to play with Leah."

Maggie, embarrassed and unhappy, didn't look at Gabe until he called "Ready?" and delivered another easy ball.

The day before Christy and Oliver were due to meet Danny Bujevski for a screen test, they decided to go up to London, leaving Jake with Mariella. Christy was reluctant to stay at Oliver's studio, and persuaded him to book a room at a small hotel in Knightsbridge. She didn't explain to him that she hated the idea of sharing the bed that she assumed he had shared with Louise. Oliver agreed on the hotel, having cleared it with Bujevski that they'd bill it to him. For the first time alone together, without children or neighbours to watch them, they behaved like lovestruck teenagers. Oliver took her sightseeing, to the Houses of Parliament, to the Tower, to Buckingham Palace, walking in St. James's Park, and finally to Harrods. Christy had said that she wanted to buy a new outfit for the screen test, but by the time they left the shop, when it closed in fact, it was Oliver who had the new wardrobe. Each item had been personally selected by Christy: three Egyptian cotton shirts, an Armani suit, a pair of pale taupe suede brogues, a blazer, chinos for casual wear, two pairs of new cords, a hazy tweed jacket—just in case they wanted him to look real British, as Christy said—and a couple of sweaters. It was a complete makeover, smoothly and efficiently handled, and Oliver was as pleased as punch. Maggie had never gone shopping with him. Maggie had never so much as darned a hole in his socks. Maggie had frequently said that they didn't have enough money for him to behave like a peacock, and that he was vain enough already, whereas Christy said it was an investment; Christy said he had to make an impression; Christy said he had a model's figure, and a movie star's face, and Oliver lapped it up.

Christy also bought a few things. She was already thinking ahead to the winter—wherever she might spend it—and picked out a pale pink cashmere sweater and some black cashmere leggings; she also bought a tweed skirt—not exactly a country or Jaegar tweed, more of a Mulberry tweed miniskirt, but it had a country aura about it. For the screen test, she chose a dress that was on the summer sale rack—a pale yellow, full-skirted affair with a cinched-in waist and a white collar. She also selected a straw hat with an immensely broad brim. Oliver was a little surprised. It wasn't nearly as sophisticated or as sexy as her normal outfits, although it gave her an innocent, girlish look that he found intensely arousing.

"Trust me, Oliver. Your producer is expecting to get a Southern belle, and I'm going to make real sure that's exactly what he gets."

"You're an old hand at this, aren't you, Christy?"

"Old hand at what?" Christy asked, batting her eyelashes, and peeping at him from under the brim of her hat.

"Manipulation."

"Why, Oliver Callahan! What a cruel and ungentlemanly thing to suggest!"

Oliver could have sworn he was standing in the middle of Harrods' millinery department with Scarlett O'Hara. The thought reminded him of Maggie—not that he'd exactly forgotten about her over the past week. He'd been waiting for her to phone. The fact that she hadn't didn't upset him, but it did annoy him. The two things that Maggie was absolutely incapable of were thinking about anybody other than herself, and admitting when she was in the wrong. There was not a shadow of a doubt in Oliver's mind that Maggie was very much in the wrong this time, and the more he talked to Christy, the more convinced he was that Maggie had failed in the one fundamental requirement of a wife: absolute rock-solid and unending commitment to her husband. Maggie had swung dramatically between being subservient and being domineering; she was either immensely sentimental or absolutely stone cold. Christy was steady. Christy had backbone, and nothing frightened her. It would never occur to Oliver to even attempt to dominate her, and that in itself liberated him.

Back at the hotel, after a bottle of champagne that Christy had ordered while he was in the shower, Oliver forgot all about Scarlett O'Hara. He was more than satisfied by the real woman in his arms. Christy was a hell of a good lover; she was amazing to look at; she thought he was a god. He loved the way she talked and laughed during sex, the uninhibited joy she took in it. Sex with Maggie had so often been warmed only by the heat of her anger; there was something reluctant beneath Maggie's passion. Here, alone with Christy, he felt blissfully content. Lying in his arms, Christy looked at him gravely, and in less than ten words, destroyed his equanimity.

"We have to talk about Gabe and Maggie."

"Why? I don't want to talk about them." Oliver was playing with her hair, trying to braid it, and making a mess of it. Christy put up her hand to still his fingers.

"Darling, this has been the best week of my entire life, but we have to talk about the future."

When other women had said these words to him, Oliver had always found an immediate excuse to leave the room, and generally not to return. When Christy said them, he kissed her.

"You're my future. I can't live without you."

"I don't want you to; but decisions have to be made. Maybe sacrifices have to be made."

"No, Christy. Not on my part. Maggie made it perfectly clear she doesn't want anything to do with me. She made that clear by sleeping with Arabin, and she expressed it most eloquently when we talked. I don't owe Maggie anything."

"I don't believe that any more than you do," she said sadly. "Maggie *will* want you back, Oliver. I know it. However much we try and pretend to ourselves that we're going to be left in peace, we're not. And there are the children to think of."

Oliver gripped her by the shoulders. "Christy, are you telling me you want to go back to Gabe?"

"No, I would hate it. It would be the end of my life. But you and I both know that we can survive half dead. If Maggie wants you back, then you have to go. For your kids. Because she's your wife. Because you are a decent man. You have to give her a chance, and you have to give her the choice."

"But what about Gabe? Are you going to give him the choice? I know what he'll choose: you. Christy, are you just trying to let me down lightly?"

"No, Oliver, I swear it. I love you." She breathed the words with her whole heart in them. "You are the only person I have ever really loved apart from Jake. Sometimes, when we're in bed, I wonder if I even love you more than Jake, and that's the thing that scares me worst of all. Even if I do, I will always put him first; you understand that, don't you, my darling?"

"Of course. I'm not jealous of Jake. It's when you talk about Gabe I get concerned."

"But Gabe isn't the important person here—if I have to, I can live with him on my conscience. It's Maggie. I couldn't live with myself if this destroyed her. I couldn't do that to another woman. I can't live with that kind of guilt, Oliver. In the end it would destroy us. You have to tell her that you are willing to go back if she wants it that way. And she will."

Oliver didn't share Christy's conviction that Maggie would want him back, but however slight the risk, the gamble was far too great. "What happens if Maggie says yes? If she comes home?"

"Then Jake and I will go back to the States," Christy said simply, keeping her eyes downcast.

"To Gabe?" Oliver held his breath.

"Maybe. I don't know. I know there'd never be another man for me, so it wouldn't much matter who I lived with, and Jake would need his father. I have ripped Jake away from his dad, after all; they both want each other. I guess my real feeling is that if I can't have you, then it doesn't matter what happens to me; I might as well do what Gabe and Jake want. I could never think of Gabe as my husband again—not like this—but, if he agreed to my going back on that basis, then I guess I'd have to go. I'm not trying to be a martyr—you understand, Oliver? The last thing I want to be is that. But I'm just not able to destroy anybody else's life for the sake of my personal pleasure. The damage is already done as far as Gabe is concerned, but it's got to stop there." Her voice was very steady and certain, and intolerable to Oliver.

"You can't mean that," he whispered aghast. "You can't talk so calmly about all this—ending. Was it just a fling to you, Christy? Did you just do it for a one-night, one-week thrill?"

"How can you think that?" She lifted her head, and Oliver saw her tears. "I love you with my whole heart. I told you the first night, that if that was all it was, it would be enough for me. Do you think I wanted to be in this mess? I've been unhappy for so long, but I can live with being unhappy for the rest of my life if I can just hold on to the idea that we love each other. Oliver, I would give anything to be really *bad*, to say I just don't care about anyone but you and me, but I can't do it! Damn it, damn it, damn it, I wasn't raised that way, and I can't get it out of my head that if I felt responsible for Maggie's misery, or your kids', it would ruin me. It would ruin you, too, and we'd be pathetic little shadows comforting each other and only together because of guilt. Don't you see we don't have a chance starting that way?"

"Why can't you accept that we have the same right to be happy that everyone else does?"

"I do. I just don't believe other people *are* all that happy. You remember what you wrote, Oliver? Maybe no one's happy. Maybe if happiness comes at the price of other people's hurt, it dies. Maybe that's how we get punished. I have thought and thought about this, and yearned for this feeling to just go away, but it isn't going to."

She was so wretched that Oliver, in desperation, heard himself make her a promise.

"Tell me what you want me to do, Christy. Tell me exactly what you want, and I promise you I will do it. I can live with all the guilt in the world, but not the knowledge that I hurt you."

"Then talk to Maggie. Make her believe that if she wants to try again, you are willing to. Tell her you want to."

"Oh, Christ!"

"You must."

"And if she says yes?"

"Like I said, I'll go. Fast."

"And the programme?"

"You'll do it with somebody else. I couldn't bear to ever see you again."

At the screen test the next day, Oliver kept thinking that this was all in vain, that before long, he would say goodbye to Christy forever. Christy looked at him with such tenderness and such courage that he felt he would weep in front of the camera. Danny Bujevski seconded Oliver's opinion that Christy was amazing to look at, and he saw something else that was even more important to him. Oliver and Christy had a chemistry that made magic. They had something elusive between them that made an observer hold his breath. They came across as archetypal opposites, he fair and angular, she dark and mysterious, the one so British, the other a blue-blood American. They seduced the camera and each other.

After a couple of hours discussing where they'd go, what sort of crew they'd need, and the likelihood of American co-finance, Bujevski was more than satisfied. As far as he was concerned, it was in the can. They had a celebratory round or two of drinks, then Oliver and Danny exited to the men's room.

"You screwing her, or what?" Bujevski got to the point before he'd even undone his fly.

"Is that relevant?"

"Okay, so you're screwing her. Lucky you. Wow. This could be big. Real big." Oliver couldn't resist a cheap sideways glance.

"Not from where I'm standing, it couldn't."

"Fuck off, Callahan. That's the problem with you hacks, you're all so far up your own arses, you can't see the bowel for the shit."

"The problem with you TV types is you couldn't use an analogy if your life depended on it."

"Who gives a shit. I don't write the fucking scripts, I produce the goods. As I said. This could be big. You could be big. You and her could be big. We could all be big."

"I think I've grasped the general drift of what you're saying, Danny."

"So. We're gonna sign a contract, okay? For any spin-offs. Say you do another trip—you and her in Scotland, or something. You and her hit New York. Whatever. You do it with us, okay?"

"If the money's right, it sounds fine to me."

Danny Bujevski shook his penis the way a Man of the Match shakes a bottle of champagne.

"The money will be fine for you, arsehole. She's not going to fuck off all of a sudden, is she? She'll be in this for the long haul?"

Oliver smiled nastily. "That's right, arsehole. She's not going to fuck off. So long as you treat her properly. She's a lady, Bujevski, not that you'd know what that means. You treat her like a lady, okay? If you know how, that is. Like a real *lady*."

Oliver left the men's room resigned to his fate. It was some small compensation that if he lost Christy, that shit Bujevski would lose her, too. Although the future looked bleak, Oliver was conscious of an unfamiliar feeling. He felt proud of himself. He felt like a champion. He felt like a gentleman. He felt like a knight in a brand-new suit of shiny armour with a spanking new white horse.

Oliver and Christy drove home to Bockhampton. They had made a silent pact not to discuss Maggie between them again, not until her decision had been made. When they pulled into the driveway, the first thing they saw was Edward Arabin's blue Mercedes with Edward standing next to it, kicking a tyre, his hand dug deep into the pockets of his cords.

"Problem with the motor, Edward?" Oliver slid out of his car and walked around to open Christy's door.

"No; I was just waiting for you. Christy's nanny said you were due back soon. Good evening, Christy."

"Hey, Edward; we haven't seen you for a while . . ."

"No. I've been busy. You're looking well."

"Oliver's been showing me the sights of London. . . . We had a grand time. Now if y'all will excuse me, I just want to check on Jake." Christy, nothing if not discreet, disappeared into the house.

"Oliver? Could you spare the time for a chat? I haven't seen you since you returned from the States."

Oliver, who had been somewhere near the top of the world a few minutes earlier, had an unpleasant sense of foreboding. "By all means," he said, with obvious reluctance. "Come in and have a drink."

Neither man spoke until they were ensconced in the den, each with a whisky in hand. From the outside, it looked like any of the countless times they had sat in the same chairs in the past, and chatted about cricket, argued about politics, or joked about the incomprehensibility of female behaviour. They both knew it was never going to be like that again. Oliver waited for Edward to open the bowling, and Edward obliged.

"I wanted to ask you what was happening. With Maggie. Between you and Christy."

"Is it any of your business what happens between me and my wife?"

Edward sighed. "I'm afraid I think it is. I do care about both you and Maggie. I am very fond of Maggie, I admit."

"*Fond* of her? Edward, you seduced my wife. You fucked her, God damn it!"

Edward, to protect Maggie, didn't quibble with the fact that he had been the seducer. "I wouldn't choose that word, myself. . . ."

"That's not the issue, is it, Ed? The issue is, you, my erstwhile friend, screwed Maggie, my wife, when I was away. Do you think that gives you the right to come over here and start asking questions and claim the moral high ground?"

Edward suddenly realised that Oliver felt under threat—that Oliver felt he deserved to be challenged over his treatment of Maggie. This represented a distinct change in the scenario.

"Nothing was further from my thoughts than moral high grounds. I have spoken to Maggie several times this week. I am concerned about her. I am concerned about you. I thought I might be able to help. Maggie forbade me to come and talk to you, but I found myself unable not to."

"It's a bit odd she's called you so many times this week, and she hasn't called me, isn't it?"

"She hasn't called me once. I have called her each and every time. Have you?"

Oliver took a big swallow of scotch, and coughed. He ignored the question.

"How is she?"

"I don't really know. You know Maggie. She wasn't giving much away. She certainly didn't want my advice. If I was pushed to say anything, I'd say she's angry."

"Angry?" Oliver leapt to his feet. "What fucking right has she got to be angry? She betrayed me—*betrayed me!* How can she feel entitled to be angry?"

"Oliver, I don't know what's happened to you and Maggie. If somebody told you, that weekend of the cricket match, that Maggie and I were having an affair, then all I can say is they lied." Oliver stared at him. "I am not denying that we slept together. We did. Once. But it was entirely of my making. Maggie didn't want to. I—" He looked down at the carpet. "I got her drunk. Very drunk. I was somewhat under the influence myself, although I don't pretend that's any excuse. She was unhappy. She felt you didn't care about her—she was alone, and miserable, and I exploited the situation for my own purposes. It was—if it's any comfort—profoundly unsatisfactory for her. In reparation, I can only say that I was deeply envious of you. I am a lonely man. I am too much of a cynic to hope that I may yet find the perfect woman. Maggie is a lovely girl. Beautiful. I have become extremely fond of her. She was upset, she needed a friend, and I abused her trust. And yours. I don't expect either of you to excuse me, but I cannot allow you to blame Maggie. You and Maggie have a good marriage. Value that. I have simply come to tell you that I'm aware my presence—so close—may make things harder for you and Maggie. I'm quite prepared to move away."

Oliver shook his head slowly, as if in disbelief.

"Oliver. You must listen to me. You and Maggie have been married for a long time. You have two children. You have a great deal that binds you together. Maggie has certain—concerns. She may feel insecure, since she stopped work. She needs—stroking. I noticed that, and I exploited it. Once. I shouldn't have, but you mustn't blame her. She loves you." As Edward talked, he could see no justice in the fact that Maggie loved her husband; he wasn't even certain that she did, but he was convinced by his last conversation with her that Maggie had decided she would work things through, and the final service he could offer her was to help her to do that. "I won't pretend that doesn't make me more angry than anything I can think of, but I know it for a fact. You've both backed yourself into corners out of pride, and I have to come forward and tell you that this is a terrible mistake. She's alone, Oliver. She's frightened."

"You said she was angry."

"It's an act. She doesn't know what else to do. She's trying so hard not to show anyone how hurt she is. She needs you."

"What does she need me for? To pay the bills? She's never given me the slightest impression that she needs me. She does nothing but undermine me—bring me down." Oliver slammed his fist against the wall. *"I'm* struggling, Edward. *I'm* insecure. It's a two-way street, these days, isn't it? I need support. I need a woman who believes in me. I need a partner, someone with strength, and conviction—I can't trust Maggie. I need someone like—" He turned, and stared at Edward, then shrugged.

"Someone like Christy?"

"Just back off, Edward," Oliver muttered. "That's nothing to do with you."

"I'm trying to help. You have a wife, you have two children—"

"You've already fucking said that. Don't tell me what I've got! I also have my own life. I have a career—I have a future—don't I deserve happiness?"

Edward stared at Oliver in amazement. When he'd come over to Bockhampton, he had had no doubt that Oliver was simply punishing Maggie for having had a fling with him. He had decided that the only decent thing he could do would be to shoulder as much of the blame as possible for Maggie's sake, let Oliver keep his pride, and then move away from the Valley. Edward had thought that if he could convince Oliver that he had wrongfully seduced Maggie, Oliver would be on the phone to his wife within an hour, and Maggie would be safely installed in Bockhampton, and the whole sorry business forgotten, within a couple of weeks. The thought had been far from thrilling to him, but Edward had seen it as his duty. Most of all, he believed that this was the best thing for Maggie, and he would have gone to any length to secure her happiness.

"Why don't you at least talk to Maggie? Clear the air. You two have always been good at that."

Oliver shrugged. "It's not up to me. Maggie makes her own decisions. She's a free agent. I just have to sit here until she has the courtesy to tell me what she's doing. That's what she's always wanted—well, now she's got it. I'm the victim in this whole bloody thing. If Maggie wants to try again, then I'll have to go along with it, won't I?"

Edward was sickened by the notion that anyone could think of living with Maggie on sufferance. Trying to explain it to himself, he asked his final question. "Are you involved with Christy McCarthy?"

"Yes, of course, I'm *involved* with her. We happen to be living in the same house, for reasons not of my making," Oliver blustered. "Christy and her husband are having—marital problems. I agreed that she could stay here until she decided what to do. She's a damn fine woman. I admire her. On top of that, she's the perfect co-presenter for my TV series. We're working on it together. Then it's up to her where she wants to go. For my own part, I have no objection if she chooses to stay."

"And what about her husband? What about Gabe?"

Oliver shrugged again. "What the hell do you expect me to say? I've never even met the man. I didn't break up his marriage. It was nothing to do with me."

"But you *are* sleeping with his wife?"

"Who the fuck do you think you are, Edward? The Chief Inquisitor? What gives you the right to come in here and ask me questions like that?"

The door opened quietly, and Christy joined them. She had changed into the short tweed skirt, a white shirt with a Peter Pan collar, and a rust cardigan. She looked every inch the Lady of the Manor.

She stepped up behind Oliver, and placed a hand on each shoulder.

"Oliver, it's all right. I'm sure Edward isn't trying to be rude." She made a gesture of apology and turned her gaze on Edward. "I couldn't help but overhear your question, Edward. I'm surely happy to tell you the truth. My marriage has broken down. It may be irreconcilable. Gabriel and I had certain problems a way back, to do with private issues—my not being able to have another baby and all; I guess it undermined what he felt for me. I am not able to give him the life and family he wants. Maybe this trip brought everything to the surface. I felt that I couldn't return with him. Oliver has been courteous enough to suggest that I might stay here until I've made some choices about what's best for me and Jake."

"I'm sorry to hear that, Christy. These past few weeks must have been difficult for you. You certainly keep your problems well hidden."

"I don't believe in washing dirty linen in public, Edward, but I think that among the three of us, we can all be open, don't you? Oliver has told me about your relationship with Maggie. Maybe you don't realise how much that's hurt him. Well, I do. Maybe it's just that Oliver and I can understand each other because we've both suffered from not being able to—satisfy our partners. It's not an easy thing to face up to, you know. As Oliver's been kind enough to understand my problems, I feel like I need to help him out here. Until—"

"Until what?"

"Until he and Maggie have the time and the peace and quiet to decide what is best. I don't think anyone should interfere with them." Christy had left her hands resting lightly on Oliver's shoulders.

Edward rose slowly to his feet. He was shaking inside, but when he rose to his full height, he looked like a painting of the wrath of God. "Oliver, you amaze me. I am astounded. I have never been married, and I have never had children, but I cannot believe that people who do can be so entirely selfish. Don't you understand? You don't have the *right* to make decisions, or choices, or whatever crap you're talking about. Neither of you are victims. From where I stand none of the four of you are victims. That is all a whitewash. You don't have choices, you have duties and responsibilities, and both of you are too damn selfish and immature to face up to them. I pity your children. They deserve better." He put one hand to his eyes as if he couldn't bear to have Christy and Oliver in his sight. "In some ways I hope you two stick together—oddly enough, you suit each other. I don't believe we have anything more to say."

"Tell me just one more thing, Edward. After that noble speech. Did you really screw Maggie when she was drunk?"

Edward looked at Oliver coldly. "For my sins, yes I did."

"You shit."

Edward looked at them both for a moment without speaking, and then left the room. They heard the front door slam, and the noise of his engine starting.

Christy coiled herself onto Oliver's lap, and stroked his hair. "You mustn't let Edward upset you, darlin'. He's just eaten up with jealousy; you know that. I'm not even sure he's telling the truth about Maggie. Something tells me—feminine intuition, maybe—he's just trying to protect her. It's all going to be okay. It's all going to work out just fine, whatever happens. Trust me."

Fifteen

A plain postcard to Maggie Callahan, Oak Ridge,
Lawrenceville, North Carolina:

*Where the hell are you? How can I stay in touch if you don't
tell me where you are and you don't return phone calls? I'm
not asking for much, Maggie—just a word.*

Edward

MAGGIE WAS IN HER ROOM CHANGING FOR THE RICHARDSES' PARTY
when she heard the phone ring, and she left it to the answering
machine. It was Edward, simply saying that he had been to see
Oliver and thought Maggie should know what had been discussed.
Maggie didn't pick up the phone. She didn't want to hear Oliver's
views secondhand, and hated the idea of Edward and Oliver discussing her as if she were some sort of disputed chattel. In truth,
they were probably fighting over Christy; winner takes Christy, and
the loser would get her as some sort of booby prize. At some point,
she was going to have to take some kind of action—Leah was hinting
at needing to get on with things, maybe going back to England,
and maybe even going back to Oz. On the other hand, Gabe was
encouraging her to stay put until the dust had settled. He had even
volunteered to talk to his son's school about taking Lily in for a
term. He seemed more than happy that she should stay and house-
sit Oak Ridge, until he had sorted out his own life. Despite feeling
that she ought to be making her own decisions, Maggie was tempted
to let somebody else take control, particularly somebody as accom-

modating and objective as Gabe. When she was dressed, Maggie went into Lily's room to read her a story and say goodnight.

Lily wouldn't look at her when she came in.

"Sweetheart, would you like to choose a story to read? I'll tuck you in."

"I don't want you to read a story now. I want you to read one later."

"I'm going out later, Lily, darling. Let's read one now, okay?"

"I don't want you to go out. Since Daddy went, you're always going out."

Leah, sorting out the children's clothes, glanced up at the scene between mother and daughter, but kept her sensible mouth shut.

"Lily, I'd love to stay with you, and I know you don't want me to go out, but I really have to."

"Why?" Lily's far from child-like eyes met her mother's.

"I accepted an invitation, darling. It's not polite to cancel at the last minute."

"You shouldn't have said you'd go if you don't want to."

"But I do want to!"

"Then you don't want to stay with me and Arthur."

"Lily, I do. I'll spend all tomorrow with you and Arthur, the whole day, I promise. But you'll be asleep soon; you don't want me to sit here and do nothing while you're asleep, do you? What would I do, just sit here and talk to myself?" Maggie tried to cajole the little girl, but Lily wasn't falling for it.

"Yes, I do. I *do* want you to sit here when I'm sleeping," she insisted.

"I can't do that, Lily. Not tonight. Don't ask me."

"Then I don't want you to read me a story. I want Leah to read it. Leah *stays* with us. You don't. I want Leah to read the story."

Maggie sighed and stood by the edge of the bed. She knew she shouldn't feel rejected and wounded; Lily was clever enough to punish her mother where it hurt most, by stating a bald preference for her nanny. It wasn't so different from Oliver's choosing to be with Christy. Lily had inherited her parents' inability to pull their punches.

"Get going, Maggie, she'll be 'right. She's just giving you a hard time." Leah pulled a story book off the shelf, and settled down to read to Lily. When Maggie bent to kiss her daughter, the little girl turned her cheek away, nestling in the crook of Leah's arm.

Gabe was waiting for her on the porch. He had ordered a taxi—
no attorney would lightly risk a drunk-driving charge—and he es-
corted her to it with a hand cupped protectively under her elbow.
When they reached the car, he opened one rear door, and Maggie
climbed in and automatically began to slide across the seat before
she realised that Gabe had closed the door and was walking around
to the other side. Maggie smiled to herself. She had spent so long
in Oliver's company that she expected gentlemanliness to stop at
opening the door. Oliver always prided himself on doing this,
whereas if he had stopped to think for a minute, he would have
realised that he caused his escort, and her dress, far more inconvenience by expecting her to shuffle across the rear seat than he
would by letting her open the door herself. Oliver took the first
faltering steps of being a gentleman, but didn't carry it through
to its natural conclusion. Gabe carried it through from A to Z.
Maggie wondered who was to blame for Oliver's misunderstanding
of the ritual. Herself? No; she'd met him too late to have any significant effect. Probably his mother. Mothers seemed to get the
blame for everything.

Gabe had recovered from his drinking bout the night before, and
was on good form at the party. Maggie put it down to the tennis
lesson; he was obviously a man who liked to help and feel useful,
and that was the least she could do for him in exchange for his very
genuine hospitality. Maggie realised that since last night, she and
Gabe had become friends—genuine friends. He didn't stay stuck to
her side all night, but he kept an eye on her, smiling at her over
the heads of the other guests, rescuing her if she looked bored or
ill at ease, and introducing her to people she hadn't yet met. Everybody asked about Christy, and Gabe handled the situation with perfect aplomb. He laughed at the coincidence that Oliver and Christy
were going to work together—"I can wholeheartedly recommend
this house swapping business to y'all, folks. I went off on vacation
with an unemployed wife, and she's fixed herself up in a new career,
and we've got two brand-new friends into the bargain!" He laughed
as he draped his arm around Maggie's shoulders, and Maggie
laughed, too. Gabe clearly had no intention of baring his soul to
the whole of Lawrenceville. He told great stories about their holiday,
and about Maggie's friends and neighbours, entertaining the party
with the account of Sir Nigel Bavington's nude gardening, and
Major Hangham's falling into the flower beds. Everybody wanted

to come and stay at Bockhampton, and Maggie issued invitations right, left, and centre without knowing whether she herself would ever return. It would serve Oliver right if he were to be invaded by an army of visiting Americans. The party might have been a dreadful strain, but Gabe made it easy for her. Far from dwelling on his own problems, he seemed to have found a new source of energy by applying himself to her welfare. After dinner, B.J. put on some music, and everybody started dancing, some perilously close to the edge of the pool. A tall and boyishly handsome doctor called Hank asked Maggie for the pleasure of a dance, and flirted openly with her.

"Your husband is a mighty fine guy, Mrs. Callahan."

"Oh? Have you met Oliver?"

"Nope, but I sure do appreciate him leaving you here with us for a bit . . . A mighty fine guy. Real dumb, though. If you were my wife, I wouldn't take my eyes off you for a second."

Maggie laughed, but when Hank suggested that he and she lead the party into the pool for a late-night dip, she demurred, and took the empty chair next to Lindy Richards.

"You look like you're having a grand time, sugar."

"I am, Lindy. You and B.J. throw great parties. I wish we could take you home with us. You'd certainly liven up Compton Purlew!"

"Beej and I don't like travelling right much, hon, but I sure hope we get to stay in touch when you go back home." Maggie nodded. "Talking of which, sugar, when *are* y'all heading back?"

"I don't really know. I'm waiting for Oliver to say what's happening—I mean, with his work. It sounds like he and Christy are trying to get things sorted out."

Lindy paused while she lit a cigarette. "Maggie, girl, I wasn't born yesterday. I've got eyes in my head, and ears, too. Gabe told us all about everything the night he got back." Maggie bit her lip, and attempted a small smile.

"Then you probably know more than I do about it."

"I know that Christy Moore has fallen in love with your husband."

"How can anybody fall in love with someone they don't know?"

"Oh, sugar; that's the easiest thing in the world. Like falling off a log. You can fall in love with anyone you take a mind to: a stranger at a party, your neighbour, your boss, your own daddy if you want to bad enough. You know what my mama used to tell me? She used to say, 'Lindy, don't ever marry for money, 'cos that won't make you happy, but go where the rich go and make darn sure you fall in love.' Not that I followed her advice none."

Maggie smiled. "Go on. Tell me more."

"I'll tell you what I know, and what I think, and if after that you think I'm an old busybody who should keep her nose out of other people's affairs, then you just tell me to keep my trap shut and that'll be just fine by me. When I've said my piece, I'll shut up. When I met your husband, I thought he was a nice guy—nice lookin', too; just because I'm over forty doesn't mean I don't have an eye for a fine piece of manhood. But between you and me, sugar, he ain't the sharpest tool in the woodshed, you hear what I'm saying? Nothing peculiar about that—in most of the marriages I know, including Christy's, and my own, it's the girls who got the smarts, not that we'd want to let on that. It beats me what's going on between Oliver and Christy—she's got something into that stubborn head of hers, and gone all out, and your fella's gone right along with it, like he's got a ring through his nose. Well now; as I see it, you can do three things. You can get your tail back there and fight for him, and maybe you'll win, or you can sit here and feel sorry for yourself and let Christy wrap everything up in brown paper and string, neat and tidy. Or, you can take a long, hard look at yourself, and fergit all about him. I mean, just fergit it! I married B.J. when I was seventeen years old. If I'd known then what I know now, d'you think I would have saddled myself with that bucket of lard? No way. You're young, you're bright, you've already got the kids, which is the only good reason fer gittin' hitched in the first place—you don't need it. My generation, hell, we didn't have no choice, so now I'm lumbered. You know, Maggie, I read an article in one of those new women's magazines, all about how unmarried women live longer, and have fewer medical and mental problems than married women. It also said that unmarried men die younger and are less happy than married men. What does that tell you, sugar? You don't need to be a Harvard summa cum laude to work that one out!" She topped up Maggie's glass from a bottle on the ground next to her chair. "Now you go have a good time, but listen to me here: you just put all this behind you, okay? There ain't nothing to stop you kicking up your heels and doing whatever you darn well please; nothing but being a scaredy-cat, and I don't think you're scared of anything."

"Oh you're wrong; I'm scared of everything, Lindy. I'm scared of myself, and I'm scared of being alone, and I'm scared that Oliver was right to dump me, and I'm scared of Christy . . . Christ, I'm even scared of my own four-year-old daughter."

Lindy studied her with piercing, narrowed eyes.

"So you ain't heartbroken? You don't feel like you can't live without Oliver?"

Maggie shook her head slowly. "To be honest, I haven't even thought about him that much. I've been too preoccupied thinking about me."

Lindy grinned, and patted her knee maternally. "You'll live. You're just gonna have to get a grip of yourself and stop all that cock-eyed scaredy stuff. You shouldn't be scared, honey; you should be clam-happy. The way I figure it, it's all out there for you. Just *go get* it."

"Lindy! Lindy, my one true love!" B.J.'s tuneless voice sang over the noise of the party. "Where's my darling girl? My arms are empty, sweetheart, and only you can fill them . . ." He was dancing by himself, his arms encircling an imaginary partner.

"Look at that overgrown kid," said Lindy with real tenderness. "I'm going to have to go do something 'fore he makes a damn fool of himself. I'm here, you dumb ox. . . ."

Couples danced slowly to some crooning ballad that Maggie didn't recognise. It had a melancholic, sentimental air, and Maggie watched the shuffling feet of the Richardses, barely moving, Lindy completely swamped by B.J.'s gorilla-like embrace. Despite Lindy's protestations at being stuck with B.J., the one thing that came leaping out of their relationship was their genuine intimacy and sense of mutual dependence. It was all very well for Lindy to grumble about her husband, but they had shared their entire lives, and now, after nearly thirty years of marriage, they not only had each other, but were bound together by a whole history of memories. There was such an aching tenderness in the way they looked at each other, in B.J.'s sentimental romanticism and Lindy's wise-cracking devotion, that Maggie felt she was spying on something not for public observation. She looked away, and for the first time realised completely what had happened with Oliver. Her marriage had died a long time ago, from that moment when she had stopped caring about him beyond whether he helped her with the house and children and came home when he said he would. She had stopped caring because at an early stage she had stopped trusting him, and she couldn't leave one of her most exposed flanks so vulnerable to assault. By not caring about him, she guarded herself twenty-four hours a day. In many ways, she was closer to Mog—or Lucy—or Edward—than she had ever been to Oliver. She had been attracted to him because he was dangerous, and unpredictable and very funny, and because he had never bored her. However strong that attraction, it had never metamorphosed into love. That was why she wasn't heartbroken now. She didn't actually miss him in her life, and there was a sense of relief in not having to protect herself from the man who should have been protecting her. For the first time in years, she thought about him objectively, and with genuine affection. After months, maybe even years, of looking inward and fending off her own growing sense of dissatisfaction, she wondered if Oliver had been miserable, too. Perhaps Oliver had suffered equal, or even greater, disillusionment of his romantic dream? Maggie didn't believe now that there was any way she could be happy with Oliver, or with a man like Oliver. Oliver needed to be admired—maybe all men did—and his ego was hellish, but maybe if she had ever really loved him, he would have been a different man. It occurred to Maggie then that men couldn't be divided into baboons and desert mice. Maybe it was the women who loved them, and the way they loved them, that determined a man's behaviour. Maggie was not at the point of holding Oliver blameless for what had happened, nor was she prepared to forgive him exactly, but she was starting to think that maybe this was all for the best—for both of them. The spell he had cast over her had snapped. She hadn't thought about him so considerately for at least three years.

"Maggie? Would you honour me with this dance, please?"

"No thanks, Gabe, I think I'll just sit this one out. Maybe later."

"Round here, it isn't considered polite to ask a lady to dance if she's already turned you down once. The way we're taught, one no means no forever. No second chances, no later. We're meant to do as we're told. So please; be kind; don't say no."

"Alright, but I'm not much good at this sort of music."

"You don't even have to move. I'll do it all for you."

Gabe took one hand in his, and slipped the other around her waist. "You looked like you were a long way aways, thinking about something real hard."

"I was. I was just on the point of deciding to call Oliver and tell him that I agreed with him. That I don't think he and I should get back together."

"You going to do that?"

"It depends on you. I don't want to do anything that would make things harder for you and Christy."

"I don't think you *could* do anything that would make things harder for me and Christy. They're just about as hard as they can get."

"Well, I'm in no hurry. If you really don't mind if I stay, I think I might hang around a little. I'd like to spend some time with the children, and try to talk to them about everything—Lily that is— and see how they feel."

"How'd you think they feel, Maggie?"

"I think they feel miserable. Have you talked to Jake, Gabe?"

"Every goddamn day. I'll say this for Christy; she's real keen that Jake and I don't grow apart. If we can't sort all this out, I'm not going to be able to put Christy, and most of all, Jake through a custody case; maybe we can have joint custody. I worry about it, though. I feel like every time I'm ever going to walk through a store, I'll be thinking, would Jake like that? Every time I see a commercial for Pop-Tarts on the TV, I'll be worrying, did Jake eat a good breakfast today? He isn't that fussed. He just asks when I'm coming back. He seems real impressed by Oliver. He told me Oliver was teaching him to play cricket."

It hurt Maggie to hear that; it made her think that the chances of Oliver's teaching Arthur to play were looking slim, and her anger surged for a moment on behalf of her baby.

"How are *you* feeling, Gabe? Really?"

He thought for a while, considering her question carefully. "When I left school, more than anything else I wanted to be a doctor. Just a small-town physician, nothing fancy. More than anything. My daddy was a doctor, and his daddy before him, and that's all I ever wanted to be. I didn't make the grades. For months, I just told myself there had to be some kind of *mistake*—someone, some examiner or administrator had screwed up real bad. I waited for a letter admitting they'd made this big mistake. It didn't come. Finally, my daddy told me I just wasn't going to be a doctor, and it was time to think of something else. That's kind of how I feel now."

"I'm not sure that I follow you. Everyone said you went to Harvard Law School?"

"I did, eventually. But it wasn't my first choice. Even now, it wouldn't be my first choice. I'd still rather be a doctor. I mean, it's worked out okay and all, I probably would have been a lousy doctor and I'm a good lawyer, but there was something I wanted real bad, and no matter what I did I couldn't have it. I'm beginning to feel that way about Christy, but it's like it's all in reverse. With Christy, it's like I got the letter saying I was accepted to med school, and then years later, got sent a letter saying they'd screwed up, and it was all a mistake, and asking for my degree back. Christy and I have been married for ten years, and I have never once doubted that we'd be married all our lives. Now I've got to think about that. I've got to think about the idea that my hopes were raised for nothing."

"Are you just going to accept it?"

"Hell no! I'm gonna appeal! I'll re-sit the exams, or reapply, or whatever I've gotta do. I just think that somebody may come along and say, sorry, pal; your number's up. It's like when every ounce of you wants to get the ten out of ten score, and you pray real hard for it, and it comes round, and you've got eight. Well, eight ain't bad. But it's surely not ten out of ten."

"Oh, God, Gabe. What an incredibly sad and sorry pair we are."

"Tell you what, Maggie. Let's you and me make a pact. Let's pretend this is the best night of our lives, and not let on how low we feel, okay? If we're gonna go down, let's go down fighting, okay?" He winked at her. "It's the Southern way."

"Okay." He twirled her round under his arm, laughing, and there were those at the party who thought that Oliver Callahan and Christy Moore McCarthy had made a very big mistake leaving their partners in each other's company.

Gabe was as high as a kite, and it wasn't to do with alcohol. She had seen the previous night how alcohol affected him. In the cab going back to Oak Ridge, Gabe sang country and western songs at the top of his voice, provoking much head-shaking from the driver, and various friendly comments about it being a darn good thing that Gabe hadn't decided to drive himself home. Yet when they arrived, Gabe leapt out of the car as sure-footed as a mountain goat and went round to open Maggie's door.

"Come into the studio, Maggie, for a nightcap." He held the door open for her. "We'll be eaten alive by the bugs if we stay outside, and I've still got some bourbon left. You didn't think I'd drunk the whole bottle last night, did you?"

Maggie settled herself on the sofa in front of the fireplace, and admired the room. "Christy really does have good taste." She felt she should be generous to Christy, for Gabe's sake. For Oliver's sake, even. She just felt generally benevolent. Maybe some chemical was kicking into her system, too.

"Yep. She's always had great taste. Except in men." He laughed.

"You're not so bad, Gabe. And I have to admit that at least at one time, I saw enough in Oliver to make me think he was the man for me."

"D'you think Oliver and I have got much in common?"

"Absolutely." Maggie smiled, and leant forward to put her glass down on the table. "Absolutely *nothing.*" They both roared with laughter like a couple of teenagers telling their first dirty jokes. "Actually, that's not quite true. You both make me laugh. And I suppose you're both good looking."

"You suppose so, huh? I'll have you know that at Wharton I was voted best-looking freshman of my year. One of the co-eds even threatened to kill herself if I wouldn't take her on a date."

"Really? No one ever did that for me at Bristol."

"No kidding? You surprise me. If you'd been at a decent, red-blooded American college, you could have had a string of suicides to your name." He winced. "Shit, that's sounds real bad, doesn't it? I just wanted to pay you a compliment."

"Thank you, Gabe; it was a pretty one, whatever it sounded like."

"You're pretty, Maggie. Real pretty." Gabe gazed at her in open appreciation, and Maggie shifted uncomfortably on the sofa. It wasn't that she felt threatened by him, exactly, but it was a long time since she'd found herself in this sort of situation, and she'd forgotten which role to play, let alone how to play it.

"I'm not making you uncomfortable, am I?"

"Heavens, no!" Maggie answered a little too quickly. "I'm perfectly comfortable. Having the time of my life." She picked up a magazine from the coffee table whose cover advertised a feature on Colorado.

"Have you ever been to Colorado, Gabe?"

"Nope." He was still looking at her admiringly.

"Really? How strange. I thought that Americans travelled all the time. . . ." She tried to keep her voice light but ended up by squeaking. Gabe smiled slowly. "Where *have* you been?" Maggie twittered.

"Here and there. South. North. West Coast."

"That must be lovely. I'd love to see San Francisco."

"Maybe I could take you. Maybe before you go back to England." He sprawled in the chair next to her, his eyes remaining fixed on her face. Maggie instinctively compared him to Oliver. Gabe was broad-chested and heavy-boned, with none of Oliver's elegant angularity. Gabe was muscular and earthy and one hundred percent solid. She didn't compare him to Edward. Edward always seemed to her to be on an altogether bigger scale than other men.

"That sounds very . . . nice. But I know how busy you are."

"No you don't. I can make time for what I want to do."

"Well, let's see, shall we? What happens, I mean. It seems a shame not to see more of the States now I'm here. I'm thinking of going to Charleston."

"D'you know how many Charlestonians it takes to change a lightbulb?"

"No; how many does it take?" Maggie prompted obligingly.

"Three. One to change the bulb, one to mix the drinks, and one to say how fine the old lightbulb was. . . ." He grinned at her. "Charleston's all about nostalgia."

"I'd love to see it."

"Now I can certainly be of service in that direction. It's just down the road a way. I know it real well. It'd be a pleasure to show it to you. There's a grand inn—real romantic—called Two Meeting Street."

"That's *awfully* sweet of you, Gabe," Maggie said in her most serious and sincere voice, "but I simply couldn't afford that sort of trip. I thought I might just take the children and stay in a motel or something."

"I'm inviting you as my guest."

"Oh. Oh, I see. Hmm. Very tempting." Maggie glanced at her watch, hoping it looked accidental. "Oh my God! Is that the time!" The words were out of her mouth before she could try to rephrase them into something more original. Gabe laughed, and shook his head at her. "Maggie, honey, there's a great big clock—maybe twelve inches in diameter—staring you in the face from that wall. We both know what time it is."

"Yes, well, I just don't want anything to get out of control, you see."

"Me neither. Are you out of control?"

"No."

"Then I'm surely not. So you've got nothing to worry about." Maggie looked unconvinced, but sank back into the sofa.

"Maggie, d'you know what I'm thinking?" His eyes were hooded, but she had the feeling that under their lids they were focused on her bosom.

"No, but I'd be willing to hazard a guess."

"Don't do that, 'cos you might guess wrong, and that would be a shame, and you might guess right, and that would steal my thunder. Let me lay it straight up. I'm thinking it would do us a power of good, you and me, to go to bed with each other. That's what I'm thinking. No strings attached, no obligations. Just a way of sealing our pact."

"Our pact?"

"Not to let everyone else know that we're hurting."

"Is that the only reason you want to go to bed with me?"

"No. 'Course it isn't. I want to go to bed with you because it's a long time since I've desired a woman other than Christy. Because you've got great legs. Because I've been a bit of a straitlaced teacher's pet ever since I was a kid and I feel like doing something reckless for a change. Because I like your eyes. Because I love the way you talk. Because you're real sexy when you're nervous, and real sexy when you're mad, and real sexy when you laugh. Because you make *me* laugh, and I didn't think I'd be doing that for a long time. Because you told Maybelle Martin that your husband was a professional wanker. Because you tricked me into thinking you'd never played tennis."

"I see. So it was just a spur-of-the-moment thing? Not something you'd considered carefully?"

"Come here, you gorgeous thing." Gabe held his arms out to her.

"Just one more question, Gabe. The Southern rule about asking a lady to dance? Does that apply to asking a lady to have sex with you, too? One refusal and you're out?"

"It sure does."

"In that case . . ." she was on the point of saying "I'd better say yes and keep my options open," because it seemed such a good line, when she looked him straight in the eyes and said, "No. I'm sorry, but this is a mistake, Gabe. Let's not do this."

"You don't want to sleep with me?" There was the faintest trace of relief in his voice, which Maggie understood completely.

"No; I don't."

"Why?"

"Lots of reasons. Some for me, some for you. You really love Christy, don't you?"

"Yes, I guess I really do."

"She's lucky. You'd lie down and die for her, wouldn't you?"

"I'd do much more than that. That would be relatively easy; putting my body between hers and a truck would just be instinct—no more than that. No; I'd kill for her. I mean it. I would commit premeditated murder if she needed it or wanted it bad enough." Gabe's expression told Maggie that he spoke in deadly earnest. "Maggie, I don't want to sleep alone. Would you just stay with me tonight? If I promise I won't touch you?"

"Of course I will, Gabe. I don't feel like being alone tonight either."

Maggie borrowed Gabe's paisley dressing gown and slipped into bed next to him. She cradled him in her arms just as she held Lily after a nightmare.

The studio room was flooded with bright sunlight when Maggie awoke the next day. For a moment or two, she couldn't understand where she was or what she was doing there. Then her sleepy mind began to focus, seeing Gabe lying next to her in the high-rise bed, and hearing a hammering at the door.

"Maggie, you in there? It's Leah." Leah's voice was insistent. Maggie leapt out of bed and opened the studio door a crack, shielding her eyes from the glare of the sun. Leah stood in the doorway, her hands on her hips and an uncharacteristic scowl on her face.

"Oh. Hi, Leah. Is it late? I'm sorry—I must have overslept."

"You sure did; it's lunchtime. Didn't you get my bloody note last night?"

"No. I never went into the house, in fact. I just decided to sleep in here."

Leah's eyes moved slowly down the length of Maggie's—Gabe's—paisley dressing gown, which reached nearly to Maggie's ankles.

"Bugger. I was sure you'd see it. Arthur's sick. He was chucking his guts up all night. And Lily's bloody boiling as well. Wanted to call a doctor, didn't I, but I didn't have a bloody number. Oliver rang—twice, and Edward Arabin called most of the bloody night— I was talking to them in between clearing up piles of chuck. Where the bloody hell were you? I rang the Richardses this morning, in case you'd stayed there. They were pretty worried until I told them that Mr. McCarthy's car was in the drive." She glared at Maggie, looking exhausted and unforgiving.

"Oh, God, I'm sorry, Leah. Let me put some clothes on. I'll be right there."

"You got clothes, Maggie, or you want me to bring some from your room? A toothbrush maybe?"

Maggie flinched at her sarcasm, but took the blow submissively. "No thank you, Leah. I'll manage."

She flung on her dress of the previous night, ignoring the wrinkles. Her head swam, and she wanted nothing more than to lie down in a dark room with a cup of tea and a few aspirin. But when you've got children—perhaps even more when you've got a nanny— you can run but you can't hide.

Maggie walked into the kitchen and found Arthur crying piteously on Leah's hip while the nanny tried to get some juice out of the fridge. Lily slept in a crumpled heap on the sofa.

"Leah, I'm so sorry. I should have come in and checked that everything was okay."

"No worries. I guess you had other things on your mind." Her normally jolly tone was clipped.

Arthur, wailing loudly, stretched out his arms to his mother.

"Leah, why don't you go and get some sleep? You must be exhausted."

"No thanks. I don't think I could sleep right now. Anyway, I need to talk to you, Maggie. You know I'm not great at keeping my mouth shut and bottling things up." Maggie slumped down at the table, and Leah, suddenly feeling a tiny bit sorry for her boss, poured her a cup of coffee.

"I've decided it's time to quit. I want to go home."

"I know you've been thinking about it," Maggie said cautiously.

"Yeah, well, I decided this morning. It was the straw that broke the camel's back; I just can't hack it anymore. Look, Maggie, I know you're in deep shit, but what you're bloody doing just isn't fair on the kids. And I'm not about to hang round watching it all and trying to pretend everything's all normal."

"I understand."

"I don't think you do, really. I know you've got your problems with Oliver. He's gone and shacked up with this American woman, from what Edward Arabin said last night. I don't want to leave you in the lurch, but if you just decided to up and shag that bloke last night, then I think it's better all round if I just get going. I don't understand what you're doing, and after last night I don't care. Lily and Arthur need at least one parent who gives a damn. I mean, what the hell have you decided to do, wife swap, or something? Who the hell gets the kids? *Me?* God knows, I love them, but I can't take this kind of responsibility. You understand, don't you?"

"Yes, I do. I know I haven't been fair."

"It's not a question of being bloody fair. Your head ain't screwed on right anymore. What *are* you bloody doing, Maggie?"

Maggie stared at her bleakly. "I just don't know. I haven't the faintest idea. Whatever it looked like, I didn't 'shag' Gabe McCarthy, and I'm not shacking up with him. I don't have any idea what Oliver's doing. I was waiting for him to call."

"Well, he called alright. And the second time, I told him you'd gone to a party with Gabe and he was really pissed off. But not half as pissed off as I was. So when he asked me how the kids were, I told him they were both sick as dogs. I'm sorry, Maggie, but I was just so bloody pissed off. I don't want to cause you any more trouble, but I just think you're all behaving like a bunch of kids—rotten ones—and none of you give two fucks about the real ones. Look at Lily; she doesn't know whether she's Arthur or Martha. All day long she bangs on about where her daddy is, and then last night, she bloody asks me if you've gone and buggered off, too. And she thinks it's all her fault, poor little mite. She's become real quiet and secretive. She's acting like she's fourteen, not four." Maggie cradled Arthur's head in her arms, rocking him. "At least that little blighter doesn't seem to know what's going on, but Lily sure does." Leah continued. "Anyway, I've said my piece, and now it's time for me to up sticks and go home."

"When do you want to go?"

"Soon as I can. I have to go back to Bockhampton to get my stuff, then I'll get the first plane home."

313

"Okay. I'll get you a ticket to London right away. We owe you your return ticket to Australia, too."

"Yeah. Well. If that's a problem, I've got enough saved."

"It's not a problem. I can buy you a ticket. If you don't want to go back to England, I'll get you a ticket straight from here, and get Oliver to send the rest of your things on."

"No, I like to clear up my own shit. I'm not good at things being out of control, if y'know what I mean. Unfinished business really bugs me."

"I understand that."

Leah turned to leave the room, and had second thoughts. "Look, Maggie. I owe you two weeks' notice. I'm not bothered if you want me to work it out. It's no big deal. It'll give you a chance to get things sorted out, and I can go back mid-September. I'm in no big rush. It's not like it's important."

"Yes it is. I think you've made your decision, and I understand it, and you don't owe me anything. If you can hang on till tomorrow, just so I can get a doctor or something, I'll get you on a flight to London tomorrow night."

"Okay. Whatever suits."

"Thanks, Leah. And I *am* sorry."

"No worries."

Maggie had no choice but to wake Gabe up to get the name and number of the McCarthys' paediatrician. Gabe sprang into action. Doctors in the States are not known for making house calls, and never on a Sunday, but Gabe persuaded Dr. Feinstein to come round to Oak Ridge within the hour. The earnest doctor assured Maggie that there was nothing wrong that a few antibiotics wouldn't cure, and simply told her to watch their temperatures and call him in the event of any material change. While he examined Lily and Arthur, he chatted to Gabe about Jake and Christy and their holiday in England, and Maggie was overwhelmed by the ease with which what seemed like such normal, calm orderly lives had been overturned by a simple house exchange. After the doctor had gone, Maggie had no time or desire to talk to Gabe about the night before, and Gabe respected the change in her mood, and left her in peace.

"I'll be in my study upstairs if you need me for anything, Maggie. Give me a holler if the kids get worse, or you need help with them, hey?"

Maggie nodded, and settled her children, spending most of the afternoon watching the video of *The Incredible Journey* again and again, with tears pouring down her cheeks. Lily and Arthur were fretful and wouldn't eat, but the drugs began to take effect, and by the evening, Lily at least seemed more like her old self. Maggie settled Arthur in his crib, and sat on Lily's bed to read her a story. Lily wouldn't choose one, rejecting all her old favourites, and finally pleaded with Maggie to make one up.

"Make up a fairy story for me, Mummy. Make up a story about a little girl called Lily."

"Alright, sweetheart. One upon a time, there was a lovely, precious little girl called Lily, who had beautiful straight blond hair, and big green eyes, and a pair of magic pink shoes."

"Did she have a little brother, too?"

"Yes she did, a little brother called Arthur, who was sometimes very naughty, and sometimes very good, but Lily loved him whatever he was like."

"And did she have a mummy and a daddy?"

"Of course she did, darling, and they loved her very much, too."

"So what happened?"

"Well, one day, Lily went for a walk through the forest, and she came to a huge, green lake."

"Like the lake here?"

"Quite like this one, yes, but much bigger, and much greener, and much more mysterious."

"What's mysterious?"

"Oh, it means all sort of strange and wonderful—a sort of magic lake. So Lily walked around the lake, and she said to herself, 'What I'd really like now is a sandwich.' "

"What kind of sandwich did she want?"

"What kind do you think she'd like?"

"Strawberry jam and salami," Lily replied firmly. Maggie smiled.

"So Lily closed her eyes, and clicked her magic pink shoes together, and said, 'Oh magic shoes, please could I have a strawberry jam and salami sandwich on brown bread. Without the crust.' And lo and behold! Right in front of her, a strawberry jam and salami sandwich appeared, and Lily ate it all up."

"Was she sick?"

"No, darling, it was a yummy sandwich, her favourite, and she gobbled it all up. And then she thought to herself, now what I'd like is a beautiful new party dress, and so she clicked her magic pink shoes together, and wished very hard, and lo and behold! A beautiful dress appeared, and she slipped it on."

"What did the dress look like?"

"What do you think?"

"I think it was green, with lots and lots of frills, and long pink ribbons."

"You're right, that's exactly what it was like. And then Lily clicked her heels together, and she said, 'And now, magic shoes, I would like a wonderful handsome prince on a white horse to come galloping up and take me away to a wonderful party that lasts forever.' And what do you think happened?"

"A prince came?"

"Well, not exactly. Suddenly, from out of the huge, green mysterious lake, an ugly old frog leapt, croaking and spluttering."

"Ugh!"

"Exactly. That's just what the little girl in the story said. She said, 'Ugh, yuck!' And then the frog spoke to her. He said, 'Hello Lily; croak, croak. You may think I'm an ugly old frog, but in truth, I'm a terribly handsome dashing prince, and an evil old witch put a spell on me and turned me into a frog, and all you have to do to make me a prince again is give me a huge great kiss on my ugly old lips and say you love me.' "

"Ugh!"

"Exactly. Pretty disgusting, wasn't it? Anyway, Lily decided it was worth it, if he really was going to turn into a prince, so she bent down and kissed the frog, saying, 'I love you, you hideous, ugly old frog.' And do you know what happened then?"

"He turned into a prince?"

"No. He laughed, and croaked, 'Got you! I was lying! I'm not a prince, I'm just a hideous old frog!' and he hopped back into the lake. So the little girl—Lily—thought she'd try again. She clicked her heels and wished for a handsome prince, and lo and behold! *Another* disgusting old frog hopped out of the lake, and told the same old story about being a prince and needing a kiss from a beautiful young girl."

"How did she know it wasn't the same one?" the rational Lily interrupted.

"It looked different. It had a big yellow splodge on its head."

"Ugh!"

"Exactly. Ugh! So this frog said to her, 'I'm a prince. I'm telling the truth. I'm not like the other lying bast—frog. I promise.' Well, Lily bent down, and kissed its smelly old head, and said, 'I love you, frog,' and once again, the second frog laughed and croaked, 'Tricked you! I'm not a prince, I'm just a smelly old frog!' and *he* hopped away, laughing, into the lake. What do you think Lily did this time?"

Her daughter considered the situation for a few moments. "I think she tried again."

"You're absolutely right. She thought, third time lucky, even though she was getting a little bit cross with her magic pink shoes. But she clicked the heels together, and wished very, very hard for a handsome prince. And lo and behold! A moment later, a truly revolting frog, far, far uglier than the other two, with black and purple and yellow splodges and blodges all over its body, hopped out, and gave a great disgusting belch. 'Hello, little girl. I may look like a stinky old frog, but I am in truth a handsome prince. A wicked witch cast a spell on me and turned me into a foul frog, but if you kiss me and tell me you love me, and if you really *do* love me, then I will be restored to my former princehood.' " Maggie heard a noise, and looked up to see Gabe leaning in the doorway, listening. She smiled at him, but Lily didn't notice the intrusion.

"Go on, Mummy. What happened next?"

"Well, Lily thought very hard, and then she said to the frog, 'Look, I've been lied to before by types like you.' And the frog said, 'This time it's the truth. I'm not lying, it's really the truth. I am a prince, honest injun.' "

"That's what Daddy says."

"What? What does Daddy say?"

"Honest injun," Lily replied smugly.

"So he does. I'd forgotten that. Anyway, where were we? Oh yes. So Lily looked hard at the frog, and wagged her finger at him. 'Look here,' she said, 'I don't mind kissing you, and I don't mind saying I love you, but I've been tricked twice before, and I don't see how I can possibly *really* love you when you're such an ugly old frog. Anyway, I'll give it my best shot.' And she bent down, in her beautiful green party dress with the long pink ribbons, and she kissed the old frog, and she said, 'I might love you one day, and I certainly like you, but that's as far as I can go.' And so you know what happened then?"

Lily shook her head, wide-eyed.

"That old frog turned into an incredibly handsome, dashing young prince, on a beautiful white horse, and he said to her, 'Thank you, lovely lady; you alone have broken the spell, because you told the truth, and said you would try to love me, but you didn't make any false promises or tell a lie. Would you be my princess and live with me happily ever after? And would you like to come to a party with me?' And Lily thought about it, very, very hard, and she said, 'No thanks, if it's all the same to you. I don't need a prince at the moment. What I really need is another strawberry jam and salami sandwich.' And that's exactly what she got. And that's the way the story ends."

"What happened to the prince?"

"Oh, I suppose he found another princess."

"And what happened to Lily?"

"I'm sure she lived happily ever after, and when she decided the time was right, she found another prince who'd never been a frog." Maggie noticed that Gabe had left.

"That's a nice story, Mummy," Lily said sleepily. "Do all fairy tales begin, 'Once upon a time . . .'?"

"No, darling, not all of them." Maggie paused. "Daddy's normally begin, 'Such a shame about the rain—I had a lot of runs in me today . . .' " but Lily was already asleep.

Maggie found Gabe on the porch, sitting in the rocker. He was reading the paper, but looked up when he heard the screen door creak.

"Hey, Maggie. That was a fine story. Maybe you should write for kids."

Maggie shook her head. "I don't think so. They're not the sort of stories most parents would approve of."

"I would. Are the kids okay? Come and sit down." He patted the chair next to him.

"They're fine. They seem on the mend at least. Gabe, I wanted to ask you a favour."

"You want to ask me if I'd get my ass back in the lily pond p.d.q.?"

"No." Maggie smiled at him warmly. "I wanted to ask you if you'd mind if I took Lily and Arthur down to the beach house for a couple of weeks. Maybe three or four, I don't really know quite yet."

"You can use it indefinitely. I don't aim to go back down there."

"I'd like to spend some time alone with them. You see, Leah's going home tomorrow. She's leaving. She gave me a bit of a lecture today—perfectly deserved—and she wants to quit."

"I can maybe help you find somebody else."

"No, the last thing I need is an employee when I don't know what I'm doing. I can't afford it anyway."

"You need money?"

"No, I just need to know what I'm doing."

"Did you know what you were doing last night?"

"Oh yes, I think so. We both did. It's not the way out, is it, Gabe?"

"Nope." He plucked at the binding on the seat cover.

"It would be another complication, if you know what I mean, and I'm just not up to dealing with anything else at the moment."

"I respect that. I guess the same's true for me."

"You love Christy, Gabe; at least you know *that*. I don't know if I love anybody."

"So you're putting in an order for a jam and salami sandwich?" His eyes creased with good humour, but there was a wistful note in his voice.

"Have you ever heard of a more disgusting combination?"

"That's kids for you."

"Yeah."

"Well, there ain't much to say, Maggie. You still got the keys to Ocean's Edge?"

"Yes, I do."

"Then you're right welcome to use it as your own. I think I'll head back to Charlotte in the morning. You got my office number and all? Just in case you need help—a doctor, whatever."

"Thank you, Gabe; I do."

"And I'll expect you to stay in touch, you hear? Don't be a stranger."

"I won't. I'll take Leah to the airport tomorrow, and then drive down to the beach."

"Sure. I may give you a call down there. Just to say hey."

"That would be great. Are you sure you're going to be alright?"

"Sure. I'm a survivor, Maggie. A born survivor, even if I am a frog."

"You aren't one—I bet you never have been. To be honest, I think of you more as a baboon."

Gabe looked mortally offended, and Maggie laughingly explained her thesis on the two types of men.

"Well, that's a bit more like it. For a moment there, you had me real worried that you thought I was some kind of ape. I mean, I know we Americans aren't meant to be as sophisticated as you Brits, but when you said baboon, it hurt me a little, I got to confess."

"You're one of the greatest gentlemen I've ever met, Gabe. A real prince."

"Nice of you to say so, Maggie. But in my experience, nice guys finish last. And I reckon there's a flaw in your reasoning about these baboon men and the desert mice men."

"What's that?"

"Men aren't born one way or the other. It's the way they get treated by their womenfolk. If I'm a baboon type, as you say, it's only because Christy moulded me that way."

"Yes, I've been thinking that myself. So you think I turned Oliver into a desert mouse?"

"I don't know about that. Don't forget I never met him. But from what you say . . ."

"You're probably right—more than you know. Maybe if I'd behaved differently from the start, or encouraged him, or not pretended I'd believed his lies, or not pretended I didn't care about him being unfaithful . . . Maybe things would have been different."

"Maybe, but it's too late for that. What do I know anyway? I've just always had a sneaking feeling that it's the female who selects the partner, and initiates things—sets the pattern, you know what I mean?"

Maggie nodded. "I know exactly what you mean. In fact, somebody else said the same thing to me not that long ago, but I didn't really take it seriously. The more I think about it, the more I think you're right."

"So next time round, Maggie, you watch what you're doing, and you set the pace, okay?" He stood up, and kissed the top of her head. "How about something for the road? A glass of wine or something, honey?"

"Just a drink?"

"I promise. I really promise. I know types like me may have lied to you before, but I'm telling the truth. Scout's honour. Let's have a drink or two, for old times' sake, and then you go to your room, and I'll go to mine. I'll be leaving before you're up in the morning."

Maggie hugged him before he went to fix the drinks.

When Maggie went to bed, she felt calm and relaxed, and, for some inexplicable reason, profoundly happy.

Sixteen

A postcard of Holden Beach to Gabe McCarthy, Winkler Barrows, Charlotte:

This is just to say thank you. Nice guys don't finish last, they're winning before the race even starts.

Love,
Maggie

P.S. Can you recommend a good lawyer if I need one?

LEAH JENKINS ARRIVED AT THE TRAIN STATION IN SALISBURY TUESday lunchtime, hoping she'd find Mrs. Mason at Bockhampton, and Oliver and Mrs. McCarthy out. Having said goodbye to Maggie and the children at Raleigh-Durham airport, she had absolutely no desire to say goodbye to Oliver, and even less to have a postmortem with him. Sadly for Leah, it was impossible to avoid. When the taxi deposited her at the Callahans' house, she found the adults plus the little American boy sitting down to a family lunch round the kitchen table. Oliver's jaw dropped when she walked in.

"Leah! What in God's name are you doing here? Where's Maggie? Where are the children?"

"They're in Holden Beach, where d'you think? They're fine. Didn't Maggie give you a bell?"

"No, she did not. What's going on?" Leah ignored him, and stuck out her hand to Christy. "Hello. You must be Mrs. McCarthy. I'm Leah, Lily and Arthur's nanny."

"It's a pleasure to meet you, Leah," Christy answered smoothly, and continued eating.

"Hi, Mrs. Mason. You're looking fab. Hi. You must be Mariella?"

"Leah, would you just sit down right now and tell me what the hell is going on?" Oliver was nearly tearing his hair. Leah took her time to sit down, greeting each of the dogs in turn, and, seeing as no one else volunteered, introducing herself to the little boy.

"Keep your hair on, Olly. No need to get your knickers in a twist." She dumped her rucksack on the kitchen floor, to Mrs. Mason's obvious displeasure. "I've quit, no big deal. I've been with you for over a year, and I decided to go back home. Maggie agreed. She's given me my ticket home. I'm just here to collect my stuff."

Joan Mason breathed an audible sigh of relief. Oliver was thrown into overdrive.

"What do you mean you've quit?" he bawled. "You can't quit. You can't leave Maggie and the kids stranded in the States without any help!" All he could think was that Maggie would be following Leah home shortly, before he'd even had the chance to do the decent thing and offer to take her back.

"Why not?" Leah shrugged. "You bloody did."

"But where are they? Are they okay? Why hasn't she called?"

"Like I told you, she had a date on Saturday night. The kids are fine. Her husband"—she gestured toward Christy—"got a doctor who got them sorted. Maggie decided to take them back to the beach after she'd dropped me at the plane. She's fine. She said to give you a message: she said to say they're all terrific, and they're going to stay at Holden for a while, and you can reach her there. She said she'd try to ring you Tuesday—today—if she got a moment."

"If she got a moment?" Oliver shouted. "The woman's fucking insane!"

"Oliver, please; your language," Christy interjected mildly. "Let Leah finish what's she's saying. Nothing appears to be out of order. I'm sure Gabe suggested Maggie go to Holden for a break."

"Oh, he suggested plenty of things alright, but it was Maggie's idea to go to the beach house. She said to tell you she was going to work on her tan. She's fine, believe me. She looks great. She said to tell you, Mrs. McCarthy, how much she liked your house."

"I'm so glad to hear it," Christy said politely, without looking up.

"So if you'll excuse me, I'll just grab my stuff and you won't see me for dust and small stones. Ol, you'll give me a lift back to the station, won't you? I'm going straight to the airport."

"No. I mean, yes, alright, but not yet. We've got to sort every-thing out; we ought to talk—"

"Everything's sorted. Maggie's paid me up to the end of the month—she insisted, even though I didn't give proper notice. Just let me get my stuff, and I'll be with you in a tick, okay? Oh yeah—before I forget, Maggie gave me a letter for you, Ol—just in case she didn't get a chance to give you a bell." Leah chucked a pale blue envelope onto the table, nodded to them each in turn, flashed a big smile, and left for her own flat.

Leah, a fast, determined, and efficient young woman, needed only twenty minutes to clear her flat of the evidence of her fourteen-month occupation. She dumped her bags in the boot of Oliver's car, and strolled down the lane to the barn, where she left a similar blue envelope in Edward Arabin's letter box.

Christy waited until lunch was over, and she and Oliver were alone. "Aren't you going to open Maggie's letter? Don't you want to know what she has to say?"

Oliver looked at her miserably. "I don't think I do. You know, Christy, I was all worked up and ready to talk to her and tell her the truth on Sunday. I don't know that I can face it now. What if she's coming back? What if she's not coming back? What if she's decided to stay with Gabe?"

Christy looked stunned. "That wouldn't have happened."

"What am I going to tell her? At least on the phone I would have had the upper hand, I would have had the initiative. Now"—he pointed an accusing, trembling finger at the envelope—"there could be *anything* in there. It's like a fucking time bomb."

Christy took Oliver's hands in hers. "Oliver, my darling, we dis-cussed everything about this all day Saturday. You haven't changed your mind, have you?"

"No. Not unless you have." Oliver said miserably.

"Then you know what you have to do. Nothing's changed. You have to do what's right, for the good of your family, however much it hurts. You have to forget about me here, and put your family first. That's what we agreed, isn't it? We were both going to do the thing that was best in the long run. No turning back, right?"

Oliver nodded. "Okay. But I don't want to open the letter. Why don't you read it, and tell me what she says?"

"I can't do that, Oliver. Much as I'd like to. Much as I'd like to lie about it, and tell you everything's going to be okay, and we can suit ourselves, I can't. It's your call. I love you, I always will, till the day I die and after, but we can't hide away any longer. You've got to do what's right. You are a *good* man. That's one of the many reasons why I love you."

Oliver visibly pulled himself together, strengthened by Christy's unfaltering confidence in his nobility. "Alright. I'm going to wait until I've taken Leah to the station, and then I'll go to The Fox in Garters and read it. I think I've got to do it alone."

"That's fine. I'll be waiting here. Don't be too long, okay? If we've only got tonight together, let's make the most of it, okay?"

Oliver put his head in her lap. "Don't say that, Christy. Just don't say it. You're going to break my heart."

"Go. Go on, go find that girl. I'm going to go take a bath." She got up from the table with a heartbreaking smile. "Hey, Oliver? Don't forget this, okay?" She chucked the letter into his lap. "And don't forget these last couple of weeks."

Oliver drove Leah to the station in silence, and she made no effort to break it. When she left, she did not extend an open invitation to Brisbane as she had to Maggie, but simply stuck out her hand, thanked him for the lift, shouldered her rucksack and suitcase, and strode off into the depths of the station. Oliver drove slowly to The Fox in Garters in Compton Ash. The pub was empty when he got there, and John, the perpetually sour-faced barman, looked irritated to have a customer.

"Hullo, Oliver. I was about to close."

"Do me a favour, and stay open, John. I'll make it worth your while. Give me a double whisky, would you?" John raised an eyebrow, but did as he was told.

"Playing this Saturday, are you, Oliver? Or are you back off to America?"

"Hmm?" Oliver was distracted. "Oh. You mean the cricket. I don't know yet. I may have to go back to the States."

"Alright for some," John grumbled. "I wouldn't mind jetting off round the world to exotic places—not that I ever get the chance, stuck behind the bloody bar all day with geezers who take two hours to drink a pint."

"You can't ever have that complaint about me, John." Oliver toyed with the envelope, flipping it over and over as he studied the one word, "Oliver," in Maggie's familiar, barely legible script.

"S'pose I can't," John admitted grudgingly. "Problems?"

"Nothing a scotch or two won't help."

"You're the boss. Don't hold with afternoon drinking, myself."

Oliver bit back the question "What the hell are you doing running a pub, then?" and took his refilled glass to the little nook at the back of the pub. He opened the envelope with trembling hands.

"Darling Ol," he read, and his few lingering hopes were dashed. She didn't hate him. She wanted to start afresh. She had addressed him with customary affection.

Darling Ol,

I've asked Leah to deliver this to you in case I don't get a chance to talk to you over the next couple of days. Leah's decided that's she's fed up with this whole situation, and wants out, and I can't say I blame her. I want it to stop, too. I have thought and thought about what's happened—I admit, in a bit of a vacuum, as we haven't talked to each other—and I think it's time we both grew up and stopped behaving like children, and faced our responsibilities."

Oliver's throat was tight. She sounded just as he expected her to sound, just as he and Christy had predicted. She was going to say that they had to try again, and make the best of things. He read on.

I know that in the past I haven't been a very good wife to you—not the kind of wife you needed, and I'm sorry about that. A lot of what has happened to us is my fault. I don't really think you walked out on me because I wrote that book—not even you can be so small-minded—nor because I slept with Edward—you can't be that hypocritical, can you?—but I can't have been easy to live with recently. I can't explain why I have failed so badly to satisfy you in the past. But what has happened over the past few weeks has made me think very hard. It's taught me a real lesson, and perhaps it has done the same for you. It is too much to expect the children to understand that we have somehow stopped loving each other—I guess that's the only way to put it; telling them that maybe we never loved each other would be just too depressing, but we do have to try to make something of our, and their, future.

"John? Can I get another whisky? A large one." Oliver didn't even hear John tut-tutting disapproval as his glass was refilled.

I'm finding it very hard to express myself. Do you realise that in six years of marriage we have never exchanged a letter? Maybe that's why it's so difficult to write to you now. Well, you always said I wasn't a natural writer, and that I tried too hard, and maybe you were right. I just never get quite to the point, do I? Now I must. As I said, I've thought very hard, and I've talked to some people, and I think we have to start afresh. I think we have to call it a day, and look ahead, and try and be happy with someone new. Maybe it would be better and braver and nobler to keep plugging away at it, but I've come to the decision that now everything's out in the open, we'll never make each other happy, and the children won't have a proper family life that way.

Oliver reread the paragraph.

I don't know if you are serious about Christy. From what her husband has told me, she seems serious about you. Maybe you two think alike. We were on different paths all the way to the altar and ever since. I think we've both known that things were very bad for a long time, and you just tried to cope by being funny and doing your own thing, and I tried to cope by being superior, and feeling wronged and not doing my own thing. It didn't work, and it's not going to work now. I just don't love you. I hope that doesn't sound bitchy—I'm pretty sure it will come as a relief, as I don't believe you have loved me, apart from a few odd moments, for a long time. So let's call it a day. Let's get divorced, or separated, or whatever suits you. I'm not bothered which one—I'm in no hurry to marry again. I don't think I'll ever want to. I'm too much of a coward to risk that kind of disappointment twice. I have to say two more things—this whole suggestion is off unless it's agreed that Lily and Arthur stay with me. I don't mean you can't see them, but I want them to live with me, wherever I end up living. Secondly, as to all the practical things like houses and money and so on, I want to spend a couple of weeks here, and then I'll probably head back to England, and we can sort everything out between us. I don't want any lawyers or other stuff. Does this sound alright? I know it's not well written, but spare me the red pen this time, okay? All you have to do is get the gist of it, and say yes or no. I really hope you say yes.

Love,
Maggie

Oliver reread the letter three times. Maggie didn't want him back. Maggie didn't want to come back to him. Maggie didn't even sound that bitter. Maggie had no hard feelings. The way was wide open. Maggie had given him carte blanche—apart from living with the kids—to make a new life for himself. Maggie was alright, she sounded fine, she was willing to come back and sort out all the details. He could give her the flat—he could give her Bockhampton, even. Well, maybe not Bockhampton. But he could raise some money on the house and give her some cash. He sat in the pub utterly stupefied. He and Christy had agreed that they couldn't fulfil their dreams at the expense of Maggie and the children. They had agreed that Maggie would naturally want her husband and home back, and that if Oliver was to be able to call himself an honourable man, then house and husband would have to be delivered to her on a plate, with all the trimmings of remorse and promises of lifelong fidelity. Oliver had wept, and Christy had wept, but Christy had been steely in her resolve, and had persuaded Oliver that there was no other decent way. And then Maggie, Maggie that he had so hated and so feared, had flung open the gates and pointed out another path. Oliver tucked the letter into his breast pocket, and walked shakily up to the bar.

"I think I *will* be playing on Saturday, after all, John."

"Not jetting off then?"

"Not for a while, no. John: do you happen to have any champagne in the fridge? A chilled bottle?"

"I've got a bottle or two of Bollinger for emergencies—not that we get much call for it from the mean bastards round here."

"Let me have one—no, two, if you've got them."

John sucked the air in over his teeth, cocking his head. "It'll cost you, Oliver. Bolly doesn't grow on trees, you know, mate."

"I don't care. I'll take it. You only live once, John."

"If you say so."

*   *   *

Later that evening, Edward Arabin sat in his garden, gazing at the river, and tapping his knee with an as yet still sealed blue envelope. He was as reluctant to open it as Oliver had been, and he feared the contents equally. He didn't fix himself a drink to steady his nerves, but just sat thinking about Maggie. She hadn't returned his several calls that weekend. He hadn't heard from her for days. When he had come home from Bishop & Moodey to find the envelope stuck in his letter box, he had assumed that she had come home to Bockhampton, and his first instinct had been to rush round to the house immediately without stopping to read the letter. But if she had written, rather than phoning him or coming in person, he could only assume that whatever she wanted to say she wanted to say officially, on paper, and he was left with the obligation to read it. He opened it with trembling hands.

Dearest Edward,
    You have been such a good friend to me, and I haven't even had the courtesy to call you back. I'm writing now because I wanted Leah to drop this off—she's flying back to England tonight—and because there are some things I must explain to you.

Edward breathed a sigh of relief. At least she hadn't come home. At least she wasn't happily cuddled up with Oliver a mile down the road at that very minute. He read on.

I have decided to stay here for a while. I went slightly off the deep end, what with Oliver finding out about us, and going haywire about my novel, and everything.

Edward had no idea which novel she was talking about. He read on.

I think I've been really stupid for a long time, and I've just now decided that it isn't all bad, it isn't something I have to live with for the rest of my life. If I've made mistakes in the past, it doesn't mean I have to stick with them, does it? I feel that if I can just admit it, just admit it was a mistake, then maybe I'll be alright. Sometimes the toughest lesson is knowing which bridges to burn and which to cross. I've written to Ol to say that I'm quite happy for our marriage to end—neither of us has been happy after all—though what does happiness mean in the long run? I'm sure I don't know. I don't know what love is all about—it's as if it's there, somewhere in the room, something familiar and recognisable, but I just can't quite put my finger on it. Anyway, I don't want you to feel at all responsible. You didn't have anything to do with it. Oliver and I should never have married, and if the fact that you and I slept together had something to do with our marriage breaking up, then at least one good thing came of it. Please don't blame yourself. When we've talked, over the past years, I've so often felt that you really understood me, and really cared, and told me so many things that I couldn't even voice to myself—I just want to say how grateful I am. I've told you how Ol constantly lied to me—about how he felt, about where he was, about who he was with, about who he *was* really—I guess that was the real problem for me. As you said, maybe I'm too romantic to ever get married. Maybe my standards are too high. Or too low. Maybe I'm too much of a coward. But I've never needed to lie to you. I don't want you to feel under any obligation to me—I couldn't bear that. I don't know when we'll meet again. I don't know what I'm going to do. I think I want to just sit here and write it out of myself. I've been thinking about your feeling that women make all the decisions. Maybe strong, sorted-out women do. I don't feel that I've made any decisions, apart from the decision not to fight for Oliver, or plead with him to come back to me. Edward, dearest Edward, I'm not sure where I'm going to end up. But for once, I'm going to try to be myself. I'm going to come back to England in a few weeks' time—I'll have to sort out some practical things with Ol. I don't expect anything from you. I don't *want* anything from you. I just feel quite overwhelmed with gratitude for all you've done to help me, and for your being there. Maybe we can get together when I get home. Home? I don't know where home is anymore.

Dear, dear Eddie, please forgive me for being so useless and such a trial. I'm going to get better. Maybe one day we'll sit together and laugh about all of this. Maybe I've reached that amazingly mature point in my life when I realise I don't need the opposite sex, or sex at all. Wouldn't that be great? I mean if you can do it, why can't I? You'll be proud of me, one day. I promise. If you happen to call me again, and I don't answer, please don't be worried. I just don't know what to say when I hear your voice. Except thank you.

With my love, as ever,
Maggie

Edward watched the river flow until it was too dark to see the river, and even then he stared at it. Despite his protestations to Oliver, and his knee-jerk fear that Maggie was happily ensconced back at Bockhampton, he wasn't that surprised that she had decided to call it quits. He had always suspected that the Callahans' marriage might be relatively short-lived, and he stuck to his belief that its end would be called by Maggie. But he'd expected—he'd wished—he'd hoped—for some indication from Maggie herself. It was a fine thing to be a friend, to be a prized and valued and special friend. Dearest Edward, she'd written. It was a rare thing to be a friend. But Edward wasn't comforted by the idea that he should settle for rarity in preference to normal, natural, and all too common love. Maggie clearly thought that he was perfectly content in his solitude. He had no doubt that he could support her materially, that he could cherish her and love her, and stick as close to her as she could tolerate. But there lay the nub of the problem. For all he knew, the last thing Maggie wanted was some man clinging to her. She had opted for freedom, as he'd always hoped she would, and was it within his rights to offer himself as a new form of shackles, however different from the last? Maggie had made it perfectly clear—he didn't need to read between the lines: if she'd wanted him, or even wanted his help, she would have asked for it. But she didn't. She didn't want *anything* from him. She couldn't have stated it more clearly if she'd told him to fuck off. She'd even said she shouldn't have to pay a price for mistakes she'd made in the past. She was right. He was clearly one of her mistakes. Maybe she was too young to understand what he was offering. Maybe he was too old to understand what she wanted.

What is maturity? In some ways, it is something quite child-like; the willingness to believe things that we can't possibly understand. Adults are perplexed that children find the twelve-hour clock so immensely confusing, and yet children find it quite easy to understand the nature of God, or death, or the absolute nature of love, because they have no need to question it. Adults have a much harder time.

On Wednesday morning, Oliver Callahan and Christy McCarthy were woken up by Christy's son climbing in to bed with them. Jake had by no means accepted Oliver as a replacement for his father, but anyone who has children, and expects them to sleep alone, and go to bed early, and say please and thank you all the time, ought to realise that children have an enormous capacity for accepting strange and unnatural behaviour. It doesn't mean they like it, but they do tend to accept it. Perhaps that is because it is forced upon them; it's hard to say. The fact is, Jake had come to accept the fact that Oliver was frequently to be found in his mother's bed, and he had stopped asking questions, and he didn't hold Oliver to his halfhearted promise. Perhaps his fear of losing his mother prompted his acceptance of his mother's friend. That particular morning, Jake snuggled up to his mother, and tickled her ear.

"Mom—Mommy—I'm hungry. I want breakfast."

"Hmm? Go back to sleep, hon. We'll have breakfast in a little while. Ask Mariella to give you breakfast. Mommy's real tired."

There were two empty champagne bottles, and two empty glasses, on the bedside table.

"Mom? Please, I'm real hungry."

"In a minute, sweetie," Christy answered sleepily. "Maybe I'll make pancakes, okay? Just let me sleep for a little bit."

"Mommy? Can we call Dad today? Can I talk to Dad?"

Christy's eyes snapped open.

"Yes, Jake. We'll call Daddy just as soon as we can. Oliver? Oliver, wake up." The one thing Christy had insisted on was that whatever time they went to sleep, Oliver put either his dressing gown or a pair of pyjama bottoms on. She didn't want any more comments about Oliver's pee-wee.

"Oliver! Wake up! I've had a great idea! Let's have a dinner party. Tonight."

"Umm-hmm. Whatever you say, dear heart." Oliver rolled over and started snoring. Christy thumped him.

"Oliver. Wake up now. Let's have a party tonight. You've got to invite Danny, and his wife of course, and some of the local people. Lucy and Charles—maybe Imogen and Curtis—Edward, we need to patch things up with him anyways—we'll need at least four people

apart from us and the Bujevskis. It doesn't really matter who. But
you've got to get on the phone. Say it's a last-minute thing. Say
we're celebrating."

Oliver propped himself up on an elbow. "What am I going to
say we're celebrating? My divorce? Our engagement?"

"No—of course not! Say it's a dinner party for your new producer. All the locals will love that. They won't be able to resist."

"My darling Christy—Lucy *hates* you. Quite violently. Hard
pressed as I am to understand how she can hate you, I do believe
she truly does."

"Trust me. If you phone and say you're giving a dinner party for
your new producer, and don't mention me, she won't be able to
refuse. I'll bet you a million dollars."

Oliver looked at her through one eye. "Have you got a million
dollars?"

"Approximately."

"In that case, I'll call the Aga Khan and the Princess of Wales
and ask them."

"Mommy, I'm hungry! I want pancakes!"

"Bloody hell!" Oliver shot up. "Is Jake in bed with us?"

"Yeah. He's over on my side."

"Good Christ, Christy, if we're to have any privacy at all you're
going to have to get him to sleep in his own bed; what's the point
of this au pair of yours? I mean, I'm fond of the lad, very, but I
never know who's listening when I'm talking to you."

"Oliver, how d'you feel like home-made pancakes with maple
syrup? Or blackberry syrup and crème fraîche? I made some blackberry syrup the other day."

Oliver groaned from deep in his gut. "Christy, my darling, there
are a couple of things you might have offered me that I would have
preferred to pancakes and blackberry syrup, but I must admit, only
a couple."

"Those things aren't on the menu, Oliver."

"More's the pity. If it wasn't for that little—"

"Angel. That little angel, I think you were going to say. So you'll
call everyone? Ask them to dinner?"

"Yes, okay, my little obergruppenfuhrer. But not tonight. Tonight, I want to spend alone. Friday night, we ask the brat pack.
I'll call them all this morning. They're not going to have any other

plans. We're the hottest item of gossip around. They'll all come like jackals."

As good as his word, Oliver called Danny Bujevski straight after breakfast and invited Danny and his wife to dinner the following Friday night. Danny accepted, but made a big fuss about his wife.

"You sure you want Gillian to come? Are you really sure?"

"Yeah, Danny, I'm sure. That's the way we do things in the country. We ask men, and amazingly, because we're such bumpkins, we ask their wives to come with them. We don't ask their mistresses, or their new secretaries, or the office slapper, we ask their wives."

"So is your wife gonna be there, Ol? I haven't met her."

"Actually, no. Maggie's still in the States, on holiday with the kids."

"And is the luscious Christy going to be there? You know, I sort of got the feeling when we were last together she had her eye on me. . . ."

"In your dreams, Bujevski. In your dreams. She's a married woman."

"Who happens to be balling you. I wasn't born yesterday, Callahan."

Oliver sighed. "She's not balling me, Bujevski. We just happen to be working together."

"Nice work if you can get it, you know what I mean, Ol? I wouldn't mind *piece* work like that myself. I wouldn't mind a *piece* of that action—"

Oliver, much to his own surprise, lost his temper. "Listen, Bujevski, you fuckhead. Christy McCarthy is a lady. I've told you that before. I dare say you haven't met many ladies in your career, but I'm going to teach you how to behave to them if I have to smash your head in to do it." A month ago, Oliver would never have exposed his sensitive side to a man like Danny Bujevski, but now he was proud of it. "I love her, God damn you. Is that just too unfashionable for you? Not very trendy for a media star, is it, to just be in love the way normal people are? Well, I am."

"Hey, hey, hey, Oliver. Cool it. It was a little joke. A man-to-man joke, alright? I respect you, mate. I admire you. I envy you. I might test you out, though. I might bring my friend Phoebe—or Freebie, as I call her."

"Just shut the fuck up, okay? Come to dinner Friday night, and bring whoever the fuck you like. I hope it's your wife."

"In that case it will be the fuck I don't like. But I'll be there."

Oliver hug up. A month ago, that last comment would have had him laughing like a drain, but now, it didn't raise even a smirk. He shivered with distaste, and that was before he decided not to pass it on to Christy. Oliver was changing. Christy had given him the courage to believe he was genuinely better than the average man, not just superficially better. Because he'd promised Christy, he gritted his teeth and phoned Edward. He called him at home, and there was no answer. He was on the point of thinking he could tell Christy he'd tried his damnedest to reach Edward, which is what he would have told Maggie, when he realised he hadn't. So he called him at work. Edward's secretary said that she expected him in later, but that she didn't think he was free Friday night. Oliver left a message, simply saying that if he was free, he was invited to dinner. His conscience was appeased, and so would Christy be. Now he had to call Loopy Lucy. She picked up the phone on the first ring.

"Hello. 622791?"

"Lucy; it's Oliver here."

Lucy forgot her principles for a moment. All sociable women, however loyal to their girlfriends, occasionally forget their principles for a moment or two.

"Oliver! How divine to hear your voice!"

"Luce, I wanted to ask you to dinner. You and Charles. Friday night."

"Friday night? That's rather short notice."

"Are you doing something?"

"No, of course we're not, you silly boy. We'd love to come."

"Good. Let's say seven-thirty for eight o'clock?"

"Glorious. Ahhh. Oliver . . . ?"

"Yes?"

"Is Maggie home, then?"

"No, she's still in the States, with the children."

"Well, I'm not awfully sure . . . I mean, don't you need a hostess? I'd be more than happy to act as your hostess . . ."

"Luce, this is really a party for a telly producer. You know, the series that Christy McCarthy and I are doing together. I suppose it's really a business dinner. Christy will act as hostess. I just wanted to have some of my friends around for support."

"I'm not sure, Oliver . . . I mean, I don't want to tread on anyone's toes, but it's very hard for me to see somebody step into Maggie's shoes just like that. . . ."

"Luce, he's a big producer. I mean big. Did you see *The Night Before Last?* Did you see *May Showers?* Did you see *Vinegar and Lemon?*" Oliver listed Bujevski's most recent productions.

"God yes!" Lucy said excitedly. "Did he do all that?"

"Yeah, he did, and he's bringing some starlet with him."

"So he's not married?"

"Only loosely."

"Well." Lucy was torn, but not for long. "Look, Oliver, of course we'll come and help you out. If you need us. You know we'll always rally round. But I must just go on the record as saying I can't possibly be nice to Christy. For Mags' sake."

"That won't be a problem, Luce. I wish you didn't feel that way about her, but if you like, I'll put you at opposite ends of the table. Then you can be as horrible to her as you like. D'you object to sitting next to me?"

"Of course I don't! Oh, Oliver! This is such an *awful* business. . . ."

"Yes, it is . . ."

"But I don't want anything to come between us. I mean, Maggie is one of my dearest *ever* friends, but you do know how *fond* Charles and I are of you, don't you?"

"Yes, I do, Luce. At least, I've nursed a fond hope that you're a little bit fond of me—that you haven't *just* been seeing me in order to see Maggie. . . ."

"Oh dear Ol! You know that's not true! We're *desperately* fond of you. It's just that I'd never be—you know—*disloyal*—to Maggie."

"I know that, Luce. I respect you for it. So we'll see you Friday?"

"Perfect."

Three down, with two clear rounds and only one no show. All Oliver had to do to keep his promise to Christy was to call Imogen. She was on the mobile in the yard.

"Mog?"

"Yes?"

"It's Oliver."

"What do you want?"

"Mog, what's the matter? You sound so . . . unfriendly."

"Yup, that's because I feel unfriendly to you, Oliver. You're no friend of mine. Look, I'm in a hurry. I'm short-handed; I've got a lot of horses to take out. What d'you want?"

"I wanted to ask you and Curtis to dinner. Friday night."

"You must be fucking joking," Imogen didn't laugh.

"C'mon, Mog! Stop playing hard to get! It's Oliver here. Your old mate? The only man who can take on Samson?"

"Oliver, I wouldn't let you ride Samson if you were the last human being on earth. I wouldn't have let you ride any of my horses if it wasn't for Maggie. As far as I'm concerned, you only get on a horse so that you can look cool. I always knew that, but for Maggie's sake, I let you ride some no-hope brute with four legs once in a while. Now I've talked to Maggie, I feel released from the obligation. So don't you come round asking me for a ride. And don't for fuck's sake ask me and Curtis to dinner."

"Well, Mog, you certainly know how to behave like a lady, don't you? You could have just said that you were otherwise engaged. You know, Curtis and I play cricket together."

"I don't give a fuck about cricket, which is the only thing you seem to be any good at. From what I've heard, you don't know a fuck about how to behave like anything but a scumbag. And while we're having this little chat, I'd just like to say that I think your articles in the *Telegraph* suck donkey dick. Okay? I just thought I'd let you know. Also, you know less than a fuck about horses. So let's have a pact, Oliver: if I get some donkey in that needs exercising, or if Curtis arranges a match that's only for quadriplegics, we'll call you. Otherwise, just fuck off, okay?" Imogen switched the phone off.

She was nothing if not genuine.

Oliver found Christy in the kitchen, poring over cookery books.

"Darling, I've called everyone."

"Are they all coming?"

"Well, the Bujevskis are—at least Danny is, and Gillian should be. Her leg's still in plaster. If she can't make it, he'll bring someone else. Charles and Lucy are coming."

"And Edward?"

"Couldn't get through to him. I left a message, but his secretary said she thought he might be busy."

"And Imogen and Curtis?"

"Yes; I spoke to Mog; sadly, they have a prior engagement. She was gutted." He couldn't bear to hurt her with the truth. As the words left his mouth, he changed his mind. He had made himself a promise that he would never lie to her. "That's not true. What she said was that I was no friend of hers, and that in fact I was a scumbag and sucked donkey dick. That's exactly what she said. Apart from the message that they wouldn't come to dinner."

"That's a real pity. I respect her loyalty. I'd kind of like to get to know her. Maybe if we give her some time to get accustomed to the idea? Well, we'll just have to ask another couple. Maybe the Hanghams? Maybe the vicar and his wife?" Christy looked so bright and happy that there was nothing Oliver could do except nod and smile. She had no idea how reluctant the locals might be to accept her. Maybe her innocence was the best strategy.

"Christy—I don't think we should be too hasty about telling them our plans . . . Let's get everything sorted out with Maggie first."

"Whatever you say, darling. You know best. You're the boss."

On Friday morning, Christy came downstairs early. Whether Oliver was prepared to announce their union officially or not, it was her first dinner as the mistress of Bockhampton, and she wanted it to be absolutely perfect. As soon as she came downstairs, she set a pot of Earl Gray tea—Oliver's favourite—to brew, and slipped outside in her silk dressing gown to get the paper and the post. She liked to take it up on a tray to Oliver with his tea and toast. Amongst the post, she saw a letter addressed to Maggie with the logo of the Worldwide Home Exchange Club. On impulse, she slit it open.

Dear Mrs. Callahan,

We hope you were among the great majority of our members who experienced a happy home exchange in 1993. If not, we hope you will try again in 1994. We wondered if you would care to write a letter of recommendation that we could publish in our next directory. It is so important to have personal testimonials, so if your recommendation is positive, or if you have any valuable tips for the Worldwide Home Exchange Club Members, please let us know. We are always anxious to hear about your trip, etc. and whether or not you were *completely* satisfied. For any letter published, we can offer a $10.00 discount towards your next car hire agreement in America. . . .

Christy put the letter aside, unable to resist a little smile at the fortuitous wording. *Completely* satisfied . . . ! She would reply to it at some point—she felt she had to—but not right now, not when she had a dinner party to cater for. She was more nervous about this dinner than she'd let on to Oliver. She knew that Danny Bujevski liked her—admired her—she knew more than that; she knew Danny Bujevski went to bed imagining her beside him. But she also knew that everyone else at the dinner party, all Oliver's local friends and neighbours, were suspicious of her. Basically, they didn't like her. They saw her as a foreigner, probably as a crass American, and it hurt her. She'd worked very hard to befriend the locals, and if she had happened to fall in love with Oliver, and he with her, she didn't see that they should damn her. Edward wasn't coming—he'd never replied to Oliver's several messages—and Imogen and her lover weren't coming either, and in her heart of hearts Christy knew that their disapproval was more to do with her than with Oliver. They would have excused anything in one of their own. Oliver had invited a couple that Christy had never met, Mike and Rachel, and Hillary, Edward's friend from Bishop & Moodey, was coming, and he was bringing a woman who was an expert in ceramics. Christy thought very carefully about the menu; she didn't want to overwhelm them, and she felt that it would be improper to have a "Southern" dinner. So she decided to cook a simple tomato tart to start, and then a fillet de boeuf en croûte, and then a traditional English pudding. To get herself back into Lucy's good books, she decided to do Lucy's plum and hazelnut crumble, despite the fact that Christy found it far too heavy for her taste.

As it happened, the food didn't matter. Everyone was far too pissed by the time Oliver had finished with them to bother about the food. Oliver had seated Danny Bujevski and Hillary next to Christy, and had claimed Lucy Wickham-Edwardes and Phoebe for himself. Christy didn't feel threatened, even as she watched Oliver flirt with the two women. At each and every flattering comment he made, he looked up and caught Christy's eye. She felt free to do her duty and entertain Danny and Hillary. The antiques expert needed no entertaining; he talked without cease about furniture, and having made a polite overture to Christy about how fascinating pre-Civil War American furniture was, he then launched into a monologue about the difference between early and late Georgian marquetry. Christy maintained an alert expression whilst trying to keep Danny Bujevski's hand off her upper thigh. Oliver, at the other end of the table, was mesmerized by Danny Bujevski's hand. It kept disappearing under the table, and he kept tensing in his chair, until he saw Christy smile, and Danny's left hand re-appear on the table top, a little redder than it had been before.

"Oliver, aren't you listening to me?"

"Sorry, Luce—I was just thinking about getting some cheese."

"But I wanted to talk to you about this book of Maggie's— Maggie told me she'd written a novel—I mean, how thrilling—I've always wanted to write a novel myself, of course; Charles always says that if everyone has one book in them, then I've got about twenty— but I hear that Maggie's actually written a book about—"

Oliver went rigid, and looked at Christy. For once he was delighted to see that she was once again occupied with Bujevski's left hand.

"Ah, yes! Well, *she* hasn't really *written* it. It's a complicated story, in fact. Not something we like to talk about. Not a book at all, just a joke Maggie and I had."

"I'm sure Maggie told me she'd written some book—just the last time I talked to her—" Lucy persisted.

"Yes, that's right, you see, that's all part of the joke. It's just a long-running joke between Maggie and me, far too complicated to explain, and far too silly."

"C'mon, Oliver!" shouted Charles. "If it's a joke, let us all in on it!" The table was silenced by the volume of Charles's voice. "We need a good laugh!"

"No, really not, Charles. It's not that kind of a joke at all. Far too personal. Not fair on Mags. Absent friends and all. Private stuff. When she gets back, she can tell it to all of you, if she wants to, but I don't think she will."

"What, Oliver? What won't she do?" Christy, distracted by Bujevski's unwanted attentions, and Hillary's banging on about Chippendale, had finally fought her way through to the conversation at the other end of the table. She thought Oliver had been talking about her.

"Just gossip, Christy. Nasty old village gossip. You're lucky you haven't been here long enough to hear it all. Thank God we didn't have the vicar and his wife after all." Oliver eased his way out of it, escaping by the skin of his teeth.

"I do wish you *had* asked the vicar," said the pouting Phoebe. "I've never met a vicar."

"Have you not, dear?" said Lucy Wickham-Edwardes helpfully. "Charles thinks he's a sort of vicar; just to pigs and things. He calls himself the vicar of his flock."

"Whoa, Lucy," Oliver warned. "We've got real human beings here for once. They don't understand your behaviour."

Lucy batted her eyelashes at Oliver, "But, Ol! It *is* truly insupportable! Can you imagine a man who walks into the kitchen at seven A.M., and says, 'I love the smell of pigs' swill in the morning'—I mean, dear God! Can anybody in their right mind blame me?"

"No, Luce, darling, I don't blame you—"

"Christy. My dear Christy. Did you ever think of an acting career? With your, ah, attributes—"

"The value of *true* Regency period furniture lies in the styling; I happen to be particularly fond of Gillows, myself—much underrated—"

"I hear you're going to be a presenter, on television, Oliver? That's *so* exciting. BBC, I hope?"

"No, my own interests is in Meissen. It's something of an obsession, I'm afraid to say."

"Ol? D'you fancy shooting tomorrow? First shoot of the season. I can always squeeze in an extra gun. That reminds me, where's Edward tonight? Thought I'd see him here and get him along."

Hillary's clear nasal voice pierced the dinner party. "He was in this morning, but barely stayed."

"I popped in at the barn this lunchtime. It was all locked up." Lucy raised her eyebrows. "Most mysterious. He didn't even have his milk order out."

"No . . ." Hillary drawled. "The message went round at the salesrooms that he'd taken some sort of leave of absence. Very offhand about it all. Wouldn't say when he'd be back. Could be tomorrow, could be next month. In Edward's case—not that I'd apply this to everyone, you understand, and certainly not myself—I'd say cherchez la femme."

"That's rather an exciting idea, isn't it? Not that we want to lose our resident bachelor, but I mean, if he *does* have a secret woman— well, that would be quite a lark, wouldn't it?" Lucy giggled.

"I don't see why," Christy spoke flatly, in ringingly clear tones.

"I don't see why it's of any interest to anyone here if Edward Arabin has a lover or not."

"Oh, Christy—you're so deliciously frank and open and—American." This was from Rachel. "Of *course* it's interesting if Edward Arabin has a new amour. It's a fresh bit of gossip."

"Haven't you got anything better to do with your time than gossip about other people's love affairs?" Christy asked coolly.

"Christy. *Dear*. It's not really gossip. You wouldn't understand, of course. It's just sport." Rachel gave her a patronising smile.

"Sport? It doesn't sound like sport to me. I call tennis sport. Maybe golf. At a pinch, football. At a real big pinch, cricket." She spoke with the voice of genteel disdain. "But the way I figure it, this ain't sport, it's just intruding into other people's private lives. Will y'all excuse me? I just want to check on my son." Before she rose from the table, Christy turned her huge eyes on Danny. "What *is* it with your hand and my leg? Has someone covered them in Velcro without my even noticing? Or is my thigh just the nearest convenient resting place?" Brushing his hand off her leg for a final time, Christy left the room. There was silence for a moment.

"Hot diggety dog! She's all woman!" Bujevski stated.

"Fuck off, Bujevski. I've told you not to touch her."

Lucy looked at Oliver, her eyes wide in admiration. "And what on earth has come over you, Oliver? What's turned you into Prince Charming?"

"Nothing. I just happen to think that Christy's right. That's all. Who wants pudding?"

"Forget about pudding," Lucy pressed. "Tell us about this transatlantic experience. You've *changed*. What did America do to you, Oliver?"

"Okay. You really want to know?" Oliver flung his napkin on the table. It was time for him to nail his colours to the mast—to Christy's mast. "I learnt a whole lot of useless rubbish. It taught me that English houses never have decent reading lights, even if they're packed with books. American houses are really well lit, but you'd be lucky to find three copies of the *Reader's Digest* in them." The company sniggered in self-congratulation. "English houses are cold, even in summer. English people are cold all year round." They stopped sniggering. "Contrary to expectations, a lot of American gadgets are more old-fashioned than English ones, but what you do get in the States is size—a bigger washing machine, a bigger dishwasher, a bigger fridge. Probably bigger pricks, for all I know. Are you all gripped? There are the obvious clichés about over-eating, and bad education, and mass culture, and crap TV. My feeling is the Yanks have it over us on all counts. You probably think I'm talking bollocks. You think I'm betraying dear old Blighty. Let me share something with you: you know why the Americans say that? Because they think it's rude and aggressive to say 'Let me tell you something.' And you know what? I think they're right. So: let me share something with you now. I've been told—I've believed—that people are the same the world over. None of these little differences about food and culture and language and traffic matter. What matters is that people are warm, and truthful, and honest, and decent, and that they care about one another, and that they're not afraid to say they care. People are the same the world over, aren't they? Like shit they are. Luce, you asked me what going to America taught me. It taught me something very simple. Americans are nicer than we are. Okay? I haven't yet worked out why, but I know it for a fact. Fact: Americans are nicer than we are. Now. Who wants pudding?"

It wasn't going to go down as one of the all-time great dinner parties. Christy never rejoined the party. But it would register as a memorable evening. It would be remembered as the night that Oliver Callahan finally stuck his neck out for something other than cricket, or someone other than himself, and ready to give credit when credit was due, the people in the Valley would always respect that.

Maggie had spent four days alone with her children at Holden Beach. She loved Ocean's Edge. Lily and Arthur were well and happy, and perhaps because of that, or perhaps as a cause of that, she was well and happy. She had set up Oliver's portable computer on the deck overlooking the beach, and when she wasn't swimming with the children, she worked away at the keyboard. She had finished *A Sad Affair,* just for the sake of finishing it, and had set it aside, and had begun work on a novel that she had provisionally titled *Our Recent Unpleasantness.* Maggie was content. She had no social life, and certainly no romantic or sexual life. She generally went to bed when the children went to bed, but occasionally stayed up for an hour or so to see the light fade over the ocean. She had made a decision; she was writing; she was doing what she wanted to do and

343

she wasn't adapting to anyone, and it felt like a release from the strain of trying to please the rest of the world. All she wanted to do was look after her kids and please herself. She put her two golden children to bed, and went into the bathroom to get ready for bed herself. As she cleaned her face, she thought she heard a car slowing down on the road behind the house. If it stopped in her driveway, it could only be Gabe. Looking at herself in the mirror, she groaned. She didn't feel like staying up and talking to Gabe. She didn't feel like making an effort; she felt like being alone. The car went on and Maggie relaxed again. It was probably the neighbour's house: people were always coming and going there. She wrapped a light cotton sarong around her and went back out to the deck to look at the ocean, and watch the evening beachcombers. It was well after dusk, and when she saw a man's shape looming up the steps from the beach she drew in her breath with apprehension. There were a few disadvantages in being a single woman alone in a house with two small children.

"Maggie? Is that you? Is this the right bloody house? I've been wandering up and down this bloody beach for half an hour asking where the Englishwoman lives."

"Edward—what on *earth* are you doing here?"

He stopped halfway up the steps, shaking sand out of his black brogues. He was inappropriately dressed in a suit and tie and carrying a small suitcase.

"I just couldn't stick it, Maggie. I was too damn angry to sit home muttering to myself, so I flew over. I couldn't bear getting some cordial little fuck-off letter from you—and on top of it all, you telling me how goddamn *sweet* and *nice* I am—what a good *friend*. It made me physically sick. And then you say that it was a mistake to sleep with me, one that you shouldn't have to live with for the rest of your life—"

"Edward, I didn't—"

"Shut up, Maggie. You had your chance. This is *my* speech. I rehearsed it for hours on the plane and during the six-hour drive to this wretched sand dune. I'm damn well going to say it, and you can just shut up and listen. Where was I? Oh yes. You also said that you had reached that wonderful state when you didn't need men anymore, and you then had the nerve to imply that I have been living in some divine state of self-elected celibacy for years. What do you think I am, Maggie? Some sort of kindly, domesticated eunuch? This is not meant to be funny!"

Maggie worked hard to keep a straight face, which was difficult, as Edward was still standing halfway up the beach steps, in his socks, and a small crowd of under-thirties had gathered on the deck of the house next door to listen to him. She shook her head seriously. "Not funny at all. You were saying? About the eunuch?"

"I've finished that bit," Edward said haughtily. "I just came to tell you that I think I was wrong about women making all the decisions and selecting partners and initiating sex. I think you were right. About the baboons and mice. I think I've just dragged myself across the Atlantic like some sort of ageing, whimpering, lovelorn baboon to tell you that I love you. To try to initiate something."

A cheer rose from those assembled on the porch of the neighbour's house. "Way to go, fella!" Edward barely glanced at them.

"Edward, do you want to come inside or do you want to finish out here?"

"Hey, lady, please let him finish out here! We don't want to miss the action—this is better than a drive-in!" A hunky teenager in surfer's gear was leaning so far over the edge of the porch railing that he was in danger of tipping over onto Maggie's deck.

"I have finished," Edward said with supreme finality.

"Okay. Then let me tell you that you were right all the time and I was wrong. You were right about women. They *do* take the initiative. They do select their partners. Why d'you think I wrote that letter?"

Edward's eyebrows drew together in a heavy frown. "You mean, you *knew* I'd come over?"

"Well, I didn't *know* it, but I thought it was a pretty safe bet."

Edward bounded up the steps and kissed her fiercely. The spectators on the next porch erupted into applause and cheers of approval.

Much later that night, Maggie lay in Edward's warm arms, her head on his chest.

"Maggie, lovely, are you sure you have no regrets about any of this?"

Maggie thought carefully. "I don't have any regrets now. Up until about an hour ago I did."

"What do you mean?"

"I regretted sleeping with you at the barn."

"Oh God, Mags . . . I've dreaded hearing that."

"Let me explain why, Edward. D'you remember telling me what you thought about dreams and expectations, and reality never living up to them?"

"Ye-es," Edward said apprehensively.

"Ever since we went to bed the first time, I've been regretting it, because I felt I'd spoiled my Christmas—that I'd had it all too early, and ruined the surprise."

"I don't follow."

"Maybe you were a very obedient child. I wasn't. One Christmas—I must have been about ten, I just couldn't wait to get my presents. Early on Christmas Eve, I couldn't stop myself sneaking into my parents' bedroom—when Mum was in the kitchen cooking—and I searched under the bed, and in all her drawers, and at the back of her wardrobe until I found the stash of presents. Mum was always chaotic at Christmas—she never got round to wrapping up the presents until about three A.M., after all of us were in bed. It was incredibly exciting, even more so because I knew it was really naughty. I had a private, rushed little orgy of examining all of them, and then put them all back wherever she'd hidden them. Then I went to bed, and lay there feeling miserable because there was nothing left to look forward to on Christmas morning. Mum came in to kiss me and told me to go to sleep fast so Father Christmas could deliver all my presents. Now I think of it, I think she carried on the Santa myth until I was about eighteen. . . . That night, I lay in bed hoping against hope that I'd missed something, that there was some special present she'd hidden somewhere else."

"What a bloody little child you must have been."

"No, I wasn't! I was delightful."

He kissed her tenderly. "I know you were. You are still. Bloody *and* delightful. But I don't quite see what this has got to do with me."

"Be patient. You're even worse at listening to a story than Lily is. So Christmas morning, there I was, with a pile of presents all wrapped up but perfectly recognisable to me, and I tried my best to act surprised and delighted when I opened each one, because it meant so much to Mum and Dad. It wasn't that I didn't like my presents; there was no surprise, that's all. I'd spoiled it for myself, you see? And the pile gradually reduced, and I prayed with all my heart that there'd be something new—something I hadn't already seen. And there wasn't, and then it was over, and Dad told us to go and get dressed ready for church."

"You poor little mite. What a sorry tale."

"But it isn't a sad story, Eddie. Listen. When I came downstairs, all in my Christmas best, Dad and Mum said they needed to show me something in the garden. And Dad blindfolded me, and we went out, and there at the back of the garden, under a huge sheet with a red ribbon on it, was the most amazing rocking horse. I've still got it. It's in Lily's room back home."

"Great parents."

"Yes, they were. They are. But you don't follow the moral of the story, do you, Eddie?"

"Don't snoop in other people's bedrooms? Don't spoil surprises?"

Maggie laughed and hugged him. "It's partly that. I never snooped again. Not until you and I went to bed, that is. You see, the past two months, whenever I thought about you, I thought I'd ruined it for myself. By making love to you when it wasn't the right time, when I wasn't free and hadn't sorted things out with Oliver, I thought I'd blown it. I'd had this wonderful rushed, sneak preview of being with you, but I wasn't free, and we weren't committed, and it wasn't right."

"I'm sorry, Maggie. I should never have let myself—let you—whatever . . ."

"Don't you see, you fool? Now, when it *is* the right time—you're the brand-new dream doll's house—the climbing frame—the thing that didn't fit into the cupboard. You're the rocking horse that I'd given up hope of ever getting. And it was right there all the time. All the time I was praying."

Eleven months later—October 1994

CHRISTY HAD EMPLOYED A FRENCH INTERIOR DESIGNER FOR THE refurbishment of Bockhampton. Work had been going on for six months now, and was still far from complete. So long as it was all finished for the wedding reception, Christy would be content. The TV series—*Heading South*—had been a critical and commercial success on both sides of the Atlantic, and Christy and Oliver had invested most of the proceeds—plus some of the capital from her divorce settlement—into the renovation and redecoration of Bockhampton. As she and Oliver had attained something of minor celebrity status, Christy had been approached by both *Hello!* magazine and *Through the Keyhole*, but she had turned them both down. It wasn't just that the house was unfinished; it was to protect her son. Jake was now at school in Salisbury, and Christy wanted him to have as regular and normal a family life as was possible for the child of a TV personality.

Christy has two pressing concerns that day; the first was that she was simply going to *have* to tell Mrs. Mason that she didn't want her to cater their wedding reception—she had already selected a firm of London caterers. Dear Martin Worth had agreed to conduct a service of blessing for her and Oliver just as soon as the formalities of their respective divorces were completed. The other problem worried her more; Danny Bujevski had two ideas in development for them: one was a series with the working title, *The Swamp Fox and Other Tales of Southern Life*, which would involve her and Oliver doing a longer trip back home, following various fables of the Revo-

348

lutionary and Civil Wars. The other was a tour of the Midwest, and Christy was hoping to persuade Oliver to turn it down. She was more than a little afraid that her contribution would be significantly reduced in a Midwestern setting, and she had no wish to lose the ground she'd already gained. Now that Gabe had Jake for all the vacations—shared custody had been his sole condition for the divorce—she had way too much time on her hands, and needed to keep busy.

There was one other problem, and that was Oliver's continuing reluctance to do anything about *A Sad Affair*. It was the perfect time to launch his literary career—he'd have time to finish the book before they started the new series, and surely most publishers would leap at the offer of a good novel from a well-known journalist turned TV celebrity? Last week, Christy had even dared to talk to Maggie about it. Christy had remarked on the coincidence that both Maggie and Oliver would one day be published authors, and had assured Maggie there should be no professional rivalry between them. She saw Maggie quite regularly. They bumped into each other at school, when they were respectively delivering Jake and Lily, and Christy had taken to dropping in at the barn for a coffee from time to time. Last Friday, when Christy had raised the subject of *A Sad Affair*, Maggie had been extremely non-committal: she just said she'd never known that Oliver *had* written a novel, and advised Christy not to push Ol to do anything he didn't want to do. Christy felt a little bit irked by Maggie's reaction. The three of them had settled things quite amicably among them, and she felt it was small-minded and spiteful of Maggie not to wish Oliver well in all his future endeavors. That aside, she liked Maggie. They had a surprising amount in common. It was a shame that Oliver and Edward had never really been able to patch things up—usually the men managed to make amends when the women couldn't. Christy had decided to take the matter into her own hands. That summer, she had filled the gap left by Jake by dedicating herself to the project of getting Oliver's novel published, whether he wanted it or not. She'd got the number of an agent from Danny Bujevski and had sent what there was of *A Sad Affair* off without saying a word to Ol. He'd thank her in the long run, she was sure of it.

Only a mile and a half down the road from Bockhampton, Edward and Maggie lived at the barn in Compton Purlew. Edward had expected Maggie to want to move—at least farther down the Valley—but she insisted that she was perfectly happy at the barn. In order to have more time with Maggie and the children, Edward had resigned his partnership in Bishop & Moodey, and now acted as a consultant to them, as well as to a firm of American auctioneers. He and Maggie had made Gabe McCarthy an offer for Ocean's Edge, and had bought it six months previously with all its furniture and fittings. Maggie hadn't changed a thing at either Ocean's Edge or the barn—not a single placemat. So long as Edward was around she seemed almost oblivious to her surroundings. They had spent three months of the summer at Ocean's Edge, and had had the Richardses to visit three or four times during their stay. Edward admired Lindy and B.J. as much as Maggie did, and had no objection to Lindy's constant teasing reference to him as "that no-good cradle snatcher." He knew what Maggie thought, and that was all that mattered.

Maggie had submitted the manuscript of *Our Recent Unpleasantness* to a publisher, and had received a very enthusiastic response. She had started on her third novel, but it was going slowly; although Lily was at school—at the same school as Jake in fact—Arthur was very much under foot. Neither Maggie nor Edward discussed the idea of getting married. As far as they were concerned, they were married, and they had a peculiar superstition against the service itself. Edward was an excellent stepfather, and had welcomed Arthur and Lily into his home with open arms. His attitude to the dogs had been less wholehearted. Maggie had made it a make or break clause of living with him that if *she* came, Boomer came, too, but Edward had drawn the line at Lucius. He claimed that the dog had suffered irreparably from a dysfunctional family life, and argued that it would break Jake's heart to remove the mutt from Bockhampton. Snuff had made his own arrangements, commuting between the two households, and frequently managing to con his joint owners into serving double rations. Lily and Jake were the best of friends, and had adapted to the bizarre set-up. The people who suffered most visibly were their teachers at the Salisbury school; they had spent the night before sports' day rehearsing surnames—Mrs. McCarthy and Mr. Callahan; Mrs. Callahan and Mr. Arabin—and struggling to remember who had fathered which child. They were convinced that Edward, who had fathered none of them, was in some way responsible for all three. The situation would be further complicated when Maggie and Edward had a child of their own; the baby was due in March.

For months Maggie had been under assault from Edward, her agent, and her new editor to allow them to read *A Sad Affair*. She had resisted their efforts until a visit from Christy the week before had made her think again. She agreed to publication, suddenly reversing her earlier reservations. It would hit the shelves twelve months to the day after *Our Recent Unpleasantness*. Maggie couldn't repress a smile when she thought of inviting Oliver and Christy to the launch party.

Gabe McCarthy was now senior partner of Winkler, Barrows, & McCarthy. The original Winkler and Barrows were in fact long dead. He was glad to be rid of Ocean's Edge, although he had been happy to visit Maggie and Edward there, and had accepted an open invitation to use the house whenever Jake was over for vacations. He had hung on to Oak Ridge, having reimbursed Christy for her share of it. Although he rejected any possibility of selling the house, he spent as little time there as possible, feeling that it really needed a woman's touch. Luckily for Gabe, his super-efficient assistant, Lilah Biggs, was more than able to take over the running of the house. Gabe had dedicated himself to his career for the past twelve months and was going from strength to strength, ably assisted by the utterly dependable Lilah. He had had his son to stay for the Christmas holidays, and another two weeks at Easter, and had taken him back to Devon for ten days before returning home with Jake for the summer break. He didn't much like Oliver Callahan, but then he didn't have to see much of him. Christy made a point of phoning Gabe regularly to keep him abreast of Jake's school progress, and he received meticulously photocopied school reports, and duplicate snapshots of Jake winning the egg and spoon race at sports day. Lilah stuck them in albums for him, just like she placed new flowers on his desk every day. She said that seeing he spent so much time in his office, it ought to at least look a little more like home. Something had happened to Lilah recently; Gabe suspected she had a new man in her sights.

One day the following February Carolyn Grose, the editor of the Worldwide Home Exchange Club Directory, sat at her desk, trying to reconcile her computer records and staring at three letters. On the print-out in front of her she had listed two couples—Christy and Gabe McCarthy, and Maggie and Oliver Callahan, and three houses: Oak Ridge, Ocean's Edge, and Bockhampton. She had sent off letters after Christmas to get them re-registered for the new directory, and she had had three replies. Mrs. Christy Moore Callahan had replied from Bockhampton, saying that she and Oliver were far too busy to get away that year. Mrs. Maggie Callahan wrote to say that she herself would be in residence at Ocean's Edge, and felt it unlikely that she would exchange again. And finally, a Ms. Lilah Biggs had replied on office stationery to say that Oak Ridge was currently being redecorated, but that the house might *just* be available for the summer of 1995, when she and Mr. Gabe McCarthy were planning to vacation in Italy. Carolyn Grose was more than a little confused.